Forbidden

Forbidden

Christina Phillips

Heat | New York

THE BERKLEY PUBLISHING GROUP
Published by the Penguin Group
Penguin Group (USA) Inc.
375 Hudson Street, New York, New York 10014, USA
Penguin Group (Canada), 90 Eglinton Avenue East, Suite 700, Toronto, Ontario M4P 2Y3, Canada
(a division of Pearson Penguin Canada Inc.)
Penguin Books Ltd., 80 Strand, London WC2R 0RL, England
Penguin Group Ireland, 25 St. Stephen's Green, Dublin 2, Ireland (a division of Penguin Books Ltd.)
Penguin Group (Australia), 250 Camberwell Road, Camberwell, Victoria 3124, Australia
(a division of Pearson Australia Group Pty. Ltd.)
Penguin Books India Pvt. Ltd., 11 Community Centre, Panchsheel Park, New Delhi—110 017, India
Penguin Group (NZ), 67 Apollo Drive, Rosedale, North Shore 0632, New Zealand
(a division of Pearson New Zealand Ltd.)
Penguin Books (South Africa) (Pty.) Ltd., 24 Sturdee Avenue, Rosebank, Johannesburg 2196,
South Africa

Penguin Books Ltd., Registered Offices: 80 Strand, London WC2R 0RL, England

This book is an original publication of The Berkley Publishing Group.

This is a work of fiction. Names, characters, places, and incidents either are the product of the author's imagination or are used fictitiously, and any resemblance to actual persons, living or dead, business establishments, events, or locales is entirely coincidental. The publisher does not have any control over and does not assume any responsibility for author or third-party websites or their content.

PRINTING HISTORY
Heat trade paperback edition / September 2010

Library of Congress Cataloging-in-Publication Data

Phillips, Christina, (date)
Forbidden / Christina Phillips. — Heat trade pbk. ed.
p. cm.
ISBN 978-0-425-23808-0
I. Title.
PS3616.H45455F67 2010
813'.6—dc22
                                    2010012983

PRINTED IN THE UNITED STATES OF AMERICA

10 9 8 7 6 5 4 3 2 1

For Mark.
Forever.

Acknowledgments

I owe a huge debt of thanks to my fabulous critique partners—Amanda Ashby, Sara Hantz and Pat Posner—for their support and encouragement over the years. Even when I came close to giving up on myself, they never did, and for that they deserve mountains of chocolate, rivers of wine and a juicy pineapple. You girls keep me sane.

To my incredible agent, Emmanuelle Alspaugh, who loved Carys and Maximus and their forbidden love right from the start. Thank you for always believing, and for helping to turn my dreams into reality.

Many thanks to everyone at Berkley who has worked so hard on *Forbidden*, especially my editor, the lovely Kate Seaver; it's a pleasure to work with you. Thank you for asking the hard questions! And to Katherine Pelz for her patience in answering mine!

To Gordon Crabb and the Berkley art department—thank you for creating such a beautiful cover. Every time I look at it, I fall a little more in love!

For the wonderful friends I've made through the Romance Writers of Australia, Romance Writers of New Zealand and the online romance community—your support is invaluable and very much appreciated.

And, as always, to my husband Mark and my children, Victoria, Charlotte and Oliver—who was very excited at the thought of me writing a Roman historical until he found out it was also going to be a romance. Sorry about that!

Author's Note

It was likely the Romans who called the ancient peoples of Europe and Britain *Celts*. They would have called themselves by their own tribal names.

For clarity, I have taken the liberty of using the term "Celt" in reference to the ancient tribal peoples of Cymru as a whole.

Chapter One

Carys held her breath as her secret lover entered the sparkling waterfall, buried deep within the leafy shadows of the forest.

She pressed her fingers against the rough bark of the tree, and inched a little farther along the branch where she lay hidden from his sight.

From this angle she had a perfect view of his magnificent naked body. Even from this distance she could see the numerous battle scars that marred his tawny skin, but they marked him as a warrior. A hero who faced death without reservation and emerged triumphant.

He was the enemy of her people. And yet she couldn't tear her fascinated gaze from him.

They had never met. They *would* never meet. Such a catastrophe didn't bear thinking about. Yet she thought of this tough, brutal warrior constantly. Ever since she had first stumbled across his irregular bathing ritual three moons ago.

He turned within the shimmering rainbows of the waterfall,

fingers raking through his short black hair. Carys released her breath in a shaky gasp and her body moved restlessly against her perilous ledge. The men of Cymru had long, flowing hair. How would it feel to touch such severely cropped hair? Sharp, like the points of reeds? Or—not? She couldn't imagine. And yet she imagined endlessly.

His hands massaged his broad shoulders, and Carys's fingers dug into woody crevices as she fantasized rubbing her own fingers over his knotted muscles. It had been fifteen days since he had last been to the waterfall. She knew because she had waited here, each morning.

But the wait had been worth it, and her imagination hadn't enhanced his powerful muscles, his commanding height or his dark, exotic beauty. Her breath shortened as her heart rate accelerated, and her thighs tightened around the branch in reaction.

Slowly his hands slid over wet skin, fingers trailing through the sprinkling of dark hair that dusted his impressive chest. Lightning flickered in the pit of her stomach, and instinctively she rubbed her pussy against the abrasive bark.

Her only lover, whose possessive grip she had finally escaped three years ago, possessed no body hair aside from on his head. How would it feel to press against a masculine form so unlike any she had previously seen?

The tip of her tongue slid over her lips as her secret lover sluiced water over his rigid stomach. And then his fingers curled around his semi-aroused cock.

Carys stretched to the very edge of her branch, risking safety and the threat of discovery, but temptation was too great. She had seen naked men without number in her life, knew how insanely proud males were of their treasures, but she had never been impressed by that part of the human body before.

Not even her ex-lover's. *Especially* not her ex-lover's. And yet this man's cock, this man who would murder her without compunction if he knew who she was, held fascination beyond reason.

His fingers slid over his burgeoning penis, squeezing the dark head, and without conscious thought Carys's hand slipped between her thighs. Sweet Cerridwen, she had never wanted a man so much as she wanted this one. But she knew better than to ask her goddess to intervene, for intervention would cause untold suffering to her people.

But still, she wanted this man. With all that she was.

Even through the soft wool of her gown, her throbbing clit reacted instantly to the pressure of her finger. She sighed, and her eyelashes flickered as her hips ground against her finger, against the roughness of the tree. She imagined her Roman conqueror touching her there, spearing his finger into her wet slit, and tremors burned through her womb, tightening her muscles, spiraling through her innermost channel.

She rubbed her breasts, heavy with arousal, against the bark, and imagined his hands cupped her. Squeezed her. Pinched her nipples between his calloused fingers. Rough, battle-forged fingers. How different would they feel from the smooth hands of her previous lover?

She imagined him ripping her gown from her body, until she was naked before him. Could feel the heat of him as he loomed over her. See his eyes—she longed to see the color of his eyes—and if she lifted her hand, she could run her fingers through his short, military hair.

Her heart pummeled against her crushed ribs, blood pounded against her throbbing temples, and her wet clit ached for release against her massaging finger.

He would spread her legs. And then surge into her with his magnificent, massive cock, and she would come, as the great goddess decreed, until the stars in the heavens cascaded through her sated soul, leaving a shimmering waterfall of rainbow lights forevermore.

Hot, liquid heat flooded her pussy, and she bit down hard on her lower lip to stop from crying out. Her fantasy lover satisfied her in ways she had barely before envisaged. As her heart gradually eased its frantic beat and her breath slowed, she knew it was best he remained merely a fantasy. Reality could never compare to the joy she experienced in his arms, while safely cocooned within her mind. In her fantasy, she could orgasm. In reality, with a man, she never could.

She became aware of the sharp edges of the bark scratching her face and struggled to raise her head. A stab of disappointment, as sharp as a Druid's blade, sliced through her heart.

Her secret lover had vanished from beneath the waterfall.

She inched back along the branch until she was once again safely against the trunk of the tree. It was of no matter. Perhaps he would bathe again tomorrow, and she would be here waiting for him. Or perhaps she would have to wait another moon. There was no method to his visits as far as she could discern, and for all she knew he might never pass this way again. But she didn't want to think about that.

She was simply going to enjoy every illicit moment she could.

Carefully she climbed back to the ground, her limbs still shaky and filled with remnants of desire. But as her feet touched the leaf-strewn ground, trepidation raced along her spine, crawled across the back of her neck, and sent shivers coursing along her arms.

She was no longer alone.

The trepidation mutated into stark terror. She had trespassed into occupied territory, and the enemy had found her. Stealthily she wrapped her fingers around the dagger strapped to her waist.

She might be imagining it. But she wasn't an acolyte of the wise goddess Cerridwen for nothing. The Roman stood behind her, and was moments from slaughtering her.

And it was her own fault for not being more careful.

But she wouldn't show any fear. Wouldn't divulge any information, no matter how he tortured her. And besides, it was always possible her dagger would pierce his corrupt heart with her first thrust. She knew she wouldn't be given the chance of a second.

She drew in a breath—her last?—gathered her fleeing courage, and turned to face the conqueror.

Tiberius Valerius Maximus stopped dead in his tracks as the woman slowly turned toward him. The adrenaline pumping through him in anticipation of the chase spiked into raw sexual energy, as he stared at the one who had been spying on him for Mars knew how long.

Pure reflex kept his gladius raised, and his soldier's senses remained alert for others hidden among the trees. But his gut told him she was alone. Vulnerable. At his mercy.

He took a step toward her, emerging from the shadows into the dappled sunlight. He expected her to flee, but she remained where she was, looking directly at him as if she had every right to be there and he, none.

Slowly he lowered his gladius. He'd not imagined the spy would be so small or slender or without apparent means of defense. He flicked a glance at the gem-encrusted dagger she clutched to her side, and dismissed it. She possessed neither the strength nor ability to injure him.

Her pale lemon gown, with its square neckline, skimmed the tops of her breasts and hugged her tiny waist before falling in soft folds to just below her knee. The sunlight bathed her in a radiant glow, but her hair needed no such enhancement. Loosely pulled back from her face, it was braided into a long golden plait that trailed over her shoulder to her waist.

He took another step, barely aware he did so. Many of the local girls tied their hair in such a fashion. But threaded through this golden rope were tiny clusters of amethyst and jade, their polished edges glittering, momentarily dazzling him.

And then she moved from the sunlight into the shade. But not away from him. Toward him. And for the first time he saw her face.

For one eternal heartbeat he remained transfixed by her delicate, ethereal beauty. Golden tendrils escaped her braid and caressed her pale cheeks, yet not a hint of fear emanated.

Her serenity unnerved him. And then he looked into her wide, beautiful eyes, and primal panic whipped through him, knotting his guts and tightening his muscles. Instinctively he raised his gladius, but still he couldn't tear his gaze from her strange, unnatural eyes. *One amethyst, one jade.* Was she one of the Celts' barbaric goddesses, come to take vengeance for her people?

She flinched. Barely discernible, but his trained eye saw. Saw how she tried to hide her reaction. Saw, suddenly, the uneven rise and fall of her breasts beneath her woolen gown, a certain sign that despite the calm she displayed, in truth she feared him.

He didn't want her to fear him. He was a soldier, not a tyrant. Her conqueror and master, but he didn't need another slave.

With deliberation he once again lowered his gladius, pressed its tip against his thigh. Bizarrely, relief streaked through him at his foresight in wrapping a length of linen around his waist before hunting the spy. He cared not who saw his body, but conversely didn't want her to see how much she affected him.

And she did affect him. Despite his early-morning ritual of self-gratification, already another erection caused discomfort. He sucked in a deep breath and struggled to articulate the Celtic tongue.

"I mean you no harm."

Her glance flashed to his gladius, then back to him. He didn't need an oracle to decipher that response. Without conscious thought he took another step toward her. "What's your name?"

She pressed her lips together and tilted her head very slightly.

Maximus gave a reluctant smile. Her courage was strangely fascinating, since she had to know he could snap her slender neck with one hand if he so desired.

"So you're giving me the silent treatment?" He lapsed into the familiarity of his own language. "That makes a change, a beautiful woman holding her tongue."

Again she tilted her head and this time he laughed at the haughty glare she directed his way. "Although I'm sure there are plenty of things you'd like to say to me, if only we could understand each other." With his free hand he reached out and gently brushed a strand of golden hair from her face. The silk of her hair and the unexpected heat from her soft skin sent molten darts of animal lust from the tips of his fingers directly to his throbbing cock.

Gods. His fingers stilled against her face. She didn't try to escape. His breath burned his lungs, closed his windpipe. *Why didn't she try to escape?*

"You haven't been seen in any of the villages." He'd seen countless girls and women as the legionaries had vanquished one primitive village after another. Had even sampled a few of the prettiest himself, those who were willing to fraternize with their enemy.

Had this golden-haired vision been found, she would have been brought to him personally. The best prizes always were.

"You're no peasant." His gaze raked over her, only now recognizing the fine weave to the woolen gown, the intricate, vibrant embroidery that decorated its neckline, sleeves and hem. And the semiprecious jewels threaded through her hair were repeated in her long earrings that brushed her shoulders, the delicate necklace that clasped the base of her throat and the bracelets around her fragile-looking wrists.

Another step and he was close enough to breathe in her evocative scent of spring flowers and summer breezes. A clean, pure scent, one infinitely elevated from the stink of the masses or the claw of poverty. Or the mindless slaughter of the blood-soaked quagmires.

"Where do you come from?" He used her language although he didn't expect her to answer. This girl, whose air of fragility reminded him of a wood nymph, was from the chieftain class. Of that much he was certain. He trailed his knuckles across her cheek and gently grasped her jaw between thumb and forefinger, forcing her to look at him although she had shown no sign of dropping her gaze. "Where is your father's settlement?"

Her eyes darkened, dilated pupils almost obliterating her mystical, bicolored irises. Lust burned deep in his groin. Hot. Painful. He traced his thumb across her soft lower lip, felt the heat of her breath scorch his flesh. "Your husband's?" His voice rasped, as if he had been lost in the desert for days without liquid sustenance. As if the thought of this girl belonging to another man grazed his soul.

It made no difference if she were married or not. If he wanted her, he would have her, and to Tartarus with her entire family if they attempted to deny his desire.

The tip of her tongue moistened the seam of her lips, and he imagined that tongue slipping between his own lips, invading his mouth, and his fingers tightened around her jaw.

"I belong to no man." Her words were low, breathless, yet clear and melodic to his ears.

"You belong to me."

Her eyes never left his. "Do you take everything by force, Roman?" Her words were slow, deliberate, as if she wanted him to understand everything she said. She made an expressive gesture with her hand, encompassing the virgin forest. "My land. My people." She paused for a heartbeat. "Me?"

He rammed his gladius into the ground and cradled her face with both hands. "I don't need to take you by force, my lady. But I'll use force against any who try to keep you from me."

Her hand came between them, and the tips of her fingers touched his naked skin over the heavy beat of his heart. Her pressure was so slight he could scarcely feel her at all, and yet her touch branded him, reached deep inside and twisted his gut.

He didn't know her name. Didn't know which noble claimed her. But none of that mattered. Because he had conquered their land for the mighty Caesar and everything and everyone was now owned by Rome.

And here, he was Rome.

Her fingers grazed over his chest, as if the texture of his flesh and hair fascinated her. His hands slid from her face to her throat, and the rapid beat of her pulse against his fingers sank into his blood, an erotic echo.

"Aren't you going to kill me?" Her whisper flickered through his brain, making no sense. Had he misunderstood? His grasp of her language was far from comprehensive. An oversight he intended to remedy forthwith.

"Were you sent to spy on me?" Inconceivable anyone should send this fragile female on such an assignment, especially with only an ornamental dagger for defense. And yet the Celts were not Roman. Their women were rumored to be as ruthless as their men in battle.

He'd witnessed such himself, from those villages whose inhabitants hadn't surrendered voluntarily beneath the might of the Eagle.

She looked up at him, fearless and silent. While he couldn't imagine her engaged in bloody battle, she still had the courage of a warrior to stand up to him.

He lowered his head as his hands slid over her shoulders. "If you weren't sent to spy on me, then why should I kill you?"

Her hand flattened against his chest, as if she meant to push him away but the touch became an irresistible caress as her palm rubbed over his erect nipple. His cock throbbed at her gentle touch, and the soft linen did nothing to hide the extent of his erection. Curling his fingers around her upper arms, he pulled her against his hard body, wanting her to feel how much she aroused him, wanting to feel the softness of her skin against him.

Her lips parted in a startled gasp as he ground his shaft against her stomach. Sliding one hand down her back, he cupped her round buttock and anchored her securely against his rigid heat.

He wanted more. But for now, this sufficed.

"My beautiful, fearless Celt," he said in his own language. He squeezed her firm buttock, and she sucked in a shocked breath, even as she squirmed against him. "Would you look at me with such misplaced trust if you knew how much I wanted to rip this gown from your body?" He slid a finger between the crease of her tight little bottom, and her fingernails dug into his chest as she jerked toward him.

He wound his arm around her waist to keep her from any thought of retreat. His finger delved deeper into her hot crevice and she gave a low moan. "Do you know how much I want you, my little Celtic lady? How I want to bury my cock inside your body until I feel you writhe around my shaft? Would you let me, if I asked?"

She pulled, perhaps unconsciously, at his chest hair, and the stabbing pain shot straight to his straining erection. Gods, he needed to fuck her. But every word of her barbaric language had fled his mind, to be replaced by images of her naked beneath him as he filled every tight channel she possessed with his hot seed.

Amethyst and jade eyes stared up at him, dark with passion, devoid of fear. A man could lose his mind and soul looking into such mystical eyes. "Thank the gods you don't speak my tongue." He abandoned her tempting buttocks and his palm molded the curve of her hip. "You'd spit in my face."

Her fingers stilled in their tentative exploration of his battle-scarred chest. "Roman barbarian." The words were whispered in Celtic, yet he understood them perfectly.

His arm tightened around her slender waist, and he wound the end of her plait around his other hand. Silken strands caressed his palm and he barely noticed the sharp edges of the jewelry embedding into his skin. "Rome can teach you much, my lady." And he would start the lessons here. Now. And when his lust was sated he would take her back to the settlement so she was always readily available.

"Rome is barbaric." Her voice was breathless and she shifted against him, rubbing herself over his engorged cock. Again her language failed him, but that was of no consequence. He would show her how much Rome could teach her, and, by the time he finished, she would never wish to return to her primitive life.

He brushed his mouth against hers. She was so soft. So sweet. His tongue traced the seam of her lips, teasing for entry, pressing against the barrier of her teeth. When she finally opened to him he plunged inside, invading her heat, exploring every secret corner, and tangling his tongue around hers, stroking and stoking the scorching embers.

She moaned inside his mouth, and the sound vibrated against his flesh, sizzled along his blood and sent waves of fire coursing through his agonized shaft. Still bound by her braid he clasped her head, holding her still for his pleasure as he plundered her mouth as a ravenous man plundered the fields of Elysian.

Crushed against him he could feel the firm muscles of her thighs, and the exquisite damp heat of her pussy burned through her gown, through his linen robe, and tortured his last remnants of restraint.

Maximus tore his mouth from her, captured her bottom lip between his teeth. She panted into his face, her eyes glazed with passion, and with a growl of possession he released her lip and nibbled kisses with his lips and teeth across her face before sucking her earlobe into his searching mouth.

Her nails dug into his chest, and her earring scraped along his tongue. His hand slid up from her waist and cupped her breast, curled his fingers around the tempting fullness and imagined suckling her erect, rosy nipple until she screamed for release.

He flicked the tip of his tongue into the hollow of her ear, felt her shudder in his embrace, and slid his hand between their tightly meshed bodies. Her arousal shimmered all around, tantalizing and frustrating, edging his lust to unbearable heights.

He needed to touch her feminine folds, her swollen clitoris, the wet heat of her slit. As his finger grazed over her through the cursed barrier of her gown, he rasped in Latin, "You deserve more than a quick fuck in the forest, my lady. I promise once we're back at the settlement I'll see to your every comfort."

She tensed, as if his touch had shocked. Surely he hadn't hurt her? He stilled his finger, although every impulse urged him to explore further, to seek her hidden treasures. "Don't fear me, lady." His voice was husky, but he couldn't help that. She knew he wanted her. "I won't allow any other to touch you but me."

The very thought of another man touching her boiled his brain. She was his. She would always be his. If a husband came searching for her, the choice was plain. Surrender his wife to Maximus or die.

Her hand flattened against his chest and this time there was no pretense in the way she pushed him. "Please." Her voice was low, yet he clearly detected the panic clinging to that one word.

He dragged his hand from the apex of her thighs, although the action went against every screaming nerve in his body. Frustrated desire shredded his mind, wiped every word of her language into oblivion.

"Come with me." If only she understood him. "You know that sooner or later we'll find your kinsfolk. With me, you'll be safe." They had obviously fled to the hills to escape the invasion, but that act of cowardice had gained them, at most, only a few months of extended freedom.

And this girl was no coward. She didn't deserve to be hunted down like a rabid dog and either slaughtered in the rage of battle or taken as a spoil of war.

But she couldn't understand him and his words didn't sooth. Instead she pulled from his arms and her braid slithered around his hand before escaping.

She stood before him. It would take no physical effort to simply sweep her into his arms, toss her over his horse and take her back to the settlement. Once there, he could imprison her as an insurgent. Could have her whenever the urge gripped him.

The image churned his stomach, made bile rise in his throat. He wanted this golden wood nymph, but not at any cost. What pleasure would he derive from her total subjugation?

Chapter Two

The fear that had previously been absent now clouded her fantastical eyes. Incomprehension tore through him, melding with fiery frustration and creating a maelstrom of fury against a foe unknown. Why did she fear him *now*? What had he done to make her so afraid?

He fisted his hands but still she didn't move. Why didn't she run from him, if that was what she wanted? He wouldn't follow. Wouldn't take her captive. While he'd have no compunction in slaughtering anyone who attempted to take her from him, she had to go with him willingly.

"You shouldn't wander the countryside unattended." His throat was raw. His voice didn't sound like his own. He searched for the right words to tell her to be careful, to remain safe. To avoid the scouting parties systematically searching the hills for renegades.

But her Celtic eluded him. "Stay with your menfolk," he said instead. Perhaps they would be able to protect her. But no man could protect her as he could.

Maybe he should take her with him despite her reluctance. She would come around to his way of thinking eventually, when she saw the futility of resisting the might that was Rome.

He searched her face, unwittingly memorizing the proud angle of her jaw, her high cheekbones and her strange, captivating eyes. If he was Rome, she was Cambria, and if he took her against her will, everything that she was would die.

"Farewell, my Celtic lady." His voice was hollow, an echo of the void filling his chest and seeping through his heavy limbs. He pulled his gladius from the earth, took two backward paces, then turned and marched from her.

Carys watched the Roman disappear into the forest. Her breath stuttered in her chest and she curled her hand around her throat, the erratic pound of her pulse against her fingers echoing along every traumatized nerve.

Moths fluttered within the hollowness of her legs and she stumbled against a tree for support. *What had just happened?*

The Roman had left her. She had seen it with her own eyes and still could scarcely believe it.

She closed her eyes and sucked in long, calming breaths, attempting to regulate her heartbeat, center her psyche. Her fingers ached around the handle of her dagger and she loosened her grip, horrifically aware that not once during the encounter had she even thought to gut her sworn enemy.

Finally her pulse slowed and, with a shiver, she glanced around but he had long gone from sight. She pressed her fingers against her throbbing pussy, trying to alleviate the maddening throb of her swollen clit, but the pressure only increased the sensation, and wet heat dampened her.

She leaned back against the tree, sheathed her dagger at her waist and gazed into the leafy canopy above. Her Roman was more magnificent up close than anything her imagination had conjured.

Her finger teased her clit as she remembered his sapphire blue eyes. She had never before encountered anyone with eyes as blue as the clearest summer day.

He had told her exactly what he wanted to do with her. And when she had resisted, he had left her. Perhaps, after all, Romans did have a sense of honor.

A low cry escaped and she grasped her head, digging her fingers into her scalp. She had expected death at his hands. Perhaps brutal violation. But she hadn't expected to be kissed the way he had kissed her. Hadn't expected the touch of his hands to ignite flames in her blood or send tremors through her limbs.

He affected her more profoundly than she had dared dream. And instead of fulfilling every fantasy she harbored, fantasies she knew he shared by the dark passion in his eyes, his erratic breath and the hard, glorious erection she had felt beneath his scrap of linen, *he had left her.*

She forced herself upright. Her selfish desires had almost cost her people everything. If the Roman enslaved her, the blood shed in her rescue would haunt her forever. He had set her free and, while she knew if he'd had the slightest inkling she was a Druid—*or whose blood she shared*—he would have slit her throat, releasing her elevated his status from barbarian to her equal.

Did she dare spy on him again? It was a dangerous game. And yet one that sent dark thrills of excitement spinning through her senses despite, *or perhaps because of*, the risk of recapture.

But she wouldn't be recaptured. And even if she was, and they shared another breath-stealing kiss, she would still somehow retain her freedom.

Because this Roman possessed honor.

She retrieved her tightly woven bag from the tangled tree roots and turned and hastened through the forest, taking hidden paths known only to a select few, her sense of direction unerring as she delved deeper into the untamed wilds. Every few moments she paused, ears attuned to the slightest crack of a twig or misplaced scurry of woodland creatures. But aside from the beat of her heart, the breeze shivering through the leaves and the expected rustlings from the undergrowth, the forest was silent. She wasn't being followed, either by Roman or random villager.

Finally reassured she was truly alone, she doubled back on herself and took the direct route to the enchanted enclave of the Druids. The sacred spiral, a magical veil created by the combined power of all their gods and goddesses that pulsed from the spiritual core of the hallowed bluestones, had been their haven and hidden them from the enemy for these last seven moons.

Aeron dy Ehangwen, High Druid, stood in the center of the holy cromlech, at the heart of the protective spiral invoked during the Feast of the Dead. The fingers of his right hand drummed impatiently on the polished stone altar. Yet again, Carys had disobeyed his decree and left the security of the sanctified circle.

Rage bubbled through his veins, pounded against his temples and threatened to incinerate his brain. Did she have so little regard for her own safety? For the safety of her people? Did she not realize that if caught by the enemy, the barbarous Romans would rape her senseless before ripping her limb from bloodied limb?

Through a gap in the outer ring of the immense bluestones, he saw her emerge from the forest into the sacred oak glade. Relief tempered his anger, but not enough to quell the fire in his blood. But then, nothing could ever quell the fire in his blood when he saw Carys.

She paused beyond the inner circle of megaliths and looked his way. He doubted she could see him, deep in the shadows cast by the flat capstone roof, but he had learned years ago never to underestimate his little Carys. She had formidable powers, powers she was scarcely aware existed, but that didn't excuse her behavior.

When it became clear she wasn't going to enter the heart of the cromlech, Aeron fought against the compunction to go to her. His fist clenched on the altar, and flames licked through his chest. *She never came to him.*

He grasped the hazel rod with his left hand and stepped from the inner sanctum into the sunlight. Carys neither moved nor looked surprised to see him suddenly appear.

"So you've returned." He allowed an ember of emotion to heat his words, to show his condemnation.

"Yes." Just that one word. No hint of apology or attempt at denial. The hazel rod burned his palm, such was the pressure he exerted.

"Which village?" It didn't matter which village she had visited. They were all occupied by Roman scum. Only here, where the sacred spiral pulsed, were they safe from the invasion.

She took a step toward him. "I don't go to the villages, Aeron. I'm not that much of a fool."

She wasn't a fool at all. Except for the way she denied him.

But she wouldn't deny him for much longer. Destiny shimmered on the precipice and soon all their futures would alter irreversibly.

He held the knowledge close. She had no reason to know what he planned. None of them had reason to know.

"Then where have you been?" Against his will he strode toward her and then stopped dead as the scent of her arousal, as heady and intoxicating as the most potent of hallucinatory elixirs, drifted on a sensual breeze.

Disbelief ripped through his brain as betrayal thundered through his blood and collided with brutal force along the length of his cock. Desire and disgust warred for supremacy, but desire always simmered beneath the surface whenever Carys was near. Disgust simply fed his hunger, gave it an ugly, jagged edge.

His fingers ached to grip her shoulders, shake her till her hair tumbled free of its restraints. *How dare she fuck another?* For one incandescent moment a haze of red mist clouded his view, clouded his mind. Clouded his entire purpose. *Carys had opened her thighs to another man.*

Before he could stop himself he grabbed her wrist and jerked her toward him. Her feminine scent washed through him, musky, mysterious. *Unfulfilled.*

His senses expanded, explored. And could detect no corresponding scent of rutting male, no obscene stink of lingering masculine seed.

"You're hurting me." Her voice was calm, as if she knew he would never truly hurt her. And fuck the bitch for being right. No matter how much she insulted him, he could never raise his hand to her.

Yet.

He loosened his fingers from her tender flesh. She had not been with a man. Only with herself. The thought of Carys caressing her own nipples, rubbing her own clit and spreading her juices over her pussy caused his engorged cock to throb with painful frustration.

Still holding her wrist, he pulled her hand to his mouth and drew in a deep breath. Knowledge flared in her magical eyes, but she didn't look away.

"Is there anything you want from me, Carys?" His voice betrayed his need. If he pulled her just a little closer, she would feel how great that need was.

"No."

The single word enraged him more than if she had given him a rambling, obscure monologue as to why she no longer allowed him access to her luscious body.

No. Was that all the explanation he deserved? When he could smell the evidence of her denied desires with every breath he took?

He pulled her close despite it all. "The world is changing. To defeat the Romans we must survive and prosper, Carys." He released her wrist, and curled his fingers around her vulnerable neck. Her pulse beat against the palm of his hand. "Now, more than ever before, it's essential you allow my seed to grow within your womb."

She sighed, and her fingers clasped his wrist as, gently but with firm purpose, she removed his hand from her throat. "I'm not ready for any man's seed to grow within me, Aeron. Please, let's not have this conversation again. My answer remains the same as it has for these last three years."

He inclined his head in a show of acceptance. But only so she didn't see the fury burn in his eyes. Any other woman would weep with gratitude for the honor he wished to bestow upon Carys. Any woman but Carys herself.

"I respect your decision." The fuck he did. But the time was not yet ripe to take what rightfully belonged to him. "But remember this. When you are ready, be sure to choose your mate wisely. Our future depends upon it."

Carys only half listened to Aeron's lecture. She had met only one man who enticed her to consider the possibility of pregnancy, and she didn't even know his name.

Would a child of her body mixed with the blood of a certain Roman warrior possess his enchanting blue eyes?

It was an intoxicating notion, outrageous. Yet strangely thrilling. Had her mother, upon first seeing her father, known instantly he was the man she wished to sire her daughter?

A stab of regret pierced her. It had been an age since she'd last had the chance to talk with her mother. How much longer would they be kept separated by the cursed Roman occupation?

"Carys," Aeron said, and she blinked away the image of one particular cursed Roman to frown up into Aeron's strange silver eyes. "I fear I must expressly forbid you to set foot outside the sacred spiral."

She stiffened. "You forbid me?"

Aeron smiled but as always the smile didn't reach his eyes. "These are barbaric times. I know you wish to help the unfortunates held captive by the Romans, but the fate of the villagers is nothing compared to what the enemy would do to you, Carys."

"The enemy would never capture me." But the enemy had captured her earlier. Yet that had been her own fault, for losing concentration. Indulging her lust. Had she been fully alert, the Roman would never have been able to discover her hiding place. "I won't abandon my people. If they come to Cerridwen's Cauldron, then I'm duty bound to assist."

But for the first time in almost seven moons, she hadn't made it to the sacred spring this morning. She had become distracted. Suppose someone had risked great personal danger in order to see her today? Suppose, by her actions, someone didn't receive essential medicines and died?

Aeron gave a dismissive wave of his hand, as if the suffering of their people was of no consequence. How could he turn his back on them? She understood the need for the Druids to escape the occupation, for the invaders would never allow them to live. Proof of that, bloodied and personal, had soaked into Carys's existence long ago.

But did that mean they turned their back on the general populace? Allowed them to struggle without any recourse to their spiritual and medical advisors? Why else had they fled, if not to remain free to assist their people?

"Your duty lies here," Aeron said. "What good will you be to our people if you allow yourself to be sacrificed as an example to all?" He paused for one telling heartbeat. "Don't forget how the Romans execute their enemies, Carys."

Despite the heat from the sun, a shiver chilled her. Rumors from Britain of brutal crucifixions had circulated for years before the invasion of Cymru. And then reports reached them of the horrifying slaughter of their fellow Druids just inside their borders. The invaders had massacred them without mercy.

She thought of her Roman warrior, tried to envisage him

sanctioning such callousness. And knew, without knowing how, that when it came to Rome, he would do whatever was required.

Another shiver rippled through her, this time chilling her heart.

Her Roman possessed honor. But if confronted with the choice between saving her and serving his country, she knew where his loyalties would lie.

It pained her heart to admit Aeron was right. The people of Cymru were strong and proud, and had been vanquished only because of the superior strength of the invaders. But if the Romans publicly executed a Druid of her standing, she knew only too well the devastating effect that would have on the morale of her beloved people.

She inclined her head. "I understand." She would still visit the Cauldron. Before fleeing, she had given her solemn vow to continue aiding those in need.

But she would no longer pass by the waterfall. To do so would only invite danger of the most reckless kind. Regret speared her soul and caused a strange aching desolation deep in the most hidden recesses of her spirit.

At least she'd experienced the sensation of her Roman's large, roughened hands on her body. The feel of his sensual lips on hers. And now she knew, beyond doubt, that with the right man she *could* feel lust and pleasure as the great goddess, the Morrigan, required from her children. All she had to do was find another such man.

A man who wasn't the sworn enemy of her people.

Maximus negotiated the sprawling civilian settlement that over the last few months had grown up around the military base, and entered the gates set in the stone wall. Once on the main street, he leaped from his horse, handed the reins to an auxiliary and then marched toward the barracks. His groin throbbed incessantly, as if a horse had kicked him between the legs and then trampled over him for good measure.

It even hurt to walk, but not as much as riding from the waterfall had. Gods, if he didn't get relief soon, his balls would explode. What had possessed him to leave the golden wood nymph behind? She should be here with him now, accompanying him to one of the civilian taverns.

For one glazed moment he imagined he could feel her hand around him, guiding him into her hot, wet mouth. He barely prevented a groan from escaping.

This was madness. He'd join the legionaries on the campus and put in a few hours' hard training. Sweat and blood would rid him of this unbearable ache.

"Primus."

He pulled his attention back to the present and focused on the centurion saluting him. "Aquila."

Aquila lowered his arm. "The surveyors have returned from the border. The architects are working on the next stage of development now."

He grunted acknowledgment. How the people of these savage lands coped without decent roads never ceased to astound him.

"Maximus."

Maximus suppressed a sigh. Though Aquila was second in rank to himself, they had been friends since the age of twelve, and thus was Aquila permitted to use his personal name. It wasn't that which caused Maximus to sigh. It was the speculative gleam in Aquila's eye.

"Yes?"

"You're on edge."

That was one way of looking at it. Fucking frustrated was another. "We're still subduing the natives. Of course I'm on full alert, Aquila."

Aquila didn't look convinced. "The skirmishes have virtually ceased. They'll soon learn that life under Rome is far pleasanter than their previous savage existence."

Maximus grunted. Would his golden wood nymph also come to that conclusion?

"And I wasn't referring to the natives. I was referring to your unnatural state of extended celibacy."

Had any other centurion dared make such a comment, he would already be crippled at Maximus's feet. But no other centurion would dare.

"I'm no longer a raw sixteen-year-old who thinks with his cock." Even as he said the words, Maximus was fully aware that barely an hour earlier his cock was the only part of him functioning at optimum capacity.

Aquila didn't need to know that.

"But you are a man," Aquila said as they made their way to the barracks. "And you've been without the soft comfort of a woman for far too many weeks."

"How did you reach that conclusion?" Maximus shot his friend an irritated glance. It was bad enough his only relief recently came from his hand. Far worse that Aquila had guessed such a thing.

"Because you have an aversion to visiting the brothels. Even on your supposed day off." Aquila shot him a barely disguised smirk.

Maximus ripped off his helmet and continued marching. It was true he preferred not to visit the prostitutes who plied their trade in the civilian settlement, but he had nothing against the women earning a few coins on their backs or knees, nor the legionaries who used their services. "I have no need to visit the brothels."

"You've found a mistress?' Aquila said. He sounded skeptical.

Bicolored eyes shimmered through Maximus's mind, haunting him with everything he had allowed to slip through his fingers. "When the fuck have I had time to acquire a mistress?' He stamped into his quarters, placed his helmet on the desk and turned to face his friend.

Chapter Three

Aquila grunted as if in approval, which served only to raise Maximus's ire further. If he hadn't such a cursed sense of honor when it came to brave women, his proud little Celt would be with him now. And although she might have been unwilling at first, he could soon have changed her mind. Seduced her into giving him her body. Into becoming his mistress.

Having such an encumbrance had never appealed to him before. But now the thought more than appealed. It wrapped around his brain, branding him with erotic images of a golden wood nymph waiting for him at the end of a long day, of him teaching her about the civilized world, of them entertaining each other in bed, night after delirious night.

His training forbade him to groan at the graphic visions filling his mind, or to move a single muscle to release the unbearable pressure whipping through his blood. But his training couldn't prevent the pounding at his temples, or the accelerated beat of his heart, or the way his balls tightened with excruciating tension at the base of his engorged shaft.

"Then I have just the thing you need," Aquila said, and Maximus didn't have the first idea what the other man was talking about. Unless he knew where to find a certain Celtic lady. "Just before you arrived, the Eques Legionis returned."

Maximus jerked his head to indicate Aquila should continue. The scouting party had been gone for almost two weeks, checking the local area for renegades. It was an inevitable fact that wherever they conquered, there would always be some locals who attempted rebellion.

"They rounded up a couple of dozen peasants hiding in the hills."

"I'll interrogate the leaders immediately." It would make an excellent diversion from the current agony between his legs. And there was always the possibility these insurgents knew the whereabouts of their missing nobles. If such information was to be divulged, it was imperative he heard first. He wanted no other cohort but his own to discover his wood nymph.

"Of course. But there's someone else you might like to"—Aquila paused for a fleeting moment—"interrogate first, Maximus."

His senses went on red alert at the gleam in Aquila's eye. "Someone else?" His voice was harsh as implausible possibilities snaked through his mind. Surely the scouts hadn't found *her* during the short time he had left her?

Despite the way every inch of his tormented flesh ached to see his golden-haired Celt again, he hoped to all the gods it wasn't her. He trusted no man to keep his hands to himself when faced with such haunting loveliness. "Explain yourself."

Aquila shrugged. "They came across a vision of Venus sheltering by a stream as they returned this morning." He gave an appreciative grin that Maximus didn't appreciate at all. It was all he could do to keep himself from throttling the life from the centurion. Vile images flooded his brain of his wood nymph being violated by rutting soldiers. No matter how disciplined every legionary was under his command, the possibility always remained that lust would conquer training.

His guts knotted and again he questioned why he hadn't simply taken her while he'd had the chance. Here she would be under his protection and none would dare even to look at her for fear of displeasing him. Instinctively his hand fisted around his gladius. *Any* man who took her would feel the merciless slice of Maximus's blade castrate him.

"Unless you wish me to question her?"

"Where is she?" His voice betrayed nothing, and yet Aquila shot him a sharp glance as if something in his tone alerted him.

"I'll fetch her."

As the door closed behind the centurion, Maximus glanced toward his bunk. In keeping with his rank, his quarters were double sized, and he shared with no other. When his men gathered here in the evenings, he'd have ample time to visit his golden Celt.

He'd find her lodgings in the civilian settlement, perhaps sharing with the young mistress of Faustus the Tribunus Laticlavius.

There was a rap on the door. Anticipation heated his blood, heightened his senses.

"Enter."

Aquila brought in the reluctant captive, gently ushering her through the door. Maximus stared at her, disappointment crashing through him although logically he'd known the chances of this girl being his wood nymph were slender.

But the disappointment curdled his guts nevertheless.

"Primus." Aquila caught his eye and raised a brow. His message was clear. The poor girl was on the verge of passing out in terror.

Maximus smothered an impatient sigh. He was a warrior, not a cursed babysitter. If the girl wanted to linger by a stream, why had the scouts not left her there? It was obvious she posed no threat to Rome.

But the scouts had captured her. Therefore, it was his duty to interrogate her and ascertain she was as harmless as she appeared.

"I mean you no harm." It was the second time he'd said that to a woman this morn. Except this one looked as if she would collapse if he so much as frowned at her, whereas the other—

The other had faced him with astounding courage, even when she had thought him about to end her life.

He scowled, just as this female raised her head. Pale blue eyes widened in apparent dread and her lips trembled in soundless entreaty.

Maximus flashed Aquila a dark glare, but Aquila's attention was focused on the fragile brunette in her threadbare garments. And suddenly Maximus knew why Aquila had offered to question the girl in his stead.

He curbed his irritation. It was too late to take up that offer now.

"Sit." He jerked his head toward the chair, and then watched Aquila bring it to the girl and gently press her shoulder until she did as commanded. Maximus leaned against the front of his desk and folded his arms. "What's your name?" Was he destined to repeat himself all day? Surely as the Primus Pilus, he had better things to do with his time than terrify a native?

"Branwen." Her voice was so soft he barely heard her, but at least she had answered him. That was more than the other had done.

"Branwen." He pushed the golden wood nymph from his mind. Time enough to think of her later. In bed. To his disgust his body hardened once again.

He gritted his teeth, took a controlled breath and focused his attention on the trembling girl before him. "What were you doing at the stream, Branwen?"

Collecting water? his brain supplied with a sneer. *Bathing?*

Washing her family's clothing? Or perhaps organizing the over-throw of Rome?

Gods, he was going to have something to say to the scouts when he caught up with them.

"N-nothing." Her blue eyes darted from him to Aquila, then down at her clenched hands. "I was just—nothing."

"Just what?"

She twisted her fingers together and shot Aquila another fleet-ing glance. "My grandfather isn't well. I was just—looking for something to help him."

"At the stream?" Maximus knew there was something she wasn't telling him, but he also knew it was hardly a matter of state importance. But, important or not, it was his responsibility to find the truth.

He hoped the girl would tell him without any histrionics. He had the renegades to interrogate before he could think of breaking his fast.

"Sp-special herbs for his heart." She still didn't make eye con-tact. He shifted against the edge of the desk, and attempted to curb his growing impatience.

"Which herbs?" Aquila said, and Maximus shot him a sharp look. Aquila missed it, since he was still staring at Branwen as if she truly was the goddess Venus.

Maximus frowned down at her. She was attractive enough and no doubt would satisfy a man's needs. But she didn't possess the mystical quality of his golden nymph.

His mood degenerated further when he recalled why she most certainly *wasn't* his nymph—because he had allowed her to walk free.

"I can't—can't remember."

Gods, the creature was a half-wit. How could her grandfather hope to survive when the girl couldn't even remember which herbs were meant to save him?

"Do you live here?" Aquila said. When Branwen gave a nervous nod, he continued. "I may be able to assist." He looked at Maximus, as if just remembering his presence. "If the Primus has no objection?"

Inexplicably, a cold rage slithered through Maximus's chest and wrapped around the region of his heart. It was common practice to offer assistance in return for sexual favors. In the distant past, he'd done it himself. He couldn't understand why now the thought sickened him.

Was it because he'd been unable to find something the golden wood nymph had needed—something she needed so desperately he could have bargained her freedom with? Hypocrisy left a bitter taste in his mouth.

"The Primus has no objection." If Aquila wanted to fuck this insipid scrap, in exchange for a few herbs from the Valetudinarium, it was nothing to Maximus.

Branwen's fidgeting fingers stilled on her lap and she gave Aquila a startled glance, as if unsure as to his meaning.

Maximus jerked his head at Aquila to indicate this farce of an interrogation was finished. The girl would soon understand the terms of the bargain. It was up to her whether she wanted to fulfill them or not.

Two days later Maximus led his elite Centuria on their regular training session of a twenty-mile route march. They'd left two hours ago, all of them carrying full equipment, and still the exertion wasn't enough to alleviate the dull ache between his legs.

He increased the pace, despite the unrelenting heat from the sun and the steep incline of the terrain. This situation was intolerable. Tonight he'd hang his principles and seek relief in one of the local brothels.

As he crested the hill, he paused for a moment to scan the area.

Far in the distance sprawled a massive forest, and beyond he could just discern yet another mountain. There was nothing here to warrant further scrutiny, but as he turned to make tracks toward the nearby river, a furtive movement from the valley below caught his attention. Instinctively he raised his hand, demanding silence, and his troops became stone.

Maximus narrowed his eyes and focused. There was no mistake. The girl slipping into the sparse wood that hugged the valley was Branwen.

Senses on full alert, he turned to his troops. "Make camp," he commanded. It wasn't usual to break a routine march but that was of no consequence. A legionary had to be ready for any contingency and his men were already obeying his order.

He dropped his pack and watched them for a moment. "I'll reconnaissance the area." With that he turned and marched into the valley, not knowing why he followed the girl, aware only that he must.

She was making her way to the stream where the scouts had encountered her two days ago. Why? They had reported nothing untoward with the area. In fact they'd picked her up only for his viewing pleasure.

But she was here. And to have arrived before his men meant she must have left the settlement at dawn. Again, why would she return to the place where she had previously been captured?

The renegades he'd interrogated had not been connected with Branwen. They had, however, eventually admitted to plotting a full-scale rebellion, and, while he admired their courage, such treason couldn't be allowed to go unpunished.

But Branwen didn't have the backbone for such activities. Although he'd been mildly surprised that, as yet, Aquila hadn't managed to persuade her to share his bed in exchange for medical assistance for her grandfather.

He entered the wood, mentally recalled the map of the area

the scouts had detailed, and stealthily made his way to the hidden glade.

Maximus saw her at the exact moment the glinting stream became visible. He sucked in a shocked breath, heart pounding in his throat, echoing through his brain, and instinctively retreated behind the nearest tree.

It was impossible she could have seen him. Swiftly he removed his helmet with its distinctive, eye-catching plumage, and once again caught her in his line of vision.

Branwen was on her knees before his golden wood nymph, her fingers fluttering over the nymph's feet as if she were worshipping her goddess.

"Forgive me, my lady." Branwen's voice came to him clearly, but his focus was on the other. He hadn't imagined that haunting beauty. In reality, she was even fairer than he recalled. Lust, hot and heavy, roiled through his arteries, thickening his shaft, splintering any hopes he'd harbored of a cheap whore being able to cool the fever steaming his blood. There was only one who could quench the unnatural flames consuming him, who could satisfy the craving that clawed through every particle of his being. And she stood barely twenty feet from him.

She crouched, grasped Branwen's hands and pulled her to her feet. "It wasn't your fault." Her voice was as soft and musical as he remembered, and sent darts of sharp pleasure coursing through his body.

"The soldiers polluted the holy Cauldron with their presence." Branwen sounded on the verge of tears. "It's my fault they found her."

"Cerridwen is not found," his Celt said. "Her Cauldron's not polluted, Branwen. Any fault in this is mine, not yours. I should have been here for you. I'm sorry." She took a deep breath, and Maximus watched her breasts swell above the square cut of her gown. "Did the soldiers hurt you?"

Branwen shook her head and sniffled. "But the centurion frightens me."

His Celt frowned. "The centurion?"

"He wants to help." Branwen sounded confused. "But how can the Roman understand what ails my grandfather? I trust only you with his health, my lady."

His Celt handed Branwen a leather package. "The barbarians don't have our knowledge, Branwen. Continue administering this to your grandfather. I'll be here if you ever need to return."

A smile twisted Maximus's lips. So his lady was a healer. He decided that pleased him. But not as much as he intended she please him in the not-too-distant future.

He'd let her go once. He had no intention of allowing her to escape again. Not until he'd tasted the sweet nectar of her lips once more, or speared his fingers through her long hair, pulling it loose from its restraints and feeling the silky softness envelope him in a halo of gold.

"Go now." His Celt held a note of command in her tone. "But not the way you came. Roman soldiers swarm upon the hill. Take the long route home."

His breath stilled, caught midchest at the significance of her words. How did she know where his men were? Did she have spies posted about the countryside?

Branwen bowed her head, clasped his Celt's hand and bestowed a reverential kiss. She then scurried away in the opposite direction.

His heart thudded against his ribs, echoed through his brain. His golden nymph continued to stand by the edge of the sparkling spring as it bubbled from a cluster of rocks, her attention focused on the direction Branwen had fled. He could emerge, capture her. She could do nothing to deny him. And yet he remained rooted to the spot, captivated by her serene profile, unable to deny her mystical hold.

She turned toward his hiding place. Stared through the trees at him. He knew she couldn't see him through the shadows of the trees and yet he felt exposed. Naked.

Intolerable. No man made him feel that way, much less a mere woman. Even a woman as beautiful as his golden wood nymph.

He saw an enigmatic smile touch her lips, as if a thought had amused her. And then she spoke. "You can come out now, Roman barbarian."

Chapter Four

Anticipation sizzled through Carys's blood as she waited for her Roman to emerge from the wood. She couldn't see him, but he was there. Somehow, she could *feel* him, deep in the most sacred recess of her soul, the same way she could feel when the wise Cerridwen merged with her spirit.

Flee. The command shivered through her mind, sharp with the acrid scent of fear. She had escaped the enemy once. To tempt fate twice was foolish in the extreme.

Except she hadn't tempted fate by returning to the waterfall. She was at the Cauldron, in the holy glade of her beloved goddess. And her Roman had discovered her there.

He marched from the shadowed depths, magnificent and terrifying in the strange, exotic uniform of his conquering race. The sun glinted on his polished breastplate and enhanced the rich scarlet of his cloak, but Carys focused on his short black hair, on his hard, unsmiling face, and finally on his unblinking blue gaze.

"We meet again." She spoke in her mother tongue, for some

reason unwilling to let him know she was fluent in Latin. She clasped her fingers together so he couldn't see how they trembled. And yet despite the shrill voice that shrieked through her mind, commanding her to turn and flee before it was too late, she wasn't afraid of what this Roman might do to her.

Only of what the consequences to her people might be.

That should be enough reason for her to seek instant escape. And yet she remained where she was, allowing him to close the distance between them, allowing her lingering chances of freedom to slip into nothingness.

"It seems the gods wish our paths to cross, my lady." His tone was sardonic, but as rich and sensual as she recalled. As erotic as any of the dreams she'd enjoyed over the last two nights.

"My gods or yours?" Her breath was tight in her chest, constricting her lungs and squeezing her vocal cords. She hoped he couldn't hear the catch in her voice, or the way her heart pounded against her ribs. She didn't want this Roman to know just how fundamentally he affected her.

He paused before her. So close she could reach out her hand and touch his battle-scarred armor. "Perhaps our gods work in harmony."

"*Our* gods?" Had she misheard? She jerked her gaze from the sensual outline of his lips and stared into his eyes. Despite her covert Latin education, she agreed with the general consensus that Romans were barbarous heathens who acknowledged no true gods—not even the all-seeing, most divine goddess of all, the Morrigan—only their own craven idols.

But if that was so, how could this Roman even suggest he acknowledged the existence of her gods?

He reached out, almost as if he couldn't help himself, and lifted the end of her braid. "Perhaps," he said, as the unbound strands of her hair slid through his fingers, "the same gods answer to different names."

He only touched her hair. And yet she could feel his touch lighting her soul. And his words ignited her brain.

"Different names," she breathed. A revolutionary concept. Almost blasphemous. And yet—strangely intoxicating, the way she felt when Cerridwen imparted a sliver of knowledge so illuminating as to be for her mind only.

His hand fisted around her hair. "Will you tell me your name now, my lady?"

It would be so easy. And yet there was power in her name. She might desire this Roman with every breath she took, but she couldn't trust him.

"Not yet." The words slipped out before she could prevent them. Before she realized what they were, what they could mean. *Not yet?* Would she, then, be able to trust him at some point?

The corner of his mouth lifted in a brief smile. "Then you intend to tell me another time?" He wound a length of her braided hair around his fist, and she stumbled forward until there was barely a breath between them. "In that case I won't demand your compliance now."

She drew in a deep breath. The earthy aroma of woods and leaves and sacred water diminished beneath the tantalizing scent of virile male, scrambling her mind. What remained of it. "I will never comply with your demands, Roman."

His blue eyes ensnared her. Surely they were the eyes of a god.

"Not yet." And then he smiled, the smile of a man supremely confident in the outcome of his prediction.

Entranced by his wordplay, she smiled back. "Not ever. I comply with no man's demands."

His teeth flashed as if he found her comment humorous. "You must have driven your father to distraction." And then his smile vanished, and the effect was as profound as if storm clouds covered the sun. "Do you defy your husband also, my lady?"

He had mentioned a husband before. Did the thought of her owning a husband irk him that much?

It shouldn't matter. And yet a thrill chased along her spine at the knowledge this proud Roman disliked the thought of her being bound to another.

"If I possessed a husband, he would know better than to issue me such demands."

His eyes darkened and his grasp on her hair tightened, but she refused to stumble before him again. Instead she resisted the pressure he exerted and embraced the needles of pain dancing across her skull.

Because the pain held a twisted element of pleasure, that spun through her mind and ignited strange tremors along the back of her neck, over her shoulders and across the exposed swells of her breasts.

"You're widowed?" His voice held no softness. Just a raw demand to know.

His smoldering gaze stoked her arousal and the tremors wrapped around her nipples in a sensual caress, tightening the sensitive peaks, straining against the fabric of her gown with unbearable need.

"I'm not widowed. I'm my own mistress, Roman."

Something flashed in his eyes, something dark and dangerous, as if her words held unknown meaning to him. He took a step toward her, loosened his hold on her hair and slipped his hand around the nape of her neck.

Calloused fingers curled around her vulnerable flesh. Strong. Demanding. *Possessive.* She tipped back her head so she could look into his face, but also to show him his predatory action didn't intimidate her.

He fascinated her. Intrigued her. Drew her as inexorably as a moth was drawn to the deadly flame. Like the moth, she would be burned. Unlike the moth, she knew her fate in advance.

And still she had no desire to flee.

"Under whose protection are you?" His voice was low, smoky, and wrapped its erotic spell around her senses.

"Cerridwen protects me." As she whispered the words, her fingers trailed along his strong, uncompromising jaw, and shivers chased from the tips of her fingers, along her arms, and to the throbbing peaks of her nipples.

His jaw clenched. Barely discernible stubble grazed her flesh and she cupped her palm around him delighting in the evocative scent of his utter maleness, the texture of his roughened skin and the hard, unyielding planes of his bronzed face.

"Do you live out here alone?" His eyes never left hers. His fingers scorched her nape. And the vibrant feathers upon his helmet brushed the swells of her breasts.

As if in a dream, Carys rose onto her toes, allowing her fingers to trace over his high cheekbone, higher, across his temple. Her breath caught in her throat as she tentatively caressed his short black hair.

Sensation sizzled through her fingertips. Softness of the red squirrel's fur yet abrasive, like his jaw. Intoxicating. She ran her palm over his head again, delighting in the strange combination of textures.

"If I don't have you soon, I fear for my sanity." His voice was raw with need. For her. Thrills shivered through her, and her need matched his.

He gave a mirthless laugh and pulled her roughly against him. His armor dug into her soft flesh, and she curled her free hand around his forearm. Such primal power in his arms. And yet he made her feel safe.

"You'd do more than tremble if you understood me," he said grimly, and only then, with a rush of awareness, did she realize he was speaking Latin. "Gods. You could do nothing to stop me from taking you. Right here. Where you stand."

She wouldn't want to stop him. She scraped her nails over his nape. Curse his foreign armor. She couldn't feel his body at all, and she wanted to feel his body. Wanted to see it, touch it. Taste and lick it. Do everything in reality that she had been practicing in her dreams for the last three moons.

He snaked his arm around her waist, and the edge of his helmet dug against her buttock before tumbling to the ground. His lips brushed against hers, hot breath mingling, and the tip of his tongue slid sensuously along the seam of her lips.

"I want to thrust my cock into your luscious mouth," he said, and sudden, shocking heat speared Carys low in her womb, painful in its erotic intensity. "I want to see you take me in, watch you suck on me. Feel your tongue stroke my length, until I pump my hot seed down your slender, tempting throat."

Vivid images flooded her mind of her on her knees before him in this sacred glade. Of her taking his rigid shaft in her hand, and guiding him into her open mouth.

She had never tried such a thing before. Had never wanted to contemplate such an activity with Aeron, despite his constant demands, and yet with this Roman—whose name she still didn't know—the notion captivated her.

His tongue teased, and she opened her mouth and sucked him inside. And imagined something hotter, thicker. Longer. She stroked him with her tongue, dug her nails into the back of his neck and clasped her fingers around his forearm.

But it wasn't enough. His armor was an impenetrable barrier. She needed naked flesh. Satisfaction. *Orgasm.*

He dragged his mouth free, panted against her swollen lips. "You can't survive out here alone, my lady. Without a man to protect you, you have no chance." He kissed her again, a deep, plundering kiss that turned her lungs inside out. Sweet agony.

Again he pulled free. "You're coming with me."

Of course she was coming with him. They would come together. She had heard of such delights. It was a magical experience, a supreme gift from the goddess, and one she desperately wished to share with this hard, tough centurion.

His hand slipped from her nape, as if reluctant to relinquish his possession. But soon he would possess her in a far more intimate manner. And she would possess him. And then they would come. Her swollen clit throbbed with anticipation and liquid heat dampened her pussy at the realization that soon—very soon—this Roman would be hers.

The tip of his finger trailed over her parted lips. "So tempting," he ground out, still speaking in his native Latin as if her language somehow eluded him. "But it's better we wait. Later I'll have all the time I need to explore every beautiful curve of your perfect body."

She licked the tip of his finger. Salty. She caught him with her teeth and drew him into her mouth. She didn't want later. She wanted now.

He gave a ragged laugh and stroked her head, clasped her plait and let her braid slide along his palm. "That's right, my little Celtic lady. Gods, you'll milk me dry." He closed his eyes and clenched his jaw, as if she caused him pain. "We need to go. Now." He spoke in Celtic and focused on her, eyes almost black with desire. And through the hot, swirling fog of arousal that clouded her reason, Carys suddenly understood.

She jerked back, panting, and stared at him. He sighed heavily as if he had expected her to pull away.

"You're not my captive," he said. "I want to offer you my protection. With me you'll have everything you wish."

He was wrong. She wouldn't have her freedom, no matter how much the Roman believed otherwise. "You want to offer me protection in exchange for"—she hesitated for a heartbeat, because saying the words out loud tarnished everything—"use of my body."

A pained frown crawled across his brow, as if he didn't much care for her analysis. "I hope you might use my body also."

She wasn't in the mood to play word games. "But I don't require your protection, Roman. I offer you myself because I want to. Not because I need something from you in return."

"I didn't mean to cause offense, my lady." Still frowning, he reached out and brushed stray strands of hair from her heated cheek. "But if you're going to be mine, then I want you where I can look after you."

Something deep inside her melted at his words. What would it be like to have a man such as this truly care for her? Look after her, in the way he so clearly meant?

But she wasn't a Roman woman who, rumor said, was incapable of making any decision for herself. Carys was not only a Celt. She was a Druid, and to willingly relinquish any of her power to another—let alone a man from the enemy—was unthinkable.

She threaded her fingers through his as he gently cradled her face. His hand was large beneath hers, yet his touch was light as thistledown.

"I can look after myself."

Something shifted in those mesmerizing blue eyes. "The scouts combed this entire area. They discovered no trace of habitation." His fingers tightened, but not enough to cause discomfort. "Where are you living?" It was no idle question. It was a demand.

Carys bowed only to the demands of her goddess.

"You know I can't tell you. I have my kin to protect against your wrath." And how great his wrath would be, should he ever discover her truth. Even crucifixion was considered too easy a death for a Druid. Aeron had seen the Roman invaders decimate her people in visions, visions that had ultimately saved all their lives.

The suspicion in his eyes faded, and his hand gentled once more. "Your kin is safe with me, lady. None of your blood could raise my wrath." He paused for a heartbeat. "But they must surrender to the might of Rome. You know this."

She stretched up and once again stroked his short black hair. Back and forth. As if he was a harmless puppy. Entranced by the sensations skittering over her fingertips, and the mesmeric quality of his intense gaze, she offered him a wondering smile.

"You know I can never surrender, Roman."

His calloused thumb caressed her cheek. "You, my lady, need only surrender to me."

Flame licked through her womb, caused the muscles in her

damp channel to contract with need. She wanted to surrender to this exotic warrior. But she could never betray her people by accompanying him to his fortification.

She caressed the curve of his ear. So strange for a man to have not even one piercing in his lobe. "And yet I remain here."

He cupped her nape once again and the warmth from his hand branded her. "You would defy me?" The words were threatening, and yet she didn't feel threatened. She felt exhilarated.

"Yes."

"I don't need your permission to take you, lady. How would you prevent me from carrying out my desire?" His grip became possessive and tension radiated from him, as if it were a living entity, coiled, ready to spring.

"If all you want is a slave, then there's nothing I can do to prevent it." Sweet Cerridwen, she didn't want to prevent him from carrying out his desire. Only his arrogant wish to enchain her. Her pulse throbbed erratically against his imprisoning hold, stirring her blood and heating her brain.

Time suspended in a shimmering haze as she returned his unwavering gaze. No breeze stirred in the sacred glade, no call of bird, nor rustle of woodland creature.

Her Roman was the only man in the world, and her future rested on his response.

His hand slid around her throat, across her collarbone, and deliberately grazed the naked swells of her breasts. She gasped involuntarily, arching toward him, begging for more. But his hand dropped from her.

"A slave?" His voice was deceptively calm, yet she could feel the hum of anger in his tone, as if her accusation offended his honor. "Is that the only way you would come with me, Celt?"

She dragged in a lungful of air, tried to rein in her cantering lust. But her mind wanted release just as much as her body. "You could come to me."

Silence, so deep, so profound, it echoed in her bones and

shattered through the stars. His eyes narrowed and brow creased, as if such a notion were astonishing, unbelievable.

As if the thought of a centurion bowing to the wishes of a Celt were beyond comprehension.

Eternity whispered with each frantic beat of her heart. And then he retreated one step. "You would meet with me illicitly?"

Her breath tangled, constricting her throat. "Yes." It was the only word she could manage. She hoped it would be enough. Already she had said too much, given him too much, and yet she couldn't help herself.

Surely she wasn't a traitor if she never divulged who she truly was? Where her people hid?

This was purely for her. To satisfy her dreams and fulfill her frustrated desires. Nothing more. There could never be anything more. The Roman would satisfy her craving for mutual orgasmic knowledge, and when they had both slated their lust she could quietly vanish within the sacred spiral.

"Why?" His voice was hard, unyielding.

"Because that is what I wish."

Incredulity washed over his features. Had he never been crossed before? "And I should acquiesce to this, simply because it's what you wish?"

Carys resisted the overwhelming urge thundering through her blood to reach out and touch his arm, or run her fingers through his irresistible hair once again. He had stepped back from her. It was up to him to make the first move forward.

"Yes." There was no other answer she could give.

Another silence vibrated through the glade, scraping along every nerve she possessed. Once again his inscrutable warrior mask shielded his true emotions as he contemplated her, as if assessing her worth as a mere spoil of war.

In his mind perhaps that was all she was.

But deep in the fundamental essence of her being, Carys knew that wasn't so. If it were, he would have taken her with him two days ago.

"What would your family do to you, if they ever discovered you'd willingly fraternized with the enemy?"

Startled by his question, she blinked at him in momentary confusion. Why would he care?

And yet he had asked the question, the one question she'd avoided thinking herself. Because she knew how violently her kin would react to such betrayal.

"They'll never discover it." She wouldn't ask Cerridwen to make this Roman hers, but she would ask her goddess to help conceal the illicit liaison. Because that wasn't being selfish. It was putting her people's safety first.

Scorn whispered through her mind, but she turned from it. Her logic was sound. Her goddess would understand.

The Roman's blue eyes incinerated her, scorching the breath from her lungs. "But what," he said in a deceptively calm way, "if they do?"

Chapter Five

Carys tried to block his question from her mind, but in a cascading flood, the images poured through.

Cold terror gripped her, ice shivering through her veins, as she recalled the fate of a Druid who had been caught spying for one of the savage Briton kings.

Nine years ago, the eleven-year-old Carys had only recently entered the sacred fold, but that didn't prevent her from bearing witness to the traitor's doom.

Spiritual isolation from the immortals would have been punishment enough for any Druid, but an example had to be made. As the sun sank behind the hills at the end of that blood-soaked day, the severed head of the ritualistically mutilated Druid was sent to her worthless lover.

But Carys wasn't a spy. Such a fate could never be hers. And yet the fear of being denied communion with her beloved Cerridwen twisted her soul.

"Answer me." His command was low. When had he stepped

toward her? Carys struggled to keep her emotions contained, the terror of that long-ago day and the turmoil she always felt whenever the Roman was near.

She dragged in a deep breath, but instead of clearing her head with the fresh scents of the sacred glade, her lungs filled with the masculine essence of raw sexuality.

"What they might do to me is nothing to what they would do if they believed I was your captive." It was true. A captive Druid was inconceivable. If rescue failed, the Druids would go to war and blood would drench the valleys. And her blood would be first.

"Do you think I fear a few barbarous Celts?" His tone was faintly mocking, but the hint of a smile touched his lips.

"No." Carys wondered if her Roman feared anything. "*I* fear."

His smile faded. A wood warbler's haunting song shivered on the warm breeze. She saw his jaw tighten, his eyes narrow. "It would never be my intention to harm your kin, lady."

She understood what he was telling her. "I know." If attacked, he would protect himself. She couldn't blame him for that.

But he didn't know her kin were the spiritual core of this land and its people, the ones who had eluded his soldiers since their invasion of Cymru. If he knew that, his intention would be far more deadly toward her.

The roughened pad of his forefinger grazed across the top of her breast, halting her thoughts, stalling her breath. His finger delved into her cleavage, and all the while his eyes remained locked with hers.

"I accept your terms, my lady." His finger slowly slid from her warm embrace, leaving her strangely chilled and bereft. And then his words settled in her mind, illuminating the darkness, eradicating the lingering tendrils of terror.

Speech was beyond her capabilities. Instead she extended her right hand, and with only the merest hesitation, her Roman took it in his large, firm grasp. He raised her hand to his lips,

without bowing his head toward her, and brushed a kiss across
her fingers.

"You will meet me here later?" It was more demand than
request, but she nodded her acceptance. How could she do otherwise? Her mighty Roman warrior had agreed to her terms.

Over her captured hand, his eyes smoldered. "There's one question you haven't asked of me, lady." She heard the challenge in his
tone, as if the fact somehow irked him.

She tried to calm her racing pulses, her incoherent thoughts.
There was a question she hadn't asked, because she hadn't thought
he would respond.

"Would you tell me if I did?" Her voice was breathless.

"You'd have to ask me first. Then you'd find out."

She darted the tip of her tongue over dry lips, saw the way his
eyes followed the movement before once again locking with hers.
"What is your name, Roman?"

The breath stilled in her chest as she awaited his reply. A part of
her was convinced he wouldn't reveal such a personal detail, simply because she refused to share hers. But another part of her, the
illogical part, wanted to know his name. Wanted to savor it on her
lips, wrap it around her mind and hold it close within her heart.

His mouth twisted into an enchanting lopsided smile, and for
one shimmering moment Carys forgot he was a Roman, the enemy
of her people, and saw only a man who had haunted every moment
of her life for the last three moons. A man she feared could, too
easily, haunt the remainder of her existence if she wasn't careful.

"Tiberius." He kissed one knuckle. "Valerius." Kissed a second knuckle. "Maximus." He turned her hand and drifted his lips
across her open palm.

"Tiberius." The foreign name sounded strange on her tongue.
He smiled once again, released her hand and stepped back.

"Close friends call me Maximus, my lady."

And what did his lovers call him?

The thought slithered through her mind. Strange, for until this moment she hadn't considered he might have other lovers back at the settlement that she'd been told now surrounded the Roman fortification.

And the thought grazed her senses, wounded her soul. Even though she knew she had no right to be so injured. What the Roman did—what *Maximus* did—when he wasn't with her was none of her affair.

"Then I shall call you Maximus." She saw his eyes darken as she said his name, and banished her troublesome concerns. She would please Maximus so thoroughly this eve that he wouldn't wish to fuck any other woman but her.

"And I shall call you"—he paused for a telling heartbeat—"my lady." And his firm, sensual lips twitched, as if he tried to prevent a smile.

"Yes." She was his lady. She would always be his lady, even after their paths diverged. But she wouldn't think of that. Not now. Not when she had other, far more fascinating things to consider. Such as discovering before tonight the secrets of satisfying a man so thoroughly he would rather fry his eyes in boiling oil than look with lust upon another woman.

"Meet me here at sunset."

Again it was a demand. From a man used to having his word accepted without question. But what did she have to question? She wanted this as much as he did. And sunset was the time she would have suggested herself.

Had he thought to ask.

"Very well."

Beneath her leather-clad feet the earth stirred and discordant vibrations shivered through her soul. Maximus's soldiers grew impatient by his absence.

She couldn't explain how she knew such things, or why the wise Cerridwen had chosen her as her acolyte. She knew only that the two were intrinsically connected, and to ignore the signs of the earth was to ignore her beloved goddess herself.

With a soft sigh she bent to retrieve Maximus's helmet. It was heavier than she expected. She brushed her fingers through the proud plumage before handing it toward him.

"My lady." He inclined his head in thanks as he took his helmet. "Until tonight." He paused, and gave her a searching look as if trying to see inside her mind and find her secrets. "Keep safe." And then he turned and marched back into the shaded woods.

Aeron bowed before the ancient Druid in the small oak grove at the outer edge of the sacred spiral's protective perimeter. As always, he hoped she couldn't see into his heart and discover the bubbling resentment that festered. But she never had before. He was a master of deception, and this Druid had no reason to suspect him of anything less than absolute devotion.

"Aeron." She held out her wrinkled hand, and he took it and kissed the fragile skin, even as his senses recoiled from the touch of her skeletal fingers. "My dearest child. Come, sit with me and tell me what you see."

He sat beside her on the moss-covered log that once, long ago, had been a mighty oak. It reminded him how all great things could fall, no matter how powerful or revered.

The old woman by his side was the most powerful and revered Druid in all Cymru. But her time was coming to an end. Aeron had seen her demise in a terrifying vision while still a child, a vision of such lucidity it had ensured his rapid elevation within the spiritual ranks.

Yet even at the age of eight he had known better than to divulge the bloodied climax of that vision. The line between savior and murderer would have been too blurred to distinguish.

"Druantia." He extricated his fingers from her possessive hold under the pretext of clasping both hands around his hazel rod. "The situation beyond the sacred spiral grows more precarious by the day. Soon the invaders will have subdued all of Cymru in a fountain of blood."

Druantia didn't answer and Aeron shot her a surreptitious glance from the corner of his eye. She often didn't answer directly, a trait he found irritating when directed at him. He was no lowly acolyte. Nor even a highly respected Druid of distinction. His place in the hierarchy was second only to hers. As such, he deserved more respect from her.

He deserved more respect from Carys.

Her name scorched through his brain, temporarily obliterating the grove from his sight. Fucking Carys with her hypnotic eyes, hair spun from sunlight and impossibly independent nature.

It was intolerable she continued to refuse him. Blood pounded against his temples, threatening his outward composure, and his hands gripped the holy hazel rod with compressed rage.

He knew that soon she would submit. His visions foretold such sweet victory, and in such visceral detail, his cock thickened with anticipation even now.

"And yet we will survive, Aeron." Druantia's voice, as fragile as a decaying autumn leaf, invaded his personal world.

Curse the hag for still clinging to this life. By rights he should possess her coveted position, for his power deserved nothing less.

Just as he deserved Carys. *And he would possess both.*

"We will always prevail." He bowed his head. Yes. They would prevail, for he would never allow their beliefs to die at the hands of the heathen invaders. But they would survive on his terms. And there was no place in his new world for decrepit old women and their ancient goddesses.

"And yet Carys still denies you."

Aeron ground his back teeth together. Only Druantia would dare throw that in his face. "She's still too young to know her own mind."

"On the contrary, my dearest child." Druantia's voice scraped along his raw nerve endings. "Carys knows her own mind very well. Don't become disheartened, Aeron. The time will come when she sees you for what you truly are."

Her one and only master. The words drummed through his brain, pounded along his arteries, throbbed along the length of his erection. It took all of his considerable willpower to remain unmoving on the mossy log, when every particle wanted to roar his frustration to the heavens.

"I trust you're right, Druantia," he said instead, bestowing a gracious smile as he imagined how easy it would be to snap her neck like the dried twig it was.

Druantia stared at him from her age-glazed eyes. Eyes that always sent shivers of revulsion skittering along his spine. "The Morrigan is never wrong, my child," she said softly. "She sees Carys is our future. And who better to share that future than you, Aeron? It is written in the stars. So shall it be."

Aeron only just prevented a sneer from escaping. *He* saw the future. And the Morrigan was no part of it.

"I'm humbled the great goddess feels I am worthy." The words choked him, but Druantia didn't appear to notice. "Can she bestow advice as to how I might win Carys back to my bed?"

Druantia considered him in silence, and he thought she wasn't going to answer. Not that he needed advice from this bitch or her redundant goddess. Carys would be his because that was his desire. And when that time came, whether she submitted willingly or not was entirely up to her, but made no difference to him.

And then Druantia spoke. "Bring us fresh moon blood from Carys's next cycle. This must be collected by your own hand, Aeron, to prevent any contamination from another."

Interest flared. The image of sequestering Carys's blood aroused him, caused his shaft to thicken and balls to ache.

"I understand." Yet he had no intention of attempting any such thing. He had no need of the Morrigan's help in this or any other matter. He took Druantia's hand and bestowed another fleeting kiss. "Thank you, Great Queen."

It was late afternoon before Carys made her daily visit to Druantia. The wise Cerridwen had not been forthcoming as to how Carys could ensnare her Roman's continued interest, but Carys knew that wasn't a bad omen. It was simply because Cerridwen wasn't overly interested in sexual liaisons.

Besides, it wasn't hard to bring the conversation around to sex with her fellow Druids. Sex was a topic they all discussed frequently, and in great detail. It was simply that before today, Carys hadn't been especially interested in the specifics.

"Carys." Druantia rose from her moss-covered log and held out her arms. Carys embraced her great-grandmother's sister, secretly sorrowing at the Druid's fragility. She sometimes feared the faintest breeze might splinter her slight physical form. "My sweetest girl. Still you put yourself in danger for your people." Pride laced the old lady's tone.

Carys helped Druantia resume her seat upon the log before sitting in her usual place at her feet.

"There isn't much danger. Cerridwen protects me, as she has always protected me."

Druantia began to unwind the ties binding Carys's hair. "Alas, child. There is always danger. Only here within the spiral are we truly protected from the invaders."

Carys gave an impatient sigh. "But what good are we here, Druantia? How can we help our people if we aren't with them?" She turned as Druantia began to gently tug her fingers through her still-damp hair. Hair she had washed with scented flowers for the pleasure of her Roman.

She shivered and thrust the thought aside. She couldn't think of Maximus now. Not when she was in the presence of Druantia, and in the sacred grove of the Morrigan herself. She forced her mind back to the present. "How much longer do we have to hide?"

Druantia continued to unplait her hair. Normally Carys found the ritual soothing. But this afternoon she couldn't be soothed. Because all she could see was an endless existence stretching before her, where she could never be allowed the true freedom her soul craved.

"Darkness is descending." Druantia's voice was hushed with sorrow. "Everything we cherish is on the cusp of oblivion. How else can we protect our ways, Carys, except by shielding them from the Romans?"

Carys turned to stare at the great Druid. "But for how *long*?" Maximus hadn't derided her religion. Why couldn't it be possible for the Druids to educate the Romans into the light? Was that truly such an impossible dream? That they might, someday, live in harmony with each other?

Druantia sighed, a soft, wistful sound that sank into Carys's soul and ached with everything they had lost. "I fear for us, Carys," she said, and Carys held her hand, tracing her fingers across the delicate skin that barely covered the veins beneath. She didn't want the great Druid to fear. Because if she did, what hope remained for them all? "I fear what will happen once I continue with my journey."

"There are still many steps for you to take before that happens." Carys couldn't imagine Druantia no longer being in the physical world. Didn't *want* to imagine it.

Druantia shook her head, and confusion creased her face. "My grandmother, your own foremother, Carys, had eyes the color of the sky and the earth. Just as you do. The great Morrigan chose her as her acolyte at the age of ten."

Carys knew that, had heard the family histories many times. But Druantia liked to tell her stories, and so she said nothing. What was there to say? She knew Druantia had expected Carys to be chosen by the Great Goddess. And yet, far from being chosen, she'd always felt inexplicably rejected.

"The eve you were conceived, the Morrigan herself came to me."

Carys's breath stilled in her breast as shock ricocheted through her senses. This she *hadn't* heard before. Was her mother aware? Yet she knew she wasn't, for there were no secrets between them. Was *anyone* aware? Visions were not generally kept from those to whom they pertained. And unless she was deeply mistaken, this vision of Druantia's had a great deal to do with her.

Druantia stroked her drying hair. "She told me the child would have eyes from the sky and the earth. And that you would one day be the light in the darkness, the one who led us into the new future."

Shivers coursed over her arms, made the hair on her scalp rise. Even the wood warblers ceased their distinctive trilling, and the ensuing eerie silence screamed through her mind.

"But I'm not a leader, Druantia. I'm a healer." *Surely that wasn't the reason why the Morrigan had never honored her with her presence? Because she was a* healer?

Druantia peered at her through her clouded vision. "I knew, in my heart, the Morrigan had chosen you for her acolyte from the moment of your conception. Our goddess is not one to give up what is rightfully hers. And yet upon your birth she allowed Cerridwen to claim you." Druantia's brow puckered. "Why? You were destined to lead our people, Carys. Why did the Morrigan turn from you?"

Chapter Six

Maximus decided to indulge in the bathhouse before meeting his Celt. That she would be waiting for him he had no doubt, although logically his certainty made no sense.

Besides, if she didn't appear, he would simply tear the countryside apart until he discovered her whereabouts. It couldn't be that hard to find her, not if she were living with her family. Some traces could be uncovered, and how his scouts had missed them astounded him. Twice he had encountered her within a five-mile radius. She had to be hiding somewhere in that vicinity.

Aquila settled himself onto the neighboring bench in readiness of his own massage. "Are you intending a night in the town?"

No. He was intending a night in his Celt. He grunted as the masseur kneaded his knotted muscles.

"Possibly."

"Want some company? I know where there are some pretty girls who are more, uh, selective about those whom they favor."

Maximus eyed him. "What of the girl, Branwen? Is she still refusing you?"

Aquila's grin faded and a frown took its place. "Mars take her. I can't work her out at all. She answers me if I speak to her, and appears not to be repulsed by my presence." He shifted impatiently. "And yet if I attempt to touch her, she flees as if she believes I might ravish her."

Maximus snorted. "And nothing could be further from your mind, naturally."

Aquila scowled as if he didn't appreciate Maximus's humor. "I've no wish to hurt her. Gods, I've a good mind to give her whatever herbs her grandfather needs without any form of promise from her." He paused for a moment. "That's if she could remember what they are. She seems very vague at times."

"Perhaps she genuinely doesn't know what they are."

"Then what was she doing by the spring?" Aquila's gaze sharpened. "You think she was meeting someone there?"

Fuck. He hadn't meant to put that idea into Aquila's head. He didn't want any more searches of the area, not unless he decided his Celt needed to be flushed out for whatever reason. "I meant she doesn't appear to be in full possession of all her senses. Perhaps she simply doesn't know their names."

Aquila's scowl deepened, as if Maximus had just insulted him. "I believe her senses are intact. She is merely traumatized by the events of the last year and still in mourning for the death of her sister in childbirth."

"So you've given up on her?" He rolled his shoulders in appreciation of the masseur's ministrations and imagined his Celt giving him a full-body massage instead. Both of them oiled and naked. His lips curved. Somehow he would find a way to make that fantasy reality.

Aquila raised himself up on one elbow. "Is the Primus interested in Branwen for himself?" There was a distinct undercurrent of hostility in his friend's tone, and Maximus shot him a calculating glance.

"Not in the slightest. She's hardly my type, Aquila."

"Indeed." Aquila's tone was scathing. "And yet I've seen that look in your eye before, Maximus. If you wanted her, why didn't you take her the other morning? They brought her back for you, after all."

Maximus waved his masseur back and sat up, remembering only just in time to cover his erection with the towel. If Aquila saw that, he would never believe Maximus couldn't give a shit about his precious Branwen.

"If she interested me, I would have taken her." He rearranged the towel since it didn't appear to be doing its job. "Although I doubt she would have accepted me had I offered, so you can take your vine stick from your arse and find better use for it."

Aquila rolled onto his back and clasped his hands behind his head. The length of his erection almost rivaled Maximus's own.

At least Maximus could anticipate slaking his desire this night with the one who haunted his thoughts. Aquila, poor bastard, would have to seek relief from a whore. That knowledge was enough to temper Maximus's irritation with his friend's banal accusation.

"Go fuck a pretty girl," he said, laying a hand on Aquila's thigh. "It will help clear your thoughts. Then look at your Branwen again, and see if she still fills your loins with lust."

Aquila grunted, as if Maximus's wise words didn't much assist. Winding the towel around his hips, Maximus rose from the bench, only to come face-to-face with the Legatus, similarly disrobed.

"Sir." Maximus nodded in greeting at the imposing middle-aged man he had known his entire life, and hoped the commander wasn't about to embark on an impromptu military discussion. It had been known to happen, and was one of the reasons the Legatus preferred using the communal baths to his private bathhouse, but this evening Maximus wasn't in the mood for such distractions.

Aquila struggled to sit up, but the Legatus waved him back and then sat upon Maximus's recently abandoned bench.

Fuck. Maximus reined in the impatience threatening to steam his blood and sat beside his commander.

"I've just received word from the Senate," the Legatus said, hands splayed on his knees. "They wanted to know whether we've eliminated all the cursed Druids in the area."

The Emperor was obsessed by the Druids, and Maximus agreed their ferocity in confronting the Legion had been unexpected. "We haven't come across any since the border skirmishes."

The Legatus raised his eyebrow. "They were rather more than skirmishes, Maximus. Fucking Druids have a death wish."

Maximus conceded the point. Not only had they fought furiously; they had also rallied the villagers in the vicinity who appeared in thrall to them.

"We've discovered no evidence of further Druid activity locally." They'd found plenty of evidence that the Druids had fled the area before the Legion's arrival, which was somewhat at odds with the behavior of the previous group of Druids they'd encountered.

The Legatus grunted and hooked a finger at a pretty dark-eyed masseur. "They're long gone. I told the Senate in my last communication that they had doubtless scurried across the water to their heathen isle."

"It's the logical conclusion." Maximus agreed with his commander. Had the Druids attempted to escape over the border into Britannia, the legionaries would surely have captured them.

"Of course it is. The Druids pose no immediate threat to us here." The Legatus unwound his towel as the masseur approached with her oils. "Undoubtedly at some point we'll need to crush their stranglehold across the strait, but we're not at that strategic point as yet."

Maximus rose, and his commander arranged himself facedown on the bench.

"You informed the Senate of this?"

The Legatus grunted as the girl began to oil his back. "I did." Then he opened one eye and looked up at Maximus. "Meet with me after assembly tomorrow. We have matters of import to discuss."

It was both dismissal and permission to continue with his plans for the night. Maximus gave a sharp nod of respect and turned on his heel, instantly relegating the bloodthirsty Druids to the back of his mind.

He had an assignation to keep.

Carys peered through the arched entrance of the gigantic circular mound of earth, within which they all now lived, toward the cromlech. Aeron, as always, prowled the perimeter of the monoliths as if he were their self-appointed gaoler.

She ducked back inside and leaned against the smooth earthen wall. Her friend Morwyn, an acolyte of the Morrigan, clasped her hand in sympathy. "Aeron?"

"He doesn't usually stand guard until just before the sun sets." And there were almost three hours until then. Plenty of time to ride to the Cauldron and undertake the necessary preparations.

But only if she could slip past Aeron unnoticed.

Morwyn squeezed her fingers. "I'll distract him for you." A knowing smile lit her face, which caused Carys to give her a searching glance. She had told the older woman she needed to see someone urgently, with the implication that it was a medical emergency.

So why did Morwyn have that look of barely suppressed glee on her face? As if she guessed Carys was going to meet a secret lover?

"Thank you." Carys decided to give more credence to her deception. "Because I've given my word, Morwyn. It's imperative I see this person."

"Of course it is," Morwyn said, nodding far more vigorously

than the situation warranted. "And Aeron will never let you leave if he sees you." She stepped to the threshold before turning back. "I'll lead him away from here," she whispered. "But hurry. I don't have what he requires to maintain his interest for more than a few moments at most."

Carys watched Morwyn saunter toward Aeron, and wondered why he had never shown any interest in her. Morwyn made no secret of the fact she wanted Aeron in her bed, and it was a source of much good-natured teasing among their fellow acolytes.

Not that the dark-haired, vivacious beauty ever lacked for bed partners. And neither, until fleeing to this sacred place, had Aeron. But, since his tastes favored the young of either sex outside their spiritual circle, as far as Carys could gather, he'd been celibate for the last seven moons.

That could, she supposed, be the reason why he had started to press his attentions on her again.

She suppressed a shudder at the thought of once again becoming his lover. And wondered why, of all the acolytes, he had chosen her as the only Druid he ever fucked.

"Aeron." Morwyn's voice interrupted her thoughts. She watched the other woman run her arm along Aeron's, saw the way he imperiously brushed her touch aside. "I had a dream—a vision. I need your guidance."

"I'm not your mentor. Speak to Hywela."

"This is different. I need to show you something."

Pure reflex caused Carys to glance over her shoulder to ensure Hywela, the High Druid of the Morrigan, wasn't within earshot. Hywela, the niece of Carys's grandmother, most certainly wouldn't approve of Morwyn assisting Carys in her deception.

That she would disapprove of Carys's meeting with a Roman in the first place went without saying.

But the passage that led into the ancient underground chambers was empty. And Morwyn was leading a clearly reluctant Aeron in the opposite direction of the gateway to the outside world.

Carys sucked in a quick breath, gathered up her embroidered bag, and hurried through the cromlech.

Leading his horse, Maximus emerged into the glade and his heart slammed against his ribs at the ethereal scene. The gathering dusk swirled, but a dozen small lanterns were arranged in an oddly compressed cluster, the flickering golden flames and aromatic curling smoke enhancing the mystical creature who stood in the center.

He tethered his horse, his eyes never leaving her face. Raw lust tightened his loins, lengthened his shaft, and without further hesitation he stepped toward her.

For one dizzying moment the world undulated, as if suddenly plunged beneath clear water. The effect froze the breath in his lungs, caused his heart to stutter in his chest and sent eerie shivers chasing along the back of his neck, but before his brain could make sense of the phenomenon, it had passed, as if it had never occurred, and once again the world was steady, solid.

And his Celt awaited him.

She moved, but not toward him. Instead she walked around the perimeter of the perfect circle formed by her delicate lanterns, a *spacious* circle, as if the land had expanded between one breath and the next—*gods, he was half blinded by lust*—until she paused before the gap through which he'd entered. She knelt, still keeping him within her line of vision, and placed a small rock on the ground between the two lanterns.

His soldier's mind sharpened at her action, an insistent dagger in his cortex, demanding answers. Instinctively feeling that something beyond his understanding was happening. *And her lanterns had definitely clustered around her feet as he'd approached.*

But it was fleeting, instantly obliterated by the knowledge that the woman who had invaded his life two days ago and refused to leave was now within his power.

Without a word he held out his hand. Was it his imagination or did she hesitate for a moment? But then her hand was in his, small, fragile. He curved his fingers around her, holding her captive.

"My wood nymph." In this setting, how could she be anything else? He kissed her fingers, his gaze meshed with hers, and the glow from the lanterns and the strange luminous smoke made it hard to distinguish the fantastical colors of her eyes.

"My Roman invader." Her voice was breathless, seductive, as if his slightest touch was enough to arouse. The knowledge pleased him. He pulled her forward.

"I wish only to invade you in the most pleasurable of ways." He watched her pupils expand, dark passion rising. For him. "Unbind your hair." He wanted to see her hair falling loose over her shoulders. Needed to feel the silken curls slide through his fingers.

"You unbind it." Her whisper broke into his erotic fantasies. A smile curved his lips.

"You argue with me, even now?"

She looked up at him. He'd forgotten how diminutive she was. How infinitely dainty, as if she did indeed possess the blood of a nymph.

"I think I'd like to feel you unbind my hair." Her confession stirred his already heated blood, and his smile evolved into a grin.

"Then how can I refuse?" He released her hand and turned her around, and tugged on the soft length of leather at the end of her braid.

Dropping the leather to the ground, he slid a finger between her bound tresses and teased them free. There were no strands of jewels threaded through tonight. Her soft hair slipped over his fingers. Strangely sensuous. He continued up her braid, releasing each segment with slow deliberation until he reached her nape. Without warning, she shook her head, and her hair shimmered in the lantern light, a glowing river of living gold.

He stepped back. Her hair skimmed the curve of her buttocks, longer than he had imagined. And infinitely more beautiful.

She looked over her shoulder, her face framed by curling strands of exotic silk.

"Did that please you, my lady?" His voice was husky with need. But he would play her games for a little longer, if that amused her.

"Yes." A simple word, and yet it possessed the power to spike unadulterated lust through his groin, painful in its suddenness, in its shredding intensity.

Perhaps he wouldn't be able to play her word games for much longer. He cupped her jaw, soft skin over fragile bone.

"Come here." He accompanied his words with pressure, forcing her to turn and face him. "Do you intend to talk all night?"

"I'm not the one talking, Maximus." Her fingers traced over his, as he held her face in the palm of his hand.

He laughed, despite the throbbing agony between his legs. "Can you never open your mouth without contradicting me?"

And then he imagined her open mouth enclosing him. Gods, that would still her incessant chatter. He resisted the instinctive urge to thrust her to her knees, to demand she satisfy his clawing need.

There was time yet to satisfy both their needs.

"Would you truly want me to agree with everything you say?" She trailed her fingers along his jaw, as if the texture of his skin intrigued her. And then she reached up onto her toes and repeated her actions over his head.

He lowered his head for her, amused both by her words and her obvious fascination with his hair. Women had often run their fingers over his head, but never with such a look of awe on their faces.

And although he couldn't imagine why his hair so entranced her, he found her obvious fascination oddly erotic.

"It makes life a lot simpler when a woman obeys her man without question." He raised one eyebrow, waiting for her response. Knowing his proud Celt would never allow such a statement to pass by unchallenged.

Her fingers stilled in his hair. He saw her struggle to keep the smile from her face. And then she trailed her finger over his brow, along the length of his nose and across the seam of his lips.

"Are you my man, Maximus?" Her finger paused at the corner of his mouth. So temptingly close, he could almost taste her sweet flesh.

"For tonight, my lady, I'm all yours." His hand slid from her face to clasp her nape. "And you are mine."

Carys wrapped his words around her heart, savoring them, secreting them away in hidden corners of her mind. She knew he spoke in lust, but it didn't matter. She could imagine he wanted more than raw sex tonight, could pretend he was driven by emotions more sacred than pure masculine need.

"For tonight," she whispered, just so he knew they were equal on that point. Although the truth was she wouldn't mind being his for eternity. If only that wasn't such an impossible dream.

He gave a low laugh. "Always you must have the last word. Very well, we are each other's for tonight, if that appeases you, my lady."

Before she could assure him it did, he captured her lips, as if anticipating her thoughts, but thoughts no longer mattered, not when her Roman held her in such a close embrace, or teased her willing mouth with his tongue and nipped her tender flesh with his teeth.

Shivers skittered along her skin, hot shivers that mirrored the heat in her blood, the fire in her womb. She flattened her palm against his broad chest, delighting in the hard muscle beneath his linen tunic, the thunder of his heart against her fingers.

She slid her arms around his body. Granite strength and primal power radiated from every pore, thrilling her feminine senses, making her feel safe. *Protected.*

And yet she was the one who protected them both from untoward attack, here inside her own sacred circle.

Her Roman could never discover such magic.

She pushed it from her mind, concentrated on the moment, on having him in her arms, of feeling his hard body surround her.

Concentrated on the spiraling sensations spinning at the juncture of her thighs. Such sweet, terrifying sensations, part pleasure, part pain. And wholly exhilarating.

"I want you naked." His breath was hot against her swollen lips. "Your naked flesh against my naked flesh." He drew back, only far enough to stare into her eyes. "I want to strip you, my lady. Strip every garment from your body."

Liquid heat flooded her pussy at the wild look in his eyes, at the passion in his words and the way his hands covered her buttocks in a hard, possessive hold.

He hadn't asked permission. And yet, in his way, he had. She drew in a shuddering breath, caught the strange scent of his foreign soap, so unlike the scent of flowers her people used, and yet shockingly arousing by its very difference.

"I want to strip you too." She could barely speak, her heart hammered so violently against her lungs, and yet he heard, for she saw his predatory smile.

"No." He covered her hand as she attempted to loosen his tunic, and his other hand molded the curve of her bottom. "Not yet."

He began to unthread the laces of her gown. For such a large man he managed such an intricate task with dexterity. She glanced down at his fingers as they loosened her clothing, then up into his face. He caught her eye and gave her a disarming smile that sank into her soul.

His fingers slid to her shoulders and slowly eased her gown over her arms. The night was mild, but still she shivered as the air caressed her naked flesh. Another moment and he exposed her breasts to his view, and Carys hitched her breath, part with nerves, part anticipation.

For an eternity he gazed at her, and the heat emanating from him warmed her skin, and the shivers became tremors of need.

"Don't fear me." His voice was husky, and he trailed one finger across the swell of her breast, and gently circled her sensitive areola.

She gasped, clenched her fists. How could so fleeting a touch ignite such fierce desire?

"See how your nipples crave my touch?" He grazed the tip of his finger across her erect peak and she dug her teeth into her lower lip to stop herself from crying out.

She wanted to touch him. But she was bound by her own gown, her arms trapped by her sides. Sweet torture.

Slowly he lowered his dark head. His lips brushed across her throbbing bud. Then retraced his sensual path, this time with the tip of his tongue. Hot. Wet. And when he looked up at her, abandoning her aching breast, the air skittered over her damp skin, and again her limbs quivered with reaction.

"My lady." Desire vibrated his voice, hummed in the space between them. He inched her gown over her arms, exposing her belly. She caught her breath as his hands skimmed her hips, and then her gown slithered without hindrance to the grass.

Sweet Cerridwen. She was naked before him. Flame flared between her thighs as she saw him look at her there, at the place she wanted him to look. To touch and stroke and make her feel everything she had only ever experienced in the sanctuary of her own mind and familiarity of her own hands.

He inhaled a ragged breath before tearing his gaze from her pussy. "You're more beautiful than I imagined."

The tip of her tongue dampened her dry lips. Now was the time to pose provocatively, flutter her eyelashes and tease him by playing with her nipples, her clit.

All this she knew. And yet she remained immobile before his scorching gaze, paralyzed by the intensity of the moment.

He cradled her face. Had she imagined that slight tremble? Surely her Roman would never tremble before her. And yet he had. And the knowledge thrilled.

Chapter Seven

"You've haunted my thoughts since the first moment I saw you." His voice was oddly hushed, and his thumb gently caressed her cheek. "I've wanted this. But I don't want you to be afraid of me, lady."

She swallowed, so hard when her mouth was as dry as the leaves in autumn. Perhaps every drop of moisture in her body had gathered between her thighs.

Instinctively she pressed her knees together, but that only increased pressure on her clit, and she gave another involuntary shudder.

"I'm not afraid of you, Maximus." Her voice didn't sound like her own. So breathless. So aroused. She pressed her face against his hand, to show him how much she craved his touch, and was rewarded when he once again resumed gently stroking her heated skin.

"And yet you tremble like a virgin on her wedding night." His fingers stilled, as if a thought had just occurred to him. "You're not a virgin, are you, my lady?"

How could he think such of her? Despite her nakedness she drew herself up proudly. "I am not." His insult stung, but perhaps he didn't realize what his question implied.

She took a deep breath, noticed how his attention slipped to watch her breasts. "Maximus."

When he didn't immediately return his focus to her face, she cupped his jaw, until he once again looked at her.

"I'm a Celtic woman," she told him. "I worship the goddess and all her gifts she bestows upon us."

Just because she hadn't enjoyed those gifts while Aeron grunted over her didn't mean she had ignored the goddess. Even if the goddess ignored *her*. At least whenever she pleasured herself she never experienced discomfort or dull dissatisfaction. But Maximus didn't need to know that.

"The goddess?" Confusion briefly clouded his features, as if he didn't know to whom or what she referred. She reminded herself he was Roman. His ways were different from hers.

"I offered my virginity to the goddess six years ago," she said, just to clarify that she was a woman and not a girl. He may not have intended to slight her; her knowledgeable tutor had explained how Roman men idealized girls ignorant of the goddess's delights, but the slight rankled nevertheless. "I tremble with need for you, not from fear of you."

The tense expression hardening his features relaxed and a smile of pure masculine pride curved his lips. Carys smiled back, relieved he had believed her. For as much as she wanted to take everything this Roman had to offer her, a part of her did fear.

Feared that, even with him, she might be unable to attain the heights of pleasure for which she so longed.

With great economy, Maximus shed his cloak and tunic. "Touch me," he commanded, but his hand was gentle as he trailed his fingers along the line of her jaw.

Touch him? She wanted to feast upon him. Greedily she devoured his well-defined muscles, the tawny gleam of his skin that the lanterns enhanced to a mystical glow, and traced her finger over one of his many battle scars.

He made an odd sound in the back of his throat, and she glanced up at him, frowning. "Did I hurt?" She couldn't decipher whether he had groaned from pain or—but surely not—stifled a laugh.

His lips twitched and he appeared on the verge of saying something. But then he shook his head.

She flattened her palm against his warm skin, thrilling to the masculine texture of flesh and hair. "I don't wish to hurt you," she said, knowing she wasn't, knowing she could never hurt this Roman even if she wanted such a thing. But it felt strangely erotic to turn his words back on him.

"Nothing you do could possibly hurt me." His body was tense beneath her hand, as if he held his base male instincts under iron control. "You may well kill me, but you won't hurt me."

Carys glided both hands over his chest, delighting in the way his hair tickled her palms. The sensations shimmered along her fingers, along her arm, and tightened her erect nipples still further.

"I won't kill you." She reached up, caressed his shoulders, then skimmed her hands along his firm biceps. "You have a beautiful body." Even she could hear the awe in her voice, but she couldn't help it. He had a body made for worship. And she was willing to pay homage.

He gripped her arms and pulled her roughly to him. "My body is ready for yours." Raw lust sprang from every syllable. "Play with me later, my lady. Allow us to slake our desire first."

Her breasts crushed against his chest. She gave an experimental wriggle, and her nipples chafed against his rough hair. "Yes." She whispered the word against his shoulder and then looked up. "Yes."

Large hands roamed over her back, exploring every dip of her waist and swell of her buttocks. "I'll fuck you as no man has ever fucked you before."

His hot promise sent darts of desire streaking through her

swollen clit. She believed him. More truly than he would ever know.

"And I'll—" Her response tripped in her throat, and she stared at him mutely. How could she promise him something she had no way of knowing she could deliver?

A smile of pure evil tipped his lips. "What will you do, little Celt? Tell me." It was a demand. "Tell me now." And then an entreaty.

His softened tone was her undoing. "I'll fuck you as no woman has ever fucked you before." Her nails dug into his flesh as she whispered her promise, her desire mingled with rippled threads of trepidation at the thought of failure.

Against her belly his rigid shaft grew even thicker, although she could not believe such a thing possible. And trepidation of another kind shimmered.

"I know you will." His hand covered her rounded cheek and squeezed her flesh possessively. "And by the time I've finished with you, you won't even recall the names of your previous lovers, let alone how well their cocks satisfied you."

He spoke in Latin, as if he didn't want her to know of his wish. But she heard and understood, and secretly thrilled at his pledge.

"I want you now." Once more in Celtic. He stroked her hair from her face, stared intently into her eyes. "Beautiful wood nymph." Again he slipped into his mother tongue. "I wanted to savor every moment with you this first time. But I fear for my sanity if we wait much longer."

Every word he uttered sent new tremors of delight along her nerve endings. She slid her hand along his arm, threaded her fingers through his and attempted to tug him.

He resisted her efforts to lead him to the blankets she'd arranged on the ground.

"You're not going anywhere." His fingers tightened around hers; his body remained rooted to the spot. "And you still haven't touched me, my lady."

She traced the outline of his lips and deliberately caressed her body against his. Not touched him? He was clearly addled by lust. "I made a bed for us," she said, and used her finger to point in the general direction.

His eyes narrowed slightly, as if her foresight astounded him. "A bed?" he echoed. "Out here, in the wilds?"

"Yes. Come." Again she attempted to tug him, and this time he acquiesced.

"A bed." He sounded on the verge of laughter, although she couldn't imagine why. And then she did. Of course, it was all very well for men. They could fuck anywhere in comfort. But if she was on her back, she would rather not have sticks and stones digging into her.

"It's softer." She didn't like the defensive note in her voice and tried to extricate her hand from his.

He tugged her to his side and speared his fingers through her hair, gripped her skull and prevented her from moving.

"Thank you." He still sounded as if he wanted to laugh out loud. "My aching bones will appreciate the comfort you've provided."

He *was* laughing at her, inside his head, and she didn't know why. Where had he expected they would have sex? "I would rather not copulate in a tree," she said, because there was no comparison between pleasuring herself and having a huge Roman plow into her while clinging onto a branch.

And then he did laugh out loud, but before she could be offended he wrapped her in his arms, in a hug of such bone-crushing intensity the air in her lungs evaporated.

"It hadn't occurred to me to copulate *in* a tree," he said, his voice muffled as he buried his face against her hair. And then his lips were by her ear. "But perhaps one day we might try that. What do you say, my funny little wood nymph?"

Carys wasn't sure if she liked him calling her that. Was he mocking her?

"I don't know. I might fall off." Her arms were pinned along the front of her body. All she could feel with her fingers were his massive thighs.

She wriggled her fingers against his flesh. His muscles flexed with appreciation.

"You wouldn't fall." His voice was rough. "I'd catch you, my lady. I will always catch you."

His words soothed her wounded pride and she softened against him. She loved when he said such things to her.

"Take me to your bed." He loosened his hold on her, but still kept his arms around her. And when she brought him to her make-shift bed, he knelt on the blankets, taking her with him.

"You see?" Her voice was breathless as she wound her arms around his broad shoulders. "Much softer than the hard ground."

"You thought of everything." His hands cradled her face, strong fingers holding her firm. "How many others have you captivated this way, lady?" He spoke in Latin, not expecting an answer, and yet she longed to give him one. Instead she slid her fingers over his nape, and up into his short, spiky hair.

"But no more." His rough words in Latin stoked fires within her soul. "Do you understand me?" His Celtic was suddenly heavily accented, as if his control had slipped. "No other men for you, lady. I'm the only one you will share your bed with, here or anywhere else."

"I understand." She hoped he felt the same way afterward. But for now, she could savor his demand because it made her feel cherished and wanted and infinitely desirable.

He muttered a curse in his own language before capturing her lips in a crushing kiss, plundering her open mouth in an invasion at once sweet and savage and overwhelmingly possessive.

One strong hand held her still for his mouth and teeth and lips to explore, his tongue tangling with hers, sliding against the roof of her mouth and sending shock-filled tremors dancing through her heated blood.

His other hand trailed down the side of her body, molding the shape of her ribs and her hips and sparks of raw desire ignited along every inch of sensitized flesh he touched.

Fingers splayed between their melded bodies, hard fingers that demanded access to her most intimate secrets. She sighed into his mouth, twisting restlessly against his probing finger, and then gasped as he found her throbbing nub.

"So wet." He growled the words into her mouth. "Hot and wet, ready for my thrusting cock."

She angled herself against him, and moaned when he rewarded her by circling her engorged clit with his searching finger.

"Tell me what you like." His hot words scorched her lips, ignited her brain.

"I like this," she panted, gripping his hair and his skull with such force her muscles protested. "I like how you touch me. I like how you make me feel."

Even her own fingers couldn't give her such sweet pleasure as her Roman was.

His laugh was ragged. "Good. Now tell me what you like."

She moved her hips, and he responded by gently holding her sensitive clit between thumb and finger. Goddess, she would die of delight.

"You." It was all she could manage, all she could think beyond the thudding pleasure enslaving her body.

He released her from the precipice of sweet agony and trailed his fingers over her wet pussy, back and forth, dipping into her hot channel before sliding out and over her pussy yet again.

She whimpered against his mouth, felt his lips curve into a smile. His hand slipped from her face to hold her nape.

"Lie down." His command left no room for protest, but she didn't want to protest. If she didn't lie down soon, she feared she might fall. "I want to look at you."

He helped her lie upon the blankets, hands still firm around her nape and cupping her sex. She clung to his head, but he didn't have enough hair to wind around her hands and drag him to her.

Her hands slithered over his neck and onto his shoulders. His smile was predatory. Possessive.

"I'm not going anywhere, little nymph." He claimed her parted mouth, stroked his tongue along the inside of her lips and then broke free.

He towered over her, bracing his weight on his hands, his dark head and white teeth filling her entire world. She dug her nails into his shoulders, in an attempt to make him cover her, claim her, make her his.

Instead he resisted her efforts with another of his disarming smiles.

And then, without warning, he lowered his head and sucked her nipple into his mouth, and she reared in shocked reaction, gasping her pleasure, raking her nails along his rigid biceps.

Teeth grazed her, spiking her pleasure to unknowable heights, pleasure and pain, so intermingled, and yet she felt no fear, only a clawing demand to shatter this spiraling need that careered through her body like a living entity.

His mouth abandoned her breast, and chills skittered across her wet peak, but he moved lower, jaw scraping over her belly as he looked up at her.

She shifted restlessly. "Maximus." She wanted him to take her now, while she felt so wet and ready. If he fucked her now, she knew she would come. How could she not?

She needed to come, or die from want. And she wanted to come with Maximus inside her, not with the poor substitute of her own finger.

"I'm here." His rough growl caused her womb to clench. Goddess, couldn't he tell how much she needed him?

His tongue dipped into the hollow of her navel, then moved downward.

Her fingers fluttered over his retreating head. "Maximus," she said again, unable to keep the trepidation from her voice. She didn't want him eating her pussy. Aeron had spent endless moments doing such things, and even now the memory distressed her.

Hands on her hips, he finally looked up at her again. "Spread your thighs for me."

Despite knowing what was to happen, her pussy quivered with anticipation. Perhaps, with Maximus, the experience wouldn't be so uncomfortable?

She eased her thighs apart. Maximus straddled her, so she couldn't open too wide. Perhaps he didn't mean to do the things Aeron had at all.

Maximus shifted so her legs were now on the outside of their embrace. And then he kneed her left thigh farther apart, exposing her to his heated gaze.

Chapter Eight

Carys held her breath as she gazed at Maximus kneeling between her parted thighs. He appeared transfixed, and primitive desire ricocheted through her clit, vibrated along the neck of her womb.

Gently he traced his finger along the outer edge of her lips, but made no move to devour her with his mouth. Her hands dropped to the blanket. But she continued to watch him, fascinated by the way he openly admired her body.

"Beautiful clitoris." Heavy desire soaked with male satisfaction drenched his voice. "Swollen with passion."

Another violent quiver seared through her pussy, coiled around her painfully erect nipples.

"Will you not take me now?" The words were uneven, barely audible, and filled with desperation.

"Yes. I'll take you, my lady." Maximus spared her a brief glance. His eyes glowed almost black with lust, and Carys ached to hold him in her arms, against her body, and shatter around him.

He shifted his weight, kneed her right thigh open. Carys

shivered with dark delight. Her neck ached from her unnatural position, but she couldn't lie back. Couldn't stop watching her Roman looking at her.

He parted her folds with tender fingers, and her heart thundered in her ears; blood pounded through her arteries. She was fully exposed for his viewing pleasure, and the ardent expression on his face assured her the pleasure was intense.

As she watched him lower his head, an incoherent sound of protest lodged in her throat. He stilled, looked up.

"I mean only to kiss you."

Flash memories of Aeron slobbering like a rabid dog over fresh meat taunted her. She flicked her tongue over her lips, blinked away the image and focused on her Roman.

On Maximus.

"Yes." She didn't know whether her words meant anything to him. Would he continue if she denied him permission?

And she realized it didn't matter. Despite her reservations, she wanted him to taste her. To lick her. To kiss her throbbing clit.

His dark head was between her thighs. She sucked in a suddenly panicked breath, tensing her muscles for the onslaught. And then the tip of his tongue teased her sensitive bud, damp pressure, soft yet firm, encircled her in a swirling caress, and pleasure obliterated her lingering doubts.

His lips surrounded her; a kiss such as she had never dreamed existed. A ragged sob spilled from her, and she blindly groped for him. Touch, sweet Cerridwen, she needed to touch him, to hold him.

And then he was there, poised over her willing body, gazing down at her with a fierce, possessive expression as if she belonged to him now and forever and he would never allow her to escape.

He thrust into her, and her muscles clenched involuntarily as the air hissed from her lungs, her heart stuttered in shock and the blood stilled in her veins.

Her fingernails dug into his shoulders and all she could feel was his great size invading her, stretching her, *tearing her apart*.

He froze, stared at her in lust-drenched confusion. "Venus." He sounded horrified. "You said you were no virgin, my lady."

She didn't have the strength to be offended. It was all she could do to gasp a breath before blackness descended.

"I'm not."

She felt him begin to ease back, and clung onto his shoulders in desperation.

"It's been three years since I welcomed a lover, Maximus." She hadn't wanted to confide that to him, but better the truth than have him think she'd never taken a man before.

"Three years?" She could feel the tension radiating from him as he remained completely still above her.

"Yes." Experimentally she flexed her internal muscles around him. Already the discomfort of his sudden penetration had eased.

He let out an agonized breath. "You're so tight. I didn't intend to hurt you, lady."

"You didn't." He had, but only momentarily. "Truly, I am not injured, Maximus." But she would be, if he decided he no longer wished to continue.

Braced on one forearm, he tenderly brushed tendrils of hair from her cheek. "Three years without any man inside you makes you almost a virgin."

She slid her fingers through his wonderful short hair. "But you're inside me now."

Slowly he lowered his hips, and his shaft slid farther inside. Still stretching her long-unused muscles, but the sensation of being filled, of being expanded to her outermost limits, no longer caused discomfort. Only breathless wonder and a rising spiral of renewed need.

"Gods." The strangled word tore from his throat. "You hug my cock so tightly. I can feel every tremor from your sweet heat wrapped around me."

She hooked her ankles over his powerful thighs, felt him move farther inside her.

"More," she panted, knowing he held back but wanting everything he had to offer. She shifted, wrapped her legs around his hips and enticed him closer.

He resisted, but strain etched his features as his fierce gaze singed her.

"Stop." His command was hoarse with need. "I'm at the edge, lady. *Stop moving.*" Sheer desperation vibrated every word.

Primordial power whipped through Carys as she stared into her Roman's tortured face. She could see the struggle tearing him apart, the desire for release and the need for control.

Fingers splayed against his skull, she jerked him toward her as she tightened her grip around his hips.

"I won't," she promised against his lips. His breath came in ragged gasps against her cheek. Thrilling her to new heights.

"You're not ready." But his body surrendered to her demands and his cock surged into her, nudging the entrance to her womb, his heavy balls slamming against her stretched, sensitized flesh.

She reared upward, barely aware of her reaction, knowing only that she had to be closer, inseparable, melded with this tough Roman warrior.

"Fuck me, Maximus." She clawed his shoulders, his biceps. "Take me. Make me come."

He braced his weight on both hands and she took advantage to slide her arms around his back. Gripped his buttocks. Pulled him ever farther into her hot, willing body.

His groan of impending defeat set her senses ablaze, and when he rocked into her, the base of his cock ground against her clit, stoking the blaze to an inferno.

He pulled almost out of her body, then rammed her so hard shooting stars exploded through her mind. The friction between her thighs radiated throughout her core, her heart, her lungs, and spiraled through her aching breasts and taut nipples.

For one sparkling moment of eternity she hovered on the precipice, and then she tumbled into the void, spinning out of control, sensation cascading along every nerve she possessed, and she could feel Maximus's cock impaling her as her slick heat convulsed around him.

"Fuck me, sweet Celt." His voice, raw, demanding, shattered her mind. "I'm coming inside you. Fill you with my hot seed." And he thrust into her, hard, powerful, and his roar of release filled her senses as his maleness filled her womb.

Chapter Nine

Maximus pounded into his wood nymph's tight channel, giving her every last drop of essence, draining him dry, wringing his soul with the fury of his possession.

His roar of satisfaction echoed in his ears, vibrated through his brain and trembled along every sated nerve.

Control long since vanished, he collapsed onto her welcoming body, so soft, so hot. Burning still, with slaked desire. Enclosing him in a scented mist of raw sex and unbridled passion.

Through the fire that still licked through his brain, he became aware of her smallness. Her fragileness. Against his desire he heaved himself onto his elbow and studied her delicate face.

Gods, she was so beautiful in the ethereal light that bathed them both. As desirable as a nymph of the goddess of love herself.

His cock, still buried in her tight, wet tunnel, stirred. Venus, he wanted her again already.

Her eyelashes fluttered open, and although he couldn't see the colors of her eyes, their beauty still awed him.

"I came." Her voice was hushed, as if the fact astounded her.

He laughed softly and wound a damp lock of her hair around his finger.

"I came too," he said. "A most satisfactory outcome for us both, I believe."

She pressed her hand against his heart. He liked the way she touched him, the way she looked at him as she touched him, as if it gave her great pleasure.

"We truly did come together." Her whispered words, in genuine wonder, aroused him further. "It was even more magical than I had dreamed."

He stilled playing with her hair. "Was this your first time?" To be sure, it was rare he came at the moment of his partner's release. Usually he ensured they came first. But with his golden Celt his control had shattered.

Thank the gods he had still satisfied her. She deserved nothing less after the immense pleasure she'd given him.

"Yes." Still, the wonderment laced her voice. He smiled down at her, pleased she hadn't shared mutual orgasm with any other man.

Her hand rubbed over his chest, as if she couldn't help herself. As if his hair held an impossible attraction for her.

"It is different, coming with a man inside." She looked up at him, wide-eyed with newly discovered knowledge.

He frowned slightly, unsure as to her meaning. "Different?" He shifted his hips, and his cock showed its appreciation by swelling further, pushing against her tender flesh.

"Yes." She seemed to think that answer enough, but before he could demand she explain further, she clenched her internal muscles around him, wiping his question from his mind.

"Gods." His voice was ragged. "You have the touch of Venus, my lady."

Her hand reached up. Instinctively knowing what she wanted, he lowered his head, so she could gently stroke his hair. Odd how so simple a gesture could be so arousing, when performed by his Celt.

"Your goddess of love." It wasn't a question. She trailed her fingers along his jaw, and he saw her lips curve into a strangely shy smile. Something tugged deep in his gut, painful, almost sexual and yet not.

"The Morrigan never blessed me so before."

The name was vaguely familiar. A heathen three-headed goddess the Celts worshipped. Certainly incomparable to his divine Venus.

He would never insult his wood nymph by telling her so.

"Tonight both our goddesses blessed us." And he was ready, more than ready, to be blessed again. He slid his arm around her waist and swiftly reversed their positions, and grinned at the startled expression on her face.

"Oh." Her voice was faint as she stared down at him, and her glorious hair tumbled over her shoulders, enclosing them in a scented river of gold.

He cupped her hips, holding her still. Poised above him she looked like a goddess from Olympus, enjoying the charms of her mere mortal lover.

"Take me deep inside you, lady." Still holding her hips, it would be too easy to force her down the length of his shaft, but he waited agonizing moments, wanting, needing her to be the one to make the first move.

Slowly, as if she had never done such a thing before, she inched down his erection until he was utterly enslaved by her slick heat. Enveloped in a tight embrace, she contracted around him, the sensation so exquisite a primitive roar scraped along his throat, echoed through his mind, shattered the remnants of his restraint.

He dragged his hands over her waist, cupped her breasts as she hung over him. Felt her move, matched her rhythm, slammed his hips against her, molding her tender flesh to fit his size and take his length. Her nails tore his shoulders, and through a haze of lust he watched her eyes widen, glazed with passion, saw her lips part, felt the heat of her ragged breath against his face.

"Maximus." She gasped his name, as if in wonder, and it was too much. With a primordial growl he abandoned her breasts and cupped the rounded cheeks of her delicious bottom, and rammed his cock into her, claiming her, possessing her. *Branding her his.*

And sanity shattered.

Arms wrapped around her shoulder and waist, Maximus heard the uneven gasp of her breath against his neck, the erratic pound of her heart against his chest. He tightened his grip around her quivering body, but was too sated to move farther.

"You belong to me." He said the words aloud, claiming her even if she didn't know it. "You will always belong to me."

"Yes." Her soft response satisfied his male pride. And then, within a heartbeat, he stiffened.

"You understand me?" He had spoken—still spoke—in his native tongue.

Her breath puffed against his neck, as if her exertions this night had thoroughly exhausted her. And despite himself, male pride heated him once again.

"Yes. I always have." Again she answered him in perfect Latin.

Gods, what had he said to her the other day, believing her oblivious to his words? He couldn't recall. But he did know he hadn't wanted her to understand.

"Why did you lie to me?" He traced his fingers over the curve of her waist, and felt her shiver.

He should have ensured his cloak was within reach. He didn't want his little Celt to become chilled.

"I didn't lie." She snuggled against him and her hand curled around his shoulder. "You assumed, and I allowed you to do so."

He conceded that perhaps she was right. "Your grasp of my language is impressive."

This time he felt her sigh. "It was thought prudent to learn the tongue of our approaching enemy."

He stroked her hair, which curled over her shoulders. "I don't wish to be your enemy, my lady."

She was silent for a moment. "Nor I. But you will always be the enemy of my people, Maximus." Infinite sorrow clung to her words, as if she somehow knew that for a fact.

He banished the thought. "In time, even your kin will accept us. Already much of the populace are benefiting from our presence."

She began to trace swirling patterns on his shoulder. "Maybe that's true. But it doesn't mean you've been accepted."

He rolled her onto her back, pinned her beneath his heavy body. She gazed up at him, fearless.

"If your family surrenders, they won't be enslaved." He would make sure of that. "We could use the knowledge and loyalty of the nobles, my lady."

"That would make us traitors to our own people."

Bracing his weight on one hand, he cupped her face with his other. "No. You could help bridge the chasm between your people and ours."

Pain filled her eyes. "You make it sound easy. But you'd wipe out our culture without a second thought. Destroy our way of life forever."

He traced the outline of her lips. "No. You can still worship your gods alongside the gods of Rome."

She frowned, clearly confused. "Reports of your conquest reached us long before you arrived in Cymru. Of the blood-soaked battles and merciless slaughter of all who opposed you."

"I'm a soldier, lady," he said, gently playing with her beautiful hair. "We fight when opposed. I can't lie and tell you otherwise."

A ragged sigh wracked her body. "My kin will never surrender, Maximus."

He fisted her hair. She was only a woman, and as such had

little power in her family. He knew that. And yet the fact she was so adamant her kin would never consider surrender irked him.

"In Britannia, many nobles retain their exalted status." True, they paid tribute to Rome but that was a small price to pay for an improved standard of living.

Again she frowned, but not in confusion. For the first time she looked offended by his words. "We are not Britons, Roman."

Her haughty tone amused him, wiped clear his irritation with her cowardly family.

"No. You're a stubborn Celt, and you belong to me. And as such I should take you back to the garrison tonight and never allow you to leave."

She melted beneath him. "But you won't." She sounded so confident he wondered how she would react if he put his threat into force.

He had no intention of dragging her back by force. Not yet, anyway. Only as a last resort should all else fail.

A strange flicker caught his attention, and he glanced up to see one of the lanterns fade into darkness. His wood nymph gasped and pressed ineffectually at his shoulders.

"You're not going anywhere. Stop complaining." He settled himself more securely over her wriggling body. If she continued so, he would have no option but to fuck her once again.

"Maximus." She stilled beneath him, but her eyes captured him. "I have to go."

"And I said no."

She tilted her head to one side. "I don't *want* to leave," she said. "But if I'm missed tonight, I may never be able to escape from them again."

Sudden anger shot through him. So her family kept her prisoner. "Then come with me. You will never have to escape from them again." Despite what she believed, he could keep her safe.

Safer than she could possibly be wherever it was her cursed kin were hiding.

She cradled his jaw, a fleeting caress. "You misunderstand. They bind me with love, not chains." She sighed. "If I disappear, they'll think terrible things. I can't do that to them, Maximus."

He could. Easily. "You'll meet me here again." It wasn't a question. "In three nights." It was the earliest he could manage. Curse her. He didn't want to wait three nights.

For a moment she appeared surprised at the wait, as if she'd expected to see him tomorrow. If she agreed to return with him now, then she *would* fucking see him tomorrow.

"I'll be here."

Yes, she had better fucking be there. Otherwise he'd rip the entire valley to shreds until he found her. And her fucking family.

"Maximus." Her soft voice pulled him back to the present. She had a strange smile on her face, but in the gathering darkness it was difficult to determine her precise expression.

"What?" It was a growl. He couldn't help it. No woman had ever annoyed him so.

"I'll be here waiting for you." A silken caress that soothed his wounded ego. "I'll always be here waiting for you."

He sucked in a deep breath, savoring the scent of crushed flowers, fresh sweat and hot, abandoned sex. Her promise appeased him. For now.

"Very well."

Carys shivered as her Roman finally rolled off her, severing contact. She had the powerful urge to pull him back, entice him inside her again, because his withdrawal left a gaping chasm, cold. Lonely. Extraordinary sensations that gripped her body and confused her mind.

A second lantern flickered and died, and Carys jerked up. She had little time before all the lights extinguished and the smoke's magic, hallucinogenic properties vanished, allowing Maximus to realize, should anyone pass by the circle, that they were invisible to the world.

She caught sight of her gown lying some distance off. Her Roman reclined on the blanket, propped up on his elbows, watching her as a predator watched his prey.

He clearly had no intention of collecting her gown for her. On hands and knees she crawled across the grass, aware of his intense gaze on her exposed buttocks. She gave an exaggerated wiggle of her hips and glanced over her shoulder to catch his reaction.

His eyes clashed with hers. "Do that again." His voice was eerily calm. "And see where it lands you."

The temptation to do just that was strong. But the watchful look on his face assured her that if she pushed, he would take. And she couldn't afford to linger much longer.

She crushed her disappointment. Safety was of paramount importance, and she wouldn't allow herself to risk discovery through mindless lust.

"I don't wriggle to order," she said instead, and grabbed her gown as Maximus made as if to rise. "No. There isn't time." She hastily pulled her gown over her head. Maximus remained on the blanket, but she could see every muscle tensed as if he was waiting for the slightest provocation to pounce.

"You don't appear to do anything to order."

She tugged her gown straight, threaded the ties at her breast.

"Not when they're given by a man." She flashed him a teasing smile. Heat bloomed deep in the center of her being at the sardonic grin he tossed her way. As if he didn't believe her but was prepared to indulge her fantasy.

"You had best start learning how to obey orders given by *this* man."

She sat back on her heels, knowing she didn't have time for such flirtations and yet unwilling to shatter the moment.

"It's possible," she said, "I may make an exception in your case."

He laughed. She knew he hadn't meant to, knew he was still angry with her for refusing to go with him. But still he laughed at her, as if he couldn't help himself.

Chapter Ten

Two more lanterns gutted, and panic licked around the edge of her heart. She grabbed her bag, which was usually filled with dozens of medicinal herbs and lotions but tonight was used only for the lanterns and protective bluestones and certain feminine essentials.

"Maximus, get dressed." She shot him an anxious glance as she gathered up the dark lanterns and potent bluestones. "There are only a few moments left before all the flames die."

He didn't move, and his gaze never left her. "Are you afraid of the dark, lady?"

His question was so unexpected, she paused, an illicit shard of bluestone in hand. "No, not at all." And it wasn't completely dark. The moon gave plenty of illumination.

He rose to his feet and she stared up at him, committing his magnificent body to memory. She barely flinched when a fifth lantern sputtered.

"Yet you bathed us in light to keep back the night." He sauntered toward her, naked and proud and clearly ready for her again.

Her gut clenched with painful need. It was no longer safe. No matter how much she wanted to feel his hard body possess her again.

"This is a lover's circle." It wasn't a lie. It just wasn't the entire truth.

He crouched, picked up a dead lantern and handed it to her. As she took it, his fingers closed over hers. "I'll ride with you back to your people."

"I can't let you do that." She didn't try to pull away from him. Didn't want to pull away from him. But she couldn't allow him to accompany her to the sacred spiral either.

"It wasn't a question."

She stroked his roughened jaw with her free hand. "I'll be perfectly safe, Maximus. I know these hills and valleys intimately. They are my friends."

He scowled, as if he considered such sentiments absurd.

"You're a woman. You shouldn't be wandering the countryside alone at night."

She decided to try another angle. "If you accompany me, I'd be a traitor to my kin." Her thumb grazed over his rigid jaw. The very fact he hadn't instantly refuted her words proved he recognized her loyalty even while it displeased him.

She sighed, as the conflicting emotions collided in her mind and ignited her body in a maelstrom of renewed desire. Her refusal on this point had little to do with him being a Roman. Even if she'd taken a man from one of the villages as her lover, she still could never have allowed him access to the sacred spiral.

"So you intend for us only to ever meet here?"

She didn't want that either. But what choice did they have?

"It's better than never meeting at all." At least, it was for her. She hoped he felt the same. His body certainly appeared to agree with her.

His brow crinkled as if their conversation bemused him. Or perhaps he simply wasn't used to making compromises. Especially not with a woman.

That thought fluttered through her mind, disturbing her on a fundamental level. Did he truly see her as unworthy of such respect?

"Your sense of honor irks me greatly." He was still frowning and there was iron in his voice. Carys dared to stroke his hair with the palm of her hand and shivered with delight as the now-familiar sensation tickled across her flesh.

He pulled from her reach with evident impatience. "Don't start something that you have no intention of finishing." He snatched up another lantern and pinched the guttering flame between thumb and forefinger before thrusting it into her open bag.

"I'll finish you in three nights."

"Assuming I'm prepared to wait that long."

Her heart thundered in her chest, outraged by the suggestion. She clutched the bluestone, unheeding how the jagged edges drew blood, scarcely able to believe he had uttered such a thing.

"You would take another woman in the meantime?" How dare he even consider fucking another woman after the magical night they had just shared?

And despite her limited personal experience she knew how well she had satisfied him.

His lips curled as if he thought her amusing, but since that was impossible Carys could only assume the uneven illumination was playing tricks with her eyes.

By the goddess, she would poke *out* the eyes of any woman who dared touch her Roman. She raised her fist, still clutching the sacred shard of bluestone.

"Answer me!"

There was no mistaking the self-satisfied smirk on his face now. Irrational anger pumped through her blood at the realization he was laughing at her. She knew she was being irrational, because why did it matter so much?

He was only a man, and her enemy at that, whom she was using to satisfy her carnal longings. What he did when they weren't together was of no consequence whatsoever.

But still the anger bubbled in her veins. And if he dared vocalize his mirth, she would—she would *hit* him.

"Does my little wood nymph have a temper?" His voice mocked her. "Does the thought of me pleasuring other women make you jealous?"

She slammed her fist against his chest. It was as if she'd slammed her hand against pure granite.

"Does the thought of me pleasuring other men make you jealous?"

His grin vanished and he curled his fingers around her arms in an iron grip. "Don't even jest about such things." There was a deadly note to his voice. "I wouldn't hesitate to disembowel any man who takes what is mine."

Her breath came in uneven gasps as she stared at his grim expression. Her white-hot fury curled up on itself and, within a blink, evaporated into the insane desire to giggle.

"Nor I any woman."

Perhaps he heard the suppressed laughter in her voice, as his frown darkened further. But his grip on her arms lessened. He appeared thoroughly confused by her reactions, and she didn't blame him since she was confused herself.

All she knew was that the realization that he hated the thought of her being with another man made her hot and wet inside.

"I can wait three nights." His voice was gruff and he finally released her. "The image of you disemboweling another of your sex is more than enough to keep my cock to myself."

Early the following morning Carys stirred as dappled sunlight danced across her closed eyes. She pulled the blanket over her head, and couldn't prevent the groan from escaping.

She felt as if she had been trampled by a wild horse. Every muscle ached, every tendon pulled, her right hand felt as if it had been crushed by an avalanche and her pussy throbbed, raw and swollen.

With a small grunt she gently fingered her tender flesh. Imagined Maximus fingering her, and, despite her discomfort, a smile of feminine satisfaction curved her lips.

She had never felt so wondrously sexual before. Every particle of her body was branded by Maximus. She could feel him in her bones, smell him on her skin. Hear his masculine roar as his orgasm rocked them both to the stars.

Now, at last, Carys understood that dreamy look in her mother's eyes whenever she spoke of her father's scorching touch.

For a few indulgent moments she continued to tease her sensitive clit, luxuriating in the warm scent of sex and lust that bathed her body, clung to her clothes and permeated the blankets. And then reality intruded.

"So here you are." Morwyn's voice. Carys inched the blanket to her nose and squinted at the other woman, who was looking down at her with a barely suppressed smirk on her face.

"I'm not yet ready to rise." Carys began to cover her eyes again. She should have picked a shadier spot to sleep in last night. There were too many gaps in the tree canopy here. And did the warblers have to be so vociferous?

Morwyn snorted with evident glee. "I can see that, Carys." And then she settled herself at Carys's head. "So tell me. Was he good?"

Carys sighed in defeat. There was no point lying. She reeked of sex. "Very good."

Morwyn smiled with satisfaction. "It's about time you found yourself a lover. The Morrigan will be appeased. There's nothing as fulfilling as having a man's cock buried inside you, now, is there?"

Memories of Maximus filling her warmed her blood, cause her pulse to quicken and lips to curve. "No." And then she felt the need to qualify. "Depending on who the man is."

"Yes." Morwyn leaned in closer. "And who is he, Carys? One of ours?" Her dark eyes gleamed with curiosity.

Carys pushed herself upright, with some difficulty since her muscles screamed in protest at the slightest movement. "No."

"I didn't think so." Morwyn twirled a long raven lock around her finger. "Although even if he was, the need for secrecy would still be prudent."

Carys couldn't argue with that. Even before they had been forced to flee into the forest, Aeron's possessiveness toward her was more than enough to quell any other man's interest.

Notwithstanding that he'd fucked around whenever the fancy took him, and she had severed their ties two years and five moons prior to their flight. He still appeared to imagine he retained rights over her, when the truth was he never had.

"It's easier if no one knows." Carys leaned back against a tree and yawned. Sweet Cerridwen, but she was exhausted. "Then there's less likelihood of him hearing a whisper."

"Your secret is safe with me." Morwyn kissed the tips of her fingers to seal the promise. "Now, tell me how you met. Is it someone I know?"

Carys dearly wanted to confide, but knew she never could. "He is newly arrived at the settlement around the Roman fortification." Almost true. Not quite a lie.

She could live with it.

When Morwyn finally left, after having extracted enough erotic details to satisfy her probing questions and a promise to meet for morning tea when the shadows shortened, Carys examined her aching hand. Now she remembered why it hurt so much.

She'd punched Maximus.

Across the palm, dried blood streaked, and shock arrowed through her heart. The bluestone. Had she damaged it?

Heart thundering in her ears, she dragged her bag over and

carefully pulled out the soft leather pouch. After glancing around to ensure she was still alone in this part of the forest, she quickly examined the sacred stones.

They appeared to be unharmed. With a relieved sigh she quickly slid them back into the pouch.

Of course, if anyone did see the stones in her possession, they would assume they were merely ordinary bluestones. As such they commanded due respect for their spiritual significance, but these stones were far from ordinary.

She had stolen them after the terrifying ceremony at the Feast of the Dead when Aeron had fused the powers bestowed by their immortals to invoke the sacred spiral.

Carys stroked the leather pouch with humble reverence for its contents. Even now, seven moons later, she could scarcely understand why she had done such a thing. Yet she had felt compelled. As if the broken shards, scattered across the ground of the cromlech, had called to her.

And perhaps they had. Without their protective magic, shielding her and Maximus from unexpected discovery, last night could not have occurred.

Fingers clasped around the pouch, Carys hesitated. Did that mean the gods had foreseen and approved of her liaison?

She wanted to believe it. And yet she wasn't convinced. The Romans had invaded their country. Enslaved their people. How could their gods approve of anything but the utter destruction of the enemy?

But she didn't want to think about that. She thrust the pouch deep into her bag, and her fingers brushed against another leather pouch.

Blood flooded her cheeks and her heart kicked against her ribs in shocked disbelief. How could she have forgotten something so fundamentally important?

She dragged it from her bag, pulled it open and stared at the contents of her emergency pack of cleansing creams and special herbs. She had assumed that, after leaving Maximus, she'd come back here, bathe away the evidence of their liaison and prepare the preventative tea.

Instead she'd been so exhausted all she'd managed was blessed oblivion.

She couldn't return to the cromlech and risk encountering Aeron in her current state. Dawn drifted over the valley and she didn't have much time before the risk of others finding her escalated.

Ignoring the way her body protested, she sprinted to the nearby river.

Carys found Morwyn at her favorite meditative spot some distance from Druantia's oak grove.

"Are you still going to the Cauldron?" Morwyn said as she placed two highly decorated cups on the ground.

"Yes." Carys shot her a glance as she sat beside her and began to prepare her herbs and bark for infusion. It was obvious Morwyn knew that Aeron had forbidden her. As if he had any right to forbid her to do anything when it concerned her personal goddess.

"I've always thought it odd," Morwyn said as she picked up the pot suspended over her small fire, "how the Cauldron was excluded from the protection of the sacred spiral."

Carys dropped her prepared herbs into her cup and picked up the dried bark. On that fateful night, as the shattering violet waves had radiated outward from the double circle of bluestones, it had never occurred to her that her beloved Cauldron wouldn't be included.

"I sometimes think Aeron deliberately eliminated the Cauldron from his protective spells." She didn't have any evidence, and her feelings were illogical. But she had never been able to shake them.

Morwyn frowned as she poured the hot water into her own cup. "Not every Druid's sacred place was enclosed, Carys." She replaced the pot on its stand and dropped the protective handling cloth on the ground between them. Then she gave Carys a calculating look. "Although most were, certainly."

"And he expected me then, and expects me now, to simply abandon the holy spring." She hadn't believed him at first, because aside from the spring being Cerridwen's sacred Cauldron of Wisdom, it was her own personal haven. She meditated there, practiced her training for endless hours. Felt safe and loved and, most of all, close to Cerridwen.

"Then he will continue to expect in vain." And Morwyn gave a little snort as if the thought of Aeron being crossed pleased her.

Carys peeled a strip from her bark. "Although if the Cauldron had fallen within the protective circle, none of the villagers could have continued to meet me there."

Morwyn shrugged. "You'd have found another holy place, Carys."

Yes, she would. Although she was only an acolyte with barely ten years' training, people trusted her with their health problems. For two years she'd been treating a growing circle of patients and she'd been furious when Aeron had assumed she could simply abandon them at a moment's notice.

A smug smile tugged at her lips as she recalled what else she'd done in her most beloved of places. Had Aeron enclosed the Cauldron, she could never have invited her Roman there.

Luxuriating in the illicit glow warming her core, she made to drop the prepared bark into her cup. And paused. The herbs already there were arranged into the unmistakable shape of a womb, save for a few sprinkled pieces in the center.

An eerie shiver chased along her arms. But perhaps it wasn't so strange. Not when this preparation would clean out her own womb of Maximus's potent seed.

Yet still she hesitated.

A flutter of darkness made her jerk up, and she sucked in a shocked breath as the raven landed less than a stone's throw away. Symbolic of the Morrigan, in her guise as the War Goddess, the raven prophesied both devastation and regeneration. One black, glittering eye observed her, as if sizing her up, before it suddenly took to the air. *Was this a sign that the goddess truly was appeased? Had her orgasm with Maximus been with the Morrigan's blessing? Did this mean the Great Goddess would no longer disdain Carys's existence?*

"Goddess save us." Morwyn gripped her arm in a painful grasp, and Carys stared in transfixed silence as one black tail feather fluttered to land at her feet.

The potent omen couldn't be ignored. It foretold fertility and new life.

Morwyn's grip intensified. "War," she whispered, staring at the feather in horror. "*Death.*"

Chapter Eleven

Aeron stood by the stone altar, palms pressed against its cool surface, his hazel rod at his feet.

He didn't know how many hours he had remained in this position. Only that now, as glimpses of the future fluttered behind his closed eyes, other Druids approached.

Anger stirred at the disruption, at the distortion in his visions. The cromlech was the center of the Druids' spiritual connection with the gods, but it was more than that to him.

Since the age of eight, when he'd received irrefutable proof via his bloody vision of his importance in the future of the world, the cromlech had become his own personal bastion of power.

His hands fisted. The others would disperse when they saw he was engaged with the gods. They would assume he was communing with the mighty god of the Otherworld, Arawn. Or perhaps the warrior god Camulus or Taranis, god of thunder, as to ways of beating the Roman scum and bringing peace once more to the valleys.

Contempt for his fellow Druids seared through his arteries, pounded in his mind. As a chosen acolyte of Arawn, he had always been a favored one of both Camulus and Taranis. But in the depths of his soul he had long ago abandoned those weak deities. They were nothing when compared to the one true source of power that had spewed forth those insipid gods, which bound all life together, which had shown itself to him on the longest day of summer twenty-five years ago.

His eyes snapped open. Morwyn emerged from the mouth of the great mound, and when she realized he looked her way, she gave an exaggerated swing to her hips.

Revulsion curled his belly. He knew it wasn't Morwyn herself who repulsed him. It was her calling. Whenever he looked at her, at the maiden aspect of the Morrigan, he saw only the wrinkled crone.

A shudder crawled the length of his spine. Soon, the triple goddess would be relegated to her rightful position in the circle of existence.

Crushed beneath his feet.

He hooked a finger at Morwyn and, as he knew she would, she sauntered over, tossing her long black hair over her shoulder.

"Good morn, Aeron." She braced her hands on the altar, the disrespectful whore, and angled herself so he had a clear view of her ample cleavage.

He offered her an icy smile, when all he really wanted was to swipe her undeserving hands from the sacred slab.

But she was Carys's special friend. And his major recourse for discovering what Carys did with her days. For almost fifteen years he'd nurtured the tenuous ability he possessed that enabled him to keep mental track of her whereabouts. It was a power he cherished; one many would covet had they known of its existence. A power that had inexplicably vanished the night he'd created the sacred spiral. Even now he couldn't fathom how such a fundamental error had occurred, but one thing was certain. It had nothing to do with his flawless incantations that night.

"I trust you weren't troubled by disturbing dreams again?" He feigned interest, though he didn't care whether Morwyn's visions drove her insane or killed her. All that interested him was why Carys hadn't returned to the mound last night. She'd never before slept out in the forest.

"I slept like a babe." Morwyn fluttered her eyelashes at him.

He knew she lied. Currently she was fucking the brains out of Gawain, a fellow Druid, and whatever she may have done last night, sleep wouldn't have been a major factor.

"Have you seen Carys this morn?" He had never been a great one for small talk, and over the last few moons it had grown increasingly more difficult to converse with his inferiors.

He didn't have time for mindless chatter. Only information.

Morwyn straightened, as if his question didn't please her. "We shared tea and broke our fast."

Something in her manner alerted his senses. He leaned toward her across the altar.

"And?" His voice was persuasive. He could be very persuasive when it suited.

Her brow creased and she nibbled on her lower lip. He waited in silence for her to continue.

"We were touched by the raven's eye."

Shivers skittered across his skin as excitement tightened his chest. "You or Carys?" Of course Carys. Morwyn was nothing compared to Carys, in beauty, in power and in potential.

Morwyn hugged her waist as if the recollection disturbed her. "The raven eyed Carys. But then, when it took to the wing, it dropped a tail feather at her feet."

Aeron's heart stilled for one eternal moment, then slammed against his rib cage as the significance of the omen penetrated.

"How did Carys react?" He kept his voice calm, but inside victory thundered. The raven, with its gift of prophecy, frequently inhabited his visions of bloodthirsty conquest, the bird and its flock picking over the broken carcasses of their slaughtered enemy.

If the raven had singled out Carys for its token, then Aeron's destiny was assured.

In the midst of carnage, Carys and the fruit of her womb would belong to him.

He no longer cared why she had slept outside last night. It had been a prelude to what had followed.

"She didn't." Morwyn sounded confused by Carys's reaction to the bird. "Aeron, I know what the raven portents. There'll be more fighting and death before this is over, won't there?"

He forced himself to respond, to drag his lustful thoughts from once again possessing Carys's body. Except the next time he did so, he would also possess her mind. Her soul.

Her freedom.

"This will never be over until the strait churns with Roman blood."

"Celtic blood also." Morwyn's whisper was filled with sorrow.

Aeron drew back, folded his arms across his naked, blue-daubed chest. "The gods are with us, Morwyn. They'll protect us against the heathen invaders."

Aeron gripped his hazel rod in frustration. After leaving Morwyn— who assured him she had not the faintest idea where Carys might be—he mentally searched all the holiest places within the vast confines of the sacred spiral, attempting to pick up a glimmer of her aura.

But there was nothing. And while the severance of his spiritual connection to her meant he could no longer pinpoint her exact location, when he invoked the mighty power of Annwyn—a power that no other even imagined could be enslaved—he always knew whether or not she remained within his specified limits.

The fucking bitch had defied him yet again.

Rage filled his chest and compressed his heart at the knowledge she had escaped to her precious Cauldron.

He didn't care that she loved her Cauldron. He didn't even care
that she loved ministering to her fucking useless patients. What
tore at his guts was the fact she thought nothing of disobeying his
direct orders.

Gritting his teeth, he glared around the cromlech. He had
always known how attached she was to the sparkling spring in
the hidden glade. She felt the same affinity there as he did with the
cromlech.

He understood. It was part of who Carys was, part of her mystical power that even now he could scarcely comprehend.

Because of that, he had specifically enclosed the Cauldron of
Cerridwen within the parameters of the sacred spiral. Then, he
knew, Carys's anger would be appeased at the enforced captivity.
She wouldn't be able to see her patients but at least her sanctuary
would be eternally available for her meditations.

And he would always know where he could find her.

But the spiral had fallen short. The Cauldron was now outside
his power. And Carys, alternating from one holy place to another
during the course of a single day, could never be found when he
wanted her.

He reined in his smoldering fury. *Patience.* For twenty-five
years he had waited for his time, and he was a master of patience.
In less than three days, during the shortest night of the sacred
wheel, the old gods would fall, the enemy would crumble and *his
time would come.*

"Enter."

Maximus entered the Legatus Legionis's office and saluted.

"Primus." The Legatus acknowledged him and then indicated
he should sit. "I received communication from the Emperor yesterday. I've been promoted to provincial governor."

"Well deserved, sir." And unsurprising. With only one Legion
in this province it made sense to appoint the Legatus.

The commander jerked his head in acceptance. "And Faustus has been reappointed to Rome."

Maximus remained silent. He knew what was coming.

The Legatus leaned back in his chair and regarded Maximus through narrowed eyes. "That means the post of Tribunus Laticlavius is vacant."

"Sir."

"How old are you, Maximus?"

The commander knew exactly how old he was, considering he was his father's second cousin. "Twenty-seven, sir."

"Five years older than Faustus."

Again Maximus remained silent. It was an undisputed fact the commander's nephew, Faustus, was indeed a full five years Maximus's junior.

The older man tapped one finger on his desk. "The Emperor has seen fit to promote you into the vacant position. Congratulations, Maximus."

"Thank you, sir." He was now second-in-command of the Legion. A tight knot of pride glowed deep inside his chest, but he kept his features clear of any such expression.

"Of course, if you'd gone about your career in the right way, you'd be looking toward your own quaestorship by now." The Legatus gave him a dark scowl, which almost instantly broke into an approving grin. "You're old to be appointed Tribunus, but what the fuck. Your experience makes up for it."

Nine years fighting his way up the centurion ranks more than made up for it. "Can I recommend my successor?"

"I thought you might."

"Aquila."

"His record is impressive." It was obvious the Legatus already had Aquila in mind for the position of the senior centurion. "Faustus is moving out within the next couple of days, so you can take over his quarters then." A gleam lit the older man's eye. "Now you've finally acquired a rank befitting your birth, I've no doubt you'll soon also be acquiring a suitable Roman wife."

The thought held little appeal. He had no need of a wife. Not when he had his wood nymph.

His groin tightened as he recalled the intense sexual pleasures of the previous night. He doubted a Roman girl of his patrician class could ever come close to satisfying him so thoroughly.

"I'd rather not." There was great feeling in those words.

The Legatus laughed, as if Maximus had shared a great joke. "Most of us would rather not, boy. But the might of the Empire must flourish, and for that we need wives."

Maximus grunted. His Celt had made it very plain she wouldn't share. Even now her vehemence had the power to stun. He'd never come across such passion from a woman before. A part of him couldn't help thinking a lady of noble birth—there was no doubt his Celt was of noble birth—shouldn't even consider such violence, let alone display it.

But another part of him—the greater part—secretly basked in the knowledge she possessed the capacity to feel so strongly.

"So long as you're discreet, there is no need to give up your mistress."

"I don't—" Maximus sucked in a breath and struggled not to scowl at the Legatus. This was what happened when commanding officers also happened to be relatives. They presumed.

For most of his military career he'd been unencumbered by such familiarity. It was only after being transferred and promoted to the rank of Primus almost a year ago, directly under the command of his father's second cousin, that he'd confronted such interference and tasted the accompanying nepotism firsthand.

Tasted, and rebelled. The same way he'd rebelled at eighteen and enlisted as a bottom-rung centurion, instead of allowing his family connections to acquire him a tribune office, as his father's consul rank demanded.

The commander laughed. "Deny it if you wish, Maximus. But it's your duty to produce legitimate heirs, and for that need you need an advantageous marriage." He shrugged. "Happens to us all. And you may strike lucky and be given a wife you learn to care for. Just don't allow her to feel threatened by any mistress. That's all."

Carys wrapped her arms around her knees and watched her last patient leave the Cauldron. Only two had visited this morn. One woman had come for her sister, whose pregnancy was causing her great sickness. And the other because she feared pregnancy and wanted to ensure such catastrophe wouldn't come to pass.

Carys hadn't probed, but received the impression the potential father wasn't the woman's husband but a Roman.

As she prepared the necessary concoction, and gave the distraught woman detailed instructions, her mind nibbled incessantly at her own fertility potential.

Why had she tipped the cleansing tea into the ground this morn?

Maximus was virile. There was no doubt of that. Even now his seed could be implanting within her, drawing her blood to his, creating the first spark of new life.

And instead of filling her with horror, the thought filled her with a strange, dreadful delight.

If she was destined to have a child, then she wanted it to be her Roman's. It would be something to remember him by, as if she would need reminding, when the time came for them to part.

Carys knew that time would come. Even if the Morrigan had tacitly bestowed her approval upon the liaison, there was no future for them together. How could there be when he was a Roman and she not merely a Celt, but a Druid?

Yet the raven had touched her with its prophetic eye, and in that moment of clarity she had seen new life spring from the carnage of war.

A warm, soothing ribbon of peace fluttered through her heart, settling her soul. She worshipped the wise Cerridwen; she believed in the truth of the raven's foresight and, suddenly, despite every obstacle between her and Maximus, she had a certainty that, somehow, their destinies were inextricably entwined.

And the only way that could possibly be was if she conceived his child.

Carys slipped through the narrow entrance between two massive oaks that marked the single passage into the sacred spiral. The wave of vertigo shimmered through her mind, as always, but vanished within a heartbeat.

She leaned against a tree, shaded from the sun, and flexed her injured hand. There were a multitude of pain inhibitors she could take, but she would take nothing that might disrupt her body's rhythm and potentially dislodge Maximus's seed.

"Carys?" The whisper floated in the air and she swung round to see Morwyn, followed by Gawain leading two horses, emerge from deeper within the forest, both wearing dull, ragged cloaks over their richly decorated garments.

"Are you going to the settlement?" It was an open secret that over the last few moons—since the Druids had realized their flight wasn't transitional, that they weren't making active plans to launch a covert assault on the occupying forces—more and more had begun to slip down to the settlement and assist their people in more unobtrusive ways.

And for all his power, Aeron never appeared to see what was happening in front of his eyes. Sometimes Carys wondered whether he even knew many of the hamlets and villages were now dead and abandoned, their occupants having discovered more opportunities awaited them around the Roman fortification.

Morwyn gave a brief nod, and then gave her a speculative look. "Why don't you come with us?"

Chapter Twelve

Carys didn't bother to hide her surprise at being asked. No one had ever asked her before, and it wasn't because they all knew Aeron considered her his private property and as such should never set foot outside the spiral's boundary.

"With these eyes?" She raised her brows in disbelief. No one ever forgot her mismatched eyes. And when Druids mingled so close to the enemy, the ability to blend into nothingness was essential.

Morwyn waved her hand in a dismissive gesture. "Then keep your eyes lowered." She nodded to the ancient blanket Carys held, which she used at the Cauldron for her patients to lie upon while being examined. "Use that to cover your head and gown."

Excitement surged through Carys, curling her stomach into knots, sending shivers along her limbs and tightening her nipples. While she visited the spring every morning, it had never seriously occurred to her to venture into the heart of the enemy's lair.

No female Druid went there alone. And no Druid had ever

wanted Carys to accompany them before, in case she drew unwanted attention.

But now, with both Morwyn and Gawain, there was no reason for her not to visit the settlement. To see the finished fortification with her own eyes.

And to seek out Maximus on his invaded turf.

Morwyn smirked. "Precisely, Carys. He won't be expecting you, and you can discover whatever you wish if you confront him in his home environment."

Carys shot Gawain a sharp glance. Curse Morwyn and her big mouth. She had promised to keep silent about Carys's secret lover.

As if she could once again read Carys's mind, Morwyn threaded her fingers through Gawain's.

"Gawain swears silence also, Carys. Don't worry."

"It's time you broke free of Aeron's hold," Gawain said. Three years older than Morwyn, he was a fully trained Druid. Had the Romans not invaded, he'd now be responsible for the training of young acolytes gifted in truth and judgment.

Instead his future, like all their futures, had been suspended in time within this sacred spiral. Forbidden to fight for their people's freedom, and denied the freedom to settle claims of injustice.

Gawain, Carys knew, had been one of the first Druids to defy Aeron's edict of total isolation from their people.

She could trust him.

They took the hidden paths from the spiral, careful to leave no obvious trail that a sharp-eyed scout might discover, and wonder about, when such trail apparently led nowhere.

Carys sucked in a shocked breath as the fortification finally came within sight. It was so much larger than she had imagined. Solid. *Impenetrable.* Made of stone as if the Romans intended never to leave, and positioned so warriors stationed in the turrets had an uninterrupted view across the countryside.

"It's as if they've been here for years." Awe threaded her tone.

"They don't waste any time." Gawain, astride the other horse behind Morwyn, sounded grim. "And the longer they remain, the deeper their poison sinks into the minds of our people."

Carys couldn't argue with that. She noticed how her patients had dwindled over the last two or three moons. As if they were receiving medical advice elsewhere.

Only the women hadn't completely deserted her. Many still came when they were in need of another woman's wisdom.

Some distance from the settlement, they dismounted. The proud beauty of their horses disguised beneath layers of mud and debris, they led them into the town.

Because it was a town. Carys had expected makeshift slums consisting entirely of ragged tents, but instead there were also many stone and timber dwellings, and more people crowded in one area than she had ever seen in her life before.

Morwyn grasped her arm and pulled her to a halt. "Hide your jewelry and dagger. Don't give any reason for the Roman bastards to glance twice in your direction."

Carys slid the earrings from her lobes, the bracelets from her wrists and the golden torque from her throat, and along with her distinctive Druid dagger buried them deep within her medicine bag.

Gawain took the reins from her. "Your blanket is slipping." He nodded to her head, and she hastily straightened the material as he thrust a stick into the ground and measured lengths of the shadow. "We'll meet here." He scrawled a line in the ground across the shadow, indicating how long before they left the settlement.

That gave her plenty of time to explore. And while she might not find Maximus—since he was probably inside his fortification—at least she could learn more firsthand about how the Romans lived and how they treated her people, instead of relying on gossip and Aeron's bitter diatribes.

Morwyn took her hand, pulled her close. "I have newborns to bless, Carys." Although she was but twenty-seven and not yet fully trained, Morwyn was the Druid closest to the Morrigan whom their people could now access.

Carys glanced around. "I'll be at the market." It had been so long since she'd wandered through markets. Until this moment, she hadn't realized how much she'd missed such a simple pleasure.

Morwyn's grip tightened and Carys raised her eyebrows.

"Carys, you're not here to wander through the market." Morwyn sounded exasperated. "Go find your lover. With him you'll be safe. But whatever you do, don't allow yourself to be accosted by any of the Roman scum."

"I've no intention of allowing myself to be so accosted."

Morwyn gave an impatient sigh. "Just stay away from them. The barbarians won't think twice about abusing you."

"Even with this revolting blanket over my head and keeping my eyes to the ground?" When Morwyn began to scowl Carys patted her arm. "Very well. I promise not to go to that market."

Because she had noticed something of far more interest. The heavy gates to the fortification, which she could see even from this distance due to its elevated position, were open.

And both civilians and military walked freely between those gates.

⋆⋇⊹⊙⊹⋇⋆

Gripping the blanket beneath her chin, heart pounding with a combination of exhilaration and terror, Carys entered the fortification. The path she trod was smooth, flat and unbelievably wide, and disappeared deep into the enemy camp.

And yet how could this be called a camp? It was another town. A walled town with the famed Roman roads, stone buildings lining each side and a public market where both her people and soldiers thronged.

She sucked in a deep breath. A tangled sensory overload assaulted her, confined animals and compressed humans intermingled with the foreign scent of an occupying army.

Belatedly she remembered she was supposed to remain inconspicuous. Standing in the middle of the road, with her head tilted to the sky and sniffing the intoxicating odors around her, was hardly the best way to achieve such an end.

That was when she became aware of the three young Roman men leering at her. She hurriedly lowered her lashes and turned on her heel. Such modest behavior went against her nature, but she couldn't risk drawing attention to herself. It would put all Druids at risk if soldiers arrested her within the perimeter of their stronghold.

She decided to hide amid the crowd milling around the market. And then a rough hand pulled the blanket from her head.

"Told you she was a fucking Venus, didn't I?" The same rough hand gripped her arm and pulled her round.

Her heart stuttered against her ribs at the contact, her breath compressed within her lungs, and her palms, clenched into fists as she grasped the blanket, felt eerily clammy.

Don't look up. The demand pounded through her mind and she stared fixedly at the man's broad chest. So long as he didn't see her strange eyes, he wouldn't think her anything out of the ordinary. It was only her eyes that made her so memorable. All she had to do was keep her lids lowered, no matter what the provocation—

"Look at that face." Another one of them spoke, sounding faintly awed. "Like a Vestal Virgin."

The first one laughed and jerked her forward. Sweet Cerridwen, would no one intercept? She darted her glance to the people busy at the market, but no one appeared to be taking much notice.

"I saw her first." With that, he tore the blanket from her and tossed it aside. Dressed in her pale green gown with the intricate golden embroidery, she felt exposed. Naked. *Vulnerable.*

"Fuck, I'm so hard I could take her right here on the street." His coarse words appeared to amuse his friends, and sent an iced shiver of terror along Carys's spine, freezing her churning stomach.

She had been born into the chieftain class, where respect for her status was as natural as the air they all breathed.

But not only was she a princess by virtue of her birth. She was also a powerful Druid in her own right, and she had never known a moment's fear for her safety since to harm her was to dishonor Cerridwen herself.

But that was before. When all she met worshipped their gods, abided by their laws and afforded her the regard to which she was entitled.

"Come on, my beauty." He finally spoke in Celtic and, with his free hand, groped her breast. Without thinking, she swiped it away, repugnance and fear skittering through her blood as she glanced wildly around for means of escape.

The only enemy she had encountered since the invasion before today was Maximus. And even though she'd expected death at his hands, her soul hadn't reacted with such primeval terror at his touch.

The men laughed as if her resistance afforded them great entertainment.

"Little cat showed her claws," said the first one, his hard fingers biting into the top of her arm. "We don't mean to hurt you. We just want a bit of fun."

"Unhand me." She spoke in Celtic, but to her intense shame her voice trembled. And still she kept her lids lowered when every particle of her being wished to glare into this bastard's face while she gutted him with her dagger.

Her dagger that, instead of being sheathed at her hip, lay uselessly buried within her medicine bag.

A fatal error on her part.

Once free from the Legatus's interrogation concerning his private life, Maximus strolled through the market. The transportation of goods was becoming less hazardous by the day, since the natives ceased their ambushes and the roads ensured swift access from the ports.

He glanced at the goods on offer. Finally luxuries were arriving that would please the officers' wives and daughters who made little secret of how much they hated being stuck in an outlying province of the Empire.

The jewelry glittered. He paused. His wood nymph liked jewelry. Closer examination proved the stones were merely colored glass, but the gold was real.

He picked up a delicate bracelet, scrutinized the workmanship. Imagined decking her in his family's emeralds and pearls, priceless pieces that would fade into insignificance beside her ethereal beauty.

But he didn't have immediate access to them. And he wanted to buy his woman a present. Seeing matching earrings, he bought them as well, and as he secured his purchases, safely wrapped in a pouch, onto his ornate belt, he wondered what Aquila would have made of it had he been around.

As Maximus left the market to take the main road back to the barracks, his attention snagged on a group of loud-mouthed, jostling legionaries crowding around a girl. For a heartbeat he dismissed the scene, since it was a familiar occurrence. Girls were becoming more open to accepting attention from the soldiers now. It was always so. And yet something made him pause. Take a second look.

Disbelief seared through his brain as he caught sight of the girl's golden hair. Without conscious thought he swung on his heel and marched over, his conviction growing with every measured step.

One of them swayed to the side and he saw her standing there, as silent as a statue of Venus. She was looking at the ground, as if the legionaries intimidated her.

A cold black rage filled his mind, momentarily fogging his vision and stilling his stride. They would soon learn better than to even look at his woman, far less invade her personal space.

Another picked up her length of braided hair and buried his nose in the unbound tresses. "Smells of nectar."

Maximus curled his fingers around his vine stick. Gods, did the dog know how close he was to losing that hand for daring to touch her?

"I'll wager her cunt tastes sweeter than any nectar," said the third, and the rage surged from Maximus's mind, chilling his arteries, swelling the cavity in his chest.

He stepped beside her. She didn't move a muscle, but the three legionaries drew back as one.

"Sir," said the one who'd manhandled her golden hair.

He ignored the piece of shit, focused on the foul-mouthed cretin. Imagined ripping out his tongue and smashing his vocal cords for daring to so insult a lady.

His lady.

"Go." His voice was even. Deadly. Two of the legionaries hastened to obey.

The third began to grin. "Sir, we were just having some fun. The girl didn't object; she was—"

Maximus's fist connected with flesh and bone and cartilage, and the legionary was on his knees with a bloodied nose before he had time to react.

"Did I give you leave to answer me?" Maximus's voice was still even. He watched the legionary scramble to his feet. A fucking disgrace to his cohort, even if his cohort was one of the less prestigious ones.

"No, sir." The legionary stood ramrod straight, blood dripping over his lips and chin.

Maximus reeled in the bloodlust raging through him, which demanded satisfaction worthy of the offense. And if he discovered this misbegotten maggot had physically assaulted his Celt, then a broken nose would be the least of his punishment.

"Meet me after evening mess." For answering back a superior officer, extra duties went without saying. Maximus would have him cleaning out the latrines for the next month, as well as doubling his training shifts.

Finally he focused his attention on her. She still hadn't moved, still didn't look at him. He slid a finger beneath her chin and forced her head up, and a thread of unease slithered through his simmering rage.

He knew his Celt was proud, was instinctively aware she'd hate him to witness any weakness. And if she hid her face because she cried, he would personally flog the legionary responsible.

She glared up at him, her eyes sparkling jade and amethyst, but no tears streaked her flushed cheeks. Without conscious thought his touch became more possessive, cupping her jaw, his thumb nudging the corner of her mutinous lips.

She was here. She was safe. *She was his.* His head began to angle toward her, aching to savor those lips against his, to reassure himself she truly was uninjured.

And she jerked back, severing contact. His jaw clenched, and his fury at how close she'd come to harm sizzled with renewed vigor.

"What the fuck are you doing, walking around unprotected?" He ground the words at her in Latin, too incensed to bother with translation.

The look of unadulterated loathing she gave him increased his temper.

"Would you keep me under lock and key, Roman?" Her Latin dripped venom. "Is that how you treat your women? Lock them away or abuse them in public?"

Mars help him, he would kill those useless turds who had accosted her and string their guts up for the crows.

"This is an occupied land, Celt." He fisted his hands to prevent himself from gripping her shoulders and giving her a thorough shake. Or perhaps he'd forgo the shaking and instead drag her into his arms and hold her close, safe within his protective embrace.

"Yes. I know." Every word a stinging condemnation.

"Look at you." He raked his gaze over her, from the top of her shining, golden head, to her full breasts that gave a tantalizing glimpse of cleavage, the dip of her waist, the swells of her hips. "It's a wonder you had only three legionaries sniffing around you."

Something shifted in those mesmerizing eyes of hers. As if she didn't fully understand his meaning.

"I kept my eyes lowered." She sounded oddly defensive. "I shouldn't have drawn unwarranted attention. I don't know why I did."

She didn't know *why*? He could scarcely credit it. "Do you not possess a mirror, Celt?" Perhaps she didn't. He would rectify that instantly. "Have you never looked at yourself in a still pool?"

Her confusion vanished. "I was disguised." Her voice was haughty and she jerked her head to a crumpled blanket that lay in the dirt.

Maximus curled his lip. "It would take more than that to disguise your beauty, lady."

And then she took a step toward him, as if she didn't realize what she was doing. "I shouldn't have to." The words were a whisper that condemned all of Rome.

Condemned him. But if he openly claimed her as his mistress, she wouldn't have to hide at all. Because no other man would dare offend her by either look or word.

"You must be aware of how you affect men." Gods, he had only to think of her to become aroused. Any red-blooded man would be eager to part her thighs, brand her as his.

She'd fucked men in the past. The thought corroded his pride. Twisted his guts. The image of her wrapped around anyone but him caused bile to rise.

And yet she'd told him it had been three years since she last took a lover.

Why?

He would find out. And ensure she never entertained another but him.

Chapter Thirteen

Carys clenched her fists in a futile effort to stop her limbs from trembling. Part of her wanted to fling her arms around Maximus, show him how grateful she was that he'd rescued her from multiple rapes.

But another part of her, the part that was inextricably entwined with the core of who she was, *what* she was, boiled with resentment.

She wasn't a weak female. And yet that was how he saw her. How he expected her to see herself.

"It doesn't matter how I affect men." She still spoke Latin, unwilling to allow any of her people to inadvertently overhear their conversation.

Not that anyone was close enough. Were they being given a wide berth deliberately? And how much more conspicuous could they be, standing in the center of the road for anyone to observe?

"It does when they don't show you respect." He still sounded angry. She couldn't tell if the anger was directed at her or at his despicable soldiers.

But she seized on his remark.

"Your *men*"—she loaded that word with all the derision she could muster—"don't know the meaning of the word respect." She sucked in a shaky breath, hid her shaking hands in the folds of her gown. "I've never been treated so—so brutally."

An odd expression crossed his face, as if his anger had suddenly vanished. Instead he reminded her of a predator watching its prey, waiting for the chance to pounce.

The analogy stung.

"My lady." His voice was gentle. As if he tried to soothe her. But she didn't need soothing. Not from him. Because she had just experienced a slice of life, a slice of raw reality that her people had faced from the moment the Romans had invaded.

While she, and the rest of her kin, had scurried like spineless cowards to the protection of the sacred spiral.

"At least the men of my people don't attempt rape on a crowded street." Her voice was beginning to rise. She couldn't help it. *Sweet Cerridwen, don't let her lose control.*

And she knew even as she uttered the words they were untrue. Some men raped. Some were caught. Punished.

But even the most degenerate would never have dared touch Carys.

Before.

Would they now? Had her world changed so irrevocably that her former status meant nothing?

No one had attempted to intercede while she was being molested. Had no one recognized her? Or had they simply looked the other way, unwilling to become involved with a Druid whose very existence might rain disaster upon their heads?

Before she realized his intention, Maximus flung his arm around her shoulders, an iron embrace, and attempted to drag her along the road.

She recoiled. "Are you mad?" Panic whipped through her, pounding against her temples. "If I'm seen with you—"

"I believe half the populace has seen you with me." But he released her, and then swiftly reclaimed her dusty blanket. "Walk forward. As if you have no choice in the matter."

Stunned that he appeared to have understood her reluctance for physical contact, she slowly obeyed.

Because he was right. She had no choice. And if anyone saw her, they would know she had no choice.

He adjusted his stride to accommodate hers. Carys stared resolutely ahead, but she saw the furtive glances in their direction. Noticed how other legionaries, and even centurions, reacted as they approached.

She slid her Roman a surreptitious glance. He appeared oblivious. As if the deference was his right.

Her stomach clenched with renewed nerves. She'd always known Maximus was a warrior who commanded respect.

And yet, despite the long-ago lessons from her tutor on such matters, she knew almost nothing of the hierarchy of his Legion. In truth, it had scarcely crossed her mind, for what did she care about his rank?

But now she had to face the fact that previously she'd managed to ignore. He wasn't simply a fearless soldier who followed orders. He was an officer who issued them.

"Here." His command broke into her thoughts as he directed her from the main street into a side road that, by the look of it, housed the barracks.

He pushed open the door to their left, waited for her to enter. The room was quite obviously used as a military base with a large desk at one end, a smaller table at the other, and detailed maps nailed to the walls.

Carys shot the maps a second look. They were *frighteningly* detailed. Just how much longer could the Druids remain hidden within the spiral's protection without the geographical anomalies raising suspicion?

She dragged her attention from the maps as Maximus pulled out a chair. "Sit."

"No." Carys straightened her already rigid spine. Even if every strained nerve welcomed the thought of collapsing into a chair, the last thing she intended was to obey any more of Maximus's orders.

His look was calculating. As if he guessed her thoughts. She tensed her muscles further, ignoring the way they ached in protest.

She wasn't one of his subordinates, and she refused to bow to his dominance. He could beat her as he beat his legionary, but she would still be his superior because *she was a Druid* and he was nothing but a barbarous, murderous invader.

It curdled her stomach to admit that, perhaps, Aeron had been right when he'd told her no Roman could ever look upon her without wishing to fuck her before killing her.

"My lady, please sit." His voice was gentle, at odds with the granite planes of his face, the watchful look in his eye.

She flicked him a resentful glance, then stiffly lowered herself onto the proffered chair.

After a moment's strained silence where he stared at her and she refused to meet his eyes, he turned and opened a chest. In her peripheral vision she watched him extract a pottery amphorae and goblet.

As if she would drink anything he offered. She would take *nothing* he offered. Not now that she'd been subjected to how the Roman scum abused those whose freedom they had crushed.

Besides, she would never let Maximus see how badly her hands shook. She gripped her fingers tighter, and pressed her hands into her lap.

He diluted the wine with water before crouching in front of her and handing her the goblet. "The wine will calm you."

She gave him her haughtiest look. "I don't need calming, Roman. But I suggest some of your men need castrating."

And by the Morrigan she would wield the dagger herself.

His jaw tensed. "Had they raped you, I would castrate them personally and force their cocks down their throats."

The painful lump lodged in the center of her chest eased marginally. Just as all Druids were not the same, neither were all Romans.

She took an unintentional sniff at the wine, and its rich bouquet snared her senses. Perhaps one small sip would steady her.

As she took the goblet, Maximus wrapped his hands over hers. For a moment she considered protesting, but it was only her head that protested. Her wounded pride.

Her heart and soul took comfort from the warmth of his fingers, the strength she knew those hands contained. And so she allowed him to lift the goblet to her lips and took a reviving sip of the deep amber wine.

"How often do you come into the settlement?" His voice was neutral. It wasn't a demand, just a question.

"Today's the first time." She looked at him over the rim of the goblet and, despite everything, melted at those impossibly blue eyes. "I imagine it will also be my last."

There was no doubt it would be her last. Once Morwyn and Gawain discovered she had been marched off by a senior centurion—and they would discover it; too many people had witnessed her humiliation to keep such a thing hidden—they would think the worst.

And whatever story she concocted when she saw them, nothing would change the fact she had been noticed. Just because she'd escaped the enemy this time didn't mean she'd be so lucky a second time.

There was no chance Morwyn or Gawain would risk letting her accompany them to the settlement again. And if today taught her nothing else, it was the brutal reality that she wasn't safe walking through Roman-occupied territory.

Maximus's eyes darkened. "How could your father allow you to come into the settlement by yourself?"

Carys decided to ignore his obvious implication that she required male permission before she went anywhere. "My father is dead."

Tension radiated from him, as if he instinctively knew her father's death was linked to his beloved Rome.

"I'm sorry." The words sounded strange from his lips, as if he rarely uttered them. And the words he left unsaid hung heavy between them.

She stared into the liquid gold of the wine, unsure of how she should respond. Part of her wanted to tell him about her father. And yet another part urged caution.

Would she forever be torn between the logic of her brain and the feelings in her heart for this Roman?

In the end her heart won with barely a skirmish. There was so much of herself she could never share with Maximus. Yet this, if she guarded her words, was something she could.

"He died soon after the Roman Legion crossed the border into Cymru."

His hands tightened around hers, as if he thought she might follow her disclosure by tossing the contents of the goblet in his face. "I regret your loss."

An odd pain speared her heart. His forbidding expression told her more clearly than his stilted apologies that he expected her to hate him.

She should hate him. The enemy of her people, the murderer of her father. Yet from the first moment she'd spied him beneath the waterfall her feelings for this Roman had been nothing short of treasonable.

"We heard he fought bravely." There was quiet pride in her voice. She had met her father infrequently as a small child, and that had been more than ten years ago, but although she didn't love him the way she loved her mother, he was still blood of her blood.

And he had been killed by the Romans. Perhaps even by Maximus's own hand.

Yes. She should hate him. Hate him with such virulence that she'd sooner take her own life than allow him to touch her. But she'd done more than allow him to touch her. She'd taken him inside her body, the first man she had independently chosen for such an honor, and more than that, she knew, in this strained echoing silence that drummed against her ears, she had taken him inside her heart.

Maximus maintained eye contact. "You heard true, lady. They all fought bravely. And yet still I regret the loss of life. I wouldn't wish to cause you pain intentionally."

"I know." How strange to say that to her enemy. Yet she knew he meant his words, just as she meant hers. "It was a battle. You won." It would always hurt, forever leave a scar on her soul, but hating Maximus could never change the past.

Only the future.

The eerie whisper shivered through her mind and she froze. *The thought wasn't hers.* Disbelief meshed with shock, momentarily paralyzing her. Sweet Cerridwen, was the goddess here with her now?

And what did Cerridwen mean? That Carys should hate her enemy—or that she should not?

"Had the Druids not driven the people wild with bloodlust, the carnage would have been greatly reduced." Maximus's grim voice rammed through her brain, shattering the tenuous connection with Cerridwen—*yet there had been no connection after those cryptic words*—forcing her back to the present.

"The Druids?" Her tongue could barely articulate the words as dread trembled through her soul. Her father had been one of the greatest Druids in Cymru. It was the reason her mother had allowed her favorite lover's seed to grow within her womb.

Her father had led the revolt against the invading army. They'd received sporadic reports in the following weeks from spies and those who had escaped the slaughter. The bloodied accounts mirrored Aeron's visions in spine-shuddering accuracy, adding to his already formidable authority.

When he'd told them the time was upon them to seek the

sanctuary the gods had offered, there had been little dissent. The gods favored Aeron. They would show him how to defeat the enemy once they were safely within the sacred spiral.

And they were still waiting.   ·

Maximus took the goblet from her, placed it on his desk, then enclosed her chilled hands, as if he wanted to protect her from whatever words he next uttered.

"We offered honorable surrender. The Druids refused to even contemplate our terms. They fought like creatures possessed."

A heavy weight expanded within her chest, hurting her lungs. Hurting her heart.

"Is there such a thing as an honorable surrender?" Her father would never have surrendered. She may not have known him, but she knew of him. And her mother had chosen him because of his inspiring spiritual power, because of his incomparable beauty and because his courage, even as a boy, was legendary.

"Yes." Maximus's blue eyes didn't waver. He sounded completely sincere.

She choked in a breath. "Would you have surrendered if the positions were reversed, Maximus?"

His eyes flickered the merest degree. But it was enough, as if she'd needed evidence. Of course her brave Roman centurion would never have surrendered because, as for Druids, surrender was never an option.

And then he honored her with the truth. "The Legion never surrenders, my lady."

Chapter Fourteen

Maximus waited for her response, knowing she saw the hypocrisy of his words although until this moment he'd failed to recognize them as such.

But she didn't say anything. Simply stared at him with those bewitching bicolored eyes, and he had the sudden conviction she could see beyond a normal mortal's vision; that her eyes could see into the hidden depths of his soul.

An eerie shiver snaked along his spine, in much the same way as it had when, as a child, he'd been forced to visit oracles back in Rome.

Spiritual connections unnerved him. He understood the strength of Mars and might of Jupiter but for him they were tangible concepts, intrinsically linked to victory and the Empire.

Lesser gods were honored, but since the age of eighteen he'd not had much use for them. And even less use for the heathen gods worshipped in the provinces in which he'd served.

But this Celt, with her golden hair, air of fragility and

unwavering gaze, forcefully reminded him that he knew little of her culture. Her beliefs. *Her purpose.*

And then she blinked, and the illusion of being in the presence of *something* he couldn't explain splintered, vanished, as if it had never been.

He dragged in a deep breath. Of course it had never been. It was simply relief she was unharmed combined with a failing attempt to dampen the sharp arousal that fired his blood.

Despite the simmering desire that demanded he pull this tantalizing woman into his arms and fuck some sense into her, his military brain snapped back in time. Nobles and peasants had fought side by side, all whipped into a frenzy by the savage, blue-daubed Druids.

They still hadn't worked out the hierarchy. Were Druids socially superior to the chieftain classes? The few prisoners they'd captured had refused to talk, closing ranks and deliberately obfuscating.

And the peasants, what remained of them after that bloody battle, were too traumatized to make much sense at all, apart from the obvious fact they were equally terrified and deeply reverential of both sectors of their ruling classes.

"Thank you." Her voice was soft, but cut into his recollections with the force of a blade.

He trailed his hands up her arms. Her skin was warm. Silky smooth. He ached to taste her, to reassure her she would never be harmed while under his protection.

She was certainly under his protection now. Even his brave Celt would have to admit to that.

"For what?"

Her fingers traced over his hair; her breath whispered across his skin. "Not lying to me."

He cradled her delicate jaw. How easy it would be for a man to snap her neck. Something tightened deep in his gut at the image of this woman being in any man's power but his. Of being at the mercy of any man but him.

His brain seethed with fragmented visions, and his stomach twisted with inexplicable spasms, but his fingers remained gentle.

"I would not dishonor your intellect with lies, lady."

A smile touched her lips, as if his words were unexpected. "Am I no longer a barbarous Celt, Roman?"

He pulled one of her curls that framed her face, and then trailed the end across her cheek. "You were never a barbarian."

Her eyes darkened; her breath shortened. His cock hardened unbearably at her obvious arousal, but there was something he needed, something he wanted from her. Something that didn't involve the searing delight he would find from plunging into her hot, welcoming body.

Again he cupped her face, found himself drowning in the magical depths of her eyes. "Tell me your name."

She didn't pull away. Didn't break eye contact. Her fingers stilled on his head and he could almost hear her thinking. Turning over his demand in her mind, as if contemplating whether or not to satisfy his curiosity.

But it was more than mere curiosity. The need to know her name consumed him. Ate into his brain.

It would be easy enough to discover, now that she had been seen with him. But he didn't want to find out her name from another.

Illogical, since the outcome would be the same. And yet it would be entirely different.

And so he waited.

Her breath puffed out as if she had reached a decision, and her hand dropped to his shoulder. "Carys."

"Carys." He savored the taste of her name on his tongue, and found it pleasing. Exotic. "My lady Carys." Yes, the sound of it pleased him greatly.

The tips of her fingers scraped across his neck, and she might just as well have scraped her nails over his throbbing shaft for the way his body responded.

She leaned toward him until their noses almost brushed. "My lord Maximus."

Lust speared through his groin, and gripped his balls with exquisite agony. "Finally you recognize your master."

She nipped his bottom lip, a shocking sensation that seared the length of his swollen cock. Instinctively his hands tightened around her, and her delicate bones branded his palms.

"I have no master." Her whisper was uneven. "But I have you."

It was enough. Because it was the same. "No more games, Carys." She was where he wanted her now, and he had no intention of allowing her to leave. Let her brothers and uncles try to claim her.

They didn't deserve the honor of protecting her, when it was blatantly obvious they were even unable to curtail where she wandered.

He ignored the flaws in his reasoning. Had her male relatives had complete control over Carys, then he would never have met her in the first place.

She gave him an odd smile, almost as if she found his words quaint. But before he could take issue with that ludicrous assumption, her lips captured his.

Gods, sweet torture. His heated brain imagined peeling her gown from her body, spreading her over his desk and displaying her luscious, rounded buttocks for his personal pleasure. He'd part those silken cheeks with probing fingers, discover her swollen folds and bury himself in her, up to the hilt, until his balls slapped against her tender flesh.

He was vaguely alarmed to hear a groan escape his throat, and pulled back from her clinging lips before he forgot who he was, where they were, and how high the risk of discovery was.

"I want you, Maximus." Her whisper blazed through his blood, sending every nerve into volcanic meltdown. "I ache for you."

It was impossible she ached for him as much as he ached for her. But every word she breathed stoked his fire higher, and if she continued to tell him how much she wanted him, *how much she needed him*, within moments he'd lose what little control he retained and take her here, on the chair, or the floor, or even up against the fucking wall.

He dragged his eyes from her heated gaze and focused briefly on the position of the large window. From this angle Carys was partially concealed by his desk. Although the window didn't look out onto a thoroughfare and afforded a degree of privacy, a curious passerby looking in would still see him crouched before her, cupping her face, but from the waist down she was hidden.

Anyone could storm through the door. But nobody would dare.

He slid his hands over her shoulders, then briefly molded her full, tempting breasts. She sighed and pressed herself into his palms and, with an audible swallow, he forced his hands to her waist.

Hidden.

"Maximus." She gripped his wrists in a surprisingly strong grasp and attempted to force him up. "I want you to cup my breasts. Stroke my nipples."

"Be quiet." He barely recognized his own voice. "If you speak, I'll lose control." And if he lost control, he risked compromising Carys's reputation. One glance through the window from a passing legionary would be enough.

Her fingers speared through his hair as he inched her gown up her thighs. "I want you to lose control, Roman."

It hurt to breathe, never mind talk. Why did she insist on talking?

"Put your hands on the chair." It was a harsh command. The soft, warm heat from her thighs blazed from his fingertips straight to the engorged head of his throbbing cock.

"I don't want to." But her hands fell to her sides where she gripped the edges of the chair. Her thighs parted beneath his searching fingers and her breasts heaved erratically with each shuddering breath she took.

Higher. He grazed against her soft curls, felt the dampness slick her hot pussy. Her eyelids flickered and her teeth dug into her top lip and she leaned back in the chair, head lolling, raising her hips for his invasion.

"Look at me." A guttural demand. One hand curled around her thigh, keeping her still, and with his other he spread her lips and imagined how she looked, with her body opened for him. Only him.

His heart thundered. Blood pounded. Brain teetered on the edge of insanity.

"You torture me." Her words were slurred as she raised her head as if it pained her neck to support it.

"You kill me."

"I'm glad." She offered him a sultry smile and widened her thighs. "Torture me further, Maximus."

If he didn't die first. Gods, could he risk taking her into his adjoining room? And yet too many had seen them enter his quarters. He was on duty. He was the fucking Primus, by Mars. He couldn't afford to disappear for a quick roll with his wood nymph.

With Carys.

At least here a cursory glance would confirm nothing untoward was happening. Because he would give no cause for any to question her virtue.

Or his integrity.

He cupped her sex and she ground into his palm, her eyes dark with passion, her breath gasping between parted lips. Her clitoris bloomed against the pressure of his thumb, like a precious bud opening, and wetness bathed the straining head of his penis.

Blood stained her cheeks a pale rose and her thigh muscles tensed beneath his steadying fingers. He circled her erect nub, teasing, stroking, never breaking eye contact, and the scent of her arousal, of her impending orgasm, drenched his senses.

"Maximus, stop." Her hips bucked into his hand, denying her uneven whisper. "I don't want to come like this—I want you to—"

"Come for me." He would make her forget the terror and revulsion she'd experienced at the coarse hands of his countrymen. In time he would do more, but for now this was all he could offer.

Still she resisted. He could feel her resistance as her thighs trembled, fighting the rising waves of pleasure, and how she gripped the chair so tightly her knuckles whitened.

"No. I want—"

Stubborn. The word blazed through his mind. Didn't she realize he was in imminent danger of unmanning himself before her? Couldn't she simply accept what he wanted to give her?

He slid a finger into her wet channel and barely prevented groaning aloud. At least she stopped talking, but her gasp of shock and the way she clenched around him did nothing for his crumbling control.

Another finger. Another gasp. Another mind-shattering clench of her strong internal muscles.

She bucked against his hand, and he increased the pressure against her swollen clitoris. Gods, he wanted to see her, watch her as she came for him, but watching her face as her hot sheath contracted around his thrusting fingers was just as arousing. Her pupils obliterated her jade and amethyst irises, became unfocused, yet she maintained eye contact with him, as if he was her lifeline, her god, *her master.*

"Carys." It was the only word he could articulate. The only word that pounded through his throbbing brain. "My Carys."

Liquid heat flooded over his fingers as she convulsed around him, but she made no sound apart from a strangled gasp before digging her teeth into her lip.

He kept his thumb against her pulsing clitoris, milking every last exquisite shudder from her. And every shudder reverberated through his body, arrowing directly to his agonized cock, ratcheting up the tension until he knew his balls were on the cusp of exploding.

Slowly he pulled his fingers from her grasping warmth and

stroked her damp curls. *Wanted to see her.* His iron will faltered. The chances were slender anyone would see them for the brief moment it took to raise her gown and satisfy his burning need.

And yet if they were seen, Carys would be considered a whore.

He reined in the ravening lust threatening to devour his sanity. He had plans for Carys, and tarnishing her reputation was not among them.

Later. He could look at her for as long as he desired and discover the true color of her sweet pussy in daylight and not lamplight—*later.*

Moments passed, and Carys's erratic breathing finally slowed. She slid her fingers over his hands. "You didn't let me wait for you." Her voice was languid, sated, yet held an undercurrent of disapproval.

He dragged his fingers against the flesh of her thighs. She didn't loosen her hold. "I will allow you to return the favor very soon."

Awareness sparked in her eyes and she glanced at his crotch. She would see nothing—his armor hid all evidence—but the realization that she knew exactly what he had in mind caused his loins to convulse with need so acute his entire body pulsed with agony.

She licked her lips and leaned forward. "Is now soon enough?"

Mars, she *would* kill him. The image of Carys on her knees, taking him into her mouth, incinerated what little remained of his control.

The sharp rap on the door barely registered as his gaze locked with Carys's. Not until the flicker of alarm creased her forehead did reality rip through his fantasies, and recall his splintered senses.

With a strangled curse he pressed her knees together and straightened her gown. Rising to his feet had rarely engendered such discomfort. Thank the gods his armor concealed his arousal, although if he grew any harder, he feared he'd poke a hole through the silvered plates.

"Enter." He sounded rabid. He was rabid. He also ensured he stood in front of Carys so the intruder would be unable to see her properly.

One of the clerks entered. "Sir." His eye contact never left Maximus for a moment. "The Tribunus Laticlavius requests your presence in his quarters."

Maximus attempted to modify his scowl but it was impossible when he required all his willpower to remain upright. "I'll be with the Tribunus directly. I have a matter of import to finalize first."

"Sir." The clerk saluted and left, as if he couldn't wait to leave Maximus's presence.

With a muttered oath, Maximus turned back to Carys. She sat with ankles crossed, hands folded on her lap, looking like a chaste, golden-haired maiden of Venus, and he found it incredible to believe that mere moments earlier she had spilled her shattering orgasm over his exploring fingers.

It was the wrong thing to remember, when Faustus awaited him.

Fuck Faustus. He had Carys to deal with first.

He marched into the adjoining room, scrubbed his hands in the jug of water and contemplated tipping the lot over his head. Or crotch.

He doubted either action would manage to quench the fire raging through his veins and expelled a long breath. Carys would never realize the extent to which he was punishing himself for the behavior of his men toward her.

When he returned to her, she was no longer sitting demurely on the chair. Instead she was examining one of the maps of the local area that was nailed to the wall.

She swung round on hearing his approach, and for a brief heartbeat looked oddly guilty.

He brushed the thought aside, irrationally annoyed she should feel guilty for the pleasure he'd given her. There would, after all, be plenty of time later for her to pleasure him. They would have all night.

Another wrong thought. Gods, his loins *hurt*.

"Carys." He mentally winced at the harshness of his tone. Somehow he couldn't help the clawing frustration shredding his voice.

She didn't appear cowed by his growl, as she came toward him, as if she was about to embrace him.

Hastily he stepped back. His control stretched only so far and was already dangerously frayed.

"I will make arrangements for your immediate accommodation." He sounded as if he were issuing a punishment. When he attempted to smile to soften his words, he could manage only a glower.

"My accommodation?" A wary expression clouded her face, as if she misunderstood him. Gods, he needed relief. He sucked in a deep breath and attempted to focus on something other than his throbbing cock.

"I am—distracted," he managed to grind out between gritted teeth. "Let me clarify. You're here now, and I have no intention of allowing you to leave."

She wrapped her fingers around his clenched fist. "I'm sorry." She sounded troubled. "I know you're hard with desire and unable to think clearly, Maximus."

He broke into a sweat. No woman had ever uttered such words to him. Jupiter, he'd doubted until this moment a woman could even *comprehend* such a thing.

It was unnerving. And yet, because the woman was Carys, also shockingly arousing.

"I'm perfectly capable of thinking clearly." He'd sooner rip out his own tongue than admit anything less to anyone, never mind to Carys. Of their own volition his fingers tangled with hers. "Once we're formally together, your safety will be assured."

Her thumb stroked his. A sign of surrender. *At last.*

Chapter Fifteen

"Maximus." She drew his hand to her face and gently rubbed his knuckles over her cheek. Her surrender was sweet, and it was sheer torture he didn't have the leisure to enjoy it.

But later he would indulge every blessed moment of her surrender. And reassure her that, in reality, she surrendered nothing.

"These rooms are only temporary." In that moment he knew he could never be satisfied with Carys living in the settlement. She belonged with him. "We'll have larger quarters before the week ends."

Her fingers tightened. "I want to stay with you." Her words were barely above a whisper, and yet she looked in torment as if she had just admitted treason.

"Then all is well." He resisted dragging her into his arms to comfort her. He wasn't sure why she required comforting, but he was sure that if he held her, he would be unable to stop himself from taking her.

"But I can't."

He heard her words. But they made no sense. Perhaps she had misunderstood him. "I'm not giving you the choice, Carys."

She let out a ragged sigh, and brushed her lips over his captured thumb. He remained rigid before her, not trusting himself to move a muscle.

"My kin—"

"Your *kin* should take better care of you." He didn't try to hide the rage simmering through his blood. He could scarcely believe she still dared argue with him over this matter. How could she even contemplate leaving him?

Did she truly imagine he would allow her to go?

Instead of shrinking before his wrath—which would, he acknowledged grimly, have infuriated him further—she clasped his fisted hand to her breast.

"Would you truly wish me to cause my great-grandmother's sister such pain?"

He glared at her, uncomprehending. Her great-grandmother's sister? Surely such an ancestor couldn't still be alive. "By Mars, woman, what are you talking about?"

Far from flinching at his tone, as virtually everyone else he could think of would have done, her face softened.

"She is strong of spirit, Maximus, but this is her ninetieth summer. If I don't return, I fear what my absence might do to her."

Her ninetieth summer. Despite the heat pumping through his veins, an awed chill snaked along his spine. He'd not believed attaining such an age possible.

"Then you'll send her a message, assuring her all is well." With his back to the window, blocking her from sight, he dared to cradle her face with his free hand. "She must have other descendants, closer in kin than you."

Carys leaned into his palm. Her eyes never left his. "Her

daughters are all continuing their journey. And they had no children of their own." Their journey? Did she mean they were all
traveling? "My grandmother is her closest kin, but she is frailer
than her mother's sister."

The chill from his spine wormed into the pit of his stomach,
and curled into an icy knot. "What of your brothers, Carys? Your
uncles?" And yet he knew what her answer would be, and the knot
tightened.

"I have no brothers." Regret flickered in her eyes. "No sister
either. I dearly wanted a sister, Maximus, but my mother wanted
no other children."

Her mother wanted no other children. Had her father no say
in the matter?

Yet he couldn't mention her father. Not when the knowledge
that his Legion was responsible for her father's death weighed
heavily on his conscience.

"Your mother is there also?" Dread seeped from his twisted
guts, chilling his blood, tormenting his brain. Yet still he resisted
allowing the thought to push through his mind and gain substance.

For a moment he thought she wasn't going to answer. "No."
Her voice was oddly hollow. "She left before the invasion to visit
distant kin." She sucked in a quick breath. "But my cousin and her
son are." She paused, and a soft smile tilted her lips. "He is but
three years old."

Maximus stared into her lovely face in horrified disbelief. The
only male relative she had was *three years old*.

She lived somewhere out in the wilds with three other women—
one of whom was frail and the other surely hovering close to
Erebus—and a small child.

He'd assumed when Carys and her kin had fled the invasion
that her male relatives were behind it, and damned them for their
cowardice.

But instead Carys had escaped with the female members of her family. Had all the men perished alongside her father? Was that what she wasn't telling him?

His hand fisted against her soft flesh. "You know eventually you'll have to leave your haven." His knuckles traced the line of her proud jaw. "You can't hide forever, Carys."

Her fingers tightened around his hand, which she pressed against her tempting breasts, and pain filled her eyes. "I know."

He wanted to crush her in an embrace or shake her until her brains rattled, or find the words to convince her that her duty *did not* lie with her vulnerable female relatives.

Words he would never utter, even if such words existed. Her loyalty earned his respect, even as it drove him insane.

"You know?" He gave a brief, hollow laugh. "And yet still you insist on hiding like common criminals."

She sighed heavily, and shook her head. "You're right, Maximus. We can't hide forever. And we won't. I know, in my heart, this can't go on for much longer."

"Then end it now."

A frown creased her brow. "It's not yet time. I can't explain. I wish I could. I only know the end is approaching and—there's nothing I can do to change that."

Shudders crawled over his flesh, as if the wings of Mors brushed death across him. He braced his muscles against the unnatural reaction and rationalized her words.

She wasn't speaking of the end as gods would have it. She merely knew that, sooner or later, her hiding place would be found by *him*.

"Who accompanied you here?" His question was harsh. A command. He couldn't help himself. Frustrated desire mated with impotent fury at the knowledge that yet again he would have to allow Carys to leave.

Intolerable. And yet there was no choice. He knew she was a healer, although her youth precluded that she could know much of any use. But if the health of her elderly relatives relied on her skills, such as they were, how could he refuse to let her go?

"Why do you want to know?" For the first time she sounded wary, and he gripped her shoulder, unreasonably stung she should think he intended harm to any of her blood.

"You didn't venture here on your own."

She didn't immediately respond, and for one eternal heartbeat he thought she was going to remain silent. *Did she not trust him?*

"No."

"Carys." Her name was a growl in his throat. She knew he would never harm her kin. He'd sworn such to her on more than one occasion. How dare she doubt his word?

"With two companions."

He sucked in a long breath, attempted to smother the leaping rage consuming his chest. She had been answering his question, not his thought. Was this woman turning his mind? Could he no longer think clearly?

"When must you return?" He couldn't believe he was asking such a thing. He didn't want her to return to her people. And yet if she didn't, he knew she would never fully be his.

"Very soon." He gained little satisfaction from the fact she sounded reluctant. "Maximus, they're sure to have heard I was taken by a centurion. I can't allow them to worry unnecessarily."

He knew what she was saying. She couldn't be late. Did she think he intended to prevent her from leaving, after everything she'd told him?

He glared into her eyes. And saw the truth.

She knew he wouldn't keep her against her will. Perhaps she'd always known that, even before he'd reached that conclusion himself.

The thought didn't improve his temper.

"It's not safe for you to walk around the settlement alone."

Her fingers twitched around his hand, and he unclenched his fist, and cupped the weight of her breast.

"I know." She sounded irritated, but her breath hitched as he tightened his hold around her luscious globe.

"I forbid you to stroll through the markets and streets unaccompanied." Not until she accepted the mantle of his protection would she be safe from further molestation. And even when all knew she belonged to him, he would procure her a constant companion.

Her eyes flashed mutiny. She opened her mouth, and then shut it again, and he could *feel* her mind working furiously as her jaw clenched beneath his palm.

"Answer me, Carys."

Her breath escaped in an indignant puff. "I won't stroll through the markets and streets unaccompanied, *Maximus*." She put exaggerated emphasis on his name. "But only because I have no desire to be manhandled by obnoxious Romans."

He rubbed his thumb over her nipple, and even through the wool of her gown felt her nub harden. He wasn't sure whom he was punishing by his actions. Her? Or himself?

"And you will meet with me at the spring in two nights."

She shifted, so her breast pushed more insistently against his thumb. "*You* will meet *me* at the spring in two nights."

His thumb stilled against her. Her eyes mesmerized him. And then he tweaked her erect nipple until an involuntary gasp spilled from her disobedient lips.

"Meet me in two nights." He'd be damned if he would agree with her demand, when she refused to bow down to his. She was a woman, *his* woman, and as such shouldn't even question him, let alone presume she could have the last word.

And then she lifted his hand from her breast and grazed her lips across his knuckles. Her breath was hot against his flesh, her lips soft. And her eyes never left his.

"Come to me in two nights." Her whisper caressed his skin, soothed his injured pride. Although why that should be so, he couldn't fathom. Yet again, she was determined to undermine his authority.

Long moments passed. She was so small, so fragile. What did it matter if he allowed her this one small concession?

He pulled her hand up. Kissed each finger in turn. "Yes. I'll meet you at the spring in two nights, Carys." And then he couldn't help himself. "Don't be late."

Chapter Sixteen

Carys hurried toward the meeting place, knowing Maximus's gaze followed her. She wouldn't be surprised if he followed her physically at a distance, but she refused to confirm her suspicions.

Heart thumping, she ignored her good sense and glanced over her shoulder. Strolling nonchalantly through the outside market, within easy shouting distance, was Maximus.

She caught his eye and relayed the frigid message that she didn't appreciate him following her. He merely raised one eyebrow and made as if to approach her.

Goddess, didn't he realize what a precarious position he was placing her in? If Morwyn or Gawain guessed the centurion she'd been accosted by was now stalking her, how long would it take for them to deduce he was also her elusive lover?

She tugged the blanket more securely around her face, her mind feverishly concocting plausible scenarios. It was imperative she give her friends no reason to suspect she and the centurion had passed anything but the most cursory of exchanges.

And then she collided into a hard, solid body.

"Carys." Gawain gripped her arms and peered at her, his face contorted with a mixture of alarm and relief. "Thanks the gods. We heard you'd been arrested."

Morwyn pushed him aside and enveloped Carys in a bone-crushing hug. Over her shoulder Carys searched for Maximus's telling presence, but he had vanished into the crowd.

"I wasn't arrested," she said as soon as Morwyn allowed her to draw breath. Before she could say any more, her friends flanked her and urged her forward, toward the boundary of the settlement town, horses in tow.

"We should never have brought you," Gawain said, and Carys saw his sharp glances piercing through the throngs, as if searching for legionaries. Or centurions.

Once outside the town, Morwyn turned to her. "Sweet goddess, Carys." Carys was horrified to see tears in her friend's eyes, but before she could comfort her, Morwyn cupped her face. "For you to be so violated." She sucked in a quick breath. "The Romans will pay for this with their blood. I promise you. And the one who touched you will have his entrails strung up for the crows."

Blood flooded Carys's face. Could Morwyn smell the lingering trace of arousal on her? "I wasn't raped, Morwyn."

Morwyn stroked her cheek, as Gawain slung his bulky pack over his horse, his face a deadly mask of fury.

"We heard how you were abused in public, dragged from the streets." Morywn sucked in a ragged breath. "How dare they think they can behave in such a barbaric manner?"

Formless terror surged through her, a *knowing* that if she didn't appease Morwyn's sense of outrage, if she didn't convince her friend that she hadn't been violated, catastrophe would befall them all.

She grasped Morwyn's shoulders, and the blanket slithered from her head and tumbled to the ground. "It's true I was accosted by three Roman louts in the market. But the centurion drove them off." And then she couldn't help herself. "None of our people came to my aid, Morwyn. They all looked the other way."

"Things have changed, Carys." Gawain shot her a hard look before taking the pack lashed to Morwyn's back and securing it to the second horse. "Do you think the centurion swine would have thought twice about running anyone through who attempted to cross him?"

"I'm not talking about the centurion," Carys said without thinking. "He didn't abuse me. It was the legionaries who attacked me."

They both stared at her as if they couldn't understand her distinction. Suddenly realizing she was defending Maximus and not being subtle about it, she bent to pick up the blanket, to snatch a few vital moments to compose herself.

"What did the centurion want with you, Carys?" Gawain's voice was low. Even. She shot him a probing glance but his face was impassive.

She decided to go for the truth. Partially. "He wanted to ensure I was unharmed."

Morwyn gave a disbelieving snarl. "Unharmed? When they march into our lands, murder our people, rape our women—"

"Did he interrogate you?"

Her heart pounded against her ribs, yet it was slow, drawn out, and echoed eerily in her mind as if she was separated from her body and connected only by each amplified beat.

"He asked my name."

Gawain's eyes narrowed. "Is that all? He didn't ask you anything of where you come from? Who you are?"

Sweat trickled along the length of her spine. Sweet Cerridwen, how could she answer? She had no wish to lie to Gawain. But how could she explain what had occurred in Maximus's quarters?

It was impossible. She couldn't confide in her friends, yet she owed them more than this.

She took Gawain's hand, maintained eye contact. "He asked

after my kin. I told him the truth, yet told him nothing. He didn't hurt me, Gawain. He's—I feel he is an honorable man."

He was silent for a moment. "The Romans have no honor, Carys." He sounded resigned. "The gods saved you today. We must give thanks for that. And give sacrifice to Arawn that Aeron never discovers what happened to you today."

Carys didn't care if Aeron discovered she had been into the settlement or not. Lately, whenever she thought of Aeron, a hard knot formed in her chest, and, since meeting Maximus, her years of buried resentment toward the older man had finally sparked into life.

"Perhaps he should know." Morwyn swung herself onto the horse and Carys followed, since Gawain's horse was more burdened with goods from the town than theirs. Morwyn glanced over her shoulder at Carys, then across at Gawain. "If he thinks the Romans have violated his beloved Carys, then perhaps he'll be more inclined to share when, precisely, he plans to attack."

Carys sighed inwardly. She knew her friend was sore that Aeron still, for unfathomable reasons, wanted Carys in his bed. But she couldn't understand why Morwyn obsessed on wanting to fuck Aeron when it was clear to all how much Gawain adored her.

Aeron, Carys believed, adored no one but himself. And despite his declarations of undying devotion for her while they'd been together, she'd never *felt* the emotion from him.

But then, she had never felt anything with Aeron. It was as if he was an abyss. Her relief after finishing their relationship had been so profound, she felt as if she'd been reborn into a more vibrant, tactile world.

"*If* he plans such an attack." Gawain's expression was stony.

Morwyn jerked, shot Carys a disbelieving glance. "If?" she repeated, once again focusing on Gawain. "How can you doubt, Gawain?"

Carys chewed her lip and stared resolutely ahead. Until recently she'd been eager to fight the enemy, help drive them across their borders.

But now she was torn. She wanted freedom for her people. But she also wanted Maximus.

An impossible dilemma. One she couldn't imagine ever reconciling.

Gawain gave a mirthless laugh. "How can you *not* doubt, Morwyn?" His voice was harsh. "How many moons have we hidden away like rats on a ship, waiting until the time was right? What time? When will it be right?"

"But—"

"The *right* time," Gawain persisted, "was the moment the barbarians invaded our lands. We should have stood firm, as our kin did at the border."

"Our kin all *died* at the border," Carys said. "Aeron saved us from that at least, Gawain."

"At least they died a noble death, defending their people and land."

Morwyn twisted round and frowned at Carys in clear confusion. "But Aeron received visions from the gods," she said, glancing back at Gawain. "Only when all the planets are in alignment will we be able to drive the enemy from the valleys."

Gawain turned to stare at them. His eyes were hard, his expression grim. "I have the greatest reverence for Aeron's visions. He foresaw the slaughter. Ensured we escaped unscathed from the following onslaught." His lips thinned. "But this retreat was supposed to be temporary, while we gathered our powers and united the spiritual forces. Now we've waited so long the very people we're pledged to protect are bowing voluntarily to Roman rule."

Shivers raced across Carys's arms, despite the warmth of the day. All she could see in her mind's eye were those maps on the walls of Maximus's quarters.

She'd studied them during the few brief moments he'd left her alone. And been transfixed by how meticulously the landscape was captured.

And yet not captured. The entire section protected by the spiral had not been mapped. Because, as far as any casual observer could see, there was nothing there *to* be mapped.

But no matter what her fellow Druids believed, the Romans weren't stupid. And Maximus most certainly wasn't stupid. How long would it be before he realized there was something very wrong with the geographical markers beyond her spring? And how long before someone, somehow, stumbled across the one and only entrance to their sacred retreat?

Maximus waited until Carys and her companions left the settlement before turning to keep his appointment with Faustus.

When the tall, fair-haired man had embraced her, a bolt of pure fury swept through him. Had she lied? Was this man her lover?

And what the fuck was he doing there? Carys had mentioned no man. Only female relatives. It had taken a considerable measure of willpower to remain out of sight, when every instinct demanded he make himself known. Make *them* know that Carys was his.

The thoughts churned his mind as he marched through the main street, barely acknowledging the way legionaries went out of their way to avoid him.

The dark-haired woman had to be Carys's cousin. And the man her husband. It made sense. Although considering how Carys's relatives had fled before the invasion, it made *no* sense why a man would allow his wife and her cousin to enter the enemy's lair.

And then allow Carys to wander alone. The rage surfaced again, fueled by his steaming lust. How many spineless men were hiding behind the skirts of frail, ancient women? Manipulating Carys so she felt honor bound to remain with them?

In what other ways were they manipulating her?

He rapped sharply on Faustus's door, scarcely waiting for permission to enter before marching inside.

"Gods," Faustus said, pottery amphorae in hand, staring across the room that bore more resemblance to a senator's reception than a military office. "You nearly took the door down, Maximus. Wine?"

So this was a social visit. He didn't feel social. He felt like demolishing something. "Celebrating?" He tried to modify his tone, but only partially succeeded.

Faustus diluted the wine before handing Maximus an exquisitely crafted glass goblet, which had been specifically imported from Rome along with numerous other luxuries Maximus considered unnecessary.

He resisted the urge to shatter the fragile object and instead drained the contents in one go.

"Wouldn't you be celebrating if you were leaving this barbaric land?" Faustus curled his lip in disgust and refilled Maximus's glass with wine and water. "By Jupiter, I can't wait to return to civilization." He waved Maximus toward a chair before sprawling on another. "The Senate awaits."

"Good luck to you." Maximus drained the second glass and slammed it onto the unnaturally tidy desk. The thought of taking his own place in the Senate didn't appeal, but then, he wasn't Faustus.

"With my military record, I won't need good luck."

Maximus declined to answer. Faustus's military record was negligible, but since it happened to encompass the last year when they had defeated the Druids of Cambria and conquered a good portion of Britannia's windswept western peninsula, he knew Faustus's assertion was correct.

"And now you're taking my place," Faustus said, "you'll only have to suffer this life for another year at most. I'll ensure the Emperor knows of your exemplary conduct, Maximus."

Maximus grunted. If Faustus was waiting for thanks, he could

wait until Tartarus froze. Maximus was very aware of his own conduct and didn't appreciate the character assessment from someone
who believed twelve months in service qualified him as a veteran.

Faustus shot him a frown. "Sit down. There's a matter I wish
to discuss with you."

Gritting his teeth, Maximus sat and ignored the discomfort
between his legs. But since the ache in his balls radiated throughout his entire groin he wasn't entirely successful.

"There's been a change of plan." Faustus set his goblet on the
desk and unaccountably avoided eye contact. "I'll be leaving for
Londinium this afternoon."

That caught Maximus's attention. "So soon?"

Faustus shrugged. "My uncle believes there's no point in staying longer than necessary. I can't disagree with that."

So from tomorrow, he would no longer be the Primus. He
glanced around the room, knowing other—private—rooms led
from this one. Quarters more than suitable to house Carys in
comfort.

"I have a favor to request."

Maximus focused on the younger man, who was frowning as
if something other than the anticipated return to Rome was on his
mind.

"Yes?"

Faustus cleared his throat, and then pulled a small pouch from
his belt. He dropped the leather bag onto the desk. "I would ask
you to give Efa this, as a sign of my regard."

Maximus glanced at the pouch, then stared at Faustus. "You're
leaving without telling her yourself?"

Faustus made an impatient gesture with his hand, but still
avoided eye contact. "If I tell her, she'll only become hysterical,
Maximus. If you explain the situation, she'll accept it without
making an exhibition of herself."

Maximus pulled Efa from his memory. He'd met Faustus's
young mistress on only a few occasions over the last three months

and she seemed a quiet, timid little thing. But who could tell how a woman would react upon learning her lover had abandoned her?

He fingered the leather pouch. Felt the weight of the coins within. "You don't want to leave her."

Faustus finally looked up. For one unguarded moment Maximus witnessed the naked longing in the younger man's eyes, and shock speared through him as he realized the truth of his semi-idle comment.

"What does it matter what I want?" Faustus said. "I'm heading back to Rome and my intended wife. There's no future here for me. I've always known it."

"You could apply for a transfer. Take Efa with you into Britannia."

Faustus stared at him as if he thought he'd gone mad. "Britannia?" he repeated. "Gods, I'd go insane if I had to stay in the army indefinitely, Maximus. I'm not like you, loving the life. I'm only here to further my Senate career."

He thought of Carys. Of never seeing her smile again, of never hearing her contradict every word he uttered.

An odd pain twisted his guts.

"Have you not considered taking Efa back to Rome with you?" Would he take Carys back to Rome with him? Would she even consent to go to Rome if he asked her?

"Fucking Jupiter." Faustus poured himself more wine and swallowed it neat. "Of course I have. I have the means to set her up in style; she would want for nothing." He shot Maximus a scowl. "The old man forbade me. Said it would besmirch the honor of my dear bride to return with my mistress in tow."

Maximus's fingers clenched around the pouch. He didn't have to wonder how Carys would react to *his* future bride. She had already told him, in graphic detail.

"Then have Efa come to you later."

Faustus picked up the amphorae and studied it. "That could

take months. It's best I end it now, without leaving Efa false hope of a future together."

Maximus narrowed his eyes as he considered Faustus's words. "A few months are nothing. At least she'd be with you. That's what you want, isn't it?"

Faustus replaced the amphorae on the desk and leveled a dark glare in Maximus's direction. "I want to take her with me because she's a good fuck, Maximus. Gods, my cock aches every time I think of her delectable mouth around me."

Maximus emitted an unintentional grunt, as the image of Carys's delectable mouth around *him* invaded his thoughts.

One day, *and soon*, he was determined for that fantasy to become reality.

"Then have her follow you in a month or two. You'll be married by the time she arrives, won't you?" Maximus couldn't see why Faustus saw obstacles. If he wanted Efa, then he could have her. He'd just have to wait for her; that was all.

Faustus expelled a disgusted breath. "You haven't seen my bride, Maximus. Two years ago, when I last paid my respects upon the anniversary of her eleventh year, I had never seen such an unappealing creature in my life. The thought of fucking her withers my balls."

"Then close your eyes and think of Rome." Maximus eyed the amphorae, then decided against another glass. So far the wine, far from deadening the lust in his loins, had fed it.

"It would take more than Rome to get it up for her," Faustus growled. "Acquiring a suitable mistress is a priority. You understand, now, how I can't wait months waiting for Efa. It wouldn't work."

Perceptions adjusted. Maximus frowned. "You only want to take Efa with you for one reason." Even as he said the words, his brain questioned his response.

Why else did a man take a mistress if not to satisfy his carnal desires? It certainly wasn't for the purpose of procreation. That was why a man married. To beget heirs for Rome.

Faustus gave a short laugh, devoid of amusement. "What other reason is there?"

Maximus attempted to prevent the scowl from darkening his face. There was no other reason, although he knew well enough that some men felt far more than mere lust for their mistress.

For a moment, he had imagined Faustus one of them. Apparently, he'd been mistaken.

"I thought she might stimulate your brain with her scintillating conversation." He infused each word with derision, although whether he was deriding Faustus for his cavalier treatment of Efa or himself for his uncharacteristic descent into seeing more than existed, he couldn't say.

This time Faustus's laugh sounded genuine. "There's not a lot of time for conversation while I'm pounding between her thighs, Maximus."

Maximus refused to respond. Faustus didn't appear to notice.

"Scintillating conversation?" The younger man grimaced. "Is that how you entertain your whores, Maximus? By *talking* to them?"

The sudden vision of hammering his fist into Faustus's smug face assaulted him. Only the knowledge that the other man had no idea of Carys's existence prevented him from smashing his superior officer's nose across his aristocratic cheekbone.

He swept up the pouch. "I'll pass on your message in the morning." As he attached the pouch onto his belt, his knuckles grazed another package. The jewelry he'd bought Carys.

Fucking Mars. Would nothing go to plan when it came to that woman?

Chapter Seventeen

Back in his quarters, Maximus flung the pouch of coins onto his desk in disgust. He couldn't work out why he was so mad.

Certainly, the unintentional slur against Carys rankled but he knew Faustus hadn't meant it personally. No one knew of his involvement with Carys. And when they did, none—not even his superiors—would even consider slighting her name. To do so would be to insult the honor of Tiberius Valerius Maximus himself and all that entailed.

Something else boiled his blood. Something he couldn't rationalize. Couldn't comprehend.

Something connected to the way he'd misinterpreted Faustus's regard for Efa.

It nagged the edge of his consciousness, like a tick from the tropics of Carthage burying into his brain, distracting his purpose. Somehow connected to Carys, although that made no sense because Carys wasn't Efa and he wasn't Faustus.

Would *he* ever send another to tell Carys he was leaving? That they would never see each other again?

With a livid curse he snatched up a sheaf of papyrus and glared at the most recent cartography.

Would he take Carys back to Rome, whatever objections were raised, when the time eventually came for him to take his place in the Senate?

He forced himself to relax his grip on the papyrus before it disintegrated.

Yes, he fucking would.

Even if the objections came from Carys herself.

He ignored the sliver of his brain that reminded him how stubborn Carys could be. Ignored the fact that while, for the moment, he was unencumbered by a faceless fiancée, that state was unlikely to continue.

Mainly he ignored the gnawing certainty that Carys wouldn't hesitate to make her displeasure known if he told her she was going to Rome where she'd be ensconced as his official mistress.

He sucked in a deep breath, and focused on the meticulously sketched map. He had yet to take over the reins of the Tribunus Laticlavius. Why in Tartarus was he thinking about an impending marriage?

It would take his father months to secure a suitable match. Possibly even years, considering the scandal surrounding the way he'd left Rome nine years ago. And with any luck the female chosen would be so young, she would be unable to wed for several more years.

Yet still the disquiet hovered, like a low-lying fog across a marsh, distorting his thoughts, clouding his senses.

Because of a woman.

It was ludicrous. There was a time and place to think of women, and now was neither. Again he glowered at the map, narrowing his eyes as he tracked various landmarks and compared them to his mental images.

Carys was only a woman, like any other woman. And yet she was like no woman he had ever before encountered.

The *damn woman* was driving him out of his mind.

There on the map was the glade where they'd fucked so exquisitely. And there was the waterfall, where he'd first encountered her, the waterfall that reminded him of his family's country estate in the Bay of Naples.

And—something wasn't right.

He strode to the wall, where an enlarged map of the area was displayed. The valley. The secluded glade. The waterfall. All checked out.

But still, something grazed the outer edges of his brain. He searched further, stared at the ridge of trees beyond.

He remembered seeing that forest from a distance as he'd stood on the hill looking into that valley. But according to these maps, there was no forest. Just a line of trees and then another cursed mountain.

His brain clicked the image into focus. A chill slithered along his arms.

There *was* a mountain beyond those trees. But not anywhere near as close as this cartography suggested.

It was inconceivable such an error had been made. And yet the evidence was here, nailed to the wall and embedded in his mind's eye.

He rolled up the map. There was doubtless a simple explanation as to why acres of forest had been omitted, but before he hauled in the scouts and cartographers, he'd double-check the area himself.

And it had nothing to do with the illogical sensation echoing through his bones that this glaring discrepancy had, in an inexplicable way, something to do with Carys.

"I need to meditate."

Gawain shot Carys a probing look. "Meditate within the spiral, Carys."

Carys glanced at the flawless blue sky, then around the green valley and approaching forest. Since leaving the Roman settlement, nerves fluttered incessantly in the pit of her stomach, danced through her veins and vibrated against her temples, making her constantly on edge. As if something not of the mortal world watched her with a malevolent eye.

"I need to be close to Cerridwen." Then perhaps the eerie sensation of being followed, even though she *knew* they weren't, would disperse.

"Cerridwen will come to you within the spiral," Morwyn said, and gave her hand a comforting squeeze. But it didn't comfort; it merely heightened Carys's certainty that if she didn't communicate with her goddess, and soon, she might never experience that immortal touch again.

Panic flared. She had to discover what Cerridwen had meant by those cryptic words, *only the future*, she'd uttered in Maximus's quarters. And the most sacred place was Cerridwen's Cauldron.

Reaching around Morwyn, she pulled the horse up and slid to the ground before her friends could voice another objection. "Cerridwen calls."

"Then I'll accompany you." Morwyn made to dismount but Carys laid her palm across her friend's thigh.

"I need isolation." She couldn't risk Morwyn discovering anything about Maximus, and who knew what Carys might disclose if she ascended into trance?

"Then I'll remain outside the Cauldron's sacred circle. But you shouldn't go alone."

"Morwyn." Gawain's voice held a note of warning. "If Cerridwen wants Carys alone, then she will protect her."

Morwyn's brow furrowed. "Something feels terribly amiss. I can't explain, but ever since we left the settlement I feel as if a dark cloud hovers above us."

"The Roman stench," Gawain said, but Carys caught Morwyn's eye and saw understanding dawn.

"Speak with Cerridwen," Morwyn said, grasping her hand and squeezing her fingers until they tingled. "Find out how we can dispel this evil once and for all."

Gawain growled in his throat, as if he had his own ideas how they could dispel their enemies, and Carys merely nodded. She couldn't confide what she really wanted to ask her goddess.

"Come, then." Gawain swung his horse around. "Let's take the supplies back and be astounded once more at how Aeron believes our dwindling stocks have been miraculously replenished yet again. If he even notices."

Morwyn shot Carys an odd glance, as if Gawain's escalating antipathy toward Aeron both confused and concerned her, before she followed Gawain's lead.

Carys pulled the blanket from her shoulders, sucked in a deep breath and headed upstream toward the spring. The sensation of encroaching darkness was palpable, and now that she knew Morwyn had also sensed the suffocating presence of something beyond her understanding, the need to seek her goddess's advice became more urgent than ever.

By the time she reached the Cauldron, her heart pounded against her ribs with a combination of fear and exertion. Sinking to her knees, she opened her embroidered bag and sought the special root. She had no business having one in her possession, but the same compulsion that had urged her to collect the slivers of bluestone had also compelled her, on that memorable night, to sequester one from Aeron's own stocks.

Her hands trembled as she prepared the concoction. She was being reckless. Perhaps selfish. But despite knowing she was breaking their laws, she continued with her task.

She trusted Cerridwen implicitly. Her goddess would protect her from discovery, both from her own people and any wandering Roman.

Aeron gripped the stone edges of the altar as a wave of impending devastation washed through him. The sensation was so sudden, so acute, it sucked the air from his lungs and sent splinters of ice ricocheting through his heart.

A cold sweat prickled his skin. His stomach roiled and bile scalded his throat, but no vision catapulted him into the heart of the phenomenon.

Children's squeals shattered the moment and he dragged open his heavy eyelids and glared at the two culprits, who scampered from the cromlech as if Arawn himself had emerged from the Otherworld to silence their tongues.

He couldn't take this for much longer. The cromlech was sacred. The cromlech was *his*.

Since the Roman invasion, the cromlech had become more social than sacred, as if his fellow Druids were forgetting its special significance to their way of life.

To him.

But soon balance would be restored. They would once again take their place in the world. And the cromlech would, once more, become his personal refuge.

He closed his eyes, attempted to recapture the shimmering threads hovering just beyond the reach of his conscious mind. A darkness loomed, but it wasn't a familiar darkness. Revulsion skittered along his nerves, caused the hair to rise on the back of his neck.

The scent of feminine malevolence drenched the encroaching fog, tainting him with the stench of millennia of matriarchy.

The Morrigan.

Instinctively he ensured his true nature was concealed, the way he'd concealed his beliefs and convictions for the last twenty-five years. No Druid, no god, and most certainly not this goddess could discover his purpose until it was too late for them to do anything but bow to his will.

Her skeletal touch grazed his soul, but didn't linger, as if she either was unaware of his presence or attached so little significance to him as to render him unworthy of further scrutiny.

Since the latter was inconceivable, Aeron knew it was his own formidable shields that protected him from the goddess's all-seeing eye.

Sweat beaded his forehead. The Morrigan wasn't searching for him. But she was searching for something.

For someone.

On the spiritual plane the black fog swirled, and for one heart-shuddering moment Aeron saw into the center of the Morrigan's focus.

Chills raced along his spine, cooling the sweat on his skin, freezing the blood in his veins.

She searched for Carys.

Hidden in the shadows of the trees, Aeron watched Gawain and Morwyn enter the sacred spiral. The other Druids thought him unaware of their excursions into the enemy lair. But why else did they imagine he'd allowed this passageway if not for the purpose of access when it came to replenishing their supplies?

He ignored the fact that the fracture had created itself in the instant he had released the great power from the bowels of the earth. His original intent had been to isolate them absolutely, but in the same way the spiral had failed to enclose Cerridwen's Cauldron, it had also left this slice of the forest unprotected.

As if the spiral had its own agenda. But since Aeron was the master in this extended manipulation of the elemental forces, that also was inconceivable.

Carys wasn't with her friends, but instinct told him she had been with them earlier. While he knew no Druid would allow her to go as far as the Roman settlement, he also knew he was alone in his condemnation of her escaping to the Cauldron as often as she did.

Therefore, Morwyn and Gawain had left her at the Cauldron on their way to the settlement. And she had to be there still.

Wrapping his cloak around his shoulders, he silently left the sacred spiral. The Morrigan, in a dark cloud of fury, searched for Carys. And could not find her.

He intended to discover why. On both counts.

Maximus reined in his horse and stared over the valley toward the forest. From his vantage point on the crest of the same hill where he'd stood only yesterday, the extent of the forest was beyond doubt. Looking down upon it, even from this distance, the tree canopy spread for miles.

He consulted the map. When he discovered who had charted this region, demotion would follow punishment. Such a blatant discrepancy between their intelligence and reality could cost lives. Roman lives.

Quelling his anger, he urged his horse forward. How many other areas did he need to double-check? Where the fuck had this particular cartographer learned his so-called craft?

Pulling up on a lower ridge, he once again scanned the surrounding area. An invisible fist punched through his heart as disbelief slammed through him, but still the message his eyes transferred to his brain made no rational sense at all.

The forest had physically shrunk.

He sucked in a deep breath, shielded his eyes from the glare of the sun. But still the heat haze hovered over the forest—*what remained of it*—no forest at all, merely a wooded area as depicted by the map grasped in his fist.

His heart hammered against his ribs, sweat slicked his skin, and his mouth dried of all moisture, as if he'd just completed a marathon training session. But a training session was something tangible, something he understood.

This—could not be understood.

He retraced his path, eyes narrowed, watching the forest. And as he once again reached the summit of the original hill, the forest inexplicably expanded.

Eerie shivers raised the hairs on his arms and back of his neck. What dark magic had he uncovered?

Chapter Eighteen

Carys stared at the minuscule portion of mashed root in her small wooden bowl and a slither of apprehension chilled her. Such powerful aids to bridge the chasm between mortals and gods were used sparingly, during sacred ceremonies. The results could never be anticipated, and as such no untrained Druid was permitted to use them unsupervised.

As a Druid only halfway through her training, Carys knew only too well that without a powerful link back to the earth, she could end up forever lost in the spiritual abyss revealed by the magical properties of the root.

But she would be careful. For a start, she wasn't making the required preparations for a ritual with all the bodily and spiritual cleansing such undertakings required. She intended to swallow only the minutest amount, just enough to open the doorway and allow her access to the upper realms.

Smothering the lingering thoughts that persisted telling her she was merely twisting words to suit herself—*because of course she wasn't*—she trickled fresh water into the bowl and stirred the contents with her finger. Meditation was all very well but couldn't guarantee a connection, and she desperately needed a connection with Cerridwen.

She inhaled slowly, then licked her finger clean. She needed only the merest taste, just enough to let her—

The breath jerked from her lungs as she catapulted through the misty veils, without warning, without even swallowing the forbidden mixture. Faster she sped, landscape merging into an emerald blur, and she could feel the wind on her face, whipping through her hair, and yet she could also feel the grass against her legs where she sat, frozen within her mortal body, at Cerridwen's Cauldron.

She tried to call for her goddess, reach her with her mind. But Cerridwen remained beyond her grasp.

Panic flared. If Cerridwen wasn't here, how had she crossed the chasm so swiftly? She could feel her finger still in her mouth, could taste the magic as it seeped into her tongue, but couldn't move a muscle, on either the spiritual or physical dimension.

All movement ceased. Heart pounding with sudden realization of where she was, Carys stared at the forked path before her.

A beautiful maiden materialized, and Carys trembled, in her mind and her soul and the core of her being. Despite all she had experienced during her years of training, despite the numerous occasions Cerridwen had graced her with her presence, the Great Goddess, the Morrigan herself, had never appeared to her. And Carys had never before entered her most divine of domains. *Was this further proof that the goddess had decided to welcome her into her sacred embrace?*

The maiden turned, showed Carys the face of the Mother. And then she turned again, to present the Crone.

Carys tried to prostrate herself on the ground, but she had no body, no will over her mind, no substance. And although, incomprehensibly, the eyes of the Crone bored into her with malice, Carys had the eeriest conviction the Morrigan couldn't see her at all.

The Morrigan looked down the path that led into the far distance. As Carys followed her gaze, she felt the warm, familiar comfort of the ages envelope her, caress her with their combined love and knowledge of all that was and all that could be.

Her ancestors, the spirits she called upon whenever she required their assistance.

Her kin. The powerful women of her line who had gone before her.

And relief rushed through her. The Morrigan, who had never once honored Carys with her presence, had come to her at last. Whatever Carys had done to offend the goddess was clearly forgiven; otherwise why would the Morrigan show her how intrinsically and intimately they were linked?

Carys attempted to show the Great Goddess her gratitude, but as if she was still utterly unaware of her presence, the goddess turned to the fork in the path.

For one terrifying moment Carys saw the fork through the eyes of the goddess. Both paths led into the future. Her people's future. But the choice of that future hovered in the balance, shimmered on the edge of the precipice, and could as easily shatter into oblivion as bloom into everlasting life.

Ice clawed through her heart, both physical and spiritual, cleaving the realms together, spinning impossible scenarios through her pounding brain.

She didn't want to see the future.

But it made no difference, as her soul, her mind, her spiritual entity coalesced into an image of her physical self and *shoved* her bodily along the left-hand path.

Flames engulfed her, searing her skin, singeing her hair, and instinctively she raised her arms to protect her face. Black smoke billowed, war cries ripped through the foul air, and water boiled with blood and fury.

Druid and Roman fought, and an immense and terrible knowing slithered through her, coiling around the essence of her being, leaving no room for doubt or disbelief. The battle she foresaw was not merely for land or pride or some faceless barbaric emperor.

The battle was for survival of everything her world had ever known.

And it was a battle her people could never win.

Mesmerized, Aeron watched Carys from the far side of the stream. There was no doubt in his mind as to what she had sucked from her finger, as her instant ascent into trance was impossible otherwise for a mere acolyte. The fact she shouldn't even be in possession of such magic barely concerned him—at least now he knew why the Morrigan searched for her. To punish her for her disobedience.

Without taking his fascinated gaze from her, he slowly advanced. Even by taking the magical root, such instant ascent was unusual. But then, Carys was no ordinary woman, no ordinary Druid. If the gods allowed her such rare honor, it reinforced his conviction—as if he had ever doubted—that she was meant for him.

He crouched before her, stared into her glazed, blinded eyes. "Carys?" But he didn't expect an answer. She was too far beyond the mortal realm to be aware of his presence.

But perhaps he could still glean information from her.

"Where are you?"

Her body jerked, as if she heard. He grasped her wrist and pulled her bloodied finger from her mouth. Her lips remained parted, full and pink and bloodstained. No longer denying him access.

Lust burned his arteries, blazed through his groin, as he imagined capturing those lips with his mouth. Her breasts rose and fell with each erratic breath, and it would take only one sharp tug of her ties to once again feast upon her beautiful, tantalizing flesh.

Heart thudding in tandem with the blood pounding through his loins, Aeron opened her bodice and sucked in a shuddering breath as he revealed her full, rounded globes.

Still as perfect as he recalled in every one of his heated, lust-fueled dreams.

He laid aside his hazel rod and roughly pulled her gown from her shoulders, exposing her more fully to his gaze. She made a small sound of distress but nothing more, as if she knew, deep in her soul, that he had the right to touch her as he saw fit.

And of course he had the right. Since the moment he had first noticed her as a child of five, he'd been entranced by her strange eyes, her golden hair and infectious laugh. Then eighteen years old, he had already been well on his way to accruing power and prestige and any woman or boy he so much as glanced at.

But from that day he'd set his sights on the young princess. The girl whose noble birth was so far removed from his own humble origins that such a joining was beyond contemplation.

Except Aeron had overcome his poverty-stricken beginnings, thrown off the shackles of serfdom by virtue of his astounding abilities, and been accepted into the hallowed ranks of the Druids while still a child himself.

He rolled one rosy nipple between finger and thumb, and cupped her other breast with his hand, squeezing and delighting in the way her flesh filled his palm, perhaps more so than she ever had before.

"You should never have left me, Carys." His voice was hoarse as he stared into her vacant eyes. "I waited years for you to grow up. Years of frustration before I finally made you mine."

He sucked her reddened nipple into his mouth, grazing her with his teeth. Desire arrowed through his throbbing cock, more pain than pleasure, for it had been so long since he'd been inside her and he couldn't wait any longer.

Dragging his mouth from her, he gripped her jaw. "You don't deserve me."

She began to tremble and her eyes dilated, as if even deep in trance she couldn't deny her desire for him.

The knowledge seared him. So she could see him after all; she did know he was there, knew what he intended to do to her.

And she wanted him to.

His fingers bit into her soft skin. "I'm going to fuck you, Carys. Now. While you're communing with the gods. And you'll take my seed into your womb and our son will be blessed above all others."

Erratic pants issued from between her lips and her eyes began to water, as if in gratitude that he was prepared to forgive her the last three years of denial.

He eased her down onto her back, pulled her gown up, exposing her thighs and her glorious pussy. He wanted to fuck her every which way in every hole she possessed, take her as he had never taken her before, because she had never allowed him to.

But time was short. He needed to fill her now, while she walked in the realm of the gods, and if he waited too long, he'd spill his precious seed before he even entered her.

Grunting with need, he freed himself, kneed her thighs farther apart. After today she would never again deny him. And he could indulge in every fantasy that had haunted him for the last fifteen years.

"Welcome your master home," he said, and positioned himself above her open, willing body.

Chapter Nineteen

Maximus didn't know what compelled him toward the glade where he'd encountered Carys. There were other, more direct, routes to the inexplicable forest, but still he urged his horse through the narrow wooded path where he had previously followed Branwen.

Dismounting, he walked the last few feet to the edge of the wood. Through the gaps in the trees he caught glimpses of the stream, but no Carys.

Why had he expected to see her here?

Only because he had wanted to.

And then he did.

His entire body stilled, blood, breath, his very heartbeat. His gaze locked on the scene, seeing yet not quite believing, understanding but unable to comprehend the evidence filtering through his numb brain.

She lay on the grass, her hair cascading around her head like a golden halo, while a man spread her legs as if he had every right to do so.

Nausea rode him. He balled his fists, ignored the sweat drenching his body.

Carys with another man.

Unthinking, he dropped the reins and took another step forward, relinquishing the shelter offered by the trees' shadows.

How could she take another man?

Acid churned his gut, unlike anything he had ever experienced, seeming to eat into the region of his heart, leaving great, gaping holes of fire.

It was deeper than rage. Sharper than damaged pride. It was as if he suffered from acute indigestion and severe food poisoning, and the reason for his physical indignities lay spread-eagled on the ground, just feet from where she had lain open to him so recently.

Giving herself to another.

It was hard to breathe. He sucked in a lungful of oxygen but the air seared him, as if tainted with the foulest smoke.

But still he moved forward, although gods knew why he didn't simply yell his anger and impale the Celtic bastard on his gladius.

And then turn his weapon on her, the lying bitch.

Each step took a century, yet he was upon them before her blond lover had the chance to take her. And in that one blazing moment, Maximus saw through his tortured disbelief.

Carys lay unmoving on the ground, her arms tethered to her sides by her ripped gown. Her eyes were vacant, dilated, and stared unseeing into the sky. Blood smeared her lips and cheek.

Fury scorched his veins, obliterating the inexplicable aches within his body into a solid, recognizable core.

His woman was being violated.

He gripped the stranger's long hair, ripped him upward and smashed his fist into the shocked face. The Celt reeled backward, stumbled into the shallows of the stream. Maximus took a step in his direction, his mind filled only with the image of vengeance, of slicing this creature's balls from his groin and forcing them down his misbegotten throat.

He had promised Carys, and he kept his promises. It mattered not whether the perpetrator was Roman or Celt.

Gladius in hand, he advanced. Strange silver eyes glared back at him, the malevolence so potent he could feel it singe his skin.

"Prepare to die, barbarian."

The Celtic barbarian bared his teeth and, for one spine-shivering moment, Maximus was reminded of something, something that shimmered just beyond the veil of memory.

Rasping breaths from behind him stilled his pace. Carys sounded as if she could scarcely breathe. She needed his help.

But her attacker stood mere feet away, as if daring him to advance. It wouldn't take long to mutilate this bastard, to avenge Carys.

The rattling gasp she gave sent chills along his flesh, and with one last glower at his quarry, he retraced his steps, never taking his eye from the Celt until he reached Carys's side.

He risked tearing his glare from the Celt to look down at her. Another bolt of anger seared through his heart, but additionally a sliver of fear gripped his gut. *What had the Celt done to her?*

She lay as if unconscious, and yet her eyes remained open. Every instinct, born of his heritage, his years in the army, *his core of honor*, demanded he exact retribution from her attacker.

And yet Carys needed him.

Grinding his teeth, he sank to his knees and tugged her gown over her thighs, covering her exposed flesh. In his peripheral vision he saw the barbarian retreating, heard the splash of water, and his fingers tightened around his gladius in readiness.

But the coward made no move toward him, instead vanishing into the far side of the woods.

May Mars strike him down. It crucified him to allow an enemy to escape, but Carys—for Jupiter's sake—what in Tartarus was wrong with Carys?

Still clenching his gladius in case the Celt made an unexpected return, he attempted to cover her breasts, but the material snagged around her arms, impeding his one-handed efforts. He leaned over her and frowned into her glazed eyes.

"Carys?" His voice was barely above a whisper. She made no sign that she could hear him, and somehow that was even more unnerving than her vacant stare.

With a finger that unaccountably shook, he gently wiped the blood from her lips. He could see no cut or bruising upon her face, but that meant nothing. He, Tiberius Valerius Maximus, had failed to protect her when she had needed him most.

He ripped the fibula from his right shoulder, barely acknowledging how the clasp tore his flesh and spilt his blood, and pulled his cloak free. With one sharp glance across the stream to ensure the Celt wasn't making a stealthy return, he placed his gladius on the grass.

Sliding his arm beneath Carys's neck, he lifted her from the ground and slipped his cloak around her, covering her chilled body. Still she didn't acknowledge his presence, but merely lay there as if she were a beautiful, malleable corpse.

And then a strange, pungent aroma drifted in the air, taunting his consciousness with an elusive familiarity.

Pinpricks of alarm raced through his blood, although he couldn't fathom why, only knew in the most elemental recesses of his soul that the cloying aroma clinging to Carys was somehow *wrong*.

An iron fist wrapped around his lungs, crushed his ability to breathe. Sheathing his gladius, he gently lifted her, holding her close to his body. Smothering his natural instincts that urged him to ignore his suspicions, he lowered his head and drew her breath deep into his constructed chest.

For one shattering moment he was catapulted back to his childhood, back to the sacred temples of the oracles with their swirling incense and magical flames.

Comprehension flooded his brain. And then flames of another kind roared through his lungs, expanded his chest and scorched his sanity as the realization of *what* the barbarian truly was punched through his consciousness.

On the other side of the stream, hidden within the shade of the trees, Aeron watched as the Roman scum lifted Carys as if she belonged to him, and strode back the way he had obviously come.

Aeron gripped his hazel rod, imagined it was the invader's neck. How dare the cretin throw him aside, as if he were of no account? And how dare he touch Carys, soiling her flesh, polluting her spiritual journey?

Grinding his teeth, he arrowed malevolence across the stream, searing the Roman's retreating back. Fucking coward, to attack him when he possessed no weapon, when he was unprepared, when he'd been about to take Carys and impregnate her with his son.

Rage broiled through his gut, ignited his veins. And now the Roman would fuck her instead, fill her with his foul seed, corrupting the sanctity of her womb.

Air hissed between his clenched teeth. She would never conceive a Roman brat. He would see her dead first, honor preserved.

But first he would deal with the Roman abductor.

When he was sure he was alone, he emerged into the clearing, hazel rod angled slightly above the ground. The answer was here, somewhere. He could feel the certainty humming through his bones, and, although he didn't know what he sought, that was of no consequence.

He would know when he found it.

The hazel rod jerked and Aeron sank to his knees. Hidden among the grass a gold barbaric broach glinted. And smeared across the sharp clasp: Roman blood.

Maximus rode back to the settlement, one arm wrapped around the still-unconscious Carys. A dozen fragmented thoughts churned through his brain, but this wasn't something he could conquer through superior might, or fight with physical strength, or lambaste with logic.

For this, he needed a priest.

An auxiliary took his horse and Maximus shouldered his way through the locked door of his new quarters.

He lowered Carys onto the bed, tugged her gown into some semblance of modesty across her breasts and then hovered by her side. He didn't want any messenger to know of his business, yet how could he leave her alone to go to the temple, when she was so vulnerable?

"Maximus?"

Maximus straightened and turned toward the bedroom door where Aquila stood. The one man he trusted above all others. Sometimes the gods answered a prayer before it had even been uttered. "Aquila, fetch me the priest."

Aquila glanced at Carys. "The priest? What's happened, Maximus? Who is this woman?"

Mine.

He strode toward Aquila and glanced through the door to ensure they were alone. "She was attacked. By a Druid."

"You captured a Druid?"

He fucking should have. "He escaped."

"How do you know he was a Druid if you haven't interrogated him?"

He should have caught that bastard. "He drugged her with elixir of the gods. She looks awake, yet is unaware of our world."

"You saw this happen?"

"I didn't need to see it." His voice was sharp. "She reeks of the essence of the oracles. As for the Druid, there's no mistake." He should have realized instantly what the creature was, as soon as he'd seen him stumble into the water. "His stance was unmistakable, even without the blue-daubed nakedness of the ones at the border."

"You say she was attacked. But perhaps she's his woman. She could lead us to where the Druids are hiding."

"She's not his woman." The thought was repellant. "He was about to rape her as I arrived."

Aquila regarded him through narrowed eyes. "How did the Druid evade capture? If he was alone and vulnerable with his cock hanging out, I fail to see why—"

Maximus grasped Aquila's arm. "She's mine." He saw confusion and then comprehension flare in the other man's eyes. "And I have every intention of capturing the barbarous Druid and exacting vengeance."

"You know you'll be questioned as to why the Druid escaped." Aquila's voice was low, but filled with meaning.

Of course he knew. "The priest is bound by vows. I'll ensure his silence on the matter."

Carys's head slumped to the side, facing him. His heart jerked against his ribs, but instantly he saw it meant nothing. She was as unaware as before.

"I wouldn't trust the priests we have here to keep your counsel." Aquila sounded grim. "They're looking for any leverage to ensure their speedy return to Rome."

"Then I saw no Druid." Maximus shot his friend a feral glare. "Do you understand, Aquila? There was no Druid."

Only the tightening of Aquila's jaw betrayed his personal feelings on the matter. "I understand."

Maximus faced the man who had been by his side since they were both boys in Rome. "Ensure you do understand. I'll have no whispers circulating that Carys has anything to do with the barbaric Druids."

Because she didn't.

A rasping breath from the bed penetrated his rage-fueled mind, and he crouched beside her.

"Carys, can you hear me?" His voice was gruff. "Do you know where you are?"

Her eyes flickered and began to water. "Mon."

The hairs on his arms shivered to attention. "Mon?" Did she mean the isle of the Druids, Mona? "No, you're not. You're here with me. In Cambria." He struggled for the Celtic translation. "Cymru."

"The Great Goddess," Carys's voice rasped as if her throat were seared by fire. "The Morrigan rejects me."

Awkwardly, he smoothed back the hair from her brow. "It's a bad dream, Carys. Your goddess will never forsake you."

"Cerridwen weeps." Carys hitched in a ragged breath and her pupils begin to contract, distilling the chilling glaze.

"Are the Druids with you?" Aquila hissed in Celtic, and Maximus gritted his teeth, incensed by the implications Aquila appeared to be making.

"The Druids?" Pain etched her face and her lashes flickered, finally dispelling the last vestiges of that eerie stare.

He felt the tension thudding from Aquila but kept his focus on Carys, as if by sheer willpower alone he could prevent her from saying something that would condemn her for all time.

Her breath strangled in her throat and her eyes widened in sudden terror. *"They all perished."*

Chapter Twenty

Carys had said *they*. Not *we*. But he had expected nothing else, couldn't understand the depth of his relief. And so he rounded on Aquila.

"She requires a woman. Fetch that girl, Branwen."

Aquila straightened, and for a moment offense carved his features, as if he resented being sent on such a mission.

"I'll arrange for her to be found."

"No." Maximus also straightened. "I entrust this to no one but you, Aquila. I don't want Carys to be the victim of any malicious gossip."

Aquila clenched his jaw and jerked his head.

"I'll find Branwen."

As soon as Maximus was sure they were alone, he turned back to Carys. She was staring at him, her eyes watering as if in delayed reaction.

"How do you feel?" Stupid question. But he wasn't used to tending sick women.

It wasn't his place to tend sick women. And yet he remained by her side, torn between relief at her apparent recovery and a sense of unease at the strange words she'd uttered as she had emerged from the elixir's enchantment.

"I don't know. Where am I?"

"In my quarters. You're safe."

Confusion clouded her eyes. "But I left the settlement." Her frown deepened. "I returned with Morwyn and Gawain and went to the Cauldron."

He filed the names away for later scrutiny. "I found you at the spring." He made an educated guess. "The Cauldron."

"I don't recall." She sounded unnerved. "What—Why did you take me from the sacred spring and bring me to your quarters?"

Should he tell her? Or leave her in blessed ignorance of the fate she'd so narrowly avoided?

Fear tinged her expression, as if she suspected the truth.

"I had no choice." It was as simple, and as complicated, as that.

Carys gripped her fingers together and tried to prevent the panic churning through her stomach from showing on her face. If he had overheard her saying something incriminating while in trance, then he wouldn't be looking at her the way he was now.

Would he?

She swallowed, her mouth dry, her throat raw and parched from the smoke-filled vision. Maximus didn't look as if he wanted to butcher her as an enemy of his precious Rome. He looked as if he was *concerned* about her.

"Why did you follow me?" The words were barely above a whisper, as the full implication shivered through her soul. How had he followed them, without their knowledge?

She wouldn't believe Maximus was the cause of that malignant presence she and Morwyn had sensed. There had to be another answer.

"I didn't follow you."

Her thoughts tumbled, shattered. "You didn't?"

"No."

She let out a shaky breath. "And yet you found me."

"It would seem our paths are destined to cross, no matter how hard you try to run from me."

The tension seeped from her body and she sagged against the wall, suddenly realizing how desperately tired she was. "I'd never run from you."

The corner of his mouth lifted in a sardonic smile. "You might want to remember that, the next time you defy my orders to stay."

He would never know how much she wanted to stay with him. Or how such a fantasy could never be. "You still haven't told me why you brought me here."

The smile vanished.

"You were in danger." His narrowed eyes betrayed the extent of his fury as they darkened with evil intent.

Ice trickled along her spine. "You saw I was in danger?" Awe threaded her voice. Even now the lingering remnants of terror scraped through her spirit as she recalled the smoke-filled, blood-drenched vision.

She had been trapped inside that vision. And something had dragged her from the pit.

Maximus. Guiding her back to the mortal realm.

Did he possess gifts from his own gods that allowed him access to the spiritual world? *Had he witnessed the vision with her?*

"Don't you remember anything that happened after you arrived at the Cauldron?"

She stared at him, as she searched her mind. But all she could recall was preparing the magic roots.

Her gaze dropped to her hands and she slowly spread her fingers. Dried blood caked the finger she'd used to stir the sacred concoction.

Slowly she raised her hand, her eyes riveted on her finger. Now she could see teeth marks ripped into the skin, could recall the taste of her blood on her tongue, her lips.

And the sheer, elemental terror of being aware of, yet being unable to flee, the fury of the Morrigan or the horrific carnage of her people.

She choked on a breath, and Maximus sat beside her on the bed and pulled her roughly into his arms, as if unaware how his armor bruised.

"Don't be afraid." His voice was hard. But his hand, gently caressing her head and sliding through her hair, was infinitely gentle. "I'll find him. You have my word."

She dragged her fascinated gaze from her torn finger and looked up at him. Something in his blazing eyes, in the way his gaze held hers with a possessive ferocity, alerted her that whatever danger Maximus had saved her from had nothing to do with her vision.

Dread coiled in the pit of her stomach. "Who will you find?"

His intense gaze flickered, as if her question made no sense. "The one who drugged you."

Relief surged through her. Whatever he'd seen, he was still in blissful ignorance of her familiarity with such sacred, forbidden knowledge.

His calloused hand cradled her face, a simple gesture and yet somehow so tenderly intimate. "The barbarian who attacked you while you were insensible upon the ground."

Her cocoon of security unraveled, twisting into knots of shocked disbelief. Her heart rate accelerated, her breath shortened, and a sensation of tightness wrapped around her chest, pressing into her lungs.

Why hadn't Cerridwen protected her?

And immediately the answer vibrated through her brain.

Because, despite whatever Carys had thought, her goddess hadn't invited her into the realm of the immortals.

"Carys." Maximus's tone was urgent and she struggled to focus on his face, and not on the horrifying prospect that she had irretrievably severed the special bond with Cerridwen by her own rash actions.

"Who—who—?" The words wouldn't articulate. Why hadn't

she known the malignant sensation of being followed, as she'd ridden back to the spiral, was because the Roman legionaries who'd attacked her that morning were tracking her?

"Don't distress yourself." His voice vibrated with leashed anger, and yet still his hands were gentle as he continued to caress her.

She tore free of his hold and forced herself to look down her body. The ties at her bodice gaped free and with a strangled gasp she pressed her hands across her exposed cleavage.

Had all three raped her, while she watched Rome rape her entire culture?

And had Maximus come upon them, as she was being so brutally defiled?

Nausea churned at the foul scenario playing through her mind and she squeezed her eyes shut, blocking out the world. Blocking out Maximus. How could she not remember any of it? How could she not *feel* the disgusting aftereffects of such violation?

"He didn't rape you, Carys. I pulled him from you in time."

There had been only one.

It was small comfort, for still he'd come upon her without her knowledge, while she had been so certain Cerridwen would ensure her safety.

But it had been Maximus who'd saved her. Maximus who had protected her honor. Relief, regret and revulsion churned, and a lingering aftertaste of the sacred root against her tongue caused her gut to contract. She struggled to the edge of the bed as sweat slicked her skin, feverishly pushing Maximus, but he refused to be pushed.

She gave up. And vomited the contents of her stomach over the floor.

When Aquila finally returned with Branwen, she slunk into the room as if she expected to be eaten. Maximus curbed his irritation and forced a smile.

"I understand you know the lady Carys."

Branwen's nervous glance flicked to the bed where Carys slept the sleep of the exhausted, not the enchanted.

When the pause lengthened and it became apparent Branwen wasn't going to reply, he stepped toward her.

"The lady Carys," he prompted.

Branwen began to tremble. "No, my lord."

He refocused his attention, which had strayed to Carys. "What?"

"I don't know her, my lord."

He couldn't believe this shaking excuse for a female had the audacity to lie to his face. "Indeed, I believe you do."

"The Tribunus Laticlavius wishes you to personally attend to the lady Carys, Branwen."

Branwen shot another fearful glance at Carys. "I'll tend to the lady." Her voice was barely above a whisper.

Maximus decided to make Carys's position crystal clear. "The lady is my mistress. She is to be accorded the respect due to her elevated status."

His words had an unexpected effect. Instead of looking suitably impressed that she had been chosen to attend to his woman, Branwen visibly jerked, as if he'd just imparted a shocking edict. The glare she tossed his way, before dropping her gaze to her feet, smoldered with surprising passion.

What was the matter with her? Anyone would think he'd just insulted Carys, by the way Branwen behaved.

He turned to Aquila. Much as he wanted to stay with Carys, duty called. "Ensure she understands," he said, reverting to Latin. "I'll arrange for the door to be repaired, food and drink to be delivered, but no one is to enter until I return."

Carys stirred, and frowned when she saw Branwen peering at her, her eyes wide and fearful.

"My lady." Branwen hitched in a sob. "Thank the gods you're awake."

Carys glanced around, but there was no sign of Maximus. "What are you doing here, Branwen?"

"The centurion brought me." A faint blush brushed her cheeks and she avoided eye contact. "But it's the other one—the Primus, although he's called something else now—he's imprisoned you, my lady."

Branwen sounded so horrified, Carys had to hide a smile. She clasped the younger girl's hand. "I'm not a prisoner. The Roman saved me from attack."

"Whatever he did, he plans to dishonor you." Branwen sank to her knees. "He's going to use you, our princess, as his mistress."

Pain tightened her chest. This was why she and Maximus could never have a future together. Her people would never accept his, could never contemplate a noble, a *Druid*, succumbing willingly to the enemy's bed.

"I won't allow myself to be used." She tugged on Branwen's hands, urging her to rise. "I can look after myself."

"You must escape." Branwen glanced wildly about, as if the means would suddenly appear. "Before he returns."

"Yes." It hurt to speak. Hurt to know that, once again, she was running from Maximus when all she wanted was to stay by his side. How many times would a man as proud as he forgive her?

With Branwen's assistance she stood up, and the room tipped over. She gasped, staggered back, and sat heavily down on the bed again.

"My lady?" Branwen looked petrified. "What—what did the Roman do to you?"

It wasn't the Roman. She had brought this on herself.

"I haven't eaten since I broke my fast." How long ago that seemed. "I can't go anywhere until I've regained my energy."

After a simple meal of fruits and freshly baked bread, she stood, thankful the world no longer rocked like a boat. It would take her hours to reach the spiral, and the prospect of such a long walk filled her with dread.

Suppose she was attacked yet again? It was unlikely in the extreme Maximus would miraculously appear for a third time to save her honor. The next time, she would have to rely on her skill with her dagger.

Where was her medicine bag? Had it been left at the Cauldron? She'd have to rescue it first thing in the morning. And since her dagger was in her bag, she picked up the knife she had recently used to eat with. It was sufficiently sharp. It would slice through clothes and flesh with equal ease.

She turned to Branwen. "I want you to do something for me."

"Anything, my lady." But fear caused the younger girl's eyes to widen and voice to tremble.

"It's a small thing, but important. I want you to promise me that you'll tell no one I was here today."

Branwen blinked a couple of times, as if she had expected a far more terrifying command. "Of—of course. Whatever you wish."

"This can't become common knowledge. If word reached my fellow Druids, another battle would rage. Do you understand?"

But before Branwen could respond, the door burst open, and Maximus entered.

Chapter Twenty-one

For a moment Carys stared at him, as if his appearance completely unnerved her. An unsavory thought skulked through his mind. Had she been planning to leave him, yet again?

"Maximus." She smiled at him and placed a knife on her plate. The cynical section of his brain noted it made an effective weapon.

He strode toward her, banishing his suspicions. Even if Carys had planned to leave, she certainly couldn't now.

"You look well." He took her hands, caressed her knuckles with his thumbs. "How do you feel?"

"Much better." She responded in Latin and glanced at Branwen, as if uneasy by the girl's presence.

It didn't make sense. He knew they were acquainted. It was the reason he'd insisted on the girl in the first place. So that Carys would wake to a familiar face.

But she obviously didn't want Branwen privy to their

conversation, and so he reverted to Latin. "I've arranged for domestic help. A cook will arrive later to prepare our dinner."

"I've just eaten." She attempted to free her hands.

"Fruits and bread." He dismissed her recently eaten meal with a jerk of his head before turning to Branwen, who, by the look on her face, appeared in mortal agony.

"That will be all, Branwen," he said in Celtic. "You may return in the morning to tend to your mistress."

Both women tensed as if he'd just uttered something outrageous. But neither said a word as Branwen bobbed her head and scurried from the room.

"Why does she pretend not to know you?" He released Carys and began to remove his armor.

"Perhaps she thinks it unsafe to confide in Romans."

He grunted. "Then she needs to become more proficient at lying."

"Branwen believes you intend to dishonor me."

He linked his arms around her waist and pulled her toward him. The scent of her hair reminded him of summer forests. "Is that what you think?"

She slid her hands over his chest, rested them against his shoulders.

"I think," she said, as her fingers played a seductive tattoo against his shoulder blades, "if you were going to dishonor me, you would have done so already."

His lips brushed her forehead. He had an erotic encounter planned for Carys tonight, and it didn't entail taking her while he was sweaty from the day's exertions.

"You're safe from abuse now."

"I was always safe from abuse before."

Why did she always throw that in his face? Times had changed. She no longer lived in that world where her status as a noble's daughter protected her from the base lust of man.

He refused to acknowledge the tug of guilt. If his Legion hadn't conquered Cambria, then another would have.

"By morn, all will be aware you're my mistress. Any lack of respect shown to you will be a personal affront to me."

He'd planned on saying more, but the confusion on her face gave him pause. "Do you understand?" He wasn't sure she did.

"Yes. But I'm not your mistress, Maximus."

Did she truly have to disagree with every word he uttered? He sighed heavily and attempted to make her see reason.

"It's the only way I can protect you."

She opened her mouth, as if to dispute his words. And then a faint blush stole over her cheeks and her gaze wavered.

Instead of triumph at the knowledge she recognized his words as truth, only bitter-tinged regret coursed through his veins. He wound a lock of her hair through his fingers and gave a gentle tug.

"I can't turn back time. This is all I can do for you."

"My people won't view it as a token of respect." She traced a finger along the line of his jaw. "They'll only see that—that I've been subjugated by the enemy."

The word grated his bones, offended his sense of honor. He'd made Carys his official mistress today to ensure every Roman knew her worth, accorded her due respect and accepted her position in his life.

He hadn't considered the feelings of the Celts, since they were of little consequence.

Except they were of consequence. To Carys.

"They'll soon learn you're far from subjugated." Why had she used that word? The more he considered it, the more it irked him. "I doubt you could subjugate yourself to any man, even if your life depended on it."

"I know that." She sounded serious, whereas he had spoken half in jest. Then again, she was so proud, perhaps she would rather face death than slavery.

Irrationally the thought pleased him.

"We both know I'm with you because I want to be with you. But as far as Branwen can see, as far as any of my people will see, I'm your prisoner."

"In that case I'll arrange for you to be clapped in irons first thing in the morning."

Instead of smiling, she frowned as if she didn't think much of his humor. "This is no laughing matter. I didn't want my people to see this."

His amusement with their conversation vanished. "Because you're ashamed to be seen fraternizing with the enemy."

It was scarcely a revelation. And yet the knowledge scraped through his gut, leaving an odd pain in its wake.

"Ashamed?" Carys's frown intensified, as if she struggled to comprehend his meaning, and then her face cleared and she sighed. "I should be ashamed of my actions. But I'm not. And." She hesitated for a brief moment before flicking him a strangely furtive glance. "I know I betray my people every time I come to you, every time I even think of you. But I can't help it."

Something, a band of unused muscle perhaps, contracted deep inside his chest, causing a peculiar sense of serenity to seep through his limbs, soothe his brain.

He cradled her jaw. "You're not betraying your people. In time, Romans and natives will come together as they are in Britannia, as they did in Gallia. It's the way of the world, Carys."

Pain shimmered in her unearthly eyes. "It's the way of the Roman world. While you strip my land of her gold."

⊰⊱⊷✦⊶⊰⊱

He refused to tell her where they were going. Carys gave up asking and wound a length of linen over her head and across her shoulders.

"There's no need to cover yourself so." Maximus sounded irritated, as if he wanted to show her off like a coveted prize.

She hooked a finger into the linen draped across her mouth and pulled it free. "I've explained my reasons to you. The least you can do is respect them."

"It has nothing to do with respect. Sooner or later your people will have to come to terms with your new status. I don't see why that can't start now."

It couldn't start now because she had no intention of ever letting her people see her with Maximus. The knowledge caused a dull ache deep in her heart but that was something she knew she'd have to learn to live with.

"Not tonight, Maximus." Her voice was soft. She knew it would take nothing for him to rip the linen from her head, to march her from this dwelling to wherever he wished them to go.

She also knew he never would. Her Roman was strong, proud and honorable and, although she couldn't explain her conviction, she knew for him to use his physical strength against her would somehow diminish his worth in his own eyes.

His features softened, almost imperceptibly. "Keep your disguise tonight, if it means that much to you." He tugged the linen across her mouth. "Perhaps it will stop you answering back so readily."

They walked along the broad main street where earlier that day the markets had flourished. Again she marveled at how swiftly the Romans had constructed such a massive stronghold on her land, a walled town with so many stone buildings she could scarcely believe it.

Gawain was right. They should have stood up to the enemy from the start, not given them time to build this formidable fortification.

But then she would never have met this fascinating, intriguing man by her side.

They stopped outside a large building set back from the road, and Maximus rapped on the door, which was immediately opened.

He ushered her into the dwelling and, despite herself, she couldn't help admiring the luxurious interior with its polished slab flooring, so different from the home where she had grown up. Did all Romans live in such style?

"Maximus." A male voice jerked her from her reverie, and she glanced up to see a dark-haired middle-aged man dismiss a slave with a flick of his hand before turning back to them.

"Sir." Maximus's fingers tightened around her shoulder, as if he half expected her to flee. Or perhaps he was more concerned she might attack?

She pulled the linen aside and lifted her head, forcing eye contact with this Roman barbarian, and satisfaction stabbed through her as shock rippled over his features.

"My name is Carys of Cymru." Her Latin was perfect. She'd been taught it from a babe, one of the few requests of her absent father who'd traveled through Gaul as a youth and foresaw the power of articulating the encroaching enemy's language.

The Legatus's eyes gleamed with appreciation, and before she realized his intention, he took her hand and raised it to his lips.

"It's a pleasure to make your acquaintance, Carys of Cymru." His lips brushed her knuckles before he relinquished his hold. "I welcome you into my home." He continued to look at her, but spoke to Maximus. "Everything is prepared. You won't be disturbed."

Maximus wound his arm around her waist as he led her farther into the house. She didn't want to admire the Roman architecture, but the galling truth was that this home of the conquering Legatus, a home that, less than a year ago, hadn't even existed, far surpassed her own now-abandoned dwelling that had been in her family for generations.

They entered a small courtyard where a single building stood, with a slave who opened the door at their approach.

Carys stiffened and fumbled for her linen that draped over her shoulders.

"There's no need to fear," Maximus whispered against her ear.

"All the slaves are from Rome. Your secret remains safe in this house."

She heard the edge of mockery in his voice but decided to ignore it. "I trust you're right." Because if word escaped that she was a willing guest in the home of the Commander of the Legion, the repercussions would be horrific.

"I'm always right." His breath tickled her ear as he ushered her through the door.

She stumbled over her feet and stared at the vision, speechless with awe. Her tutor had told her of such luxuries, but secretly she always assumed he exaggerated. But he hadn't. A room, so large she could scarcely comprehend, spread before her with countless lamps flickering and smooth columns soaring to the ceiling.

And taking up a vast expanse of the multicolored, tiny-tiled floor, was a sunken, water-filled *lake*.

Maximus eased her farther into the bathhouse and shot her a glance. The look of disbelief on her face was priceless.

"Nothing to say?" He hid his amusement, immensely satisfied his surprise appeared to enthrall her.

"I've never seen anything like this before." Her voice was hushed, as if she spoke in the presence of the gods.

He cast a cursory glance at the bath, and tried to see it through her eyes. "You should see the public baths in Rome. Now, they are truly magnificent."

"*This* is magnificent." She shot him a scandalized look. "And it grieves me greatly to admit that."

He grinned and unwound the linen from her shoulders before handing it to one of the attending female slaves. "This is but a small private bath. Barely large enough to satisfy the Legatus's family." Its construction had been a priority for the comfort of the Commander's wife and daughters, but its minuscule scale and lack of marble was, he knew, an irritant to the patrician ladies. "But more than adequate for our needs tonight."

She angled her head and appeared to be studying the mosaics

adorning the floor. "It's very pretty." She sounded as if the confession pained her.

He gripped her shoulders, pulled her toward him. "Don't analyze it, Carys. Just enjoy it. Tonight, this is for us."

"Oh." She raised her eyebrows in mock astonishment. "Do you mean to ravish me, Roman?"

"Only if you behave yourself."

"Alas. I never behave myself. I thought you knew that by now."

He laughed. Much as he enjoyed fucking Carys, he enjoyed her conversation almost as well.

Except when she contradicted him. *Naturally.*

He untied her bodice, never breaking eye contact. Gods, her eyes bewitched him. They would bewitch any man.

But no man would dare touch her. Not now.

Without turning from her, he spoke to the slaves. "Leave us." He had no need of slaves tonight. Not when he wanted to administer to Carys's every need himself.

Chapter Twenty-two

He pulled back from her welcoming body, but long enough only to tear the constricting clothes from his own. He watched her rake her gaze over his chest, before fixing it upon his groin.

He stifled a groan and clasped her outstretched hand before she managed to rip all control from him. "Later." The word rasped against his throat. "First, we bathe."

"We could bathe afterward."

"For once," he said, as he led her to the steps descending into the bath, "obey your master without question."

The teasing smile on her face vaporized as her toe hit the water. "It's hot." She sounded aghast, as if she'd never before experienced such a thing.

He knew she hadn't. And yet her Latin was so perfect, her beauty so refined, it was hard to remember she was a primitive Celt and not a Roman noblewoman.

"You'll enjoy it." He took her free hand and urged her toward him. Gingerly she took another step, and the water lapped over her ankles.

"I'm enjoying it already." She continued toward him, and, as the water enclosed her, her face radiated sublime pleasure. "I've never copulated in water before. Have you?"

The curve of her succulent rear filled his hands, although he had no recollection of sliding his arms around her.

"Not recently." Not since he'd been thoroughly seduced in his family's bathhouse at the age of fourteen by a beautiful slave girl of his mother's.

"Oh." A frown flicked over her features as if the thought displeased her. He squeezed her tempting globes, simultaneously forcing her pussy to rub against his rigid shaft. Her frown vanished. "Then at least I know such a feat is possible."

"It's possible."

"I want to make love with you in every possible way."

A heat, which had nothing to do with the steaming bath, pulsed through his blood, stiffening his engorged cock to an impossible degree.

"That can be arranged." He cradled her bottom, caressed her smooth, wet skin, and attempted to recall what he wanted to do with Carys.

Her fingers stroked his neck, speared through his hair, and her stiff nipples rubbed and jerked against his chest with every tantalizing move she made. And then her lips found his, so sweet and right, and her tongue demanded his surrender and he acquiesced to her invasion as she probed, explored and sought to conquer.

He thrust back, sliding along the length of her tongue, penetrated her mouth, felt her moan vibrate through his brain, and his hands roamed over her back, her shoulders, before once again gripping her delectable bottom.

Her fingers dug into his scalp, an erotic agony, and then she powered into him, knocking him off balance, sending his arse sliding onto the step of the bath.

Winded, he attempted to regain his footing and his dignity but Carys's hold around his head tightened, and with a hop she wrapped her legs around his hips, bracing her feet against the step.

Gods, she was seducing him. Sharp arrows of fire ignited his groin, hardened his balls, and a primitive growl seared his throat as her hot slit teased his engorged head.

"Is this good for you?" Her panted question made no sense. He grunted in response, jerking his hips in an effort to slide into her welcoming heat.

Her thigh muscles flexed, and she evaded his tactical maneuver.

"Do you like the feel of me on you?" she persisted, and he stared at her through a haze of red-tinged lust, incomprehension pounding with every thud of his heart.

"Yes," he snarled, since she clearly required an answer. "Do you like the feel of me?" He neither expected nor required a response. All he needed glittered in her passion-filled eyes.

"I love the feel of you." As added torture, she ground her hips, sweeping her pussy across his straining shaft. "Your cock fills me, in a way I had never before imagined."

He gripped her bottom, a warning that he was on the edge. "Then let me fill you again, Carys, to remind you how much you need my cock inside you."

With a ragged gasp she plunged onto his shaft, so sudden, so exquisite, his sanity shattered.

"So big." Her hands slid down his neck, and her fingernails gouged his flesh. "All I can feel is you."

And all he could feel was her tight channel clasping him, sucking him into a haven of pure sensation.

Her thighs flexed as she raised her hips, bracing her weight against the step upon which he sat, fucking him as if she were a water nymph and he her captured mortal.

He leaned back against the side of the bath, soaking in the

sight of her straddling him, her hands on his shoulders, her breasts tantalizingly close to his mouth as she plunged along the length of his shaft.

"Tiberius," she panted, as she sank onto him, taking his entire length into her body. An involuntary groan shuddered along his throat.

"Valerius." She retreated, until only the tip of his throbbing head remained clasped inside her wet cleft.

"Maximus." She thrust down violently and flung back her head, lips parted, eyelids fluttering, as her glorious pussy clenched around him in endless waves of infinite delirium.

He gripped her hips, plowed into her, his cock pulsating with primeval intent, lightning coursing through his arteries, blood pounding against his temples. Rome receded, the Empire crumbled, but none of it mattered because all that mattered was that Carys was here, safe with him, and fucking him as he had never been fucked before.

His frenzied thrusts claimed her, branded her, and finally filled her with his scorching seed. One hand tangled in her hair, grasped her head, forced her to him so he could taste her lips, savor her tongue, devour her sweet cries of passion.

Eternity shimmered in the heated air, nebulous and fragile. The lingering scent of lust filtered into his sated limbs, cocooned his drifting mind.

Carys.

Chapter Twenty-three

Arms wrapped around her, he held her securely against his body, her soft breasts crushed against his chest, her heartbeat thundering in tandem with his own.

She belonged to him, and nothing but the gods could take her from him.

Carys lifted her head from his shoulder. "How did I compare?" Her voice was breathless, her eyes still glazed.

He brushed her wet hair from her face. When he regained his strength, he would unbraid her hair, allow it to float free in the water. "Compare?" The word was idle. He had no idea what she was talking about, and didn't much care.

"With the other times you've made love in water."

A satisfied smile curved his lips. "Favorably." In truth, there was no comparison, but he had no intention of confessing that to her.

"Only favorably?"

He sighed indulgently. "You don't need me to tell you how good you are." And then his indulgence evaporated as comprehension surfaced. "Your technique was such that I find it hard to believe this was your first time in a bath."

Instead of rushing to reassure him of the fact, a slow smile lit her face and caused her eyes to sparkle. A scowl crawled across his features at her unwarranted response.

"I'm gratified you thought so."

Gratified? "That was not intended as a compliment."

She settled herself more comfortably against his groin, which was becoming more uncomfortable by the moment. "It was a compliment, for which I thank you."

He held her bottom in a punishing grip. Something that had plagued him since the previous night gnawed at the forefront of his mind, demanding to be satisfied no matter how much the answer would grate.

"How many men have you fucked?"

Her smug smile wavered as if she hadn't expected that. "I could ask you the same question."

He bared his teeth in a mockery of a smile. "I don't fuck men."

With reluctant fascination he watched a rosy blush spread across her cheeks, as if his question truly bothered her.

And again he had to remind himself she wasn't a Roman noblewoman. Her culture was different from his, and a wellborn Celtic woman wasn't condemned for taking lovers before she married.

"You know what I mean." Her voice was haughty.

He wrapped his arms around her waist. "It doesn't matter how many women I've had."

"Then it doesn't matter how many men I've had."

He was not a Celtic barbarian. And he wanted—no, he demanded to know how many men had fucked his woman.

"Carys." The word was a warning, low and dangerous.

She raised her chin defiantly. "Why do you wish to know?"

He didn't want to analyze why he wanted to know. What did

he expect to do with the information once in his possession? Hunt the men down and gut them?

He'd taken women from many cultures in the past, and never before had he cared about their previous lovers. So why did the thought of Carys being with another man affect him so profoundly?

It didn't make sense. And yet he couldn't let it go.

"You're my mistress. It's my right to know."

"I didn't ask to be your mistress." With a suddenness that took him by surprise, she pushed at the step with both feet, severing bodily contact. "And you have no rights over me whatsoever."

Before she could flounce away he caught her by her arms, swung her around and pinned her into the corner of the bath. Irrational anger warred in his brain. Why did Carys resist his offer? And why did her refusal irk him so?

He stared into her defiant eyes, and a shiver inched over his skin as he recalled the lifeless expression she had harbored earlier that day.

And remembered the Celtic barbarian looming over her prone body, ready to ravish her while she hovered on the brink of unconsciousness. The barbarian who would pay with his lifeblood when Maximus discovered his heathen lair.

A memory stirred, soothed his wounded pride. "Why haven't you enjoyed a lover for the last three years?" It was inconceivable to him that, in her morally relaxed culture, she had chosen to remain celibate.

He didn't think she was going to answer. He ran his fingers along her arms, and noted with satisfaction how her nipples visibly hardened.

She let out an exasperated breath. "I don't owe you an explanation." Her eyes narrowed in clear provocation. He decided to ignore her challenge, and continued to caress her arms, up and down, a soothing gesture, and eventually her glare faded.

"No man pleased me." Her voice was lofty, but he caught the

furtive glance she shot his way before she stuck her nose in the air and looked over his shoulder.

His fingers paused against her wet skin and his brain took over from his ego as something occurred to him.

"Perhaps your lovers were boys, not men." Why that should appease him he didn't know, but somehow the thought of Carys fucking boys her own age, rather than older, experienced men, didn't tie his guts into seething knots.

She made a sound of disgust. "He was certainly a *man*."

Something in her manner alerted his senses. "He?" He strove to make his voice casual, so she would elaborate further and not decide to be stubborn yet again.

There was a heartbeat of silence as Carys stared at him. The tip of her tongue moistened her lips. "They." Her voice was husky. "I meant *they* were men. Not boys."

She was lying. The certainty was as clear in his mind as if Carys had told him so herself.

But why would she lie to him about the number of men she'd had?

"Did your . . ." He hesitated for a brief moment. He had almost said *Did your father*, but he didn't want to drag up her father now, not when he knew his Legion was responsible for the man's death. ". . . parents give you to this man when you were a young girl?"

The thought shouldn't rile him, and yet his blood boiled at the image. In Rome, among his patrician class, arranged marriages were commonplace. Young girls were often married to older men, and until this moment he'd never given the girl in question a second thought.

But then, the girl in question had never been Carys.

Her brow creased, as if his question mystified her. "Of course not. How could my mother *give* me to anyone? I'm her daughter, not her slave."

"So you went willingly with this man."

"Of course I did." She sounded surprised, as if she couldn't imagine there being another logical response. "All my kin were in favor of the union, despite the differences between our lineage."

Now he understood. "So he used his superior status to leave you no choice." Bastard.

Carys gave him a strange look. "I could have denied him, and no one would have forced me to go with him." She stroked her fingers along his chest, almost as if she was unaware of her action. "He was older than me, and powerful. Very powerful." For one unnerving moment her eyes lost focus, as if this man's power still retained a hold over her.

Twisted rage coiled his belly. "So you fucked him for his power."

Carys didn't spit in his eye, or knee him in the balls. Incredibly, a smile curved her lips. "I didn't need his power."

He pressed her against the side of the bath, his cock hard and hot and throbbing as it scorched her tempting belly. "Then why did you fuck him when you didn't want him?"

Her smile wavered. "Why do you think I didn't want him?"

He raked his gaze over her flushed face. "You don't speak of him as a woman would speak of her first lover whom she had desired above all others."

Or was he mistaken? Did he want Carys to admit she had felt nothing for this man, simply to appease his *ego*?

Mars take him, since when had his fucking ego been so fragile?

Her smile disappeared entirely and a haunted expression flared in her eyes for one heart-stopping moment.

"I didn't desire him." The words tumbled from her lips as if she had never spoken them before, and she shot him a defiant look. "But he fascinated me. And for two years he had watched me constantly, telling me how we were meant to be together." She sighed heavily. "By the time I was ready to offer myself to the goddess, he was the only man willing. All others had been warned off by him."

He slid his hands from her shoulders and threaded his fingers between hers, beneath the hot water. His simmering rage against her family, against this faceless man who had abused his position of power to force his attentions on her, struggled against restraint.

"How long were you with him?"

"Three years."

Three years? Shock ripped along his spine at the implications.

"You were betrothed to him." It was a statement of fact.

She blinked in obvious surprise. "No, certainly not."

Rage of another sort seared his chest. "He didn't offer for you?" How dare he use Carys for three years without also legalizing the union?

She raised her eyebrows. "Offer for me?" she echoed. "He wanted to tie the knot, if that's what you mean. He was obsessed with becoming my husband."

The rage stumbled, confusion rocked. "You refused him?" How could she have refused? How had her father allowed her to refuse?

"Of course I refused him." Carys stared up at him as if she couldn't believe he had asked such a thing. "I didn't love him, Maximus. And although he claimed to love me, I believe he loved my status more."

Despite the heat of the water, a chill shivered over his exposed flesh. "What is your status, Carys?"

Her lips parted, but she didn't say anything. Then she swallowed and shook her head, as if shaking off droplets of water. "You must know I'm not of the peasant class."

"Yes."

"He—was. But he was very clever. And he became powerful in his own right. For many men that would be enough but he—he wanted more. He wanted me."

Maximus struggled to process all the information she'd just imparted. But from it all, only one fact burned through his brain.

"You didn't want him, yet you let him fuck you for three years." If her father had demanded she acquiesce to the more powerful man, then of course Carys would have had no choice in the matter. He understood that. It was the way of the world.

But the other man had not been more powerful, and her father had demanded no such thing.

Carys looked affronted by his accusation. "He was the only one available for me," she said, as if that explained everything. "Besides, I thought it would get better the more we did it." A frown flitted across her brow. "But it didn't. He said it was me, that I was deficient."

Gods. Maximus glared at her in disbelieving comprehension. Was she saying she hadn't even enjoyed fucking the old bastard?

"You certainly aren't deficient." It was likely the man was so decrepit he could barely get his cock up, never mind use it effectively.

"Thank you." She offered him an oddly shy smile. "After I finished with him I didn't want another man. And then when I did, I was afraid it would be the same as it was with Aer—with *him*." She sucked in a long breath. "That's why I didn't take another lover. I know it's not a valid excuse. I know the goddess wasn't happy with me, but—"

"But." He disengaged their fingers and placed one across her lips, silencing her. "You've only ever had one other man beside me."

Her face flamed, as if he'd just insulted her.

"I'm not going to apologize for it." She hissed the words at him and he grinned at her, as he pressed her more securely against the bath's edge. Why she considered an apology necessary was beyond him, but perhaps it was yet another obscure Celtic custom.

"Then don't." He had other things on his mind. Things he had planned to do before Carys had so deliciously distracted him with her enchanting seduction.

Her breath quickened, although he knew by the look on her face she fought against her body's reaction. "There were a great many men who wanted me after Aer—after I was free," she said, as if that knowledge would astonish him. "Despite the fact he threatened to disembowel any who so much as touched my hand."

Maximus grunted. The thought of disemboweling the old lech was certainly tempting, but not nearly as tempting as the thought of seducing Carys as thoroughly as she had seduced him.

"Even if we had to meet in secret, they would still have met with me."

He laughed. He couldn't help it. "I believe you. What man in his right mind could resist you if you so much as glanced his way with interest?"

Carys gave him another of her haughty looks, as if she thought he was making fun of her. "Just so you are perfectly aware, I *am* a desirable woman."

"I'd have to be dead not to know that."

Carys could feel the proof of his knowledge burning against her belly. His eyes were dark with mounting desire, and it would be easy to melt into his embrace and take everything she could from him before their worlds tumbled into ashes.

But he had laughed at her. And she didn't understand why.

"You're not shocked by my lack of experience." She hadn't intended to ever say such a thing to Maximus, but since he'd now discovered her secret shame, and didn't appear concerned by it, she realized she needed to discover why.

He laughed again, a deep, rich baritone that, despite its lack of respect, sent delightful shivers skittering over her naked flesh. She stared up at him, thoroughly confused, until his moment of insanity passed.

"As far as I'm concerned," he said, still grinning as if she had just told the most hilarious joke, "you're as pure as a Vestal Virgin."

Her stomach fluttered, twisting between bemusement and innate offense. And yet Maximus meant no insult by his comment; she could see that by his eyes, by his smile, by the tone of his voice.

She swallowed down her stinging retort. Her shame.

"It's not something I'm proud of." The words rasped against her throat and she was relieved when Maximus didn't laugh at her again but instead began to frown.

"You've lost me." He sounded concerned. And then his frown darkened as comprehension dawned. "You're still ashamed of being with me."

His comment was so far from the truth she almost laughed herself, despite the way she also wanted to dive under the water and hide.

She flattened her hands against his chest, thrilling to the way his wet hair caressed her palms, the way his steady heartbeat vibrated through her blood.

And in that moment of connection, she understood.

Chapter Twenty-four

The breath hissed between her lips and a shiver slithered along her spine. Maximus had his own gods, his own culture and customs, and they weren't hers.

He laughed because he thought she was flirting. Not because he mocked her beliefs.

He possessed no knowledge of her beliefs.

Her head dropped to his shoulder so he wouldn't witness the blood flooding her cheeks. She'd had no need to explain to him. No reason to justify her lack of lovers.

And yet she'd told him the most intimate details. Things she'd never spoken of before. *And there had been no need.*

A mortified groan escaped and she resisted when he forcibly maneuvered her upright.

"Well?" His demand was harsh and she attempted to recall why he looked so mad, when she knew it had nothing to do with the way she'd slighted the Morrigan for so many years.

"I misunderstood." She had the overwhelming urge to screw

her eyes shut but refused to allow herself such luxury. "I thought you laughed because you found humor in my lack of homage." She sucked in a shaky breath. "But I was wrong. I think." And she shot him a desperate glance.

There was an excruciating silence as he raked his gaze over her burning face. She curled her toes and attempted to pull her hands from his chest, but Maximus pressed even closer, so they were meshed together and it was impossible for her to move a muscle without his permission.

Finally his scrutiny eased and he brushed an errant curl from her cheek. "There's much about you I don't yet understand." His voice was gentle. "But I would never knowingly mock your ways." He hesitated for a moment, as if searching for the right words. "I know your gods are important to you. I regret my actions made you think otherwise."

The trembling knot of agony in the center of her chest eased, by a merest degree. "I should never have confessed to you." Could she ever live it down? And not only had she shared her darkest secrets with Maximus; she had also come perilously close to telling him the entire nature of her status.

A shiver coursed through her. No matter how he professed to respect her beliefs, he would never respect her right as a Druid.

"Carys." His whisper was an erotic caress along her soul. "I'm happy you confessed to me."

The constriction in her chest ebbed and she realized she no longer minded Maximus knowing of her lack.

Because Maximus didn't consider it a lack.

She took a deep breath. "Then I'm glad I told you."

He tugged on her braid and began to unbind her wet hair. "You can tell me anything."

If only that were true. But she smiled up at him anyway, because she knew his offer was genuine. And knew how easily she could succumb and spill the most devastating secret of all.

She moaned in protest when, after his fingers had worked magic against her scalp, he slid his arms around her and carried her from the bath. "I don't want to go." She wanted this night to last forever, because tonight might be all she would ever have.

But he ignored her and she curled against his chest, squeezing her eyes shut against the world, against the knowledge that soon she would have to leave him once again. And this time he might not deign to take her back.

He lowered her to her feet and swathed her in a huge length of absorbent cloth.

"It's warm." She snuggled into the decadent softness. "Romans don't care for the cold, do they?"

He swiftly dried himself with another towel, his blue eyes never leaving hers. "Does the heat displease you?"

"I didn't say that."

"Then we Romans have our uses." He indicated a stone bench covered with yet more towels. "Lie down."

Hiding a smile, Carys dropped her covering and stretched out, arms over her head, one knee provocatively bent.

"On your front."

Her seductive smile wavered. Was he going to take her from behind, like an animal?

She rolled over, and wondered if she was in the right position. But if she wasn't, then Maximus would soon show her. It was a relief to realize she didn't have to pretend experience of such things, when the only knowledge she possessed came from gossip with friends.

Muscles tense with expectation she pillowed her cheek on her hands and raised her bottom into the air. Maximus made an odd choking noise and pressed the flat of his hand on the small of her back, until she was once again prone.

"Don't move again." It was a command. "Gods, Carys. You don't make this easy for me."

She watched him grab a small amphorae from the nearby stone plinth.

"Are you ready?" But he scarcely waited for her uncertain nod before he straddled her, his knees on either side of her hips, his calves imprisoning the length of her legs.

And then his hands swept across her shoulders, firm, warm, slick with oil, and a shocked gasp shook her entire body.

"Relax. This is supposed to be enjoyable."

His fingers massaged her stiff muscles, a rhythmic, tantalizing motion, and with another expulsion of air the tension seeped from her rigid limbs.

His powerful legs imprisoned her, a willing captive, and corded muscles branded her back as he flattened himself onto her, his engorged shaft scorching her, and the pleasure of his touch sank through her skin, her muscles, and into the center of her heart.

And threaded through every touch, every gasp, every delirious sensation, the stark knowledge glittered that he was more to her than a lover who had taught her the wonders of sex. More than the man who had wiped away the uneasy feelings of inadequacy she'd harbored for the last six years.

More than her enemy, the conqueror of her people, the embodiment of Rome who would destroy everything she held dear.

And as he administered his magic to her feet, and she tried in vain not to grind her hips against the towels that hugged her throbbing clit, she finally acknowledged the truth.

She loved him. And that love could kill her.

Chapter Twenty-five

Maximus rolled Carys onto her back, and she stared up at him through glazed eyes, her lips parted, her breath a series of erratic gasps.

Gods, what had possessed him to start this? In theory he'd assumed it would be arousing and enjoyable. It was most certainly arousing, but the abstinence made the pleasure a knife's edge of agony.

She shifted her leg, hooked around his shoulder, pinning him against her welcoming heat. He braced his weight on his free arm, prepared to once again resume control.

And then he glanced up at her.

Her body gleamed in the ethereal flicker of the lanterns, her breasts full and proud, crowned by rosy nipples. And her head was raised, looking back at him, as beautiful and desirable as any artist's depiction of Venus.

"Come here." Her whisper echoed around the bathhouse, wrapped its sensuous command around his mind. He couldn't recall why he had to resist, why he had to refuse her open arms.

"I haven't yet finished." But he made no move to reassert control, because the vision before him was too tempting to disturb.

She gripped his throat with both hands and pulled. Without knowing why, he followed her lead, gliding up her slick body, the oil sliding onto his skin, warm and fragrant.

He towered over her, his wood nymph, his Celtic lady, his Carys. "Why do you never do as you are bid?"

"Because"—Carys gasped as she flexed her thighs and dug her heels into his backside—"I'm not your slave, Maximus. I'm your woman."

He sank into her and she cried out and grasped him to her, meshed as one. The oil he had massaged over her willing flesh coated him, their slick bodies coming together in rising frenzy.

"My woman." He growled the words into her flushed face. Found satisfaction she, like him, knew her place in his life.

"Always." He barely heard her breathless response, but her meaning intoxicated his senses, sent the remnants of his control spiraling into the abyss.

And with every thrust, every touch, every mind-shattering moment of orgasm, he showed her how completely she was his woman.

Always.

⊰⸙⊱

Legs entwined with her love, Carys hovered on the blissful edge of sleep. Surely, tonight she had conceived his child. The moon phase was favorable, her body receptive. All that stood between conception and barrenness was the wrath of her sweet Cerridwen.

She closed her eyes, focused her mind. Begged forgiveness for her transgression, begged Cerridwen to intercede on her behalf with the Morrigan.

After all, wasn't she now worshipping the Morrigan in the way the great goddesses had always demanded? Didn't that count for anything? Didn't it make up for the way she had taken the sacred root without proper ritual or permission?

For a moment she recalled the terrifying fury of the Morrigan as she stood at the crossroads. The impotent rage as she had looked into the future. The eerie certainty that, implausibly, the goddess somehow held Carys accountable.

That was impossible. Why would the Greatest Goddess of them all blame Carys for something so utterly beyond her control? *And why had she looked through her as though she weren't even there?*

"Carys." Maximus's lazy voice jerked her back to the present and her eyes snapped open. He was propped on one elbow, looking down at her with a satisfied smile on his face. "What's the matter?" He traced a finger across her brow, and she realized she was frowning.

She drew in a jagged breath and relaxed her muscles. She could pretend all was well, or she could tell Maximus the truth.

There was so much she could never reveal to him, so she decided on the truth. At least, part of the truth. She couldn't confide her fears regarding the Morrigan with him—she didn't even understand them herself.

"I was asking Cerridwen to forgive me."

His smile slipped a notch. "For sleeping with the enemy?"

She puffed out an exhausted laugh. "No. I fear I offended her earlier today. It was nothing to do with being with you."

Except that was a lie, because it had everything to do with being with Maximus. She decided that didn't count.

He grunted in clear disapproval. "I respect your devotion to your goddess, but would prefer you didn't think of her while still glowing from our union."

She reached up to cradle his jaw. "I can scarcely think of anything but you."

His frown vanished. "Better." He reached across her, his

powerful chest scraping across her sensitized breasts. "Where in Tartarus is that strigil?"

She breathed deep, savoring the scent of man, of fragranced oil and hot, sweaty sex. Why did the one she had finally given her heart to have to be a Roman? How many stolen moments from time could they enjoy before they were discovered?

"Now, lie still." Maximus loomed over her, and from the corner of her eye she caught sight of a curved blade glinting in the lamplight.

She held her breath as he gently scraped the strigil over her oiled skin, and watched him meticulously clean the blade after every spine-tingling sweep.

How many women had he pleasured this way in the past? His touch was so sure, his technique so skillful, he must have had plenty of practice.

It didn't please her, despite the fact she was now the beneficiary of his expertise.

"You're frowning again." He waved the strigil under her nose. "I trust you're not communing with your Cerridwen while I slave here for your every comfort."

"No. I was simply wondering how many women you've done this to before."

"This?" He glanced at the strigil, as if he'd never seen it before. "Do you think I was a slave in Rome?" The corner of his mouth twitched, as if he found the concept amusing.

"I don't know what you were in Rome." She knew he had been no slave. "All I know is you command your soldiers here in Cymru."

"In Rome," he said, gliding the blade along the curve of her breast, "slaves would take care of such menial tasks." He flashed her a grin. "I'm gratified we're not in Rome. This experience far exceeds my expectations."

"Then you also are not of the peasant class." But she knew that already. His bearing was regal, his attitude that of one who expected deference as his right. It went deeper than military rank. It was in his blood, his bones. His heritage.

"Does it matter?"

It shouldn't. And yet it did. Not because she wanted him to be of similar status to herself. But because she craved to know everything she possibly could about him.

"Do you miss your kin?"

He flicked her an amused glance. "Believe me, distance is a virtue when it comes to my father."

She tried to imagine living so far away from her own relatives, being unable to see them whenever the desire arose. Her mother, who had visited distant kin on the Isle of Mon ten moons ago and intended to be gone only a short while, became stranded once the invasion spread, and Carys missed her wise words, her infectious laugh and irreverent sense of fun more every day.

"Is that why you joined the Legion?"

"I was always destined for a brief sojourn in the military." The strigil brushed perilously close to her pussy and she tensed involuntarily. He glanced up. "It bestows honor on one's family."

"So you only joined up to honor your family?" That meant he hadn't voluntarily become a soldier or conquered her land.

"I didn't say that."

"Then why did you join?" But she didn't really care. Because if he had not joined his famed Roman Legion, they would never have met.

"If you insist on knowing, I ran away to join the Legion when I was eighteen years old." From between her legs he shot her an evil grin. "To prove that I could."

She speared her fingers through his short hair, rubbed the spikes over her palm. "You rebelled."

"You're not supposed to laugh." But he looked as if he was on the verge of laughing also. "It's unheard of for the son of a prominent senator to be a mere centurion in the lowest cohort. I'm astonished my father didn't disown me entirely."

"I'm sure he's proud of your success now." She rubbed his head again. "Surely it's honorable to work your way up the ranks?"

"Not for a patrician." He pushed his head against her hand, as if encouraging her to continue. "The parents of my betrothed were so scandalized they ensured all of Rome knew of my appalling behavior."

Carys dug her fingers into Maximus's scalp as her bubbling laughter vaporized. "Your betrothed?" She dug her fingernails in further and ignored the pained expression on his face. "You're married?"

Why had that not occurred to her before? Of course he was married. He wasn't a common foot soldier. He was an officer. And a Roman patrician.

And he probably possessed a perfect Roman noblewoman as his wife.

Her stomach churned with sudden distress. Had he also fathered children with the weak-minded harridan?

He twisted his head from her grasp. Laughter gleamed in his beautiful blue eyes, and her fingers clawed as the tempting vision of gouging them from his sockets thudded through her mind.

"Careful." He waved the strigil at her as he knelt between her spread knees. "I don't like that look on your face."

"I asked you a question." She propped herself up on her elbows and glowered at him.

"At the time I joined up, my *betrothed*"—he emphasized the word and offered her an inappropriate grin—"was three years old. Her parents were offended that her future husband was a common centurion and severed the contract."

Carys narrowed her eyes. "And?"

"And they demanded recompense from my family." The humor faded from his face. "I'm not proud of that. But my father and I had just had another gods-awful fight, and all I wanted was to get away."

Carys didn't care about his father. "Were you given another wife?"

The corner of his mouth twitched as if she had just said something amusing. "No other family would touch me after my former betrothed's parents had finished blackening my name."

"So you don't have a wife waiting for you back in Rome?"

Although why it mattered, she wasn't going to analyze, because it wasn't as if *she* could ever be his wife or bear his recognized children.

No matter how much she wanted to. *That didn't make her a traitor.* She couldn't help how she felt about him.

"Jupiter." He clasped her waist, and the bone handle of the strigil dug into her skin. "I do not possess a wife in Rome or anywhere else." He paused for a moment as if reassessing his declaration. "And I don't intend to have any such encumbrance for a good many years yet."

She sucked in a long breath and willed her heart to stop hurting. There would be plenty of time, years, eternity, for her heart to ache once she and Maximus were severed by fate.

She couldn't let her feelings come between them now, couldn't let her newly discovered love create barriers when their time together was fraught with so much jeopardy beyond her control.

Besides, he wasn't married. He had no wife.

She smiled and rubbed his head once again to indicate her forgiveness. "Why did you and your father fight?"

He eyed her, as if weighing up her sudden shift in mood. "You ask far too many questions for a woman." He jerked back when she dug her nails in his scalp once again. "But if you insist on knowing, it was because I wanted to join the Legion and work my way up the ranks on ability and not connection."

His explanation was in no way amusing, but still the overwhelming urge to giggle assailed her. "I see."

"By Mars, you have no respect." He didn't sound displeased as he rolled her over. "But you will."

She closed her eyes, relished the way he scraped the oil from her shoulders. In Rome he had been despised for his choices. But, even though those choices meant he had willingly fought for his Emperor, had willingly invaded her beloved Cymru, he'd risen to his present rank through his own ability, blood and sweat. Not because he was the favored son of a powerful senator.

A smile curved her lips. He was her Roman conqueror and she loved him, even if such an admission fluttered on the wings of blasphemy.

Chapter Twenty-six

Later, as the slaves dried her and massaged scented oil into her hands and arms, she cast a longing glance at the bath. Would she ever enjoy such a night as this again?

"That isn't mine." She waved her hand at the long white tunic one of the slaves brought to her.

"Indulge me." Maximus's lazy voice drifted toward her. "Just for tonight, my lady."

He looked magnificent and utterly foreign in his tunic as two other slaves draped a long toga decorated with a broad purple stripe around him. She glanced again at the proffered garment, torn between asserting her rights as a Celtic Druidess and a secret, shameful desire to wear this Roman creation.

No one would know. So she allowed the slaves to dress her, allowed them to comb and twist and manipulate her hair in elaborate Roman style.

And Maximus, from his semi-reclining position on the bench, never took his smoldering gaze from her.

Dusk had fallen by the time they left the Legatus's dwelling, for which she was thankful as Maximus had made it clear she wasn't going to wear the concealing length of linen this time.

Not that it mattered. The only others they passed were Romans who, after glancing her way and catching sight of Maximus in his senatorial glory, hastily averted their eyes.

Such was the power of her Roman's word. Once, her word had commanded similar respect from her people. Would the world ever return to the way it had once been?

With a shiver she recalled the horrifying vision she'd endured earlier that day. Had it truly shown her the future?

She had to speak to Druantia. Ask her advice. Beg the Morrigan's forgiveness for her trespass, and offer any sacrifice so she might once again gain sweet Cerridwen's favor.

Iced sparks dug through her heart as the rash promise vibrated in her mind. Instantly, she refined her pledge. She would do anything Cerridwen or the Morrigan demanded, fulfill any obligation the goddesses required.

Would sacrifice whatever was within her power to give. *Anything but Maximus.*

As they entered Maximus's quarters, the enticing aroma of roasting meat greeted them. She sniffed appreciably as he led her into another room that had a low table surrounded on three sides by couches.

He picked up a small leather pouch from the table.

"This is for you."

Enthralled, Carys unwrapped the leather. Nestled in the center, gold and green glinted up at her.

"Maximus," she breathed, enchanted that he had bought her a

gift. She sank onto one of the couches and spread the leather across her lap so she could more easily admire her treasures.

He sat beside her, his hard thigh snug against hers. "Do you like them?" His voice was gruff, as if he wasn't used to asking women such a thing.

She picked up the delicate bracelet, and the green stones glittered in the lamplight. "I've never seen anything so pretty," she told him, and it was the truth, for despite owning numerous bracelets, necklaces, earrings and ankle chains, none of them had been chosen specifically for her by Maximus.

"One day I'll buy you the real thing. But for now, I'm glad you approve."

She laughed and held up one of the long, sparkling earrings. "I love them and shall always treasure them. Thank you."

He fastened the bracelet around her wrist, and she slid the earrings through her naked lobes. She shook her head and the sharp stones jiggled along the length of her neck, brushing her shoulders.

"They suit you." He scrutinized her. "I knew something was missing earlier. You weren't wearing any of your own jewelry."

She thought of her precious gems hidden within her medicine bag, and hoped no one would find the bag before she managed to reclaim it. Not because she feared losing her jewelry, but because of the illicit bluestones it harbored.

Her breath caught as a truly magnificent idea illuminated her mind. *She could offer the bluestones to the Morrigan.* It was a sacrifice, for it meant she could never again prepare a magical meeting place for her Roman, but she would give them up, and willingly, if the goddess desired.

Besides, she no longer needed to meet Maximus by the Cauldron. So long as she was discreet, she could meet him here, in his quarters.

She smothered the thought before it could manifest and find its way to the Morrigan.

The game was roasted to perfection and served with a sweet, fruity sauce she'd never before encountered. She didn't recognize all the vegetables either, obviously strange Roman imports, but could find no fault with their flavor.

"You don't look comfortable, Carys."

She glanced over at him, as he reclined on the couch. "Neither do you." She'd always sat upright while eating and couldn't imagine how the Roman way could be anything but detrimental to the digestive process.

"You'd be surprised how comfortable I am. You should try it and see for yourself."

"Thank you, but I prefer not to be awake all night with a stomachache."

He gave a soft laugh and toasted her with his goblet. "Then I will have to teach you how to handle correct etiquette."

She raised her eyebrows. "*Roman* etiquette. And why should I wish to learn that?"

"I don't know." He regarded her with a thoughtful look on his face. "Perhaps it's because you look as if you were Roman-born. I could take you into the highest echelons of society and no one would guess otherwise." And then he offered her a sardonic grin. "Unless, of course, we attended a banquet. Then you'd give yourself away in an instant."

She smiled sweetly. "The likelihood of my attending a Roman banquet is remote."

There was a pause, as if Maximus was considering his response. Although what was there to consider? It wasn't as if this conversation was serious. It was lighthearted flirting.

"Carys." He replaced his goblet on the table. "Tell me how you speak Latin as if it were your mother tongue."

It wouldn't hurt to tell him. It was no secret, after all. "My father brought a scholar back from Gaul the moon after I was born." The scholar had also been a Druid of some distinction, but Maximus didn't need to know that.

He frowned, as if her explanation didn't clarify. "This scholar had a remarkable grasp of Latin. You have no accent at all."

It had been another stipulation from her father. That she learn the Roman language as if it were her own.

She decided Maximus probably didn't need to know that either, as it cast unnecessary speculation as to her father's motives.

"That's because he was a Roman himself." She sipped the wine, savoring the way it warmed her throat. "But when he grew to manhood"—when the Druidic visions had begun to turn his mind—"he discovered his father wasn't the man he had always believed. He was, in fact, only half Roman."

"I should like to meet this scholar of yours."

She flicked him an assessing glance, but he didn't look as if he suspected anything untoward. And why would he? There was no reason for him to assume her dear Gaius had possessed Druid blood.

"Alas, he continued his journey five winters ago." Her breath hitched in a regretful sigh. "He was ancient when I was a babe, Maximus. But his knowledge was vast."

There was a respectful silence. "He taught you well."

Carys batted away the irritating tickle against her nose, but it trailed over her cheek and into her ear. With a groan she opened her eyes, to see Maximus looming over her, teasing her with a feather.

Instantly, her senses overflowed with alarm. She had intended to leave during the night, as soon as Maximus had fallen asleep, but their lovemaking had exhausted her so thoroughly it was she who had succumbed first.

"Don't look so distressed." He abandoned the feather and smoothed her hair from her cheek. "I regret having to wake you, but I fear I require your presence."

Carys swallowed her trepidation. Panicking wouldn't alter the fact she had remained outside the spiral all night. She could only hope she hadn't been missed.

"My presence?" Her gaze caught his, and warmth flooded her chest, smothering the remnants of unease. She had spent the night with her Roman, and deep in her heart she could never regret it.

"Yes." A scowl crawled over his features. "I have an unsavory duty to perform. I believe your—uh—soothing talents may be called for."

"My soothing talents?" Was he mocking her? But he didn't look as if he were jesting. He looked as if he were struggling to contain his temper.

"Pray don't repeat every word I utter." He tugged on one of her ringlets, a reminder of the way her hair had been twisted and coiled the previous night. "It's hard enough to ask this favor without you laughing at me."

She hadn't been laughing at him, but at his words laughter bubbled through the warmth heating her heart.

"What favor do you require, Roman?" She trailed languid fingers over his shaven jaw, and regret speared through her that he was already dressed.

His scowl deepened, although he threaded his fingers through hers and rubbed her palm more roughly against his face.

"A woman's touch."

Carys winced as Branwen combed through the multitude of tangles her vigorous night had created. After Maximus had painstakingly removed every last pin, she'd forgotten to braid her hair. And this was her punishment.

"Forgive me, my lady," Branwen muttered. From the moment she had arrived, and Maximus had left for a meeting with the other officers, she'd refused to make eye contact, as if secretly shocked Carys still remained within Maximus's quarters.

She gritted her teeth as Branwen fought the ringlets and began to braid her hair. It was none of the girl's concern where she slept. How dare she judge her?

Yet Branwen judged her as all her people would judge her. Carys gripped her fingers together and refused to think on it.

She wasn't hurting anyone. She wasn't betraying anyone. All she was doing was spending as much time as she possibly could with the man she loved. And she had no intention of apologizing for that.

Maximus trusted her to be here when he returned. He *needed* her. Her failure to wake during the early hours had been a sign that she should never run from him again.

"Are you ready?" Maximus entered the bedroom and shot them a curious glance, as if he could feel the whisper of hostility tainting the air.

"Yes." Carys slid her new earrings through her lobes and stood, once again dressed in her own gown. Goddess only knew how Branwen would have reacted if she'd seen her dressed in the Roman finery. "Where are we going?"

"Into the settlement."

Her irritation against Branwen faded. How could she accompany Maximus into the settlement? Someone would be sure to recognize her. She shot Branwen a glance, but the girl stared at the floor as if she were a deaf-mute.

Maximus made an impatient noise and threw a length of linen onto the bed. "Wrap this about yourself if you must." He didn't sound happy about the prospect. "We have to leave."

Swathed in linen, Carys stepped outside, and a centurion snapped to attention. She stiffened in affront, and as soon as they were out of earshot she rounded on Maximus.

"Do you set guards to watch my every movement now?" She hadn't intended to leave before he returned. She'd given her word she would help him with whatever unsavory task he needed to perform. But why hadn't he trusted her?

"What?" He shot her a clearly bemused glance. She jerked her head toward his quarters and raised her eyebrows.

His frown cleared. "All Tribunes' quarters are guarded, Carys. It had nothing to do with watching your movements."

Mollified, she resumed walking. It was just as well she hadn't attempted to slip away during the night. She would never wish to mortify Maximus by being caught in such an undignified manner by a guard.

"Are you going to tell me where we're going?"

Was it her imagination or did Maximus wince? Intrigued, she stared up at him, but once again his face was impassive.

"I've been ordered to pass a message on to a young woman."

It was obvious the order irked him. And why would a great man like Maximus be ordered to do such a thing anyway?

"That's a strange order for a Roman Tribune." He'd told her of his promotion last night, and she'd heard the quiet pride in his voice and shared it, because he was Maximus, and berated her pleasure because he was also the enemy of her people.

He tossed her a dark look. "It's more in the nature of a favor to a relative."

"And what's the message?" She heard the censure in her tone, but made no attempt to conceal it. Was Maximus going to tell this unfortunate woman his relative wanted her in his bed? And had he brought *her* along as proof such an arrangement could be amicable?

Maximus scowled, although whether at her tone or the nature of his assignment, she couldn't be sure.

She halted and hooked her finger in the linen covering her face so her words would be perfectly clear.

"And what will you do if this young woman refuses, Maximus? Because I won't try to encourage her to go against her will. If that's the reason you brought me, then you have sorely misjudged me."

And she had misjudged him. The hurt wormed into her heart, but she refused to sag, refused to break eye contact. Refused to let him see just how much his actions wounded.

"By Mars, what are you talking about?" He sounded irritated, and pressed his hand against the small of her back in an attempt to urge her forward. She remained immobile. His jaw tensed, but he didn't exert more pressure. "I brought you with me, Carys, to comfort the poor girl should she become hysterical at the news her lover has departed for Rome."

She continued to favor him with her haughty glare, while her brain stumbled over that new information. Maximus took advantage of her confusion by once again urging her forward, and this time she let him.

Were local girls now embracing the enemy? She'd always known some would have no choice but to attach themselves to the brothels that would have inevitably sprung up to accommodate the needs of the Legion. But was it also tacitly acceptable for a young woman to take a Roman soldier, an officer, as her lover?

She could scarcely imagine such a thing. Wouldn't the girl be castigated, condemned? Or had her people's attitudes really changed so radically?

A swift glance at Branwen's stony countenance confirmed her turbulent thoughts. Regardless of how her people felt about a peasant girl fraternizing with the Romans, when it came to their nobility, to the Druids, such a coupling would be entirely unacceptable.

It was still early, and as they entered the settlement, Carys lowered her head so as not to attract unwanted attention. But deep inside, a thread of resentment bubbled. Why should she have to hide her face, as if she were ashamed of her love?

The thought was treason. She knew that. But still the resentment festered.

Maximus ushered Carys into the timber-built tavern where Faustus had accommodated his mistress. Gods, this task galled him, but he had promised, and the abandoned girl had certainly earned the gold coins Faustus had been magnanimous enough to leave her.

The tavern keeper directed him to the room where Efa stayed, and then cast a speculative look over Carys and Branwen. Maximus shot him a deadly glower, which the Celtic bastard chose to ignore. Had he really once contemplated installing Carys in such an establishment?

"Do you wish refreshments to be brought through?" And again his gaze slid over Carys.

Filthy dog. He reined in his temper, knowing Carys wouldn't thank him if he smashed her countryman's teeth down his throat, no matter how much his insolence deserved it.

"We won't be staying." He maintained eye contact until the other dropped his gaze and shuffled away.

"Did she love him?" Carys's whisper was so low he strained to hear.

He stared at her, appalled. "I hope not." If Efa loved Faustus, the possibility of her dissolving into hysterics magnified alarmingly.

Carys exhaled. "Maximus. She can't know we're together. You simply requested my presence, as I am a Celt and you need—a translator."

Her insistence on keeping their relationship a secret was beginning to piss him off. "And suppose I refuse to pander to your whims?"

"Then I shall remain here, and you can face the woman by yourself."

Chapter Twenty-seven

She had an answer for everything. He should, by rights, assert his authority and show her who her master was, but unaccountably a perverse portion of his mind enjoyed the way she stood up to him.

"It would take no effort whatsoever," he said softly, "to ensure you entered the room with me."

Instead of trembling with fear, as any other woman might, she smiled sweetly. "If you consider me your slave, Maximus, then perhaps that is exactly what you should do."

He had never considered her his slave. Had never wanted her as his slave. And with a slither of disbelief he realized she had once again got her way.

He rapped sharply on the door. "Efa knows I speak your barbaric tongue. Your translator idea won't work."

Carys's breath hissed between her teeth. "Then you brought me along for propriety's sake."

Before he could respond to that, the door opened and Efa

blinked up at him, in obvious confusion. Her black hair coiled over her shoulder in a long braid and her face looked unnaturally pale.

"My lord." She hovered uncertainly, her eyes apprehensive. Then she noticed Carys, and her entire face stretched with horrified disbelief.

He tensed. Over the last few months several officers had taken mistresses. To his knowledge, the women hadn't been unduly harassed by the Celts as they began to understand the advantages that embracing Rome and all she could offer entailed.

While he'd pandered to Carys's desire for concealment, deep down he'd thought she was overreacting. But the way Efa gaped at her, the way he could feel the girl's shocked antagonism rolling from her, splintered his previously held convictions.

And this reaction came from the ex-mistress of a Roman Tribune, a young woman who had willingly fucked Faustus and accompanied him whenever he had wished it. It was hypocritical and unbelievable, but if Efa directed such venom toward Carys, then how in Tartarus would the general populace respond toward her?

Carys stepped into the room as if it were her right, and, feeling entirely out of place, Maximus followed her, Branwen taking up the rear.

"I regret meeting you this way, Efa, while in such company."

It was odd hearing Carys speak the Celtic language when he was so used to her fluent Latin. He flicked his glance toward Efa to see how she took the slight against him, but she didn't look appeased.

"The Roman accosted me while I communed with Cerridwen."

He shot Carys a dark glare. It was all very well attempting to soothe the dark-haired Celt's feelings, but *accosted*? That was harsh.

Efa's hostility wavered. "You aren't with him?" Her voice was low, as if she didn't wish him to hear, so he kept his expression blank and glanced with feigned interest around the Roman-furnished room.

"I came here to see you."

It was uncanny how she didn't lie, and yet also managed not to tell the truth. An unsavory notion whispered through his mind. Had Carys used this tactic on him, without him realizing?

"Forgive me, my lady." Efa bowed her head. "I know you would never—I—Forgive me. I'm not myself this morn."

His interest sharpened. Efa's demeanor was suddenly servile. And although he knew Carys was no peasant, that her family was of the chieftain class that in Roman society would equate to the nobility, there was something else going on here.

Something he couldn't see. But, unaccountably, he could feel it, humming in the air, sparking along his senses.

An eerie shudder inched along his spine.

"The Tribune has a message for you." Carys turned to him, and he saw the disapproval glinting in her eyes.

He cleared his throat, mentally cursing her. Did she think he was enjoying this excruciating encounter?

Efa also turned toward him, but fear tinged her face. "Is my lord Faustus well?"

"He is quite well." Maximus's voice was gruff, and he frowned at her, as he imagined stringing Faustus up for putting him in such an awkward position. "He is on his way back to Rome."

"Rome?" Efa pressed a hand against her breast. Gods, he hoped she wasn't going to faint. Thank Minerva he'd thought to bring Carys along.

He pulled the pouch of gold coins from his belt. "He wanted you to have this."

Efa stared at him uncomprehendingly. Maximus swallowed and proffered the pouch a little closer. "As a token of his regard."

Carys made a noise that sounded suspiciously like a snort, and he favored her with a quelling glare that, naturally, she ignored.

"Faustus has left me?"

Sweat prickled across his brow. What had possessed him to agree to Faustus's outrageous request?

"Yes."

To his vague horror, Efa swayed as if she were about to collapse. Carys gripped her hands, steadying her, but as she did so an incomprehensible blend of emotions washed over her face: elation, relief—followed instantly by iron purpose.

"Sit down." Carys's tone brooked no argument, not that Efa looked capable of disagreement. Maximus watched Carys settle the younger woman on a chair, still holding her hands. "It'll be all right, Efa. You have no need to fear."

She would have no money problems either, if the wretched woman would take the gold. He dropped the pouch onto a side table and flexed his fingers. He hoped Carys wouldn't take too long to calm Efa. He needed to resume his tribunal duties, but before then he wanted to ensure Carys was safely back in his quarters.

"He didn't say he was leaving." Efa sounded on the point of tears. Maximus shifted uncomfortably.

"Forget the Roman." Carys sounded as if she meant it. He looked at her. *Did* she mean it? Somehow he'd imagined she would be more sympathetic to Efa's distress. But then, what did he know of women's distress in these matters?

Efa gave a sob. Carys crouched before her. Maximus stared in growing confusion. What was going on?

"Efa." Carys's voice had softened. "You must put the Roman behind you. You've the future to think of. You must be strong, for the sake of your babe."

Maximus stared at her, and as the weight of her words thudded into his brain, he dragged his gaze to Efa. She hadn't moved, hadn't responded, simply sat on her chair with a vacant expression on her face.

He dropped his gaze to her flat belly. Fuck. She was pregnant? How could Carys know? By the look of it, even Efa didn't know. She certainly wasn't showing.

Branwen moved to Efa's other side and patted her shoulder, as if offering comfort. Maximus had the overpowering urge to march from the room and leave the women to it, but he was a Tribune, and he couldn't leave before this situation had been satisfactorily resolved.

He cleared his throat. "Are you with child, Efa?"

Efa shivered. "If my lady says so."

He'd already concluded Carys was a healer. She obviously had more skill than he had given her credit for. Although how she had discovered such a thing about Efa without an examination was beyond his comprehension.

Perhaps it was another mystical Celtic way Rome had yet to master.

"We won't speak of it now," Carys said gently. "But I'll see you later today, or tomorrow, and we can discuss what you wish to do."

Her words washed over him as he focused on her profile, and stark realization dawned. For all he knew, Carys also could be pregnant. *With his child.*

Heat flared through him. The possibility had never occurred to him before this moment. The first time he'd taken her, he'd assumed—in a distant, unimportant corner of his mind—she had taken feminine precautions to ensure against such catastrophe.

He'd known she was no whore, but she was a Celt and their ways were different, their women less constrained than those of noble Roman birth.

But Carys had known only one other man besides him. And been celibate for the last three years.

Yet she was a healer. Doubtless she knew of such things. *But suppose she did not?*

"I don't know what to do." Efa pressed a hand against her belly. "How can I have Faustus's babe if he's not here to protect me?"

"Will your kin take you back?"

Efa flicked Carys a despairing look. "Not with a bastard to feed."

Shit. His muscles were so knotted they pained him, and he desired nothing better than to vanish from the room. He was an interloper, eavesdropping on intimate female conversation, and the experience was torturous.

Carys stood, extricated her hands from Efa's and collected the pouch he'd left on the table. "Here." She placed the pouch between Efa's listless fingers. "This is yours. And remember. There's no need to burden yourself with a reminder of Rome if you don't wish it."

He definitely shouldn't be listening to this conversation. But he was rooted to the spot, unable to move. Unable to take his eyes from Carys. She no longer reminded him of a well-bred Roman lady. She was a Celt, a foreigner, a woman who knew things he could scarcely comprehend, a woman whose every word this peasant girl not only believed, but respected.

Efa shuddered and her fingers clasped the pouch. "My lady, I do want the babe. It's the only thing I'll have of Faustus to love."

Carys nodded and stroked a gentle hand along the girl's arm. "Then I shall find alternative arrangements for you, Efa. I'll make a sacrifice to sweet Cerridwen and beg her favor."

Efa gripped Carys's hand and kissed it reverently. Ragged claws crawled along Maximus's spine at the gesture, which hovered perilously close to worship.

Women's concerns. The words thundered through his brain, obliterating the strands of doubt. He had never witnessed anything like this before, and by Jupiter he never wanted to again. Efa was frightened and Carys offered comfort. Of course the peasant girl was grateful. Of course she would show her gratitude in such a way.

He was seeing shadows where there were none.

"If my lady has no objection,." Branwen sounded hesitant, as if unsure of Carys's reaction. "Efa could stay with me. There's only my grandfather at home."

A look of wonder flashed across Carys's face, as if Branwen had just uttered something extraordinary. "A babe," she whispered, and the hairs on his arms shivered at her tone. "Efa, what do you think of this arrangement?"

"I suppose." She didn't sound entirely convinced, but Carys didn't appear to notice as she reached out and took Branwen's hand.

"The babe will strengthen your grandfather's heart, restore his will to live. Truly, Cerridwen moves in the most mysterious of ways." And she smiled radiantly, as if all the ills in the world had suddenly been cured.

"Carys." His voice was harsh, an unwelcome intrusion, but he couldn't stand any more of this womanly talk or adoration of the barbarous Cerridwen. "We have to leave."

"Yes, of course." Carys agreed so quickly he was unnerved. He'd expected her to argue, to say she couldn't possibly leave Efa alone in such a state, or that she needed to make arrangements for the girl's relocation.

He didn't trust her swift acquiescence.

"Branwen, you'll stay here with Efa to ensure she has everything she needs." Carys spoke with quiet authority, as if she had every right to issue orders to Branwen. To the girl *he* had acquired to be her own personal maid. "I want Efa out of here and installed in your home as swiftly as possible."

"Yes, my lady." Branwen seemed just as eager.

Carys glanced over at him. Something about her had changed since they'd been in this room, and although he couldn't fathom what, he could feel the difference in her, an inner energy, as if a lamp had been ignited in her soul.

"My lord Tribune."

It took him a moment to realize she was addressing him. "What is it, Celt?" He infused each word with as much disdain as possible. See how she enjoyed being on the receiving end.

The corner of her mouth quirked, as if she struggled not to smile at his attempt at offense. "Does everything in this room now belong to Efa?"

Everything in this room had the touch of Rome. Faustus had undoubtedly furnished its entirety from his own pocket. "It does."

When they finally left the tavern, Carys had to restrain the urge to fling her arms around Maximus and tell him how much she loved him.

Cerridwen had returned.

Even now, she could scarcely believe it. But there was no doubt. Cerridwen had been with her, had shown her the spark of life within Efa's womb, and how to smooth the life-path of not just Efa, but Branwen's grandfather also, whose heart still trembled with the loss of Branwen's sister and stillborn child.

"I thought you didn't want to draw attention to yourself." There was an odd note in Maximus's voice, as if he was torn between frustration and amusement.

"What?" She glanced up at him, floundered in the beautiful blue of his eyes and again wanted to claim him for her very own in front of the world.

"You're all but dancing. Not that I particularly disapprove, but people are staring."

She immediately reined in her exuberance. "Thank you for bringing me." She kept her voice low. "Cerridwen awaited me there."

A frown flashed over his face, as if he didn't think much of Cerridwen. But she wanted him to love her goddess, perhaps not as *she* loved her, but enough so she could tell him of Cerridwen's great wisdom and generosity.

And forgiveness.

Joy bubbled through her heart once again at the knowledge Cerridwen had forgiven her transgression. Truly, she would give great sacrifice to her goddess. Anything she desired.

Almost anything.

"Efa didn't know she was with child, did she?"

She dragged her attention back to the present. "No. But it *is* very early. She'll feel the changes in her body soon enough."

His jaw tightened, as if she'd given too much information for comfort. "How did you know, Carys?"

She opened her mouth to tell him exactly how she'd known, when a slither of alarm alerted her senses.

He was her beloved, and she defied her people to be with him. But he was still Rome, and Rome was the enemy of her blood.

The euphoria dimmed. There would always be some secrets she must keep from him. For both their sakes.

"I'm a healer, Maximus. I've always had a particular affinity with feminine conditions." It wasn't a lie. But it wasn't the whole truth either.

"And what of you?" He was still frowning, but concern threaded his words.

"Me?" She tried to understand what he meant, but failed. "What of me, Maximus?"

He pulled her to a stop, his hands on her shoulders. "You might also be with child."

If only.

But as she stared into his unsmiling face, the certainty gripped her that Maximus would be appalled by such an occurrence.

She sucked in a deep breath. "There's no need to fear on my account. I would never burden you with such an encumbrance."

"Burden me?" His eyes narrowed as his frown intensified. "That's not my concern, Carys." He sounded offended, as if she had deliberately misunderstood his meaning.

So what did he mean?

"Maximus, you don't have to worry about it." But even as the words left her lips, a chill shivered through her.

Just days ago she'd been so sure their liaison would be of short duration. How could it be anything more? Sooner or later the Druids would rise against their oppressors and, with the fury of the gods to guide them, obliterate the enemy forever.

But what if the long-promised attack never occurred? Her heart lurched in strangled delight at the prospect of being able to see Maximus indefinitely. But then what of her plans to conceive his child? Would he still desire her as her body changed or would he lose interest?

"I'm not worrying for myself." His fingers tightened around her shoulders as if he wanted to give her a good shake. "I'm thinking of you. Did you—uh—take precautions?"

He looked tortured, as if the conversation crucified him. As if Roman men usually never spoke of such matters.

She smothered a sigh and pressed her hand against his heart. "I know what to do. All is well, Maximus."

Back at his quarters, Maximus stared at Carys in growing disbelief. "You'll stay here," he said, "until I return."

"So I'm your prisoner?"

He ignored her inane accusation. "How can you think of leaving?" He just prevented himself from adding *me*. "Every time I turn my back, some rutting male attacks you."

She flushed, and far from feeling victorious he felt only a rising sensation of dreaded frustration.

"If you lend me a suitable weapon, then I'll be able to defend myself."

He almost laughed in her face, but not with amusement. With derision. How could a woman as fragile as Carys hope to compete against a full-grown man blinded by lust?

"You're no warrior maiden, Carys." He meant it as a compliment, for what did he need with one of those heathen females? But Carys stiffened in clear affront, and he realized yet again he'd managed to insult her culture without intent.

He let out an impatient breath, battened down his irritation and took her hands. "I mean no disrespect. But I can't allow you to wander the countryside unprotected. Look what happened yesterday. If I hadn't found you when I did, you would have been raped—perhaps even murdered." A nauseous chill invaded his stomach at the image and he banished the thought with a shudder. He would never allow Carys to put herself in such danger again.

"That won't happen again." There was a note of iron in her voice, as if she had reached a decision of which he had no knowledge. "I learn from my mistakes, Maximus. It was wrong of me to go to the Cauldron and—" She cut herself off, and blinked as if she had forgotten what she was about to say.

"Then let me hear no more of your insane wish to leave." He relinquished her hands and turned, intending to ready himself for the day ahead. Where in Tartarus had the slave hidden his favorite fibula?

"Do you think I won't return to you?"

He flicked his gaze over her, from the top of her golden head, her delicate features and enticing curves, to her leather-clad feet. How could a woman who looked as ethereal as Carys possess so stubborn a spirit?

"Is that what you believe?" She rested her hand on his arm, demanding an answer.

Impossible female.

And yet, deep inside, an illogical certainty formed. He knew she would return to him. She would always return to him.

But only if he allowed her to go of his own free will.

A dull throb pounded at his temples. Women were there for comfort. For convenience. They were not supposed to cause a man headaches and make him question his own integrity.

But Carys would never be merely a convenience. She would never accept his word as her law, unless it suited her.

Once again, he was back at the waterfall and the choice was his. Force her to his will, or allow her to go.

He circled her wrist with thumb and forefinger and removed her hand from his arm. "I shall provide you with a horse and weapon. If you allow any harm to befall you, I'll kill you myself."

She flashed him an inappropriate smile, rose onto her toes and brushed a teasing kiss across his lips.

"You'll never have any need to kill me."

Her words echoed in his mind, an ominous refrain.

A shudder inched along his spine. *Madness.* He would never harm Carys, whatever trouble her foolhardy behavior caused.

She was his woman, his responsibility. And whether she liked it or not, in the eyes of Rome her actions were his.

Chapter Twenty-eight

As soon as Carys reached the Cauldron, she saw her medicine bag where she'd left it. She dismounted the mare Maximus had acquired for her and hastily gathered her scattered belongings together, whispering prayers of gratitude and love to Cerridwen for protecting her possessions from scavengers.

She dug into the bag and retrieved her dagger, and secured it at her waist, next to the one Maximus had given her. Never again would she allow herself to be so vulnerable.

Aeron sucked the noxious fumes deep into his lungs, holding the smoke within his physical body, freeing his spirit to commune in the astral plane.

Gwydion, the warrior magician, the greatest of the enchanters, whispered caution through his mind. *They hadn't come this far to shatter their illusion of allegiance to the old gods yet.*

Soon. But not today.

Aeron bared his teeth but dampened down his rage and derision toward the swarming multitude of gods and goddesses he'd pretended to worship most of his life.

Only Gwydion, master illusionist of the immortals, knew his true heart. Only Gwydion had seen his pure spirit at the age of eight while he writhed in the torturous grip of his revelatory vision.

Gwydion, who had taken the terrified boy and protected him, nurtured him, taught him how to hide his fear, feed upon his disgust and gain strength from his deceptions. Gwydion, who had loved him before any of the other gods deigned to acknowledge his existence.

The god of illusion had instructed him well. For even Gwydion did not know the entire scope of Aeron's plans.

It was not yet dawn, and the cromlech was blissfully deserted, allowing him uninterrupted meditation. The Roman scum's blood was even now fermenting in the sacred bowl, mingling with his magical concoctions, the acrid odor weaving through the air, sending out its malevolent tentacles.

The Roman would be drawn into its mystical web. Without his knowledge he would be led to the sacrificial altar. And there, at the appointed time, Aeron would rip open the enemy's ribs and slice his filthy heart from its moorings.

A dramatic and auspicious start to the battle that would eradicate Rome from the soil of Cymru.

He felt Morwyn's approach, like the scuttle of spiders across the nape of his neck, before she came into sight. He focused his concentration on the bubbling sludge in the bowl, but the edge of his awareness prickled.

Morwyn had not retreated when she saw him engrossed. She was standing beyond the outer ring of the bluestones, waiting for him to acknowledge her presence.

Strands of consciousness intertwined with the nebulous odor, feeding, assessing.

The target had been located.

With a long, outdrawn breath Aeron's tightly coiled muscles relaxed and his fingers flattened against the cool stone of the altar. *Justice would be his.*

Only then did he open his eyes and turn to Morwyn. She came toward him without her usual exaggerated swagger and, unaccountably, the lack needled him.

Perhaps he should fuck her here, on the ground by the sacred altar, show her what she had long coveted. Except Morwyn wasn't Carys, could never be Carys.

Carys was now as soiled as the land of Cymru, raped and violated, unworthy of nurturing his precious son.

The rage erupted through every pore, every orifice. He wanted to smash Morwyn's face for being here when Carys wasn't. Wanted to fill her wretched womb with putrid maggots, because Carys's womb was polluted and Carys's womb was the one he wanted. Needed.

Craved.

"Aeron?" Morwyn sounded unsure, and if there was one thing Morwyn was, it was sure of herself. He reined in the fury, and it steamed through his blood, scalding, blistering.

"What is it?" Years of practice ensured his voice remained neutral, despite the havoc wrecking every burning point of his body.

"Have you seen Carys?"

Instantly his senses sharpened, searching for hidden meaning in her words. "Since when?" He glanced back at the bowl, feigning disinterest.

"Since yesterday. I couldn't find her in the mound last night."

Morwyn hadn't witnessed the scene at the Cauldron. He sucked in a measured breath, waited for his heart to resume its normal beat.

While he had every right to take Carys, with hindsight he had, perhaps, been a little hasty the previous day. Had the Roman not interrupted, Carys would have conceived his son. But would she also have had the audacity to cry rape?

A chill shivered through his groin. Knowing Carys, such blasphemy was very possible. And despite his power, despite his position, he was not yet omnipotent, and had Carys accused him, his balls would be ripped from his body and burned before his eyes for daring to touch their precious princess.

Even though she was his. Even though she would always be his, even after he slit her throat and watched her tarnished blood gush over the smooth stone altar.

"Aeron?" Morwyn's sharp tone dragged him back to the present, dragged him back to the harsh reality that he had lost Carys to the Roman. That even now the Roman was fucking her, using her body, pumping his rancid seed deep into her womb.

"No doubt she slept out in the forest." He began to gather his various implements together, unable to trust himself to look at Morwyn in case she saw the malice burning in his eyes.

"I've checked her favorite places." There was no mistaking the worry in Morwyn's voice, and finally he wondered why. If she hadn't seen the incident yesterday, if she had no idea that Carys was currently the sex slave of a perverted Roman weasel, then why was she so concerned for Carys's safety?

He veiled his eyes and looked up at her. "Then perhaps she spends time with a lover."

Morwyn's eyes widened, as if in shock. Her lips moved, as if she tried to speak, but no sound emerged. He waited with false patience, to see if she swallowed such an outlandish explanation for Carys's whereabouts.

"A lover?" Morwyn's voice was unnaturally high. "Oh. I— That hadn't occurred to me."

Of course it hadn't occurred to her, because Carys had never taken another lover since leaving him. But now it served his purpose if Morwyn believed such a lie.

He was not yet ready to disclose she had been abducted by the enemy. And he would never divulge the true circumstances of her abduction to anyone, least of all a female acolyte of the cursed Morrigan.

Carys led the mare through the gap in the spiral, and whispered words of comfort to soothe the creature's agitation. The vertigo caused by the sacred protections still affected her even after all these moons, but for one who had never passed through before, the shift in perception shocked.

She kept to the outer rim of the spiral. The last thing she wanted was to approach the cromlech and risk being seen by Aeron. She'd tether the mare in the glade where they kept their own horses, entwine one of her jade ribbons around the reins to claim her for her own, and seek out Druantia.

Her plan worked until she turned to leave the glade and saw a figure moving toward her through the trees from the direction of Druantia's sacred grove. He saw her the moment she saw him, and froze as if she were a spirit returned from the Otherworld.

Carys drew in a deep breath and forced herself to keep walking. She was deep within the spiral. There was no reason Aeron would even think she had only just returned into its protective sphere.

But she truly did not feel up to more of his insistence that they belonged together. She offered him a brief smile and hoped that would be enough greeting.

His continued silence scraped along her nerves and she paused and shot him a cautious glance. He was still staring at her, but not with the undercurrent of lust she had grown accustomed to over the years.

Instead, a primal claw of horror ripped into her mind and she staggered, momentarily unbalanced by the force of the emotion, by the incredulity that such emotion could emanate from Aeron.

And then the sensation vanished, as if it had never been, and she flattened her palms against her thighs in an effort to regain her equilibrium. *Had she just imagined it?*

Yet still Aeron made no move toward her. No word of greeting, or condemnation.

She flicked her tongue over her lips. Half in shadow, his face was concealed but his strange silver eyes glinted at her, as if daring her to—to do what?

Her heart thudded with breath-crushing force against her ribs, sending tremors of doubt vibrating through her gut. In all the years she'd known him, from a child when he was a youth rising through the ranks, when he first noticed her and claimed her for his own, even when she had severed their relationship—she had never feared him, because she knew, at a fundamental level, he would never harm her.

But now, suddenly, and for no reason she could envisage, an unformed fear fluttered through her soul, and for the first time she truly understood why so many of her people trembled at the mere mention of his name.

But this was madness. He would never hurt her. There was no reason why he would, no reason why he should want to. She was still in a dream thinking of her love, still wrapped in gratitude that Cerridwen had returned, and her senses were dulled.

She took a deep breath, attempted to ignore the nervous churn of her stomach. "Good morn, Aeron."

He visibly stiffened, as if her voice jolted him from his strange contemplation. *Perhaps that was it?* He had fallen into a vision, and hadn't seen her at all?

"Carys." His tone was low, emotionless. Unlike any he normally used when addressing her. An odd shiver chased over her arms and her fingers tensed against her thighs.

"I'm going to see Druantia." There had been no need to tell

him that. And yet the unbearable silence after his greeting had screamed to be shattered.

He stepped from the shadows and she had to forcibly stop herself from backing away. This was Aeron. She had known him almost all her life. And even if, for some unimaginable reason, he did wish to harm her, she was still his princess, still his social superior, still elevated from all other Druids by virtue of her powerful matrilineal heritage.

Unless he could prove her a traitor.

But she had not betrayed her people. And besides, how could he have found out about Maximus? It was impossible. She wouldn't believe it.

Cerridwen, hear my prayer.

His gaze drilled into her, as if reaching for the secret corners of her mind. "Morwyn has been searching for you."

She swallowed her apprehension. It was all in her mind. She loved Maximus, but her guilt over loving her enemy would always cloud her judgment when it came to her people. She would have to learn to live with it.

"I'll find her after I've greeted Druantia." She hoped Morwyn hadn't told Aeron of the incident involving those three Roman louts. Goddess, surely Morwyn wouldn't have confided that she'd taken Carys with her to the fortification? Aeron would be enraged.

But he wasn't enraged. He was strangely calm, but it was a calmness that ate through her nerves like starving rats shredding a rotting corpse.

"Morwyn was concerned," Aeron said, as if she hadn't responded, "because she feared you had spent the night outside the spiral."

Carys almost refuted the claim. But something stilled her tongue. *Sweet Cerridwen, guide me.* "I did."

His eyes glittered; his nostrils flared. Heat washed through her. Had she made a terrible mistake?

"Where did you go after leaving the Cauldron?"

The Cauldron? Carys stared at him as knots of alarm tightened her muscles and constricted her chest. "How do you know I was at the Cauldron?"

His unblinking gaze never left hers. "Morwyn told me."

Her heart stuttered in relief. Of course Morwyn had told him. Had Aeron witnessed the incident with the Roman lout or, even worse, seen Maximus rescue her, he certainly wouldn't be standing here questioning her as to her movements.

He would have attacked the would-be rapist himself. And then Maximus wouldn't have seen her at the Cauldron, and she wouldn't have spent the most magical hours of her life in his arms last night.

And she didn't even want to contemplate the outcome had Aeron seen Maximus at the Cauldron instead.

She realized Aeron was still waiting for her answer. "I attended a woman who is recently with child." She hoped Aeron wouldn't insist on knowing where she had spent the night, because there was a difference between omitting the truth and telling a blatant lie.

He took a step toward her, as if he couldn't help himself. "And nothing untoward happened while you were at the Cauldron?"

Had he sensed something was amiss yesterday? Or could he feel her hiding her innermost thoughts from him?

"Not that I recall." It was the truth. She couldn't recall the attack, no matter how hard she tried. She realized, belatedly, her response was lacking. "Why?" She infused as much confusion into the word as possible, but, sweet Cerridwen, how much longer would Aeron bombard her with cryptic questions?

For a heartbeat, disbelief flashed across his features, followed instantly by relief. So fleeting the emotions, so swiftly erased, she wondered if she'd imagined them.

But she hadn't. And for the life of her she couldn't understand what had just transpired between them.

"The countryside is infested with Romans." His lip curled in disdain. "Even Cerridwen's Cauldron is not immune to their poisonous touch."

"I saw no enemy. And now I must go to Druantia." She turned away and let out a shaky breath.

"Wait. I haven't yet finished with you."

She forgot about her relief at escaping his probing questions and flicked an incredulous glance over her shoulder.

"You haven't what?" Had she misunderstood his tone? It was the way one spoke to a slave. Or the way a barbarous Roman might speak to his mindless Roman wife.

Not her Maximus, though. And no Druid either.

Aeron appeared not to notice her chilled response. "You haven't told me where you spent the night, Carys."

She drew herself up and gave him her most regal look. "No. I haven't." And with that she turned and stalked off, head held high, toward Druantia's grove.

Aeron gripped his hazel rod with such force his fingers grew numb. How dare she turn her back on him? How dare she treat him as if he were a lowly acolyte, unworthy of her time?

The fucking *whore.*

Breath hissed between his clenched teeth as he watched her disappear between the trees. He attempted to calm his mind, regulate his pulses, reach for serenity.

But the image of Carys in the arms of the enemy pounded through his brain.

She didn't remember anything that happened at the Cauldron. He accepted that. But when had her consciousness returned? What had the Roman done with her?

He couldn't believe the Roman had taken her to a Celtic dwelling to recover. A Celtic dwelling where, by chance, a pregnant woman required assistance.

Not unless the barbarian preferred fucking other men, and the look on the Roman's face as he'd glanced at Carys left Aeron in no doubt as to where his sexual preference lay.

So how had she escaped her captor? It was inconceivable he had allowed his delectable slave to leave.

Unless she wasn't his slave. Wasn't with him unwillingly.

The answer flared through his cortex, splintering his reason.

Had Carys stayed with the Roman last night *voluntarily*?

Chapter Twenty-nine

Carys kissed Druantia and settled in her usual place at the elderly queen's feet.

"You've found someone at last."

Carys's breath hitched in her breast. She should have known the great Druid would see the truth. Druantia was smiling down at her, but it was a smile shadowed with doubt.

She swallowed the flicker of apprehension. "Yes." Sweet Cerridwen, don't let Druantia ask her who the man was. It would crucify her to lie to her beloved matriarch.

Druantia stroked the top of Carys's head. "And yet he is not Aeron." There was a questioning note in her tone, as if she pondered the fact.

"No."

"I always believed the Morrigan meant you for Aeron."

Carys barely suppressed a shudder. She still hadn't recovered from the odd sensation of primal terror that had whipped through her as Aeron had scrutinized her earlier.

"Aeron isn't the man for me."

Druantia's hand stilled on her hair. "The Morrigan was grieved when you turned from him, my Carys. And her affront was great when you spurned all other men afterward."

Carys clasped Druantia's other hand. When Aeron had become her lover at the age of fourteen, she had secretly hoped the goddess would honor her by acknowledging her presence. It wouldn't have mattered how fleeting that acknowledgment was. Just a small sign to reassure her that the Morrigan wasn't truly ignoring her. That the feeling of being slighted was all in her mind.

It had made no difference. During the three years she'd been with Aeron, the goddess had remained as distant as ever. If even having the High Druid as her lover hadn't caused the Morrigan to look upon her with favor, how could taking another man change that? *And how was she supposed to have known severing her relationship with Aeron would have grieved the goddess?* "But I still worshipped the Great Goddess. I tried to show her how much I loved her."

Druantia shook her head, as if Carys spoke nonsense. "You know that isn't the same. You needed a man. And if Aeron wasn't that man, you should have chosen another. But you didn't." She frowned, and her wrinkled face cascaded. "Something is fearfully wrong, Carys."

Carys tried to ignore the way her heart thundered against her ribs. At first she'd been sure the Morrigan would remain in blissful ignorance of her liaison with Maximus. Then, after she had been touched by the raven's eye, she convinced herself that the goddess was bestowing her approval.

But there had been only anger and frustration, not approval, vibrating in the air when she had entered the goddess's sacred domain. A chill clutched her heart. *Was that the reason for Druantia's distress?*

Because Carys had entered the goddess's sacred domain without permission?

"What has the Morrigan said?" Her voice was scarcely above a whisper, dread coiling deep in her stomach.

Druantia slid her arthritic fingers along Carys's braid. "Her great malevolence rolled across the land, seeking yet not finding."

"Her malevolence?" She recalled the chilling sensation she and Morwyn had felt yesterday, as they left the settlement. That had been the Morrigan? Why, then, hadn't Morwyn recognized her goddess?

"Why couldn't she find you, Carys?"

Ice trickled along her nape. "She was searching for *me*?" But she had swept right by her. Carys had felt the dark cloud of fury, the fingers of dread—how could the greatest goddess of them all have been unable to locate her whereabouts?

"I beseeched her for mercy. Begged her to give you more time. But she was deaf to my pleas in her frenzy."

Horror crawled through her heart as realization dawned. "She's angry because I'll never return to Aeron?"

Druantia's glazed eyes watered. "No. I thought, in my ignorance, she had finally lost patience with you for denying her gifts. This is why I intervened, my Carys, why I begged for her lenience." She sighed, a whispery sound not of this world. "It seems you didn't need me to intercede on your behalf."

She didn't want to ask. Didn't want to know. And yet she knew she must. "Does—does the Morrigan not approve of my lover?"

Of course she didn't. How could she have been so naïve as to imagine, for even a fleeting moment, that the Great Goddess would accept the homage and not care that Carys worshipped while fraternizing with the enemy?

Druantia cupped her cheek, a tender gesture. "My child, the Morrigan cannot see you at all. You have vanished, like the mist in the morning. She searches, but in vain. All this I saw in the blink of an eye as I begged for her favor. And yet I believe she scarcely acknowledged my existence in her fury."

"I don't understand." Carys fought the panic threatening to

choke the breath from her lungs. "How can she not see me? Am I no longer her daughter?"

"You are a Druid, as all the women of our line have been and ever will be." Druantia smiled, but still the shadows clouded her eyes. "And yet at the moment of your birth, when the Morrigan stood poised to make you her own, Cerridwen appeared and claimed you for all time. And the Great Goddess turned from you at that moment."

She knew this. All her kin did. But none of them knew *why*. "But she could always see me before." The goddess had simply chosen to ignore her. But this was a new hurt, to know that now the Morrigan no longer even saw her. And yet what of her vision? Even there, in the goddess's most sacred place, she had been invisible, a nonentity.

"Something has changed." Druantia sighed and tugged gently on Carys's braid. "The balance is shifting. I can feel it, but I can't comprehend it. It's Cerridwen the Morrigan rages against. And you are, always have been, Cerridwen's."

Carys clutched Druantia's fragile fingers as a terrible certainty gripped her. "It's my fault."

"No. Cerridwen protects you, my child. And although I can't envisage why, it is she who shields you from the Morrigan."

What had she done? If she could rewind time, she would never have taken the illicit root. Never have tumbled into the goddess's sacred realm, nor seen the bloodied visions.

The Morrigan would not have become enraged by her audacity, and there would be no need for Cerridwen to intervene. And the two goddesses would not now be locked in bitter conflict.

And Maximus would not have taken her from the Cauldron back to his quarters.

She tried to close her mind to the memories, but the love seeped into every pore, every breath, every erratic beat of her heart. He was intertwined with her soul, a part of her, and a chill rippled through her core at the knowledge that, even were she given such power to change her actions, she wouldn't.

She dropped her forehead onto Druantia's knees. "I entered the Morrigan's domain without permission."

Druantia's hand stilled on her braid. "You know that cannot be, my child. The Morrigan must have allowed you entry."

Carys choked on a breath and risked looking up. "I thought Cerridwen invited me, but Cerridwen wasn't there. I was alone, and the Morrigan—she didn't see me, Druantia."

For one terrifying moment, Carys thought she saw fear flick in the old Druid's eyes. But that couldn't be. Druantia feared nothing. She was the most powerful Druid in Cymru.

"Where were you?" Druantia breathed the words as if she almost didn't wish to know.

Carys sucked in a shaky breath. "The crossroads of life. And I saw—I think I saw—the future." A shudder attacked her, chills chased along her arms and she clasped her fingers together in supplication.

Druantia's fingers covered hers. "What did you see?"

She closed her eyes, and instantly the vision returned in all its bloodstained, fiery fury.

"The sacred Isle of Mon, drenched with Druid blood, the holy groves razed to the ground, the sisterhood vanquished."

At the deathly silence following her words, she wrenched open her eyes and stared helplessly at Druantia. "Mon burned, *Britain* burned. Our goddesses and gods writhed in agony. Everything we cherish was crushed by—by Rome."

The ancient Druid's hands trembled, and Carys threaded her fingers through the old lady's, infusing strength, but wishing desperately Druantia could offer her solid comfort in return.

She didn't want her vision to be true. She wanted her queen to refute her words, to scorn her interpretation, to reassure her that somehow all would be well.

"You stood by the fork in the road?" Druantia's voice was hushed.

"Yes."

"What of the alternate path, my child? What is our choice?"

Terror uncoiled in the pit of her belly and slithered through her gut. Sweet Goddess, Druantia believed in her vision. Believed that Mon would burn, that their ways were doomed.

Unless they took the alternate path. And no Druid would take the alternate path.

She swallowed, her mouth as dry as sunbaked rock; her chest constricted with mounting despair. She couldn't say the words, but Druantia waited.

She hitched in a ragged breath. "To embrace Rome."

Druantia recoiled, as if Carys had just spit in her face. "That can never be, Carys." She grasped her fingers in a surprisingly strong grip. "There must be more to this vision, my child. Think. What else did you see?"

"It was Rome, Druantia, the way Gaius used to describe it to me. But even without that knowledge, there could be no mistake. The wide Roman road leading into the heathen future could be nothing else."

Druantia was silent, and Carys resisted the urge to sag. Since waking in Maximus's quarters yesterday, she had kept the gut-churning terror at bay by telling herself she misunderstood the vision. That there was something she hadn't seen, something she'd misinterpreted because of her inexperience.

"Druids and Romans live together in harmony?" There was skepticism in Druantia's tone, but also something else, a hint of hope, of possibility.

She didn't want to crush that hope. Goddess, she wanted that future more than anyone could ever know.

But her vision hadn't promised anything of the kind.

"There was no sisterhood." Her voice was dull. "No fellow brethren. Only darkness encroaching upon the horizon of Rome, crawling ever closer to where I stood." She shivered at the remembered sensation of isolation. "I couldn't see far, Druantia; it was so dark. Only one flame lit the way and it was so faint, as if the slightest breeze would extinguish it forever."

Druantia's fingers tensed. "One flame." Her tone was hushed, as if the significance was clear to her. "The light in the darkness, as the Morrigan foretold. That is what you saw. No matter how this ends with Rome, we will prevail into the future."

Carys wanted to believe her. But her heart ached. She didn't want a future of bloodshed or darkness. She wanted Maximus, her kin, a family of her own. She wanted it all, and she couldn't see how it could ever be.

"How did you leave the sacred crossroad, Carys?"

Carys frowned, unsure what Druantia meant. "How?"

"Did Cerridwen return you to this realm? Or did another Druid assist you?"

She didn't answer straight away. And then knew she had no choice but the truth. "No. My lover rescued me from certain death."

Druantia nodded slowly, as if Carys's death within the vision or the fact her unknown lover had saved her did not surprise her.

"You didn't choose Aeron, the man I thought the goddess wanted for you, but if this lover could lead you from the immortal realm, then you have chosen your mate wisely."

Blood heated her cheeks, burning her skin. Druantia had given her blessing to her joining with Maximus, but if she knew who Maximus was, she would not hesitate to destroy them both.

Feverishly she sought to distract the Druid before she asked for more details of this elusive lover.

"But this is why it's my fault." She pressed Druantia's palm against her cheek, seeking comfort, seeking forgiveness for sins about to be confessed and sins she could never confess. "I trespassed in the Morrigan's realm, and that's why she no longer sees me."

An odd expression crossed Druantia's ancient face. "When did you have this vision?"

"Yesterday, midafternoon."

And as the words passed her lips, a chill stole over her body. She didn't need Druantia's reply to realize the truth herself.

"The Morrigan searched for you yesterday noon, child. Cerridwen had already protected you from her wrath before you ever entered the immortal realm."

After leaving Druantia, Carys searched for Morwyn and finally found her by the river, watching over the children as they played in the shallow depths.

"Good morn." She sat beside her friend, but Morwyn didn't answer, didn't even glance her way. "What's wrong?"

Morwyn shot her a look that sent chills along her arms. "What could be wrong? You're here now, safe and well, aren't you?"

Guilt speared through her heart and she rested her hand over Morwyn's. "I didn't intend to remain outside the spiral last night. I'm sorry if I caused you anxiety."

Morwyn deliberately moved her hand from Carys's. "You could have told me you intended to stay with your lover last night. There was no need to fabricate a tale that you wished to commune with Cerridwen on your own."

"I did commune with Cerridwen." Carys wrapped her arms around her knees for comfort. If only she could tell Morwyn the whole truth. "It was only afterward I—I returned to the settlement to be with my lover."

"I hope you enjoyed yourself." Morwyn's tone implied she hoped anything but.

She smothered a sigh. Would she forever have to lie to her friends and kin? The more she tried to protect herself, to protect her love for Maximus, the deeper into a clinging web of deceit she tumbled.

"You were right." She slid Morwyn a sideways glance. "I shouldn't have gone to the Cauldron by myself. I experienced a vision so acute, I was unaware of our mortal world."

Morwyn turned to her, no longer rigid with suppressed affront, her features softening into fascinated concern. "Alone? But, Carys, you may never have returned to us."

"I nearly didn't." She sucked in a harsh breath. "The Roman barbarian followed me. He attacked me while I was insensible. If my lover hadn't arrived, I would have died. Both in the mortal and immortal realms."

Morwyn grasped her hand. "Carys, is your lover one of our own? You can trust me. I would never tell."

"No. He's not a Druid."

"But to save you from such a fate? Surely he must possess Druid blood? Perhaps—perhaps he is unaware of it?"

"Truly, Morwyn. He possesses not a drop of our blood."

Clear disappointment clouded Morwyn's brow. "It feels wrong that your chosen one is not one of the gods' favored sons. Now, more than ever, our bloodline should be strengthened, not diluted."

Maximus, who didn't understand her ways and had little knowledge of her sacred beliefs, had brought her back from the immortal realm. And, by so doing, had proved to her queen and her best friend that he was worthy of her love, of siring her future children.

Druid or not, he would be welcomed as her husband if that was her desire.

But her desire was irrelevant, for a Roman would never be accepted within her circle.

A thought stirred. "Morwyn, I tended a woman early this morn. She's pregnant by her Roman lover, an officer. He had her installed in lodgings as his mistress."

Morwyn sighed. "It grieves me to admit, but some of our women are finding a better life serving Rome in that manner."

"But this woman loved her Roman. She wants his child."

"But does he love her?" Morwyn shook her head. "It's easy for a woman to believe herself in love when the man elevates her from the midden. They take advantage, Carys. It's not an equal relationship."

Carys recalled the haunted look in Efa's eyes at the knowledge Faustus had left. It could have been through fear of being returned to abject poverty, of resorting to working in a brothel, but in her heart she knew it was more than that. Efa loved her Roman officer, even though he was unworthy of such honor.

Her vision shivered over her. "And what if the Romans stay? What if they're not defeated? Should we forever spurn them? Should our blood never mingle? Will our people and Rome forever hate each other?"

Morwyn squeezed her fingers. "Carys, don't give up hope. Our situation is close to changing." She paused and glanced around, as if making sure the children were still safe and no other adult was near to overhear. "I'm sworn to secrecy. But you know how discontented Gawain is, how he and many of the other Druids wish to rise against Aeron's edict?"

Carys knew of the discontent. But to rise against Aeron? "Gawain wishes to overthrow Aeron?" She couldn't hide the shock in her voice.

Morwyn frowned, as if in warning to keep her voice down. "No, of course not. They want to overthrow the *Romans*. I'm not telling you anything you don't already know."

"Then what are you talking about? What's the great secret?"

"Gawain spent the night with several of the Druids. They went into trance, communed with the gods. And discovered Aeron's plans."

Her heart thudded in her chest, as a dark fog of impending devastation rolled through her. "What are his plans?"

"When the longest day is upon us, he's going to invoke the power of the spiral to wipe out our enemy. And as they run like rats from a sinking ship before the deadly wave, we will launch our attack."

Chapter Thirty

Ice chilled her flesh, ate into her bones. Morwyn spoke of the morrow.

She had to warn Maximus. But to do so would betray her people in the worst way.

Yet if she didn't, her beloved could die.

"Carys." Morwyn gripped her shoulders and forced her around. "There's no need to be so alarmed. The gods are with us, and with the power of the spiral we can't lose."

She knew they couldn't lose. And that was why her heart pounded in her chest, why her brain throbbed against her temples and why she had the horrifying urge to keel over and vomit up the contents of her stomach.

"Don't worry." Morwyn cupped her face with her hand and frowned in misplaced sympathy. "Our people will be safe from the wrath of the gods. And when the battle's over, when the Romans have fled, we can regain our lives. You'll be able to be with your lover without having to hide your face like a misbegotten hag."

She had to speak. Had to think. But all she could feel was over-whelming terror that tomorrow, if Maximus died, her life would end.

"Gawain is sure of this?" Perhaps he'd misinterpreted the signs. He, and all the other Druids who had participated in the moonlit ceremony.

Morwyn ran her palms down Carys's arms and grasped her hands. She didn't seem to notice how chilled they were.

"The gods were very clear. Tomorrow, Aeron will strike."

"Then why hasn't he told us? Why keep it a secret?" Carys snatched her hands from Morwyn and raked her fingers into her hair, gripping her skull. "How can he plan for victory if he hasn't even told us what he intends?"

"He must plan to tell us at the Renewal tomorrow."

Carys dragged her fingers down her face and curled them around her neck. Since first invoking the spiral at the Feast of the Dead seven moons ago, Aeron had Renewed its power on every holy day.

"This is madness, Morwyn." Her voice was hoarse with fear, with the stark knowledge that the end she no longer wished for was so close. "How can we plan a battle with only moments' notice? If we rush the fortification without foresight, the Romans will deci-mate us."

"No. That's where Gawain, and all the others who disapproved of Aeron's edict to wait, misunderstood. He's been communing with the gods all along—"

"We *know* that, Morwyn."

Annoyance flickered briefly over Morwyn's face, as if she didn't appreciate the acidic interruption. "We didn't know the full scope of his interactions, Carys. Where Gawain thought he was stalling, he really was simply waiting for the precise moment in time."

Once again she clasped her arms around her knees. Druantia's words haunted her mind. "Something's wrong, Morwyn."

"Yes. But tomorrow night, all will be well again."

"No." The unease solidified and it wasn't purely connected with terror for Maximus's safety. "The Morrigan would never keep Druantia ignorant of such plans. And Aeron—even if he didn't tell us, he should certainly have confided in our queen."

She remembered the apprehension that had crawled along her spine at their last encounter. If he had chosen to conceal his battle plan from them, what else was he hiding behind those emotionless silver eyes?

"Perhaps Druantia has always known." But Carys could hear the doubt in Morwyn's voice.

"I don't trust Aeron." It was tantamount to treason. But the certainty there was more behind his plan magnified with every passing moment. She'd find Gawain, persuade him to confide exactly what information the gods had imparted.

Morwyn let out an exasperated breath. "Perhaps you're simply blinded by your past relationship, Carys." There was an edge in her tone, as if she wasn't so much shocked by Carys's remark as irritated. "After all, you were convinced he'd disembowel and decapitate any man who dared to so much as look at you after you finished with him, weren't you?"

She frowned, unsure what Morwyn's point was. Aeron had made it plain to her that while he respected her decision that she no longer desired him, he wouldn't tolerate her fucking another man.

Of course, she hadn't, until recently, met another man she'd wanted in such a way, so his threats had never actively concerned her.

"I don't follow you."

Morwyn pulled a blade of grass and twirled it between her fingers. "He knows you keep a lover, Carys, and seems entirely indifferent to the fact."

Her lungs contracted, squeezing out the air, and the forest spun about her for one dizzying moment. "You told him?" The words echoed through her mind, as disbelief shivered through her breast. "How could you betray my trust, Morwyn?"

"Of course I didn't tell him."

Carys scarcely registered the offense in Morwyn's tone. "You told him I was at the Cauldron yesterday." Of course that didn't mean anything; she was often at the Cauldron, but now—now it took on special significance because what else had Morwyn told Aeron? What else did Morwyn *know*? Had she seen Maximus approach the Cauldron? Had she guessed who her secret lover really was?

Had she told Aeron of her suspicions?

"Goddess." Morwyn sounded highly affronted. "Why would I tell him we left you at the Cauldron yesterday? That would lead to admitting you'd gone to the settlement and been attacked by Roman scum."

She rested her chin on her raised knees and shut her eyes. Her guilt was clouding every word Morwyn uttered. If she didn't control her emotions, she'd give herself away.

Yet what did it matter? After tomorrow the reason for her deceit would no longer be. The Druids would once again take their rightful place, their people would be free of the yoke of Rome, and Maximus would be defeated or dead.

Rome never surrendered. Whatever Morwyn thought, the invaders would never turn and flee like cowardly rats.

Aeron could delude himself the battle was already won, but she couldn't see it ending without horrific bloodshed on both sides. It didn't matter that she knew her gods and goddesses were powerful beyond imagination.

Because Maximus, the Romans, believed the very same thing of their own immortals.

For one bone-numbing moment the sound of bloody battle filled her mind, and the stench of decay turned her stomach. Darkness descended, obscuring the mutilated bodies, muffling the cries of the wounded.

In the distance a single flame flickered, alone, vulnerable. Without knowing why she held her breath, willing the fragile light to survive the slaughter.

Do not let us be extinguished.

Shivers raced along her arms, her shoulders, danced over her scalp. *Cerridwen commands.* But her command made no sense. How could she keep a flame alight in the midst of battle, of death?

Realization hovered on the edge of her consciousness, and seeped insidiously into her coherent thoughts.

She had to thwart the Renewal of the sacred spiral tomorrow night.

Maximus spread the maps over his desk and jabbed his finger at the forest. "I want this area to be thoroughly searched."

Aquila glanced up. "Again?"

"The cartography is flawed." He leaned back in his chair and refused to rub his temples, which had ached since Carys had left this morn.

Aquila rolled up the map. "I'll see to it."

"Take only our most trusted, Aquila. I'm certain that fucking Druid's there, but if Carys's relatives are hiding in the forest, none of them are to be harmed."

"I understand." But the look Aquila shot him made him wonder how much his Primus truly understood.

"When you go, I'll accompany you." He wanted no man but himself to gut that Druid. To string him up and crucify him in the center of the settlement to show what the consequences were of violating his woman.

"There's no need." Aquila's voice was stiff with affront.

Maximus knew there was no need. He trusted his Primus to keep his counsel, trusted Aquila to bring him the Druid without arousing undue suspicion, and yet there was a terrible gnawing inside his brain, an itch he couldn't scratch, a dull sense of urgency he couldn't fathom.

An irrational *need* to return to the forest, unrelated to the consuming desire to capture the cursed Druid.

He gritted his teeth. The day was almost over. Carys would soon return—she had better soon return—and this insistent desire would recede.

He'd scout the area tomorrow. Alone.

She entered his quarters as evening descended, and only when she tugged the linen from her head and smiled at him did the corded knots in his gut relax.

"You're late."

"I meant to leave earlier. I'm sorry."

Had she just apologized? He hid his astonishment by leaving his desk and striding toward her. "I trust you didn't need to castrate any male in my absence."

"Only a dozen or so." Then she flung her arms around his neck and pressed herself against him. "I missed you."

"And so you should." He wrapped her close, savoring the fresh scent of her hair, the softness of her body, the warmth of her breath at his throat.

A strange peace entered his soul. Whatever obstacles her kin placed in her way, she had returned. Of her own free will.

The incessant throb between his temples eased, and the urge to examine every blade of grass in the forest receded.

All that mattered in this moment was Carys was here. In his arms.

Where she belonged.

As they ate, she spoke of her elderly female relatives, her absent mother, and the half-dozen children living with them. He listened, intrigued, because it was Carys who was speaking, because they were her kinsfolk she spoke of, but all the while his brain churned with unanswered questions.

How had so many people managed to stay so completely invisible for so long?

He wanted to warn her that their time was short. Soon they would be found, rounded up, brought back to face him. Since they hadn't, to his knowledge, attempted any form of insurgence, there was no need for punishment. Their lands could be reinstated, a favorable tribute agreed, and Carys would be free to stay with him permanently without fear of discovery.

Permanently.

The word threaded through his mind, lingering with seductive promise as Carys extolled the childish virtues of her cousin's young son.

Maximus was a patrician. It was his duty to one day marry and produce heirs for Rome. Yet the vision of a future without Carys in his life, without seeing her face, listening to her voice, being alternately fascinated and frustrated by her strength of will, caused an unaccustomed ache deep within his heart.

She was his mistress. An honorable status in his world. Wherever his career took them, she would want for nothing. And when he eventually succumbed to pressure and took a wife, he would install her in one of his family's villas, as far from Carys as possible.

Yet discontent lingered. Carys cherished her own culture, and being the mistress of a Roman tribune didn't please her as he'd envisaged. She had status of her own, and didn't need his protection in the way Efa had needed Faustus.

But if Carys was as vulnerable as Efa, or even Branwen, she wouldn't now be in his quarters, or causing so many conflicting thoughts to pound through his brain.

"Maximus, you're weary."

He placed his goblet on the table. "Not at all."

"Then my chatter bores you."

He laughed at that. "Why should you think that? I find your kin intriguing. I shall enjoy meeting them."

An oddly haunted look flashed through her eyes, as if she thought such an occurrence highly unlikely. He realized he didn't like concealing the fact he intended to flush her relatives out, but it was an army matter. Confidential.

Carys was intelligent, for a woman. Fuck, she was more intelligent than many men he could name. And she had to know that sooner or later he'd discover her hiding place.

She left her couch and kneeled before him, folding her arms across his thighs and propping her chin on her wrists. She looked up at him, as innocent as a Vestal Virgin and as tempting as Venus.

"But for now, you only have me."

He fingered her braid and began to loosen the colored linen strips that bound it. "For now, you're enough." Her silken hair rippled through his fingers, caressed his palm. "Come, lie on the couch with me. I'll begin your lessons on Roman etiquette."

"And yet we've finished eating." She didn't move to obey his request but continued to gaze up at him in that provocative manner.

"In that case, lie on the couch with me and we'll find something else to occupy our time."

Her lips twitched, as if she fought a smile. "I have a better idea, Roman." She tugged his tunic and raised her eyebrows suggestively.

With an exaggerated sigh he tossed his tunic aside and sat upright on the couch, thighs spread. "You're insatiable, Celt."

Her fingers trailed the length of his burgeoning cock, a teasing, tantalizing gesture.

"Thankfully, I'm not the only one."

"Remove your gown, and get up here now."

For answer, Carys slowly ran the tip of her tongue over her parted lips. "No." Her denial was breathy, seductive, and caused his groin to tighten with delicious anticipation.

Her fingers curled around his shaft. He smothered a groan and wound her hair around his hand, jerking her forward.

"There's something I want to do with you." Her voice was husky and her gaze was fixed between his thighs.

Gods. There was something he'd longed for her to do since the moment he'd spied her by the waterfall, but given her unexpected inexperience, he'd yet to voice his fantasy.

"What's that?" He could barely articulate the words for the way his blood thundered through his veins.

She glanced up at him through her lashes. "This." Her fingers tightened around him, sweet agony, and then she spread his knees with her elbows, and her golden hair caressed his thighs as she lowered herself to him.

Wet heat engulfed his engorged head and arrows of white-hot pleasure flashed along his cock, cradled his balls. He collapsed back onto the couch and raised his hips to allow her easier access.

Her tongue darted across his slit, exploring, tasting, escalating his need to insanity. Her fingernails teased his heavy balls, cupping him in the palm of her hand, squeezing, feeling his weight.

Through lust-glazed eyes he watched her, kneeling at his feet, her head between his thighs, her glorious hair a golden cloud around his hips and groin.

His fingers bit into her skull, pressing her more securely over his throbbing shaft. He heard her moan, the sound vibrating along his cock, felt her tongue licking him, felt the delirious suction of her mouth enslave him.

"Carys." Her name, guttural with primal need, tumbled from his lips. The reality surpassed even his most frenzied of fantasies, and involuntarily he thrust down her throat, losing himself in sheer sensation, in the knowledge he was inside Carys's mouth, taking her as she had never been taken before.

With a hoarse groan he wrenched his hands from her head, gripped her shoulders instead. He was on the cusp of coming, couldn't hold back, didn't want to hold back, wanted to fuck her and fill her and brand her for all time.

But still he released her, allowed her the choice, and another agonized groan seeped from his soul when she didn't pull off him, didn't retreat, but instead increased the pressure of her mouth enclosing his straining shaft.

He flung back his head and pounded into her, shooting his seed down her throat, on and on, as if it had been years since he'd last emptied his sac instead of only that morn. Stars exploded behind his closed eyes, volcanoes erupted deep in his groin, and summer sun flooded through his hammering heart.

Dimly, beyond the sound of his rasping breaths, he heard a strange gargling noise, as Carys slid her mouth from his still-pumping cock. He watched her sink back onto her heels, hand over her mouth, eyes wide with shock.

He reached out a shaking hand and pulled his discarded tunic toward them. "Here." Tenderly he tugged her hand from her face and wiped her mouth with a corner of his tunic. "Spit," he added helpfully, bunching the material for her convenience.

A light blush stole over her cheeks. She pushed the tunic away with one finger and then held on to his wrist.

"I swallowed." She sounded torn between pride and surprise by the admission. "Most of it," she added with a delightfully bemused frown.

He only just prevented a laugh from erupting. No woman had ever said such a thing to him before. But then, no other woman came close to Carys. She said and did things all the time that astounded and intrigued him.

"I'm honored." He cradled her chin and brushed a gentle kiss across her lips. He could taste himself on her. "That was an unexpected pleasure."

She flashed him a seductive smile. "I know. I wanted to surprise you. It's not something I've ever wanted to try before but you're different."

For a fleeting moment his gut twisted with acidic fire at the thought of Carys pleasuring another man in such a way. And then her words sank into his brain and he sucked in a long breath.

She had given him a part of herself she had never allowed her previous lover. He wound a lock of gold around his finger and tugged. "And so are you, Carys."

She was different from all the women of Rome. Different from every Celt he'd encountered. And as he lifted her in his arms and carried her to their bedroom, an outrageous notion filtered through his mind.

If her current status caused such antipathy among the peasants, he could imagine how her kin would react. There was only one way to ensure Carys would forever be his, only one way to ensure her undivided loyalty.

As his wife.

In the early hours, before dawn tinged the horizon, he woke. Even with his eyes closed, he was aware Carys was awake, was staring at him, and something kept him from stirring.

She moved soundlessly, obviously trying not to disturb him. Her warm breath fluttered over his jaw as she leaned over him and brushed her lips against his.

"I love you, Tiberius Valerius Maximus. I'll love you forever."

A deep sense of peace, of rightness, filled his soul as she stealthily molded her body against his. She wasn't the first woman who'd said she loved him. But she was the only one who mattered.

His earlier thought, on somehow persuading the Emperor to allow him to take a foreigner, a woman of a conquered race, as his wife suddenly seemed less inconceivable, less audacious.

Suddenly, it was infinitely possible.

Early the following morn, as Maximus watched her ride from the settlement with only slightly less irritation than he'd shown the previous day, Carys pressed one hand to her churning stomach in an effort to still her nerves.

She would do everything in her power to avert the Renewal tonight, but in case the spiral once again rejuvenated, and swept through the land in a death-wielding wave, she intended to have a backup plan in place.

In an agony of anxiety she waited at the sacred spring for patients who never arrived, before she returned to the spiral and spent the rest of the morn and midday meal with her cousin and Morwyn.

Until finally it was time to put her plan into action.

By the time she reached the Cauldron and tethered her mare, her hands were shaking. But she knew she was doing the right thing. It was the only way she could ensure Maximus would remain safe, whether a battle ensued or not.

"Sweet Cerridwen, give me a sign." She closed her eyes and waited for her goddess, but Cerridwen remained elusive.

Carys bit her lip and glanced at the sparkling spring. If her goddess appeared and told her she was following the wrong path, would she turn back? Would she allow fate her hand and risk Maximus's death?

She drew in a deep breath. This was the only way she knew how to protect her beloved. And nothing would stand in her way.

She pulled out the pouch containing the shards of bluestones. The magic incantations thrummed in her mind, the shielding spell Aeron had uttered during the Feast of the Dead when he'd activated the sacred spiral.

He used similar incantations for each Renewal, but Carys was staying with the original, as she had that night Maximus had become her lover.

She prepared the potpourri, burned the incense, meditated over each individual shard of bluestone. Unimaginable power hummed from each stone, a mere fragment of the power harnessed by the massive stones circling the cromlech, but more than enough for her purposes tonight.

Finally, the illicit incantation was complete. Aeron would have her head on a spear if he discovered she'd tapped into his power, but he wouldn't find out, and within moments her crime would be concealed by the very power she was forbidden to invoke.

She kneeled on the grass and reverently placed the first bluestone in place.

"Carys."

Her fingers froze, her breath hitched midway between lungs and lips, and a chilling terror raced along her spine. She wanted the earth to open and swallow her, swallow the evidence of her actions, but all she could do was slowly turn her head and look across to the other side of the stream at the Druid on horseback.

Druantia.

Chapter Thirty-one

She watched Druantia urge the horse through the shallow stream, toward her, and couldn't move from her knees in any attempt to hide the damning evidence. Only when the great queen beckoned her forward to help her dismount did feeling return to her numb limbs, and she dropped the bluestones in a heap and hurried to the elderly Druid's side.

"What—Why are you traveling outside the spiral?" Carys hovered around Druantia, and wondered if she could possibly bluff her way out of this. There was no reason why Druantia should know what she was doing. Not if the Morrigan could no longer see her. And surely Cerridwen didn't disapprove to such a degree that she had summoned the great Druid?

"I left the spiral to find you, Carys."

Druantia had never left the spiral before. Guilt clawed her gut. "I was coming to see you later this eve."

Druantia leaned her weight on Carys's arm. "What are you doing with the sacred bluestones, my child?"

Heat flared through her brain, burning her cheeks. Druantia's eyesight was poor. But still she knew of the bluestones, hidden in the grass.

"The bluestones?" Could she pretend not to know what Druantia meant? "I don't—"

"Carys." Druantia sighed, a featherlight whisper. "My love for you drew me here. I knew you were doing something against the edicts of the goddess, but this—What is this, my child? Do you seek to snatch power from Aeron as he invokes the Renewal?"

"Of course not." It was foolish to pretend she wasn't in possession of the sacred stones. "I care nothing for Aeron's power." She took Druantia's free hand and kissed her twisted fingers. She had promised Morwyn to keep her counsel, but her heart couldn't believe it right to keep their great queen in ignorance. "Druantia, do you know what's going to happen tonight?"

"The battle that shall not be a battle?" Druantia gave an odd smile, as if the phrase darkly amused her. "The Morrigan has long urged for such, but the gods are divided." She paused for a moment. "Last night Morwyn told me of Aeron's plans that Gawain had discovered."

"How can he plan to attack when he hasn't told us?" Carys could feel her agitation rising once again and struggled to contain it. "As far as he's concerned, none of us are aware of what he has in mind."

Druantia patted her hand, as if trying to comfort her. "I love Aeron as a son of my bloodline. He's proved his worth as a Druid many times over, despite his humble birth. I always believed you were destined for him and yet now—I fear you were right to choose another."

"But you gave me your blessing yesterday, Druantia."

"I did, and I meant it. But in my heart I still believed you'd made a mistake in refusing Aeron." Druantia peered into the sky, then studied the grass. "I was blinded by my love. For many moons the Morrigan has shown me the growing unrest among her kin.

I thought it was all concerned with the Romans. But now, my eyes are opened."

Unformed dread weaved through Carys's heart at the realization Druantia wasn't infallible, that her queen could be deceived.

"What do you see?"

Druantia closed her eyes for a brief moment. "It's Aeron who's been causing the dissent among the goddesses and gods. I don't know why. What reason can he have? And yet the Morrigan is convinced, even though she stands alone on this."

"What does Cerridwen believe?"

Druantia looked at her. Pain clouded her faded eyes. "Cerridwen hasn't honored me with her presence since the hour of your birth. I've known nothing of her for the last twenty summers."

Prickles of alarm skittered over her skin. Druantia was their queen, the great Druid, the ancient one. Although she was affiliated with the Morrigan, her power was such that she could commune with all their gods and goddesses.

Why had Cerridwen turned from Druantia?

At the same moment the Morrigan had turned from *her*?

"So tell me, my child." Druantia's voice pulled her back to the present. "Why you're using the sacred bluestones at Cerridwen's Cauldron? What is her purpose here?"

She couldn't let Druantia believe Cerridwen was engaged in subterfuge. She'd have to confide in her.

"This isn't by Cerridwen's command." She hitched in a shaky breath and hoped Druantia would at least try to understand. "I'm calling on the power of the spiral to protect my lover tonight, to keep him safe while the battle rages." *If* the battle raged, but she wouldn't burden Druantia with that added knowledge.

Druantia's wrinkles multiplied as she frowned in evident confusion. "Your lover intends to hide here tonight?"

Carys swallowed the nerves that threatened to render her speechless. "No. He knows nothing of this. I plan to—to lure him here. And then give him a sleeping draught."

"You're going to drug him and keep him hidden whilst his countrymen rid the scourge from our lands?" Druantia sounded incredulous, as if she couldn't believe she'd properly understood.

And of course Druantia hadn't, because she hadn't told the Druid the entire truth.

"I don't want him to die." The words were defiant. If Aeron had his way tonight and the spiral swept through the land, her Roman would never surrender, never retreat. Therefore, he would die.

She wouldn't allow it.

"Perhaps he would rather die than be kept from fighting for freedom by your magical potions."

"I don't care." One way or another, Maximus would survive this night. That was all that mattered.

"But what of the morrow? No man of honor would wish to live with such shame."

Injustice bubbled deep in her gut, heating her blood, rousing her temper. She refused to think of the morrow, didn't want to contemplate how Maximus would react when he discovered what she'd done, or what had happened while he'd been unconscious.

Tomorrow could take care of itself. But tonight she'd do anything within her power to ensure Aeron didn't destroy everything she loved.

"There will be no shame." But if the Romans were defeated, if they were driven from Cymru, what did she imagine Maximus would do? Stay with her? Embrace her culture, her Druidry?

"Your lover saved you from certain death in the immortal realm." Druantia's grip on her fingers became painful. "He is no sniveling coward, Carys. His love for you will die if you continue with this selfish action."

Carys snatched her hands free. "It's not selfish to try to prevent senseless bloodshed and death." And that was what she was trying to do, that was what she was *going* to do, and the only reason she intended to hide Maximus was in case Aeron still managed to Renew the spiral.

She didn't know if Maximus loved her or whether he only enjoyed her company because of the sex. It didn't matter. She loved him, and intended to keep him.

And she wouldn't think of the consequences.

"Hush." Druantia raised her finger in warning. "Someone comes." She paused, and Carys tried to calm her stampeding heart, her turbulent thoughts, and concentrate on the earth, on the subtle changes that heralded unseen events.

She felt nothing. Trepidation trickled along her nape. *Where was Cerridwen?*

Maximus dismounted as he entered the wood that led to Carys's special glade. All morn he'd ignored the sense of urgency that had throbbed in his brain since the moment she disappeared from sight, but no longer could he put off scouting the area.

It had nothing to do with regard to her safety, or the possibility that today she might not return to him. Despite the annoyance that spiked through him at the knowledge she would never simply sit in his dwelling all day and wait for his return, he didn't actively mind her visiting her kin. He knew, with solid certainty, she would always come back.

This urgency was completely unconnected with her, and focused entirely on the anomaly of the shrunken forest.

And the closer he'd ridden to the forest, the more insistent the desire to enter it became.

Even his fury for the Druid bastard, which coiled around his guts and raked through his chest every time he recalled the scene in the glade, diminished beneath that all-consuming need.

He hadn't expected to see Carys by her spring, but she was there and appeared in deep discussion with her companion.

She whirled to face him the moment he stepped from the shadows, as if something had warned her of his approach. The woman she was with also turned, and his heart ricocheted against his ribs.

Never had he seen such an ancient creature. She appeared so fragile, so wizened, he could scarcely comprehend she was still in the mortal realm.

Slowly he advanced. Tension crackled in the air and the look of frozen horror on Carys's face as she shielded the old lady from his sight was like a blade through his heart.

He halted and removed his helmet as a sign of trust. His eyes never left Carys.

"Carys, who is this man?" The old woman spoke in Celtic, and hobbled to stand beside Carys, her milky eyes fixed on him with chilling loathing.

Carys swallowed and shot him an agonized glance, as if begging him not to acknowledge their relationship. "A Roman tribune."

Every nerve tensed. Was that all the introduction she deemed necessary? All the introduction he deserved?

He tore his gaze from her and stared at the other. "My name is Tiberius Valerius Maximus, at your service." He spoke in her language and inclined his head as a show of respect for her great age.

The old woman advanced two steps, before Carys clutched at her arm and halted her progress. "And I ask again, Carys." The woman's voice was clear, strong, at startling odds with her appearance. "Who is this man?"

He watched the blood drain from Carys's cheeks, as if she too guessed the old woman already knew the answer.

"He saved me from attack in the settlement."

Not a lie. Yet not the full truth. And again he wondered whether she had spoken such to him.

A shudder rippled over the woman's frail frame, but when Carys went to comfort her, she held up one trembling hand in autocratic disdain.

Carys sprung back, as if the action scalded.

"This is the one who found you in the goddess's domain." It wasn't a question. And still those eerie eyes bored into him, as if searching out the secrets of his soul.

Carys cast him a despairing glance and he took a step toward her, wanting to support her against her antagonistic kin, but he stopped short when she sank to her knees before the old woman.

The blade in his heart twisted. Carys didn't belong on her knees. She was proud, independent, beholden to none, so why did she hold this old crone's hand in a gesture of reverence, kiss her fingers as if she begged for mercy, and look as if she was worshipping at the altar of one of her wild, heathen goddesses?

The sight offended him. More, it enraged him. And yet he could do nothing, for Carys clearly loved this wretched woman and didn't want her displeasure.

For Carys, he would hold his tongue, still his sense of injustice. But he couldn't prevent the warning glare he shot the old one's way.

"Druantia, please forgive me. I didn't mean for this to happen."

The old hag finally severed eye contact with him and focused on Carys. "Thank Cerridwen that the Morrigan can no longer see you, child. For if she could, you would be naught but dust beneath my feet."

Carys visibly blanched, and he gritted his teeth at the threat.

"I've done nothing wrong, Druantia. Please. You understand? All I've done is love."

Druantia hooked her twisted fingers beneath Carys's chin and peered into her upturned face as if searching for words unsaid. Then she gave a rasping sigh, as if the last breath from her body was escaping.

"I see the truth in your eyes. I feel the truth in your heart. But it changes nothing. Rome is our enemy." Briefly she glanced his way, and a needle-sharp pain darted through his brain, vanishing as instantly as it had began, as if the witch had somehow penetrated his core and assessed his worth.

For a fleeting moment her features softened before she once again returned her attention to Carys. "Yet Cerridwen protects you. She allowed the Roman access to physically reclaim you from the Morrigan's sacred realm. I don't pretend to understand her motives, Carys. But all I know is this."

She tugged Carys to her feet, and as the two women held hands and maintained eye contact, a shiver scuttled over his arms despite the warmth of the day.

Druantia straightened, although he could tell the action caused her great discomfort. "Whatever path you're on, my child, is the path chosen for you by Cerridwen. I can't approve of it, but I'll do nothing to jeopardize your safety." There was a taut silence, as if the words held hidden meaning. "Do *you* understand?"

"I understand." Carys bowed her head. "Thank you."

Druantia advanced toward him. For one insane moment the urge to fall to his knees before her assailed him, as if she were a female embodiment of how he'd always secretly imagined Charon would look as he ferried the dead across the Styx.

Sheer willpower alone kept him upright and rigid as she paused by his side and gave him another assessing look. Then she turned back to Carys, who hovered behind her in obvious distress.

"He is Roman. And yet my words to you remain true. Think on the morrow, Carys. The sun will always rise no matter how you wish it otherwise."

Her words made no sense to him but obviously did to Carys, as heat flared in her cheeks as if she resented the remark. But without another word she helped Druantia onto her mare and then stood by his side to watch the old woman ride over the ridge toward the forest.

He should follow her. She'd lead him to the hiding place. And yet the thought of tailing such an ancient one caused bile to rise.

He was a soldier, and he would find where Carys's kin were hiding by his own efforts. It couldn't be far. Druantia was in no state to ride for any length of time.

Yet the urge to forgo his principles and follow her anyway plagued his mind.

"Thank you." Carys curled her fingers around his arm and

smiled up at him, but he could see the tension traced around her eyes, the strain etched around her lips.

"For what?"

Confusion flared in her eyes. Would he ever tire of looking into those eyes of hers?

"For not questioning her. About where we live."

He offered her a brief smile devoid of humor. "I'm not in the habit of terrorizing elderly women."

Her smile softened, the tension diminished. "Oh, I wasn't concerned that you'd terrorize her, Maximus. I simply want to thank you for not questioning her."

"You can thank me later." He had a few ideas how she could thank him, but now was neither the time nor the place. He had to investigate why the cartography was so amiss and discover the mystery of the illusion.

But more than any of that, he had to enter the forest. It was of paramount importance. And only then could all other concerns be addressed.

"I want to speak to you about later." She hung on his arm, smiling up at him in an enchanting manner, and a part of him wanted to take her in his arms and elicit a promise from her that *later* she would accede to all his demands, whether they concerned her future status as his wife, or her future home in Rome.

But he had to unravel the puzzle of the forest.

"What about it?" He glanced in the direction Druantia had vanished. He didn't want to follow her, and yet the certainty gripped him that there was only one path into the cursed forest he could take.

Carys tugged on his arm, and with strange reluctance he turned back to her.

"I want us to have our evening meal here, by the Cauldron." She stared at him expectantly, as if waiting for his enthused response.

He flicked his glance at the spring. Recalled the first time they'd fucked. *Made love.*

His cock stirred as arousal flared through his veins. "If you wish. Tell the slaves to bring whatever you require here."

For a moment she looked startled, as if she hadn't expected him to agree so readily. "I'm preparing everything myself tonight. Just the two of us."

"I look forward to it. But now I must go."

Still she clung on to his arm, and he saw the furtive glance she cast in the direction Druantia had gone.

"So soon? Can't you stay with me a little longer?"

He wasn't fooled. "Carys, I have no intention of following Druantia. I'll find your hiding place by my own efforts." He uncurled her fingers that were biting into his flesh, and brushed his lips across them. "I understand your concern, but there's no need to fear. I'll never harm Druantia or any of your kin."

"I know." And yet he clearly saw the fear in her eyes even as she denied it.

There wasn't time to discuss it further. The urgency thrummed through his blood, pulling him onward. Briefly he wondered at the logic of his haste, but brushed it aside.

It was imperative he investigate the area, before Aquila led the First Cohort there.

"I'll see you back at our quarters. We'll come here together." He kissed her lips, and for a brief moment the urgency faded as her mouth welcomed his, but then he pulled away, replaced his helmet, and shot her a lascivious grin. "Don't forget the blankets, Celt."

⋘⋙

He couldn't place it, but there was something very wrong about this part of the forest. He'd lost count of the times his horse, a creature with nerves of iron and courage to match any centurion, shied away in clear distress from, apparently, nothing.

And yet he understood the animal's abnormal behavior, because the skin on his nape crawled with unspecified repugnance, as if malignant spirits hid behind each looming tree.

There was nothing here. No tracks, no trails, no sign of human habitation. Why was he here, in any case? All he'd intended was to once again observe the forest from the hilltop, check out its boundaries, compare them to the maps.

Instead, he'd spent Mars knew how long inside this cursed forest and he couldn't fathom why.

An odd shimmer up ahead caught his attention. Inexplicably he was reminded of the night he'd met with Carys in her special glade, but there were no lanterns casting a mystical glow here to bewitch his senses.

Stealthily he approached the phenomenon. Vertigo hit him at the same instant his horse reared in fright, a dizzying disconnectedness spinning his brain in his skull, and then a sharp, stabbing sensation pierced the side of his neck and blackness engulfed his world.

Chapter Thirty-two

Aeron slipped the blow dart into his pouch and climbed down the tree. The Roman lay sprawled on the ground, unconscious and vulnerable.

He kicked him savagely in the ribs. Fucking bastard. He gripped the bejeweled handle of his ceremonial dagger and resisted the overpowering urge to slit the barbarian's throat and watch the blood flow into the waiting earth.

The time was not yet right. Only at the precise moment when the sun set and cast its dying light into the passage of the mound, when for the only moments of the year the sun's rays penetrated to the central underground chamber, would he spill the Roman's lifeblood.

Swiftly, he encased the body in sackcloth to disguise its appearance, before winding restraints around the ankles and securing them to the Roman's horse. It was only fitting the creature should drag its master to his death.

He led the horse through the forest toward the cromlech. No

one would stop him or inquire what he was doing. A sacrifice was always required at the Renewal. No Druid would assume the sacrifice this night would possess only two legs.

A dark excitement thundered through his veins. His original plan had magnified beyond his most ambitious fantasies. To spill sacred Druid blood and cursed Roman blood during the same ceremony would ensure his position for eternity.

As he loosened the bindings from the horse and dragged the enemy into the mouth of the deserted mound, another pleasant thought intruded.

There would be no need to sacrifice Carys at the altar of retribution. Her punishment would be to watch her filthy lover die, to hear his screams of terror, his cowardly begs for mercy as Aeron, High Druid and God on Earth, gouged the Roman's eyes from his sockets, ripped his tongue from his mouth and sliced his balls from his groin.

And as the Roman lay dying, before he carved his black heart from his chest, he'd fuck Carys so the barbarian could hear every cry, every gasp, every fucking grunt and thrust.

His cock throbbed at the vision. At the possibility that despite her betrayal he might still allow Carys to live, to service his needs as his personal slave. After tonight her status would be gone, and so would her tongue.

He'd fuck her mouth but he never wanted to hear another word emerge from her lying lips.

After tonight, his word would be law. His every wish obeyed. Peasant and Druid alike would worship him as the one almighty god, and his power over the old goddesses, over their ancient matrilineal traditions, would be supreme.

The circle was complete, except for the necessary gap, and Carys poured the sleeping draught she'd prepared into a small pottery jug.

She wouldn't think about Druantia's warning. Maximus would understand she had done what she had only through love.

He's a Roman tribune. A warrior. A commander. And she thought he wouldn't care she had hidden him away in case a bloody battle raged?

Carys ignored the voice and concealed the jug in a stone crevice close to the bubbling spring.

And now she had to find Aeron and discover how to thwart his plans for tonight.

Carys stepped outside the circle and reverently placed the last shard of bluestone in place. Instantly, the grassed area within the circle contracted and vanished, as if that piece of earth no longer existed. No one could enter the circle, for no one could see it or feel it, and she dropped a pile of pebbles by the bluestone to ensure she'd recall its exact position for later.

Something made her glance up, but the sky looked perfectly normal. How high did the magic extend? She didn't really understand how it worked, only that it did, and had protected her people from discovery for the last seven moons.

Just as this illicitly wrought magic would protect her Roman from discovery.

Panic shuddered through her, harsh and shocking, as she suddenly realized how low the sun had sunk. Evening approached already. Did she have time to confront Aeron before she needed to meet with Maximus and ensure his safety?

She had no choice. Cerridwen had charged her with changing Aeron's plan, and even if she failed in fulfilling that command, at least she'd tried.

Finally she reached the outer circle of bluestones. Heart pounding, she peered toward the cromlech, but it was deserted. Of course, every Druid avoided this area on Renewal days, as Aeron required absolute privacy for his meditations, but he usually undertook those meditations in his favorite place, by the sacred altar.

She hitched in a shaky breath and tethered her mare to a sapling. There was only one other place Aeron would be so late on this day.

In the center of the mound. Preparing his sacrifice.

Cautiously she approached the cromlech. It was one thing to confront Aeron, and quite another to have him catch her unawares, and she had no intention of allowing herself to be at any disadvantage.

But as she stepped into the inner circle of bluestones, a sensation of utter despair gripped her, so violent she fell to her knees as the world spun out of control.

Cerridwen, what was wrong? It was as if all the joy had been sucked from the world, leaving behind a decayed husk of nothingness, a black void that ate into her soul, corroded her heart and chilled the marrow in her bones.

Her breath rasped her throat, echoed through her ears. Against every instinct that urged her to lie down and close her eyes and allow sleep to claim her, she struggled to her feet as her medicine bag tumbled to the ground.

"Great Morrigan, what ails you, Carys?" Morwyn gripped her arms and pulled her upright. "Are you ill?"

Carys staggered against the other woman. "Can't you feel it?"

Morwyn frowned. "Feel what? And what are you doing here? Aeron requires absolute solitude on these days."

"I need to find him." She picked up her bag and slung it across her shoulder. "Why are you here?"

Morwyn nodded to the woven basket she held. "The Morrigan's sacrifice for tonight. Usually Aeron ensures he has everything necessary for the ceremony, but obviously the coming battle's clouded his mind."

The nausea roiling through her system subsided as she recalled her purpose. "I'll come with you." It gave her an excuse to enter the mound. And once there, she would trust Cerridwen to show her what she needed to do.

"If you wish." Morwyn slid her an odd glance and advanced toward the stone altar, where five flaming torches were arranged in the sacred pentagram, and set the basket down. "There. Now we'll go and prepare ourselves for this night."

Involuntarily, Carys glanced to the sky. Sweet goddess, how had this day passed by so swiftly? If she couldn't find Aeron within the next few moments, if she couldn't somehow discover a way to avert the coming battle, she'd have to flee the spiral instantly so she could put her own plans into action.

Sweat prickled. Even if she left now, would she make it, with Maximus, back to the Cauldron in time? Ensure he took her sleeping draught and then return to the spiral before she was missed?

Every logical sense screamed it was impossible. And yet *she had no choice.*

"I need to enter the mound and speak with Aeron." She turned from Morwyn, but her friend gripped her arm and swung her around, a look of horror on her face.

"You can't do that. He could strike you insensible for daring to intrude."

Sweet Cerridwen, protect me.

"No, he won't. I have to go, Morwyn." With another anxious glance at the sky, she ran toward the opening of the mound.

Ceremonial lanterns swung from hooks inserted in the ancient earthen ceiling as she stepped into the downward-sloping passageway. But she'd gone only a few paces before she heard Morwyn running behind her.

Without waiting for her to catch up, she increased her speed, ignoring the openings that led to smaller chambers in which the Druids had lived these past seven moons.

Aeron would be in the sacred center, deep underground.

She halted at the mouth, held her breath and peered into the dimly lit chamber. It was empty. Her heart scudded, stomach churned. She was out of time; she'd failed Cerridwen, but she would not fail Maximus.

Morwyn panted over her shoulder. "Where's Aeron? There's nothing here but the sacrifice."

She'd scarcely noticed the bundle of sackcloth dumped at the outer edge of the faint illumination. The sacrifice didn't matter. And yet she stared at the dark shape with strange fascination.

"Goddess, what are you *doing*?" Morwyn sounded exasperated but Carys ignored her and crouched over the concealed creature.

"Morwyn." Her voice shook as a terrible certainty came to her. "This is a human sacrifice."

Morwyn hunkered beside her. "Of course it isn't." She didn't sound convinced, for the shape was undoubtedly human, not animal.

Carys pulled her dagger from her belt and rapidly sliced through the bindings. This was why Cerridwen had led her here. To prevent Aeron from sacrificing a human, which would somehow thwart his battle plans. And she would still have time to race back to Maximus's quarters and—

Her thoughts stumbled, backed up, choked. It couldn't be. With shaking hands, she ripped the sackcloth from the man's head, and all doubt vaporized.

"Maximus." She whispered his name as her heart squeezed with agonized denial in her breast. She wrapped her hands around his head, leaned toward him so her breath warmed his chilled flesh.

"You know him? Who is it?" Morwyn jostled against her, trying to see.

He couldn't be dead. She wouldn't let him be dead. How could she be too late to save him?

Morwyn recoiled, breath hissing between her teeth. "It's a Roman." She dug her fingers into Carys's shoulder and wrenched her back. "It's a fucking Roman, Carys. How do you know his name?"

Carys shoved Morwyn's hand away. "He's the man I love. And if Aeron's harmed him, I swear by Arawn, lord of the Otherworld, I'll have vengeance."

Morwyn visibly blanched. "A Roman?" she repeated in disbelief, but Carys ignored her, because Morwyn's approval didn't matter. Nothing would ever matter again if Maximus had been murdered to satisfy Aeron's evil sense of justice.

He wouldn't murder his sacrifice.

The realization thundered through her brain, and she pressed her fingers against his throat, searching for his pulse, her lips brushing his as she waited to feel his breath.

A choked sob escaped. He was alive. As her fingers slipped from his pulse, a sharp sting grazed her and she pulled a dart from his neck.

Rage bubbled, clouding her reason, obliterating the last lingering tendrils of terror.

She turned to Morwyn, the dart lying on her palm. "This is how Aeron took him down. The cowardly bastard."

"You love a *Roman*."

Carys pulled the flickering lantern nearer and slit open the rough sackcloth. She could see no blood, his limbs weren't oddly angled, but still she swiftly examined him to ensure there were no broken bones.

Morwyn shoved her savagely, and she tumbled onto Maximus's armored chest. Enraged, she glared over her shoulder, but Morwyn's face was twisted with a matching fury.

"What did you tell him about us, Carys, as you fucked the Roman barbarian?"

"I told him nothing of us." She ripped open her bag and hunted for a reviving elixir, trying to ignore the hurt Morwyn's accusation caused, trying to ignore the way her hands shook.

"So why is he here? How did he penetrate the sacred spiral if you didn't tell him?"

She turned back to Maximus and pulled the stopper from the

small pottery jar. The pungent aroma caused her eyes to water. *Sweet Cerridwen, let him wake.*

"The Romans aren't stupid, Morwyn. They were always going to find the way into the spiral sooner or later."

"Yes, with your help. I can't believe you've betrayed your people."

She laid her palm over his forehead, then felt his rapidly strengthening pulse. "I betrayed no one."

But was that the truth? Hadn't she, in reality, betrayed both her fellow Druids and Maximus by her actions?

Maximus gave a harsh cough and opened his eyes. And Carys knew, with soul-deep conviction, that even if she was tried and found guilty of treason by her people, she would never regret anything she'd done for the hours spent in his arms.

"Get out of my way." Morwyn pushed her shoulder and Carys dragged her gaze from Maximus to stare at the other woman.

"Morwyn, sheathe your dagger." Instinctively Carys angled herself between Morwyn and Maximus. "I won't allow you to harm him."

"You won't *allow me* to destroy the scum who've raped our land and people?" Morwyn spat on the ground at Carys's feet. "I don't need your permission, whore."

Before Morwyn had time to take a breath, Carys smashed her right fist against her jaw, and her left hammered the wrist holding the deadly dagger. As Morwyn crumpled, Carys wrenched the dagger from her hand.

"Cerridwen led me here." She jabbed the dagger in Morwyn's face before sheathing it at her own waist. "If she didn't approve of my choice, do you think she would have allowed me to find him?"

Morwyn spat blood before wiping her mouth with the back of her hand. "Perhaps you manipulate the Wise One, as you've manipulated us all."

Denial sprung to her lips, yet a terrible doubt throbbed in her mind. Had she manipulated those she loved?

She thrust the thought aside. There wasn't time to agonize over her actions now. "No mortal can manipulate the gods." Especially not Cerridwen, the wisest of them all.

Maximus rolled onto his side, kicked off the shredded sackcloth still clinging to his legs and let out a rasping groan. Instantly she turned to him, and wrapped her arms around his shoulders for support.

"Can you stand?" It was imperative they leave before Aeron returned.

He rubbed his neck where the dart had penetrated.

"How did I get here?" He cast a suspicious glance around the chamber, pausing only briefly to assess Morwyn's antagonistic glare, before refocusing on her.

"I think Aeron brought you here. But we have to leave immediately." She hoped the poison hadn't affected the strength in his legs. He was far too heavy for her to drag any distance, and Morwyn certainly wouldn't help.

"Who's Aeron?"

"Yes, Carys," Morwyn said in accented Latin, venom dripping from every word. "Tell your Roman lover who Aeron is. Tell him what Aeron plans for his precious Legion this eve."

Carys saw the sharp glance Maximus shot her way, as if he suddenly realized Morwyn was no peasant from the settlement, but an educated woman with enough status to speak to her as she pleased.

She picked up her dagger from the ground. "Cerridwen charged me to stop him, and that's what I intend to do." But first she would ensure Maximus's safety. If only he would stand up.

"Be silent!" Morwyn, once more resorting to Celtic, was on her knees and glared at her with loathing. "Cerridwen has nothing to do with this, and you know it. This is all you, Carys, wanting what you can't have."

"What does Aeron intend to do this eve?" Maximus heaved himself upright. And then his features hardened. "Where's my gladius?"

Relieved she didn't have to explain Aeron's plans, Carys glanced wildly around the chamber. "I don't know. Here, take this." She handed him the dagger he had given her the other day. "We don't have time to search, Maximus," she said, her voice rising in desperation as he gave the weapon a derisive glance. "Please, you have to trust me. We need to go before Aeron finds you."

With obvious difficulty, Maximus got to his feet. He looked as if the slightest shove would send him reeling. She pulled his left arm around her shoulders for additional support, and tightened her grip on her dagger.

"What the fuck happened to me?" Maximus stumbled against her, his balance clearly still compromised by Aeron's poisoned dart. "The last I recall I was in the forest. And then—here."

"But what were you doing in the forest, Roman?" Morwyn, stalking by Carys's side, slung him a condemning glance.

He grimaced, as if every step pained him. Goddess, she hoped she could take his weight until they were safe. Already the ache in her shoulders was spreading along her spine. "Searching for Carys's kin."

Even without looking her way, Carys could feel the surprise radiate from Morwyn, as if the truth was the last thing she had expected Maximus to utter.

"Searching?" Morwyn's voice was haughty. "Surely you knew the way to our domain, Roman."

Another step. The pressure against her shoulders eased slightly. She peered into the passageway ahead, praying incessantly that Aeron would not suddenly appear in the distant circle of light.

"If I'd known the way to your *domain* . . ." Maximus spoke between gritted teeth as if Morwyn's question, or his muscle weakness—probably both—irritated him. "I wouldn't have been searching for it."

The pressure against her shoulders eased a little more. Thank goddess, he appeared to be regaining his strength. Just a few more steps and they'd reach the mouth of the mound. *Don't let Aeron return yet.*

Morwyn gave a derisive snort. "You may have found us. But rest assured, none of us will allow you to leave."

Maximus gave a humorless laugh. "I don't require your permission, lady." His steps became surer. "How many of you are there?"

"Enough." Morwyn stamped toward the opening and then stopped dead.

"What is it?" Carys stiffened as Morwyn sank against the wall of the mound and motioned for them to keep back.

"Aeron's approaching the altar." Morwyn's voice was low. "But Druantia's with him."

Alarm prickled over her skin. "Aeron's never required Druantia's assistance before."

Maximus left her side and took up position on the opposite side of Morwyn. Carys saw him stiffen, and his fingers tightened around the dagger he held. Hastily she followed him, and held on to his arm in case he had the insane notion to race outside and attack Aeron.

"A Druid's temple." It was a statement, and as her heart catapulted against her ribs, her breath shortened with nervous anticipation as to his inevitable question.

She couldn't lie to him. She was a Druid and always would be, and he had to know that. But still her palms grew sweaty and her mind trembled at the confession she was about to give.

He didn't turn to her. His gaze was fixed on the altar, on the two people who approached their way.

"That's Aeron." Another statement. "Your High Priest."

"Yes." Her fingers clutched around his muscular biceps, as if she could somehow deflect the fury she could feel radiating from every pore. "Maximus, please. Listen to me."

He ignored her cajoling whisper. "You know him." There was

a chilling tone in his voice and she shivered, unsure how best to answer him.

"All my life." She wouldn't hide the truth from him anymore behind obfuscation and omission. She knew Morwyn was glaring at her, but what did it matter now what she told Maximus?

He'd found them out.

Tension vibrated from him, as if he held on to his temper by the slenderest of threads.

"Your High Priest, the man you've known all your life." He hissed the words over his shoulder while still staring outside. "That's the one I caught at your Cauldron, Carys. The one who'd ripped your gown from your breasts and was about to rape you."

Chapter Thirty-three

Shock punched her gut, sucked the air from her lungs. "Aeron?"
Surely she had misunderstood him. "But that's not possible."

"Not possible?" Morwyn darted across the mouth of the mound
and flattened herself against the wall behind Carys. "Of course it's
not possible. The High Druid would never do such a thing. Your
beloved Roman spews lies with every breath he takes."

Maximus never took his eyes from Aeron, and an uncanny
shiver raced over her arms. He must have been mistaken. Morwyn
was right. Aeron would never do such a thing.

"He has silver eyes, as cold as a frozen river at midwinter."

Nausea washed through her, congealing in the pit of her stomach. She recalled the way Aeron had looked at her yesterday, as if
she were a spirit from the Otherworld, and the way he'd spoken
to her, as if the inherent respect he'd always afforded her had been
obliterated.

She remembered Maximus's words as he'd tried to comfort her
when she awoke in his quarters; *the barbarian who attacked you,*

and in her confusion she thought he referred to his own country-man. His legionary. But he would never call another Roman such.

And in that moment she knew Maximus hadn't been mistaken. Aeron had come upon her while she was in the throes of a horrific vision, and, instead of trying to assist her, he'd violated her.

Her world, everything she valued, trembled on a precipice of doubt. How had he thought to get away with such a crime? Sweet goddess, it had been foul enough when she'd imagined a Roman barbarian had attacked her. But one of her own? A Druid?

The High Druid himself?

"See how he corrupts your mind and integrity with a few choice words?" Morwyn's whisper bit into her stupor. "I'll not hide here any longer, Carys. *I've* done nothing wrong."

Without thinking, Carys grabbed her arm. "Wait, Morwyn." But she could think of nothing to persuade the other woman to stay, to hold her tongue, to allow them time so she could somehow smuggle Maximus back to the Cauldron.

Maximus raised his arm in a warning gesture, and Morwyn bristled with affront. But before she could say anything, he shot them a penetrating look.

"Is this how your High Druid treats your elders?"

Still holding on to Morwyn's arm, Carys frowned as she peered outside. Aeron grasped Druantia's elbow and appeared to be push-ing her toward the stone altar. But that couldn't be so; he would never manhandle their ancient queen. It had to be the gathering dusk playing tricks with her eyes.

And yet Aeron had tried to rape her while she was insensible to the mortal realm.

Morwyn sucked in a shocked breath. "What's he doing? Druan-tia will fall. She'll break her bones. Goddess, is he mad?"

As if by unspoken command, they all sank back against the wall of the mound. Morwyn no longer appeared inclined to reveal herself to Aeron, and instead gripped Carys's arm in obvious confusion.

"I see no other Druids here, Aeron." Druantia's voice came to them clearly, as she and Aeron halted by the stone altar, a mere stone's throw from the mouth of the mound.

"They'll be here in time for the Renewal." The chilly smile he sent Druantia caused shivers to race over Carys's arms.

"As would I, my son." Druantia placed one hand on the stone altar, as if steadying herself. "And yet you were most insistent I come with you now, to meet with the other Chief Druids."

Carys dug her fingers into Maximus's arm as a terrible foreboding crawled over her scalp. His muscles tensed, as if he didn't appreciate her touch, but she didn't let go. Whatever he thought of her now, his presence gave her comfort, and she'd take that comfort for as long as she possibly could.

Aeron didn't answer, but instead knelt and removed a bowl from his sacred cache beneath the altar before placing it in the center of the pentagram.

But that didn't make sense. That was reserved for the blood of the sacrifice, and Aeron hadn't yet made his sacrifice. *And he never would.* She'd plunge her dagger into his evil heart before she'd allow him to take Maximus.

"Are you still planning to obliterate the Roman Legion this eve?" Druantia shifted, as if her bones ached.

"So you know about that." Aeron sounded amused, although Carys couldn't think why. And how much longer could they hide here, without being discovered?

"I know many things, Aeron."

"Ah, yes. Because of your long and illustrious bloodline that you can trace back to the Morrigan herself." He sounded scathing, and Carys felt Morwyn shiver, as if spirits from the Otherworld brushed through her soul.

"The Morrigan is concerned about you, my son."

Aeron placed a second bowl on the altar, by the torch signifying Earth. "There are two things I want you to know, Druantia." It was as if he spoke of the weather. "Firstly, I'm not your son. And secondly, I don't and never have given a fuck what the Morrigan thinks."

Carys's breath hitched in horrified disbelief, and as Morwyn pressed against her back in clear terror, she took the other woman's hand, the handle of her dagger clasped between them.

Druantia pushed herself from the altar and stepped toward Aeron. "The Morrigan chose you when you were but a child. The vision she gave you allowed you to be welcomed into our hallowed circle, to be—"

"The Morrigan?" He laughed as if he thought Druantia's words genuinely amusing. "That bitch gave me nothing. She plunged me into a bloodied vision and left me there, not caring if I survived or died. And I would have died, Druantia, if Gwydion hadn't pulled me from the carnage."

Carys knew of Aeron's childhood vision, but where did the magician god come into it? She'd never before heard of Gwydion involving himself in such matters—yet *he* was the one who'd saved Aeron?

"Gwydion?" Druantia's shock was clear. "You've never before spoken of that, Aeron."

Aeron gave another of his chilling smiles. "Of course not. It was a secret between me and the god of illusion. Because before he pulled me out, Gwydion showed me the end of that vision. The end that, as you'll see, I have also never shared with you."

Druantia straightened. Carys knew how such an action pained her, and yet she stood tall and proud and forced Aeron to make eye contact. "Share it with me now."

He laughed again, as if the queen's command delighted him. "I intend to. I've waited for this moment for too many years. But now the time is upon us." He advanced toward Druantia. "The time when all the fucking goddesses will be crushed into dust, when your precious matrilineal heritage will be wiped from the memories of mankind."

"No." Druantia's voice was whispery, as if Aeron's words shook her to the core of her being. Pain carved through Carys's heart at the stricken look on her face, and Morwyn gave a strangled gasp of escalating terror.

"Yes. My vision, thrust upon me on the longest day twenty-five years ago, is finally coming to pass." He gripped Druantia's arm. "It all ends with you, Druantia. Gwydion showed me how it must be. For my lineage to survive, yours must end."

Maximus pulled from her grasp and strode through the mouth, but before she could drag him back to safety, Aeron flung back the wrap hanging from his waist and brandished a Roman gladius.

Carys pushed Morwyn back and ran after Maximus, heart ricocheting as a terrible certainty drenched her. As if in slow motion, she saw Aeron plunge the gladius into Druantia, saw scarlet blood, saw Maximus wrench Aeron back, saw Druantia crumple onto the ground.

Chapter Thirty-four

Maximus flung Aeron onto the ground, and vertigo rushed through his head, causing him to reel. The poison was still in his system, tainting his blood, weakening his muscles, but he could sooner cut off his right hand than stand by and watch a defenseless old woman murdered.

Even if she was a Druid.

Mars take him, he was surrounded by cursed Druids, standing in the heart of the Druid enclave he and his compatriots had been searching for, for seven fruitless months.

Aeron, half naked and daubed with strange blue markings, regained his balance within the blink of an eye, and his own gladius mocked him in the hands of Rome's bitterest enemy.

From the corner of his eye he saw Carys and Morwyn kneeling by Druantia, but kept his focus on Aeron, who had a mad gleam in his eerie, soulless eyes.

"Sweet Goddess, you've killed our queen." Morwyn sounded on the verge of hysterics.

"She's not dead." Carys—*his* Carys, a fucking Druid, and the one thing he'd refused to allow his mind to dwell upon whenever he'd wondered about her strange Celtic ways—pulled her embroidered bag over her head.

"You won't save her." Aeron didn't take his gaze from him as he spoke to Carys. "Don't even try. Otherwise I'll prolong this Roman's death agony until you beg me to mercifully end his miserable existence."

Unbelievably, Carys hesitated. Maximus gritted his teeth. "Do what you can for her. This Druid bastard is drawing his last breaths."

In his peripheral vision he saw Carys trying to stem the blood, feverishly pulling strange packages and wraps from her mysterious bag. But the wound was deep; the woman was ancient. She had no hope of surviving.

"I thought the Morrigan wanted you to lead us into the new future, Carys." Druantia's hoarse whisper hovered in the blood-drenched air. "It's what she foresaw the night of your conception. But I was wrong, my child. The Great Goddess herself was wrong."

"Don't speak." Carys tenderly cradled the old woman's cheek. "Conserve your strength."

Her aged fingers clutched Carys's arm. "She saw your light in the darkness. *But it wasn't for her.*" She coughed wetly, and from the corner of his eye Maximus saw the scarlet stain her lips and chin.

"What's possessed you, Aeron?" Morwyn said as she cradled Druantia's head on her lap. "You'll die for this outrage. You'll—"

Aeron tossed the gladius from hand to hand, his eyes never leaving Maximus's. "Our queen murdered by Roman scum, by Roman sword. When I have his head, I'll be invincible to my people."

Maximus tightened his grip on the puny dagger. It was no match for his gladius. And he was no match for any man in his current weakened state.

Carys rose to her feet. Blood stained her gown and hands, and despite wanting to thrust his dagger through her heart for lying to him, for not telling him what she truly was, his own heart twisted with the absolute knowledge that he would sooner drive the dagger into his own chest than allow any harm to befall her.

"You treacherous murderer." Her voice shook. He had the insane urge to go to her, comfort her, to reassure her all would be well.

He remained where he was, focused on the male Druid.

"We'll string your steaming guts up for the crows, you filthy bastard."

With the speed of lightning, Aeron pinned Carys against his body, the tip of the gladius against her throat. Maximus tensed, and rage flooded his system, injecting new strength into his limbs, into his muscles. Aeron flicked his dagger a glance and sneered, as if the weapon was too insignificant to seriously acknowledge.

"Morwyn, take the bowl from the altar and catch fresh blood from Druantia."

"Don't do it." Carys's command was cut off as Aeron increased the pressure around her neck, and pressed the blade against her flesh. Scarlet bloomed.

An iced calm bathed Maximus's mind, channeling the rage into purpose as years of arduous training came to the fore.

"You're no longer a princess of Cymru, whore," Aeron said. "Keep my counsel and you keep your life. But no longer will you have the status of my lover. You'll be my slave."

A shaft of revulsion pierced his military discipline. This creature was Carys's ex-lover?

He would doubly enjoy the moment he took the cretin's life.

A shaking Morwyn obeyed Aeron's command and placed the bowl, with Druantia's blood, back on the heathen stone altar. Aeron relieved Carys of the gem-encrusted daggers at her waist before thrusting her aside with such force she lay gasping on the ground.

"A fitting sacrifice." Aeron indicated the barbaric display on the stone with a wave of his hand. "Blood of a Roman to rid my land of your plague, and blood of the last direct descendant of a redundant goddess to wipe out the cursed matriarchy."

Maximus tore one of the flaming torches from its mortise, and satisfaction flared at the surge of anger that flashed across Aeron's features.

"You don't have my blood, Druid."

Aeron snatched up another torch and poised it over the bowl in the center. "I do have your blood, Roman. Caught from the clasp of your cursed brooch."

His missing fibula. A chill slithered along his spine, but he allowed no emotion to show on his face. "A mere drop. It means nothing."

"How do you think you found your way through the sacred spiral, Roman? You can't see it, you can't feel it, and yet you weren't deterred from the area as all but Druids are."

Another chill attacked his marrow as comprehension dawned. The spiral was the powerful magic that distorted the forest, confused his cartographers. The spiral was the reason the Druids had been able to conceal their presence from their conquerors, despite being under their very noses.

"Aeron." Carys staggered to her feet, her face scratched and bleeding from where she'd fallen against broken stones. "No."

Maximus didn't know what she was talking about, but whatever it was appeared to terrify her.

Aeron lowered the torch toward the bowl. "Tell your lover to replace the sacred flame, Carys. You know what will happen if he doesn't."

"The fuck I'll replace it." He wiped the sweat from his eyes with his biceps. Gods, it was hot. Was this part of the heathen ceremony this madman planned?

Aeron dipped the torch lower, and Carys flung herself to her knees, clinging to his naked calf. "Please stop, Aeron."

Rage pumped through Maximus, a sweltering counterpoint to his scorching flesh. "Get up, Carys." It was an order. How dare she beg anything from this Druid?

The torch hovered inside the rim of the bowl. Where the fuck was all the air? He could scarcely draw enough breath to fill his lungs.

"Are you begging me, Carys?" The words were soft. Infuriated, Maximus lunged forward, and yet only managed to sway on his feet as acrid smoke filled his chest.

But there was no fire. Sweat dripped into his eyes, drenched his body, but still he couldn't move, could scarcely think, yet all the while his skin burned as if jabbed with a thousand candles.

"Yes." Her voice was strong, sure. "I'll replace the torch for you, if you replace yours."

Aeron gave a short laugh. "You must learn your new place, Carys. Slaves don't make bargains with their masters. If you want to save this Roman from frying, then you must show due respect."

Carys shot him an agonized glance before returning her attention to Aeron. "I do respect you." She didn't sound convincing.

Maximus expelled a breath that seared his lungs and rasped his throat. Jupiter, he felt as if he was being roasted alive.

A dread suspicion sliced through his brain. He shot a glance to the torch dipping inside the bowl, and his guts roiled. The Druid possessed his blood. And was using his heathen magic to burn him alive.

"Let me see how much you want to save this Roman." Aeron waved the gladius beneath Carys's chin. "Strip naked and beg me for mercy."

"Wh-what?"

Maximus staggered forward, lurched against the stone altar. "Don't do it, Carys." Every word seared flesh from his throat.

Aeron's gaze fixed on Carys's upturned face. "Remove your gown." Lust dripped from every syllable. "Unbind your hair. Grovel at my feet, you worthless bitch. Or watch him burn."

Chapter Thirty-five

Maximus concentrated all his energy on moving forward, while he focused on the mad Druid whose attention was still fixed on Carys.

She wouldn't subjugate herself so, but he had no intention of letting this farce continue. He'd crush Aeron, not only for what he was but for what he was doing to Carys.

"Aeron." Morwyn touched his arm, then flinched back as if the contact repelled. "Even if you escape the wrath of our people, you'll never be able to hide from the retribution of the gods."

"Hide?" For a fleeting moment he glanced at Morwyn before returning his silver gaze back to Carys. "This is my destiny. Why should I hide from gods whose power fades beside the one true force of Annwyn?"

"But the Universal Life Force is part of us all." Carys no longer clung to Aeron's leg. She appeared to be stealthily retreating. "It's not more powerful than our gods. It's a part of them."

"Which shows how ignorant you are." Aeron pointed the

gladius at Carys's face and she froze in her retreat. "While trapped in that childhood vision, before Gwydion plucked me from the flames, I caught a glimpse of the *source*." For a brief moment, genuine reverence threaded his words. "I've learned the secrets of Annwyn, and to control its power is to control the gods." He gave a mocking laugh. "How do you really think I invoked this spiral? From our weak, splintered deities?"

The bloodied tip of the gladius grazed Carys's forehead, and Maximus's heart slammed against his ribs as scalding fear flooded his being. The Druid was insane. There was nothing to stop him from thrusting the gladius through Carys's brain. *Mars, hear my prayer.*

And still the Druid ranted. "I allowed them to believe they were instrumental, but their combined contribution is negligible. It derives directly from Annwyn itself. I have the power to obliterate all the minor gods, and tonight I *will*."

"You can't." Morwyn sounded horrified.

"I can do whatever I wish." Aeron gave another of his icy smiles. "Gwydion showed me all that could be mine if I became his." He bent toward Carys, the gladius scarring her cheek with a trail of Druantia's blood, and the torch left the bowl. Instantly, Maximus sucked in a great, cleansing breath, and strength seeped through his trembling muscles. "But I'm no longer his," Aeron hissed into Carys's face. "And after tonight, when I no longer need him, he will no longer exist."

Another few paces and he'd be in striking range. Mars, keep the Druid focused on Carys so he wouldn't realize Maximus had regained the use of his limbs.

"And now you may strip for my pleasure."

"Aeron, I'm begging you. Please let the Roman live."

Why was she begging that piece of shit for his life? He could save his own skin. And by Mars, he'd save hers too.

"You're in no position to make bargains. See how his flesh blisters."

But the torch hovered above the bowl, and the scorching heat was bearable. He eased forward another step.

"I'll do anything. Anything you command." Desperation shivered through every word, and a shudder crawled along his spine. Carys didn't beg. Carys obeyed no man's command.

But she was doing both in the deluded hope this Druid would allow him to walk free.

As her shaking fingers pulled at the ties of her bodice, his stomach churned with revulsion, and with a primordial roar he swung his torch at the bowl, sending it crashing onto the stone plinth, severing the magic and scattering the sacrificial artifacts.

Before Aeron had a chance to draw breath, Maximus thrust the torch into his face, grinding it into flesh and bone, and as the Druid fell back, gladius flailing, the blade sliced open Maximus's arm.

Carys scrambled back as Aeron and Maximus crashed to the ground, blood thundering, pulses hammering, at the horrific screams that rent the summer eve. Sweet Cerridwen, not from Maximus. She couldn't bear to think of him so terribly injured as to emit such bone-shattering howls.

The torches fell to the ground, and the scent of roasted flesh polluted the air. As if she was captured in a bloodthirsty vision, she saw Maximus plunge his dagger through Aeron's right hand, pinning him into the earth, before he snatched up his gladius and raised it to the gold-streaked sky.

Druids rushed from the forest, weapons to hand, but froze at the horrific scene. Panting with fear, Carys crawled to Maximus, where he knelt over Aeron and covered his back with her body, protecting him in the only way she could.

But already her kin had recovered their senses; already they were screaming their war cries, advancing toward her, and all she could do was cling to his neck, and weep useless tears for the raw burns scarring his blackened skin.

"Wait." Morwyn was standing by their side, arms outstretched.

"Aeron murdered our queen. He intended to kill our princess, but the Roman saved her."

Maximus's body shuddered beneath her, as if he gave a silent laugh. "You lose, Druid. Your whole life has been for nothing."

Bile gurgled as Carys saw the ruined mess of Aeron's once coldly beautiful face. Only his eyes remained the same, silver, eerie. Inhuman.

And glowing with malice.

"You lose too, Roman." His voice rasped, snakelike. "She'll never be yours. She has no future."

"Her future is with me."

Aeron's lips, what remained of them, stretched into a mirthless smile, a black abyss filled with blood and decay. "You have no future. It's too late. The spiral turns upon itself, spewing death to all who oppose, death to all outside, *death to Rome*—"

As Maximus plunged his gladius down, Carys squeezed her eyes shut, but still felt his muscles bunch, felt the blade sear through flesh and bone as he impaled his gladius through Aeron's throat.

"It's over." He turned, took her in his blood-soaked arms, and she buried herself into his strength, his warmth, his charred, battered body. He pulled his gladius free and she looked toward the Druids, all prepared for the ceremony, all armed, all twisted with confusion and doubt and grief.

The sun dipped on the far horizon. Its last dying ray glowed with sudden purpose, arrowed between the capstone roof and the top of the sacred altar, flooded the mouth of the holy mound and penetrated the entire length of the passage into the central chamber itself.

She couldn't see it, but she knew, because as the sun set on this day, the longest day, it was the only moment such phenomena occurred.

But it didn't matter. Aeron was no longer in the mortal realm. He hadn't completed the Renewal, hadn't claimed his sacrifice.

Druantia.

A dry sob escaped. He had taken their queen, but the spiral was not renewed. It would die; their world would crumble; Rome would triumph.

A mighty roar, as if from the Earth herself, thundered from the mound, followed by a fierce wind that gusted from the mouth, ripping plants and grass and tossing stones and debris.

"What's happening?" Maximus gripped her shoulders. "The Druid's dead. Who's controlling this?"

She didn't know who or what was controlling it. She didn't even know what was happening. But as the earth shifted beneath her knees, as the wind whipped into an unnatural frenzy, and as the forest surrounding the holy hill began to shiver with the rage of deceived gods, understanding flooded through her.

"This is what he planned all along." She had to shout to make herself heard above the horrific roar. "The spiral's collapsing." Her eyes widened as she remembered the rest of Aeron's words. "It's going to kill everyone outside, Maximus. We have to warn them."

He pulled her to her feet, seemingly unhindered by the extent of his injuries. Bushes and saplings, uprooted, catapulted through the air, birds took to the skies in screeching alarm and Druids struggled to remain upright as the earth undulated beneath their feet.

Clinging to his hand, she led him through the forest, and although night had now fallen, fires blazed at irregular intervals, lighting their way. The air pulsed, like a giant lung, as if the spiral readied itself to Renew under its own terms, its own unknown conditions.

As they emerged into the clearing, a mighty thunderclap rocked the forest, an explosion so intense it might have existed only in her own mind, her own ears, except within a heartbeat the aftershock radiated outward, hurling them forward unimaginable distance.

Gasping from the impact onto the hard ground, she turned to Maximus, who still had her hand in a bone-crushing grip. Waves of malignant power rushed over them, through them, yet ultimately left them undisturbed.

"We're not going to make it." She could barely speak, her chest ached so.

"We have to try." Without letting go of her hand, he helped her up. "It's all we can do, Carys."

Within a couple of steps, she stumbled over a small furry body. A sudden blaze in the distance shed an eerie glow and she sucked in a shocked breath.

"Maximus."

All around, creatures of the forest and birds of the air lay on the ground, slain as they fled the devastating fury.

His jaw tightened and their eyes locked. But neither spoke, as if uttering the words, vocalizing the horror, would turn possibility into reality.

Even if that possibility was already the reality.

Still the belligerent waves pulsed outward, yet around them, as if they weren't there. As if *she* wasn't there. And she tightened her hold on his hand and drew close to his side, calling on Cerridwen to protect Maximus as she protected her.

Cerridwen.

"We must go to the Cauldron." It was suddenly imperative, as if the answer awaited her there.

He didn't answer, as if he knew an answer wasn't necessary, as if he knew that already it was too late to save anyone at the settlement or even beyond. Who could know how far or how viciously this distorted spiral might expand?

They crested the ridge that hid the Cauldron from the forest, and her heart slammed against her ribs, choking the breath in her lungs.

A column of white-blue flame raged directly next to the Cauldron. A flame that pulsed and throbbed with energy, which leaped up into the starlit sky, yet was rigidly contained within a perfect circle.

"What magic is this?" Maximus's voice was hoarse, as he dragged her forward. "What's your goddess doing, Carys?"

Violent wind whipped past them, and the pulsing spiral screamed at primal level as if infuriated at being diverted from its purpose. But still the great flame sucked in the wind, sucked in the spiral, sucked in the great, destructive power before it could encroach farther into Cymru.

He pulled her to the edge of the flame. It gave off little heat, and she stared, uncomprehending, at its root.

A small pile of pebbles was the only indication that shards of magic bluestone hid an illicit circle of distortion. The circle where she had intended to hide Maximus to keep him safe.

The circle that, by capturing within its compressed boundaries the devastating force that swept across the land, now protected her entire people, and the Roman Legion, from annihilation.

Chapter Thirty-six

"I created my own spiral." It no longer mattered what she told Maximus. There was nothing left to hide from him. "I wanted to save my love."

He stared at her, his face almost unrecognizable with the blackened skin and strange blue hue from the circular flame. And yet she would know him anywhere, however he looked, because she didn't need her eyes to see him. All she needed was her heart.

"Cerridwen told you to do this?"

"I don't know." Had Cerridwen guided her hand? "This eve didn't go the way I planned."

She had intended to hide Maximus here, where he would have been protected from any battle. But there had been no battle. Had Aeron ever intended for there to be one? Or had he expected to control the collapsed spiral, bend it to his will, use it to eradicate all those who stood against him?

But with his death, no longer enchained by Aeron's dark incantations, the spiral of Annwyn had erupted with rage. This magical circle, far from shielding Maximus from harm, would have imprisoned him. And as it sucked in the destructive power of the gods, Maximus would have been slain.

Because of her own selfish actions.

He looked up the fiery column, then glanced around the eerily illuminated countryside. Still the spiral pumped from the forest, and still the white-blue flame captured its fury.

"The rest of Cambria is being spared." Finally he turned his attention back to her. "Roman and Celt alike."

Was this what Cerridwen had wanted all along? The flame glowed, unnatural and hypnotic, and ice trickled over her arms.

Do not let us be extinguished.

"The flame in the darkness." The flickering, vulnerable light she'd tried to reach for in her vision. The tiny glow in the blackness of Rome.

Only the future. Cerridwen's cryptic whisper, from when she'd been in Maximus's old quarters, vibrated with shocking clarity through her brain.

Hating Maximus would never change the past. But if she had chosen to hate her enemy in the future, she would have ensured the devastating destruction of all she held dear, all she loved.

By loving Maximus, and defying her people, her gods and her fellow Druids, she'd been driven to create this illicit spiral. And by attempting to save Maximus from the Druids rage, she had instead harnessed the immortals' fury. Inadvertently, she had protected them all.

"The Legion will investigate." Maximus's fingers tightened around hers, and she let out a dry sob. The Legion would decimate her traumatized kin, no matter how brave their resistance.

"Carys, move." His voice was harsh as he tugged her brutally toward the forest. "We don't have much time. Your kin need to leave this area before the Legion arrives. Do you understand?"

She shot him a comprehending glance as they ran through the whipping grasses. "Yes." Relief meshed with awe, and she shivered with fear. Maximus was going against his beloved Rome to repay the debt of life she'd given his Legion. Would he ever be able to forgive her?

When they finally reached the cromlech—how short the journey seemed now, when there was no need to circumnavigate the area and backtrack to avoid leaving noticeable pathways—few Druids remained and Druantia's body had vanished.

"Carys." Morwyn rushed toward her and gripped her arm, steadfastly ignoring Maximus. "We've been searching for you. Hurry; we're to leave instantly for—" She snapped her lips together and shot Maximus a suspicious glance. "To where your mother awaits you."

The Isle of Mon. The Druids' most sacred sanctuary.

"No." Pain engulfed her heart, crushed her lungs, at the knowledge she might never see her mother again, might never see any of her kin again.

This was the sacrifice her goddess claimed. And it was a sacrifice that would forever wound her spirit.

But the alternative meant she would never again see Maximus.

Morwyn shook her arm. "We have to leave. Gather our strength once again. But we will come back, and we will reclaim Cymru for our own."

Panic clutched deep inside, cold and deadly. Her vision had shown her the end of Druidry. The end of everything they held dear, *unless they embraced Rome.* But how could her culture survive alongside the unrelenting claws of the Eagle, if all her fellow Druids left?

"Stay, Morwyn. You and Gawain and any others who will listen." *And let her mother return.* "Our people need us now, before they forget all the old ways."

Morwyn gave her an odd look, as if she didn't understand what Carys could mean. "They'll never forget our ways. And we'll return in a moon or less, as soon as the anger of the gods diminishes." Her tone held no doubt, as if the devastating events of this eve could be easily forgiven, easily forgotten. Her fingers tightened on Carys's arm. "Carys, you can't stay. The Romans will crucify you."

"Rome will never touch Carys." Maximus unlaced their fingers and wound his arm around her shoulders. "We're not complete barbarians. We can honor a foreign princess."

Morwyn flicked him a disbelieving glance. "The Morrigan commands we leave now," she said, turning back to Carys. "Before the cursed Romans arrive."

A chill entered her heart, shivered along her arteries, as a certainty threaded through her brain. A certainty that solidified and expanded and became absolute.

She stood at the crossroads.

The all-seeing Morrigan, who could no longer see Carys, demanded her Druids follow her down her path.

And Cerridwen, standing by the other path, demanded nothing but the continuance of her sacred Cauldron—or perhaps her Flame—of Knowledge.

By whatever means necessary.

This moment was the reason the Morrigan had turned from her at the hour of her birth.

The reason why, in that prophetic vision, the goddess had held her accountable; because Carys's destiny was entirely within her control.

She cupped Morwyn's jaw and gently stroked her thumb over her split lip. "I'm staying, Morwyn, to be with the man I love. The one Cerridwen brought to Cymru." She hitched in a shaky breath. "Tell my mother she's forever with me."

Morwyn's eyes sparkled in the light of the fires. "I'll miss you, Carys." There was a choke in her voice, and as they embraced, Morwyn whispered, "Goddess be with you, my princess."

As Morwyn pulled back and turned and fled into the forest, a great, molten rock throbbed in the center of Carys's chest. She gasped, pressed her hands to her breasts, as the agony engulfed her in a wave of despairing grief.

Maximus dragged her roughly in his arms and she clung to him, fighting back the tears, fighting back the sensation of utter isolation.

"Don't cry." His voice was gruff. "I'm sorry it came to this, Carys. But, gods, I couldn't bear to lose you." His hold tightened, crushing her bones, squeezing the breath from her lungs. "I love you, Celt." He dragged in a harsh breath. "I love you, *Druid*. Stay with me because you want to, not because your goddess commands it."

I love you, Druid. She gave a gasping laugh that sounded like a sob, but it didn't matter because Maximus accepted who she was, *what* she was, even though it went against everything Rome stood for.

"I wanted to stay with you when I thought that was the last thing my goddess wanted." She freed her arms and speared her fingers through his hair, his short military hair that fascinated her as much now as it ever had. "I'll always be a Druid, Maximus. It's what I am."

He gave a heavy sigh and slid her braid through his fisted hand. "I'll learn to live with it."

She had to tell him. "I'm glad you didn't have to betray Rome by warning my kin, Maximus. I'm glad they'd already made the decision to leave."

His fingers stilled on her hair. "It wouldn't have been betrayal. I promised you I'd never harm your kin." His sigh echoed through the core of her existence, the foundation of her love. "I'll always honor my promises to you, Carys."

And in the distance, vibrating through the earth at her feet, she felt the approach of the Roman Legion.

Epilogue

Flanked by Branwen and Efa, Carys stood in the center of the Roman road and watched the distant Legion march steadily toward her. Despite Morwyn's promise that the Druids would soon return, there had been no word from them. And no matter how close she had grown to the two women by her side, they could never replace Morwyn in her heart. Had she even reached the Isle of Mon? Would she ever discover the fate of her dearest friend and fellow Druids?

She drew in a shaky breath and concentrated on the advancing Legion. Today, Maximus returned to Cymru from his assignment in Britain. And soon, after she became his wife in the eyes of Rome, she would leave her homeland forever.

Late that afternoon, when they were once again dressed after hours of frantic lovemaking, Maximus took her hand and pulled her toward him. During the six moons that had passed since the creation of the Flame of Knowledge, his burnt skin had healed, and, although he would be forever scarred, he was still the most beautiful, magnificent man she had ever encountered.

"Come. There's something I want to show you."

A brief flash of dizziness overcame her, so swift she half wondered if she'd imagined it, but there was no imagining the absolute sense of surety that flooded her mind.

She laughed and pressed his hand against her womb. "Our daughter is conceived."

The conspiratorial smile on his face froze and his glance dropped. "You know this?" His tone was awed.

"It's fitting our first should be conceived in the land of her foremothers." She tried to keep her voice light, so he wouldn't guess how much the thought of moving and living among the heathen Britons still distressed her.

She knew there was no choice. Maximus would always go wherever he was commanded, and the only way they could be together was if he commanded elsewhere than Cymru.

It was the reason he'd been gone these last eight weeks. So Rome could have no reason to decree their union unlawful, on the grounds Maximus had taken a wife from his province.

His prejudiced Emperor had also been influenced by the knowledge she was a princess of Cymru and had been instrumental in leading Maximus to the High Druid, who'd planned to decimate the entire country.

It wasn't the truth but, as Maximus had wearily explained, it was politics. And it had worked.

"Carys." He cradled her jaw with one hand, while his other tenderly caressed her belly. "We'll return to Cambria. Many times. Our children will know of their dual heritage, I promise you."

Their children would be born Romans. To survive, she would adapt, and teach her children all she knew. And she knew that before Britain burned, they would return to Rome, and it was something she would never share with Maximus because he would insist on staying, insist on fighting, but the continuance of their bloodline was paramount and she'd allow nothing to jeopardize that future.

Druantia's voice echoed in her mind. *Selfish.*

Yes. Perhaps she was. Perhaps so too was Cerridwen. But how could it be wrong to find a way, without bloodshed, to ensure the ancient knowledge of her people wasn't lost forever?

They rode from the town on his horse, and she leaned back, soaking in the knowledge that he was back with her, where he belonged.

"When do we leave?" Aquila was remaining in Cymru, but along with handpicked centurions, Efa, Branwen and her grandfather, who'd rediscovered the joy of living during the last few moons, were accompanying them, along with several other locals who wanted travel and adventure.

"We'll be married tomorrow, and leave soon after." His arm tightened around her waist. "I know the Roman ways mean nothing to you, but this ensures you and our children have the status you deserve."

At the wood they dismounted. Why was he taking her to the Flame of Knowledge? Her people, deprived of all contact with their Druids since that fateful night, had turned Cerridwen's Cauldron into a place of pilgrimage. Carys had expected the Romans to punish the worshippers, perhaps even attempt to destroy the enigmatic Flame. But instead they too were enthralled by the phenomenon, convinced Minerva was responsible.

Minerva, sister goddess of Cerridwen. Had Maximus been right, all those moons ago, when he suggested the same gods answered to different names?

Trepidation hammered against her ribs, but she didn't know why she had the sudden, irrefutable certainty that her life was about to change forever.

Her life had already changed forever. How could it possibly alter more without her continuing on her journey?

And she had no intention of leaving Maximus behind, not yet, not for many years, until they were both ancient and could scarcely count the number of their descendants.

He led her into Cerridwen's sacred place. Her breath strangled in her throat and she clutched onto him, having the insane desire to laugh and weep, and her heart overflowed with a love so fierce it consumed the serpentine tendrils of sadness that had been a part of her since the night of Druantia's murder.

"There are Druid enclaves in Britannia." He urged her forward, toward the ivy entwined arbor of twisted branches, toward the group of Celts and Romans who stood waiting for her, toward the elderly Briton daubed in ceremonial blue, who held his hazel rod with quiet authority.

Aquila saluted, Efa smiled at her, and Branwen nodded with gentle approval. Her friends, who had spent all afternoon preparing her wedding glade.

But none of this would have been done without Maximus's approval. He was the one who had taken the time to discover her rituals, arrange for this ceremony. Despite his Emperor, despite his loyalty to Rome, he was willing to accept her heritage and culture as, tomorrow, she would accept his.

"You'll do this—for me?" She turned to Maximus, and he was blurred, beloved, her life.

He bent his head, and his breath whispered against her ear. "I'll do anything for you, my Druid princess."